WINTER TALES FROM COZY VALES

A COZY FANTASY COLLECTION #1

COZY VALES COLLECTION

L.A. SCOTT   REBECCA BUCHANAN   SELINA J. ECKERT

DEANNA AND ANGELA STUART   CASSANDRA STIRLING

KM JACKWAYS   G CLATWORTHY   NATHANIEL WEBB

BONNIE AXTON

FIREFLY TALES, LLC

INTRODUCTION

This debut collection from the cozy fantasy shared world of Cozy Vales is certain to deliver hours of holiday-themed reading!

There are many things you should know about Cozy Vales, but the two most important ones for this collection are Lantern Night and Winter's Tide.

Held every December 21st, **Lantern Night** is the pinnacle of winter holidays and the oldest and most popular holiday in the queendom. It's a rare village or town that doesn't celebrate Lantern Night in some form or fashion!

The old fashioned ritual is to light a candle in a lantern. If it burns through the night, it means you'll experience good luck. No one is 100% sure on its origins, but the lanterns are believed to ward off bad luck and are both a remembrance of the previous year and a promise / hope for the year to come. Nowadays, many people release floating lanterns instead.

The traditional words for the ritual are:

"With this light, we hold onto the memories of the past and look forward with hope for the new year. May this lantern last through the night."

Traditional greetings around the holiday are:

"May your lantern last through the night."

And the response is: "And may your light shine bright."

Lantern Night is also observed with the giving of gifts, with books to read by candlelight being one of the most popular. Unique customs for celebrating Lantern Night are observed in various communities and differ across the queendom.

Closely intertwined with Lantern Night is the holiday season known as **Winter's Tide**. This season lasts for two weeks and culminates with Lantern Night. As with Lantern Night, there are some commonly practiced traditions (decorations, parties, a more conscious effort to be kind, efforts to connect with friends and family, gratitude, etc.), but there are also local or regional takes on the celebrations.

Many vales, cities, towns, and villages have adopted unique ways of celebrating Winter's Tide, with localized custom traditions springing up all over the queendom (usually due to weather and/or geography).

Regardless of how Lantern Night and Winter's Tide are celebrated, the theme is always one of giving.

Please consider this collection our gift to you!

Learn more at cozyvales.com.

A SEASON OF GIVING
L.A. SCOTT

Dear reader, the following is a tale involving a hearth witch named Genever Wells, whose life is about to be turned upside down. But before you meet the heroine of this story, kindly allow me to properly set a stage worthy of her entrance.

At the top of the diamond-shaped queendom known as Cozy Vales is a lovely little valley named Juniper Vale with a lovely little town named Oasis (both are worthy of visiting if you have the time and the means).

Our story opens just three days before the holiday of Lantern Night, a queendom-wide celebration held on the longest night of each year. The holiday is marked by lanterns, candles, wreaths, singing, much food and drink, and gifts, but in Oasis at this time of year (mid-December), it's also marked by snow.

Lots and lots and lots of snow.

A night of falling flakes had left the town under a blanket of white. The morning was gray, and the land continued to be showered in cold kisses.

Into this scene steps our heroine, who is walking through town and craving a peppermint mocha from the Moonlit Mug Café . . .

Genever Wells crunched through snow so fresh that two inches already covered the pathway that had been shoveled clear less than an hour earlier. Not that she was complaining. She was rarely a complainer to begin with, you see, and she adored cold weather, though that was not the only reason she lived in Oasis.

The other reason was Lantern Night and the two-week celebratory season preceding it, which was known as Winter's Tide. For the residents of Oasis, and certainly for Genever, Lantern Night was unquestionably the winter holiday pinnacle. However, Winter's Tide was a highlight in its own right.

The two weeks of celebrating—someone was always throwing a party or a feast or a gala of some kind—were also marked by a constant exchange of warm wishes for the upcoming year. The entire town felt happier, lighter, and friendlier. To say it was a magical time would be an understatement.

And if you had ever experienced the holidays in Oasis, you would heartily agree.

Genever's hooded dark green cloak was made of thick wool and kept out most of the chilly air. She blinked her pale blue eyes against the gusts of wind that tugged at her long, copper-colored hair. Errant snowflakes melted against her freckled face.

Not that she minded.

However, snow collected on the cloak with such speed, Genever had to regularly shake off the accumulation. Even so, by the time the bell over the Moonlit Mug Café's door rang to announce her entrance, Genever looked closer to a snow woman than the hearth witch she was.

"Morning, Gen! Usual?" Palter Godfrey called out from behind the counter. The owner and proprietor of the Mug peered over the patrons at Genever. The café was crowded, and Palter had to nearly shout over the din of his customers, though he did so in a way that felt surprisingly polite.

Genever found the Moonlit Mug Café to be neither too small nor too large but rather just the right size for enjoying the best tasting coffee in town.

"Please!" Gen replied as politely as possible. "And make it a double. And a chocolate croissant to go."

Genever stamped her boots and gently shook her cloak. Showering Palter's customers with snow would have been rude, and Oasis was not a town of rude people . . . mostly.

The doorbell chimed again. Genever couldn't remember the last time she'd seen the place so busy. She stepped forward to make room for the newest arrival, and the mystery of the café's standing room only status was solved.

Next to Palter stood a woman dressed in a Tasters' Guild blouse and apron and holding what could only be the famous Heart of the Vale chocolate drink. The delicious beverage was no mere hot chocolate but rather the most famous drink to come out of the Tasters' Guild.

Widely regarded as the most delectable chocolate-based drink in the queendom, Genever had wanted to try one for years. She was very curious about the magical properties attributed to the drink. The guild marketed it as a general cure-all for healing minor maladies, though the process for crafting the drink and the exact magic spell used were both highly secret.

Unfortunately, the Heart of the Vale's steep price put it outside of Genever's price range, at least for the moment.

Palter had put up Winter's Tide decorations and lit candles all around the café, which gave it a very festive feel, as did the laughter and good-hearted conversations filling the air. Genever recognized several red-cheeked faces in the cafe and greeted them with a smile or a wave.

Customers who had popped in for a drink stood or sat, nurturing their beverages, eyeing the darkened sky, and considering if perhaps they should, after all, have a second round and see if the weather lightened up.

Others stood with their hands in their pockets, having ducked into the café to thaw out before continuing on their way. More than a few perused the latest edition of *The Golden Acorn*, the most popular broadsheet in the queendom. The top headline announced that Capital Crumb Bakery would soon be opening a new location in Turtle Bay Vale, which, if you had ever tried one of their elderberry fold over tarts, would understandably be headline-worthy news.

Palter was happy to let anyone stay as long as they liked and was never one to ask a current (or future) customer to leave. One might argue his kindness was overly generous, but again, Oasis was not a town of rude people.

Genever squeezed through the knot of customers ("Pardon me," "Terribly sorry," "Morning, Mr. Gable, how are you this morning?" and many more exchanges were offered along the way) until she reached the counter. The journey had taken almost exactly the same amount of time Palter needed to craft a peppermint mocha with a double shot of espresso.

"That'll be three coppers, Gen."

"The regular price is five, Palter, and that's just for a mocha."

The café owner nodded at the wreath hanging from his front door. Genever had performed a minor spell on it for success. Nothing too extravagant, as she was still learning how to manipulate aether, the ethereal energy that fueled all magic. Barely more than a little hearth cantrip for luck in the kitchen.

Palter had insisted on paying more than she'd quoted, but Genever wouldn't hear of it. She only asked a fair price for her work. There were plenty of charlatans out there as it was, tarnishing the reputations of ethical hearth witches. Genever would never allow herself to be accused of overcharging her customers, much less by the person who made the most delicious mochas in town.

Palter nodded at the door. "That's no regular wreath, and you're no regular customer."

"But you already paid me for the wreath."

Palter sighed and shook his head. "And it's brought me far more business than you promised."

Genever glanced at the woman next to Palter. The Tasters' Guild member handed over a Heart of the Vale to a smiling customer who could barely contain her excitement. The guilder nodded and ducked behind a screen to make the next one (please see the note above regarding how secretive the guild was about the recipe). A proper version of the drink required magic, which meant Tasters' Guild was one of the few guilds whose members had to be a *magical*: someone capable of wielding magic.

Now, there were many flavors of magic, much like there were many flavors of bread. But aether was the fuel for all flavors of spellcraft.

Genever nodded at the guilder. "Pretty sure she's the big draw today, not my wreath."

The café owner smiled and shrugged. "And I say I'd never have convinced her to work the counter without your magic wreath. Three coppers."

Genever would have continued arguing were it not for the other patrons. Someone behind her politely cleared their throat. Next would come a louder clearing of their throat, and if that failed to get Genever's attention, a gently spoken "Excuse me, miss, but I don't suppose you've finished with your order, have you?" was sure to follow.

Genever didn't like being on the receiving end of unnecessary charity, but she was also in no position to turn down the opportunity to keep a few extra coins in her pouch. She placed three copper coins on the counter. Each had a single mountain embossed on one side and the letters CVQ on the other.

The café owner's hand swept over the coins with practiced ease, and they seemingly disappeared into thin air. Palter was no manipulator of the aether, but it always looked like magic to Genever. He winked and handed her a waxed paper bag.

"One chocolate croissant. Give Trill my best."

"Thank you, Palter." Genever nodded at the screen. "How long is she here for?"

"Just today. You sure you don't want one?"

Want didn't come close to describing Genever's true desire for tasting the magical drink, but the lightness of her coin pouch argued against any such indulgences. Besides, if the fates smiled on her little project, she'd soon be trying her first Heart of the Vale and still have plenty of coins to spare.

"Thank you, but no."

Palter leaned close and dropped his voice. "Hey, I almost hate to ask, but have you heard from Banneton?"

Genever's lips pressed into a weak smile. She shook her head, not trusting that she could say the words without choking up. What she wanted to say was, *Yes. The Banneton Bakery School rejected me. Again. And this time, their rejection letter made it clear all future applications would be similarly dismissed.*

Palter's face went soft. "I'm so sorry. Their loss. Hey, you're still coming to my private party here on Lantern Night, right?"

Genever nodded and gently slipped the waxed bag into her cloak pocket. She literally swallowed her sorrow and offered

Palter the traditional holiday expression. "May your lantern last the night, Palter."

He gave the expected response, "And may your light shine bright." Then he added, "And you don't need Banneton to make that happen."

The tears that had threatened to spill down Genever's cheeks a few seconds ago rallied again. She smiled, nodded, and turned away before they made good on their intent.

Genever cupped the large ceramic mug and inhaled the aroma. The drink contained peppermint, dark chocolate, milk thick enough to be cream, and some of the richest espresso coffee in the queendom. She'd tried recreating the drink and never came close.

Perhaps Palter was a magical after all.

Genever moved to the bay window, where she tracked the falling snow and sipped her drink.

She really shouldn't have been spending money on mochas, even at Palter's steeply discounted price, but the drink served a handful of useful purposes.

The milk made her feel full. The espresso helped blunt her hunger. The dark chocolate wouldn't do much for her hunger but tasted delicious, which was more than enough justification, thank you very much.

Besides, the need for thriftiness was temporary. In just two days—Lantern Night—her secret project with Trill would put dozens of gold suns in their personal coffers. Coins she had planned to use to fund the cost of admittance to Banneton. The school was in Summerfrost Vale, two valleys southeast of Juniper Vale.

Depending on who you asked, Banneton was either in the top tier of baking schools in the queendom or was the most elite. The school charged simply for the privilege of applying, and they charged even more for accepting candidates.

The money was well worth it for those who graduated from the esteemed school, however, as they would easily make it all back in a year or two. Merchants and wealthy individuals flocked to hire or invest in graduates who sought to open their own shops, and existing bakeries bid furiously to snag the remaining ones.

Genever had scrimped and saved and practiced her bread baking for the past decade, all the while persistently applying to all the top baking schools, despite the costs. As a result, she was never swimming in money (and rarely had enough to do more than get her toes wet). Plus, she was now twenty-eight, which put her in the older bracket of applicants. Others might have given up, and Genever had certainly been tempted.

Then, against all odds, a year ago she learned she had some magical aptitude in hearth witchery. Genever was certain it was a sign she was destined for Banneton. Of all the magic disciplines she might have possessed, hers was a perfect match for her dreams.

After her latest rejection, however, her dream was becoming a nightmare.

Genever savored every drop of her mocha, which had neared room temperature. She returned the mug to the counter and waved goodbye to Palter, who was still facing a long line of customers.

Perhaps the café owner was right about the wreath. Perhaps her little hearth luck cantrip had been the catalyst for convincing the guilder to sell Heart of the Vales in the café. Was that so hard to believe? Genever smiled and allowed herself a dash of pride. Nothing more, of course, as hubris and magic were rarely a good combination.

Besides, she had a croissant to deliver.

Pinching her cloak at her neck, Genever pushed through the shop's door. Chimneys blew gray streams into the air, the scent of wood fires delighting Genever's nose. The top of the bell tower was still covered by low clouds and a steady flurry of snow.

Despite that, the streets were busy. One person in particular caught Genever's attention, mostly from what he was not doing: getting out of the cold.

A three foot tall goblin huddled in the nook of the café's bay window and stared inside. He wore a bowler hat and leather shoes and was dressed in a suit and vest. The golden had been staring inside for at least the last few minutes. Genever noted his clothes were in good condition but hardly adequate for the chilly weather.

Genever had encountered countless entities in Oasis. There were the usual ones—elves, dwarves, sprites, gnomes. There were the rarer ones—unicorns, brownies, centaur. And even more passed through the town each year, as well.

Later, Genever would be unable to say precisely why she felt the urge to approach the goblin. His obvious shivering? Was the holiday cheer surrounding Genever making her more attuned to the needs of others? Or was it simple intuition?

Regardless, Genever could only confirm that at that moment, she could not ignore the goblin.

"Excuse me, but is there anything I may help you with?"

The goblin startled at her voice. "My apologies. I was lost deep in thought." His eyes turned back to the window. "I'm in a bit of a pickle, and that's no lie."

"I'd like to help if I can," Genever said.

The goblin removed his hat. "My name is Nort, miss . . .?"

"Genever Wells. Pleased to meet you."

Nort leaned forward in an approximation of a bow. "Likewise. I do appreciate your offer, though I'm afraid my big troubles will require big solutions."

"Sometimes troubles appear bigger than they are."

The goblin grinned and waggled a finger in the air. "Indeed! Indeed! But in this case, they truly are nigh insurmountable. My business partner—former, it's fair to say at this point—lured me here under pretenses of some big business venture and, as soon as he had the opportunity, absconded with my money and belongings. Even took my overcoat, the rapscallion."

(Reader, it should be noted that Nort did not actually say *rapscallion*, instead using a pejorative term whose use is not suited for tender ears, regardless of the time of year but especially during Winter's Tide.)

"Oh, my," Genever replied. "How awful. Have you reported him to the constable?"

"I have." Nort nodded and sighed. "But as my former partner is almost certainly long gone from Oasis, if not Juniper Vale, the chances of my funds being returned are quite slim. I have some assets still under my name, though turning them into coins has proven most challenging."

Now, Genever was not so naïve as to believe everything Nort had said. She suspected some sort of plea for help, most likely monetary in nature, was possibly forthcoming. Even in such a polite town as Oasis, unethical hucksters, swindlers, and even flimflammers (perhaps the worst of the lot) were not unheard of.

And Winter's Tide was the perfect opportunity to prey on unsuspecting victims' sympathies, for you needed a heart of stone to walk the streets and silently ignore every request for help during the holiday season.

Genever's heart, as you most likely suspected, was not nearly so hard.

In fact, she quite believed the goblin.

"I'm on my way to meet a friend. Why don't you walk with me and tell me more? Perhaps your problem is not as impossible to solve as you might think. I often find talking with others to be extremely helpful when I'm in a pickle."

Nort blinked several times before responding. "You are the kindest person I've met in Oasis since I arrived three days ago. I would be happy for your company."

Genever saw no harm in letting Nort accompany her. If he were to ask for money, she could honestly say she had none to spare. Her pouch held only a single silver moon and four coppers, which would barely be enough to feed her and Trill until they were paid in two days. She could declare her poverty and watch Nort's reaction. That did not mean she could not be charitable, however.

The hearth witch pulled her croissant from her cloak pocket. She removed her gloves and delicately tore the pastry in two. That was to be her biggest meal of the day, but after all, wasn't Winter's Tide about compassion and gratitude and giving?

"I'm afraid I've no coins to spare at the moment, but I'm more than happy to share half of my breakfast with you."

The goblin's eyes went wide, and his eyebrows inched close to the brim of his bowler.

"Gracious, but you're kind!" He took the pastry and nibbled delicately at it. "I may not look like it, but I'm rather handy with a hammer. I'd feel much better if I could repay you in some way. Have you a stuck door that needs unsticking? Perhaps a window that won't open? I'm especially handy with drawers that don't close smoothly."

Genever noted the narrowness of the goblin's offers and wished she could point him in the direction of some drawers or doors that needed attention. She also noted the goblin has spoken in *Shar*, the most common language in the queendom. However, his voice had a slight accent Genever couldn't quite pin down.

Given the northern tip of Juniper Vale bordered two neighboring lands—The Republic of Westram and the Celestial Clouds kingdom—the valley enjoyed a constant flow of various peoples in, out, and through its mountainous borders. The goblin might have been from a neighboring vale or from clear across the continent.

Genever smiled at Nort. "Thank you, but I have nothing that needs unsticking at the moment. Please enjoy your croissant guilt-free."

"I shall endeavor, though I make no promises."

They walked. Nort ate. Genever offered him a guided tour of Oasis.

"And that's the best library in town over there. Oh, and that's one of my favorite bakeries down that alley. I used to work there."

"You don't anymore? May I inquire as to your current occupation?"

Genever laughed. "Currently, I'm working on a project with a friend of mine." She stopped herself before she completed her sentence with, *and if it goes well, we'll both make a lot of money.* "I'm heading to her house now, then on to my warehouse. Oh, and here's the Winter's Tide Market. Have you seen that yet?"

The goblin shook his head. "I'm afraid not."

"Well, you simply have to see it. We'll take a quick detour."

The town square at the center of Oasis had been transformed for Winter's Tide. Dozens of merchants and crafters had set up wooden huts with angled roofs. The square resembled a tiny winter village, if tiny winter villages sold delicious foods and drinks, sold incredible arts and crafts, and had performers singing, dancing, and telling stories.

The market was just beginning to stir, and several Oasis residents were already gathered, some huddled around the braziers burning coal and swapping the latest gossip while they waited for the huts to open. The square would be packed by lunch time.

Genever waved at a few friendly faces but didn't stop. "If you have the time, it's best at night."

"I'm sure."

"Oh, there's my friend's neighborhood up ahead."

Nort squinted. "All I see is a large stand of trees."

"That's The Thicket, and it's where my friend lives."

Ten streets east of the town square was a large park occupied by hardwood trees which were magical in some way. Theories differed as to the exact spell or ritual that had caused the trees to grow over a hundred feet tall and whose trunks spanned four or five feet in diameter.

More perplexing? The trees' ability to survive even after homes had literally been hollowed out of their core. A single tree might contain five or even ten homes, each just the right size for their small occupants.

And just who lived in this tree neighborhood? Mostly sprites, who had no problem with heights and could easily access their homes dozens of feet off the ground.

Oasis considered The Thicket a treasure to be protected and preserved, especially as sprites generally avoided settlements, much preferring to live in the wild.

Genever stopped in front of a massive oak tree and gently tapped on the tiny cornflower blue door lowest to the ground. Knocking directly on the trunk would, of course, have been quite rude.

A muffled muttering issued from inside, followed by the clash and clatter of pots and pans, which was followed by yet more muttering. Eventually, the door swung open.

A bleary-eyed and yawning sprite stood in the doorway. She wore a long dress of gauzy layers, all earth tones. Her short hair was a bright pink, and she had eyes the color of sunlit hazel.

"Morning, Trill. Got you something," Genever said. She held up the bagged croissant.

Trill was not a sprite who enjoyed the process of waking up, regardless of the hour or however much sleep had come before.

Some people never quite got the hang of speaking another language. Others spent fruitless years trying to become a singer or a musician. Despite their best efforts, the tasks remained constant sources of irritation.

So it was with Trill whenever her slumber came to an end.

Genever had learned to bring offerings of appeasement—the sweeter the better—if she planned on waking Trill before midday, which was every day since they'd begun their joint endeavor.

Trill blinked, rubbed at her eyes, and scowled at no one in particular.

"Gen? What time is it?"

"Ten o'clock."

The sprite's scowl deepened. She held out her hand. "Gimme."

Genever used a finger to sweep the snow from the porch and tore off a piece of the waxed paper. She laid the paper on the porch and placed a tiny bit of croissant on the paper. Well, tiny for Genever but nearly as big as Trill's head. The sprite stood all of seven inches tall.

The pastry succeeded in erasing most of the sprite's scowl. Trill tore off a piece and closed her eyes as she ate.

"Oh, that is divine, it truly is." She opened one eye while she chewed. "But that docsn't mean I forgive you for waking me at this insanely uncivilized hour."

"Every hour is uncivilized just after you've woken up."

"Fair point."

Genever looked at the goblin. "Nort, this is my good friend, Trill. Trill, this is Nort. We just met outside the Moonlit Mug."

"Hello," Trill said.

The goblin removed his hat and gave Trill a short bow. "Good morning."

"See you at the warehouse?" Genever asked.

The sprite made a shooing motion, as her mouth was now full of another bite of croissant. Genever waved goodbye before Trill disappeared back inside her tree home.

Despite the sprite's aversion to waking up and the need to placate her grumpiness with pastries, Genever considered herself incredibly lucky. Most sprites avoided smelly cities and noisy towns in favor of the wilderness.

On the other hand, most sprites had not needed saving from a group of incredibly distraught bees who had taken great offense at the attempt to relieve their hive of its honey. And of the sprites who had, only one had been saved by Genever in the entire history of Cozy Vales, which covered six hundred and thirty-two years.

In Trill's efforts to secure the sweet substance, the sprite had managed to get her wings covered in honey, which prevented her from flying. Worse, her efforts to free herself only succeeded in trapping her in the very honey she had planned on taking.

The bees, most indignant at the unforgivable invasion, took advantage of Trill's sticky situation.

It was at this precise moment that Genever, while out for a summer stroll, heard cries for help just off the path. Her investigation led her to Trill, who was valiantly trying to defend herself from the buzzing assailants.

With a bit of aether, Genever had summoned a gust of wind to shoo away the attackers. She then gently extricated the sprite from her self-inflicted trap. Trill rarely mentioned the incident, but when she did, it was always in hushed tones and referred to as The Great Rescue.

The pair had become close friends. So much so, that when Genever came up with her idea for growing out of season flowers and selling them during Winter's Tide, Trill was the first and only person she mentioned it to.

Thus began the Project Petunia partnership between the hearth witch and the sprite, one that hatched a plan to make a sizable profit from the upcoming Lantern Night holiday. If, that was, they could successfully deliver the large order of petunias on time and in sufficient quality.

The purple flowers were difficult to grow under any circumstances in Juniper Vale, but Trill's innate sprite abilities gifted her with not just one green thumb but two (plus eight more emerald colored fingers).

And their customer, a wealthy Oasis resident named Roderick Torbull, was thrilled at the idea of hosting the only Lantern Night party in town that would be decorated with petunias. Roderick insisted the pair keep their plans secret, as he wanted to surprise his guests with the floral adornments.

It should be noted that Roderick prided himself on hosting parties that were regularly featured in the society section of *Oasis Gazette,* the oldest broadsheet in Oasis.

Roderick had promised good payment if the pair delivered, but he'd insisted Genever and Trill cover all expenses from their own coffers. All of which explained why Genever's funds had grown as thin as the crust on a loaf of bread.

The snow had nearly stopped as Genever continued her tour and guided Nort out of the residential part of town. She and Trill had secured a small warehouse for their project. The location was not the nicest in town, and the building was drafty. The rent, however, was cheap, which meant more profits for the two ladies.

To Genever's relief, the warehouse door appeared secure, and the windows were still obscured by old editions of *Oasis*

Gazette she had glued over the glass panes. She pulled a large metal key from her cloak pocket and opened the door.

"Please, after you," she said. Genever could not imagine closing the door on the goblin, and she had barely begun to hear of his troubles. Nort followed her in. "And now that we have some privacy, I'd very much like to hear more about your situation. I have to tend to the stoves, but I'll be listening with a keen ear, have no worry."

Nort clasped his hands behind his back and gazed at the rows and rows of flower trays stretching across the entire space. He stood on tiptoes and smelled the petunia buds.

"Most agreeable, most agreeable."

Genever cast a cantrip of light. Her summoning of a thimbleful of aether came nearly as easily and unconsciously as breathing. A year ago, she'd struggled mightily to cast even the smallest spark. Now, she could have illuminated the entire warehouse as if it were daylight if she chose.

But she didn't, as that would have taxed Genever's ability to pull on the aether necessary to cast magic. She could easily burn herself out if she pulled too much too quickly, and she'd need to jealously guard that ability for the day's work ahead. Instead of lighting the warehouse with aether-fueled brightness, she lit an ordinary oil lantern to guide her around the warehouse as she began her morning ritual.

First up was a smidgeon of aether to increase the size of what was left of the croissant. Being a hearth witch presented certain benefits to someone on a limited budget, one such benefit being the ability to turn half a pastry into a full one. Or, at least, close to a full one.

The trade-off—for there was always a trade-off where magic was involved—was taste.

Magic was an exchange, a form of give and take. Forcing the half-eaten croissant into a larger version of itself was the aether's give. The take came in the form of a much blander taste, an almost complete loss of aroma, and a less substantial feel to the food when chewed.

Genever mentally repeated the words to funnel aether into the pastry and felt the energy course through her fingers as the magic did her bidding. The croissant expanded and stretched into a lumpy version of its former self. Had she spent more magic on it, she could have produced a perfect replica. However, she needed every ounce of magic she could spare to keep the flowers in perfect condition for Lantern Night.

Ignoring the diminished qualities of her magicked croissant, Genever ate the pastry while she performed her second morning task: checking the four iron stoves in the warehouse.

The ashes had to be swept away without disturbing any remaining embers. Split wood pieces and precious charcoal had to be magicked to prolong their life before being carefully placed in the stoves. Finally, the fires had to be gently coaxed back into life to maintain the necessary temperature for the flowers. Even so, the space devoured heat faster than Genever would have liked.

While Genever worked, Nort shared his sad tale, which, if you removed all the superfluous flourishes Nort inserted into his admittedly eloquent speech, boiled down to the simple fact that his life was a series of spectacular successes and equally devastating disasters.

He'd made and lost fortunes over the years and was currently experiencing a trough of tragedy (his words). He claimed to have one or properties in his home vale of Summerfrost. If the weather had been more amenable, Nort could have walked there in a week. As it was, he was stuck in Oasis.

"Asset rich and cash poor, I'm afraid," Nort said. "I have no money to get back home, and even if I did, it would take weeks before I could sell my property."

"I'm so very sorry," Genever said when the goblin had finished. "And I do so wish I could lend you some money, but I barely have enough to get me through to Lantern Night."

The goblin's story sounded implausible and was very close to the kinds of chicanery less ethical entities often employed to divorce unsuspecting victims from their hard-earned coins. But as Genever had neither money nor assets she could be separated from, she didn't challenge the goblin.

Nort held up a hand. "Tut, tut, I'll hear no more about money, nor will I tug on your ear about my financial woes. You've done more than anyone else in Oasis to help me out in my hour of need. Now, if you don't mind, please tell me the meaning of all these delightful flowers?" He walked down the first row, gently touching the buds and admiring their coloring.

"Oh, we're going to sell them the morning of Lantern Night," Genever said. "Someone is paying us to grow them for a party they're hosting."

"And what a magnificent gala it shall be if it's adorned with these."

"Well, I wasn't invited, so I guess I'll have to take your word for it." Roderick Torbull threw lavish parties but was somewhat less giving when it came to invitations. "I imagine they will set him apart this year, which is all he wants."

The rapid but soft tapping at the door announced Trill's arrival. Genever tugged open the door, which was far too heavy for Trill to open herself. The sprite zipped inside, landed on the nearest table, and began rubbing her upper arms.

"Bonnets and marmalade, but it's cold today!"

Genever ignored Trill's unusual turn of phrase. The sprite was given to uttering sayings Genever had never heard before.

"I can add more wood and charcoal in the stoves," Genever offered.

Trill shook her head. "Save it. Tomorrow's supposed to be

even colder." She landed lightly on the first table in front of Nort. "Hello again."

Genever knew Trill well enough to catch the edge in her voice. The kind of edge that wondered why she'd found a near stranger in the warehouse of Project Petunia, which was supposed to be secret.

"Hello," Nort replied. "A most impressive collection. I consider myself a bit of a lover of flora, and I must say, these are spectacular."

"Thank you," Trill replied. She turned to Genever. "So, are we going to start working or what?"

The implication hanging in the air was obvious: why was the goblin in their warehouse?

Genever opted for a reply that was not entirely truthful. "I've invited Nort to stay here today while we work."

"You have." Trill crossed her arms. "How kind of you."

Nort held his bowler hat in his hands, which were nervously gripping it. "Oh, I'm afraid there's a bit of a misunderstanding. I couldn't possibly impose on you both. I've taken up far too much time as it is. I wish you the best of luck with your project. May your lantern last the night, ladies."

Before Genever could stop him, Nort had opened the door. He turned and paused.

"If I'm able, Ms. Wells, I'll repay you for your kindness."

"That's not necessary, Nort. Please stay." Genever lowered her voice. "Don't mind Trill. She'll be grumpy until after lunch, but then she'll be as sweet as honey." That was also a less than truthful statement, but Genever hated the idea of the goblin wandering around in the cold, alone and miserable.

Nort placed his bowler atop his head and adjusted it slightly. "I'm sure, and I'll miss your company, Ms. Wells. Nevertheless, I won't be able to sort out my troubles sitting on my hands. I wish you both the very best."

And with that, the goblin was gone and the door was closed and Genever felt as if the world had turned a touch colder.

"Trill, that wasn't very nice. Why did you have to be like that?"

"Like what? Have you forgotten Roderick swore us to secrecy? We've been working on this project for months, testing and experimenting and burning through money we don't have. We are two days from delivering the goods, and you let a stranger waltz in here? What if he tells someone what we're up to? What if Roderick's big surprise is ruined? What if he decides he's not going to pay us?"

That was an awful lot of questions from such a small entity, and Genever wasn't sure where to start. She did admit that letting Nort in without at least consulting Trill wasn't the kind of thing polite partners did.

"I'm sorry for not telling you first, but he's totally harmless. And he's new to Oasis. Who's he going to tell? Besides, it's Winter's Tide. I couldn't let him freeze out there."

Trill shook her head. "What was his story?"

Genever related her encounter and Nort's explanation for his predicament. She found it less convincing this time around, though her heart still said the goblin was being honest.

"Look, it's all fine. No harm done. Let's get to work, okay?"

The sprite frowned but nodded. "You keep magicking the wood and charcoal to keep those stoves hot. I'll get to work on these flowers and keep them in check." She turned her attention to the flowers and rubbed her hands. "All right, my little lovelies, let's put a little blush on those buds, shall we? My friend here needs money to go to baking school, and if you can just hang on for two more days, she'll be mighty grateful."

Genever didn't correct Trill about Banneton. She hadn't shared the bad news with the sprite.

Trill began inspecting each of the plants, making sure there were no insects or blemishes or anything Roderick would deem unsuitable. Every plant he rejected meant fewer coins.

Genever pulled on the aether and funneled it into the wood to make it burn longer. She'd do that all day long, once every hour. Meanwhile, Trill would use her sprite abilities and knowledge of nature to keep the flowers on the verge of blooming. Tomorrow, her work would be done. The buds would blossom and be in perfect shape for delivery the day after.

The pair worked for three hours before taking a break. Genever pulled a five-day-old hunk of sourdough bread from one of her cloak pockets and broke off a small bite for Trill. The sprite tried eating it.

"Too hard. You'll need to soak it."

If she'd wanted to, she could have magicked the bread back to a fresher, softer state. Genever dipped the bread in a cup of water instead. "Better?"

"Eh."

"I'm baking another loaf tomorrow morning."

"I still want a croissant."

Genever smiled. "You got it."

THE TWO LADIES WORKED UNTIL JUST BEFORE DUSK, EACH APPLYING their talents to the project.

If Genever had been a garden witch instead of a hearth witch, she could have contributed more. But she had not been gifted with garden magic. She was a hearth witch, so she'd done the best she could with the magic she had.

In practice, that meant using her talents to make the fires burn longer with less wood or charcoal. It also meant stretching their food budget with a little aether. Any way she could use her hearth magic, she did.

"I think I'm ready to call it for today," Trill said.

"Let me bank the fires in the stove and give them a final boost."

When Genever was done, she gave the petunias a pleading look and a silent request to stay warm and pretty. She turned off the oil lamp and stepped outside, then locked the door.

The cloudy sky had muddled the last of the sun's light, but the snowflakes had stopped falling. Trill knelt on Genever's shoulder and clung to her cloak's hood while the witch walked to The Thicket.

"Same time tomorrow," Genever said after stopping in front of Trill's treehouse. "Chocolate croissant, right?"

"Chocolate croissant."

"Good night!"

Trill waved goodbye.

Genever took her time walking home. She savored the sights of the town, most of all the holiday decorations. Windows were filled with paper cutouts depicting various scenes: a holiday tree, a lantern, or perhaps a lit candle.

Some shop windows featured impressive and detailed displays, all hand cut from paper and fabric. Genever's favorite was the butcher's shop, which included silhouetted children playing in the snow against a skyline backdrop clearly meant to be Oasis.

Candles burned across the town as well, layering Oasis in twinkling lights.

Yes, the town certainly was delightfully decorated, and Genever made a long, looping path home despite the chill in the air. She was in no rush, though she was feeling the effects of casting so much magic. Despite trying to regulate how much aether she used, Genever was exhausted by the time she stepped into her single-room apartment. The small space was sparse—she'd sold some of her belongings to fund Project Petunia—but still had a warm, homey feel.

Genever cast a light cantrip and lit a lamp before selecting a handful of cut wood pieces from her diminishing bundle. She placed them in the small cast iron stove, along with one of her few remaining fatwood sticks. A fire cantrip lit the fatwood, and Genever funneled an ounce of aether-fueled magic into the wood to make it catch faster and burn longer.

The effort nearly wiped her out, but she still had some baking to do. Genever checked on her bread starter, which had bubbled and doubled in size during the day. The loamy mixture had a hint of vinegar to its yeasty aroma, which meant it was hungry and happy.

She hummed while she turned part of the starter into a dough. Two rounds of dough, actually, as she planned on delivering a fresh loaf to Palter as a gift and taking the other to work tomorrow for her and Trill to enjoy.

Baking bread was a simple exercise and involved only six ingredients: flour, water, salt, starter, time, and heat.

Baking tasty bread was less simple but within easy reach of most individuals.

Baking the kind of mouthwatering, life-changing bread Genever aspired to make was wildly aspirational. Yet, that was her goal. She wanted nothing short of baking the best tasting bread in the queendom.

Rather than use any aether to speed things along, she chose to make the two loaves without magic, though that's not to say it wasn't a magical act. The building blocks of bread—water, flour, and salt—were seemingly inert matter, as lifeless as could be. Combine them, however, and you could literally create life.

And that's what the kitchen represented to Genever. Life. Love. Warmth. Safety.

Genever's workspace was limited but more than enough for

her needs. She had a bowl, a small wooden table and a large wood board with which to mix, stretch, fold, and shape the two loaves. To save time, she abbreviated the process using some tried and true methods she'd learned over the years.

When she was done, she wrapped each loaf in a small towel and gently placed them in wicker baskets to rise overnight.

The air had warmed up enough for Genever to comfortably slip into her nightshirt and under her bed covers. She was asleep in minutes.

GENEVER WOKE WITH THE SUN IN HER FACE AND A SMILE ON HER LIPS, despite the frostiness in the air. Tomorrow, she and Trill would deliver the petunias and collect their hard-earned reward.

First things first, though, Genever thought.

She fed the stove some wood and then fed her bread starter (a cup of flour and a cup of water).

The starter had been in her family for at least four generations. Her mother said it was closer to ten, but it might have been more than that. Genever loved the idea that centuries ago, one of her ancestors had created a starter that was still alive today. And not just that, but the starter had fed thousands of people over the years.

She moved the two loaves, which had nicely risen overnight, from their baskets into two small cast iron pots. Four quick slices of her knife left a simple X-shaped pattern on top of the loaves. The cuts were both functional and decorative. As the dough baked, the gasses would force their way through the cuts instead of creating random cracks in the crust. The X was hardly Genever's most creative design, but she was pressed for time.

She covered the pots and set them on top of the stove. While the bread baked, she considered what she should do with her share of the Project Petunia profits.

Twenty-five golds could cover all of Genever's expenses for a month, two if she stretched them. They could also cover rent on a small shop off the beaten path for a few months. Or, they could fund part of the costs of opening a humble bakery, which would require equipment and lots of ingredients.

What twenty-five gold suns could *not* do was all three, or even two. Combined with the Banneton rejection letter, Genever had only one real option. She'd need to make the wind-fall last as long as possible, while she continued to scrimp and save. That would mean going back to work, and the sooner, the better.

Genever had quit her old job as a baker once Project Petunia was underway. The Friendly Loaf's owner had grumbled a bit when Genever quit, making just enough of a fuss that Genever knew she'd be missed but not so much that Genever felt guilty. Even though Winter's Tide was almost over, the owner would likely be glad to have an extra pair of hands back in the kitchen. After all, she'd once said Genever was the best baker she'd ever employed.

First things first, though. We need to deliver those petunias, or I can forget all about opening a bakery.

Genever dressed, donned her cloak, walked to the Moonlit Mug Café, and repeated her order from the previous morning. The guilder was gone, along with her Heart of the Vale chocolate drinks, though the café was just as crowded as the day before.

Genever handed over almost the last of her coins, making sure Palter couldn't see just how close to empty the pouch had become. "Business is still very good, I see."

Palter grinned. "Indeed."

"This is for you." Genever held out the loaf of bread she'd baked for him. "Serve it at your party or keep it for yourself."

Palter waggled his eyebrows. "That's a tough choice." He leaned close, his expression turning more serious. "I know you were hoping to go to one of the baking schools in Summerfrost, but you don't need them. You're plenty talented, and if you opened your own bakery, you'd be an instant success. And if it's money you need . . ."

The gesture flooded Genever's heart with gratitude, another reminder that the spirit of Winter's Tide was very much alive and well in Oasis.

"Thanks, Palter, I appreciate it. Truly. But I'll figure it out myself."

The owner handed her a peppermint mocha and a chocolate croissant. "You be sure to let me know if you change your mind."

TRILL FROWNED AND POKED GENTLY AT ONE OF THE PETUNIA BULBS. Half to herself, she mumbled, "What in the bottom of the seashell is going on here?"

"Sometimes you really don't make any sense."

"*In the bottom of the seashell* is an extremely common phrase where I come from, I'll have you know."

Genever sighed and waved a hand. "I meant about the flowers. What's wrong?"

Trill's curiosity turned to a deep concern. "Oh, this is a problem. This is a serious problem."

"What?"

"See that?" Trill pointed to a tiny white speck on the stem of an orchid. "That, my friend, is trouble with a capital P."

"Don't you mean T?"

"Tea? No, I mean trouble. That's whitecap blight, and if we move fast, we may only lose the one tray."

Genever's heart nearly stopped. An entire tray? That was going to cut into their profits, as well as Roderick's mood. "Are you sure?"

"Yes! Move it outside, quick as you can!"

The witch heaved the tray outside. The flowers didn't look that bad to her, but she trusted Trill's judgment. She put the tray on the ground next to the door and reluctantly went back inside.

"You're quite sure you can't save them, Trill?"

The sprite flicked from tray to tray. "That one goes, and this one, too."

"What? Two more trays?" Genever asked.

"It's that or lose the entire batch! Now, go, go, go!"

Genever took the pair of trays outside and placed them next to the first one. She didn't want to think about how much money she was literally throwing away. But if Trill was right—and Genever trusted the sprite's talents—they'd lose a lot more if the entire room caught the blight.

Still, three whole trays.

They might have talked their way out of one tray. But three? Roderick might be inclined to forget the entire thing and pay nothing, leaving the two ladies with lots of flowers to sell and very few coppers in their pockets.

Genever knelt and carefully examined each of the plants. In the brighter outdoor light, she could clearly make out dozens of white dots covering the plants. She scooped up snow and held it in her cupped hands until it melted, then washed her palms with the icy water. She repeated the process before stepping back inside the warehouse.

"What do you think, Trill?"

The sprite's frown dashed her hopes. "Whitecap blight

28

spreads like gossip covered in salt. We won't know until tomorrow if any other plants are infected." Trill narrowed her eyes. "Bet that goblin's got something to do with this. Did he touch any of these plants?"

"What? No. That's impossible. He couldn't have infected the plants." The sprite crossed her arms. "Okay, yes, he touched a few of the plants in the first tray."

Trill's frown deepened. "Look, I'm not saying he did it on purpose, but it seems pretty clear he infected the flowers. It's an easy enough thing to pick up without even realizing it."

Genever had to admit Trill had a point. But regardless of how the infections happened, the pair had the very real problem of saving as many flowers as possible.

"Okay, Trill, what's our next step?"

"Think we can track down a petalborn?"

Genever shook her head. "Given the weather, I doubt it. Besides, how would we pay them?"

Petalborn were gifted humanoids who could control plant growth. Genever had sought the services of one when she and Trill began formulating their plan, but she'd had no luck finding one in town. Had it been the summertime, they might have located a petalborn passing through Oasis. Given how much petalborn hated the cold, the odds of one being nearby were about as low as Genever's mood at the moment.

"Well, let's get to work, then," Trill said. "And please promise me you won't let any more strangers in here."

"I promise."

The pair had their work cut out for them. Even though Trill declared the remaining flowers to be blight-free, the flowers were looking noticeably worse. By the time the sprite said they were done, the sun had long since set. Genever could barely focus her eyes, and she seriously considered spending the night in the warehouse. The idea of walking home was daunting.

"Will you be all right going home alone?" Genever asked. "I don't think I've got the energy to walk home."

"Good thinking," Trill said, clearly ignoring the second part of Genever's statement. "One of us should stay here to make sure no one else tries anything funny."

There was nothing funny about the situation as far as Genever could see, though her brain was about as sharp as a wet sock, which she thought was something Trill might say.

"Right. Funny." Genever yawned and opened the door. "See you tomorrow morning."

Trill hovered in front of Genever and waved her finger. "Stay frosty, my friend."

Genever had no intention of staying frosty—whatever that meant—and added as much wood to the stoves as she dared. Lantern Night was still two days away, which meant the space would have to be kept heated for the flowers. After casting so much magic, Genever didn't have the energy to summon aether to make the fire last longer.

She drifted off to sleep almost as soon as she laid down on an empty table.

GENEVER WOKE IN A FULL-BLOWN PANIC. SUNLIGHT FILTERED THROUGH the covered windows, meaning it was after sunrise. That was not the problem. In fact, the problem was there was more than one problem.

First, though this was not at all unsurprising, Genever's stomach was twisting and growling in disapproval at its unusually empty state. She labeled this problem as both *Minor* and *Fixable*.

The second problem was her nose, which was quite cold. This was also categorized as *Minor* and *Fixable*, but it meant there was a different problem whose labels were *Major* and *Possibly Not Fixable*. The temperature was far too cold for the petunias.

The next problem wrinkled the witch's nose. An odor of decay floated in the air. Genever wasn't a sprite, a petalborn, or a garden witch, but even she knew this was a *Bigger Than Major* and *Definitely Not Fixable* problem.

"No, no, no!"

Genever rolled off her makeshift bed and cast a light cantrip. Even in the low light, it was clear the whitecap blight had spread to other trays. And the ones that weren't infected had suffered from the cold, their petals wilting and dark.

The flowers were completely unsellable now. Genever's small of savings—money she had hoped could turn into a generous amount of savings—had evaporated gone, as had her hopes. Even if she'd been accepted by Banneton, she couldn't have paid for her entrance.

And opening a bakery? That now seemed like a dream so far off in the distance, Genever couldn't see it with three telescopes and the tallest ladder in the queendom.

She reached for wood to stoke the stoves but stopped. What was the point now? What good would the heat provide in the cavernous space? No, she'd be better off taking it back to her apartment and using it sparingly while she figured out what to do next.

As bad as things were, Genever fretted over what she'd tell Trill. The sprite hadn't needed money, and her home was a tree and not an apartment. Trill had no rent to pay, and with the regular gifts from Oasis residents, The Thicket's residents rarely went hungry.

Still, the sprite was sure to be disappointed.

And she was. Genever knocked lightly on Trill's door, and the sprite soon stood shivering on her little porch. The diminutive entity's face turned serious. She glanced from Genever's sad expression to the witch's empty hands.

"What is it?"

"The flowers," Genever began. The words were burrs in her throat, and she tried again. "The flowers. They're all infected or diseased or dying. It's over. Our whole plan is ruined."

"Show me."

Ten minutes later, Genever stood in the warehouse while Trill darted about the trays. The sprite worked silently for several minutes before slowly flying back to her friend.

"You're right. Our goose is gone to winter, and that's no lie. The entire lot is worthless."

Genever already knew Project Petunia was a complete failure, but hearing Trill's confirmation was surprisingly painful.

"I was a silly witch to think this would work." Genever sat down cross-legged near a stove and wrapped her cloak around her. "I'm a hearth witch. I've got no business messing with flowers."

Trill patted Genever's knee. "I'm the one who was supposed to keep the flowers alive. Your job was fronting the money and maximizing our profits by using your magic."

"You mean the profits that are now non-existent?" Genever asked. It felt like a magic trick with a sad ending. The gold coins she'd expected to collect in less than twenty-four hours had vanished, just as her hopes for opening her own bakery.

Trill ignored the reply. "The rent's paid through the end of the month. We don't have to deal with this today. Come on, let's hit the Winter's Tide Market."

The words floated into Genever's consciousness like echoes down a well.

"No," she said absently. "I think I just want to go home."

"Come on, we'll swing by the stall that sells Lantern Night cakes. That elf owes me a favor. She'll give us a couple for free."

Genever silently walked to the market and stood in a daze while Trill chatted with the elf. Her mind kept pushing back at the idea that her dreams had truly died with the petunias.

"May your lantern last the night," the elf said as she pressed two small, wrapped cakes into Genever's hands. The gesture and the words pricked at Genever's eyes. She couldn't bring herself to utter the reply and simply smiled and nodded in thanks and hoped the elf would understand.

Trill and Genever nibbled at their cakes and meandered through the market, eventually stopping outside Genever's apartment. The air carried faint singing and laughter from the town square, but Genever's heart was in no condition to celebrate.

She dreaded having to tell Roderick about the petunias, but the sooner she did, the better she'd feel.

"We should let Roderick about his petunias," Genever said.

"Ugh. Do we have to? I mean, right now?"

Genever nodded. "We do. Come on."

The pair walked into the nicer quarter of town where Roderick Torbull's mansion rose four stories into the air. After knocking on the front gate and being escorted to the main house and into the foyer and down the hall and into a rather large waiting room, the pair finally came face to face with their client. Roderick was dressed in some of the finest clothes Genever had ever seen: a ruffled silk tunic, and dark green jacket and pants complete with a few flourishes of festive fashion.

"Ladies, this is unexpected," Roderick said. The dark-haired gentleman's youthful face looked confused. His eyebrows lifted as he pointedly looked around the room. "I might have said you were delivering the, ah, flowers early, but given the notable absence of my requested goods, I suppose that's not the case."

"No," Genever replied. "I'm very sorry, Mr. Torbull, but

there was an unfortunate development that has rendered the entire lot unusable."

Torbull's eyes narrowed. "Ladies, if this is some ruse to increase your price, I must say I'm most disappointed."

"Oh, no, it's not that at all!" Trill said. "The price was generous, but the flowers were infected with blight. My fault, entirely."

Genever looked sideways at her friend. The sprite kept her eyes on Roderick, who rubbed at his chin.

"Well, that is extremely upsetting. The petunias were to be my centerpiece for tomorrow's gala. Without those . . ." His words trailed off. "Ladies, you never struck me as the mischievous sort, so I'm only going to ask this once. Have you sold my petunias to another buyer?"

"No," Genever said. "We can show you the trays if you want proof." She waited for an outburst of anger or some rebuke about her failure or even another accusation. Instead, their client shrugged and sighed.

"In that case, I'm afraid our business is concluded and rather tragically, I might add. I'll need to completely redesign the entire decor for the gala, which will mean resetting the tables and, oh, this is going to be *such* a nightmare. You'll have to excuse me." Roderick glanced at a footman who had been silently standing by the door. "See the ladies out, please."

The footman guided Genever and Trill out of the waiting room, up the hall, through the foyer and entrance, across the yard, and out the gate before depositing them on the street.

"That could have gone worse, I suppose," Genever said. "Though we can forget about him hiring us ever again."

"Plenty more fish in the moon to hunt," Trill replied with a wave of her hand. "What's next?"

"I need to move the wood from the warehouse back to my

apartment. And we should clear out the flowers, maybe burn them so the blight doesn't spread."

"I can't help with that, but I can at least keep you company."

Genever smiled. "Thanks, Trill. I think I'd rather toil in solitude for a while, though."

"You sure?"

"Yeah."

"Are you going to Palter's party at the Mug tomorrow night?"

"Maybe," Genever lied. The idea of enjoying an evening surrounded by laughter and happiness felt as impossible as getting into Banneton. Her stomach growled at the possibility of a hot meal and a peppermint mocha, but her heart quietly shook its head in disapproval.

"Well, swing by my place if you do."

"Promise."

"And look, I know things feel really hopeless, but they'll turn around. Trust me."

Trill flew off, and Genever walked to the warehouse to begin cleaning up the mess. Her thoughts were scattered and darted about as quickly as Trill did when she was excited.

Genever wanted to trust her friend, but at that moment, she simply couldn't. How could things possibly turn around? Genever was essentially broke. She could let the warehouse space go, but she'd have to pay rent if she wanted to keep her apartment. And she'd need money if she wanted to pay rent. And she'd need a job to have any money . . .

Her thoughts tumbled and rolled around her head, which was almost certainly why she hadn't noticed Nort approaching her from behind.

"Ms. Wells! I say, Ms. Wells!" The goblin raced across the

snowy ground and stopped, nearly breathless, in front of her. "I've been looking all over for you."

"Why?"

"I wanted to see how your project went." He nodded at the warehouse's door. "Your flowers, I mean."

"See for yourself." Genever replied. "But those trays should give you an idea."

Nort stepped around the infected flowers Genever had put outside the day before and followed her into the warehouse.

"Oh, my," the goblin said, then he repeated it. "Oh, my."

He walked the rows of tables while Genever stacked the remaining wood by the door and began cleaning up. The flowers would have be disposed of, and given the blight, she'd have to burn the trays, too. She might not be a garden witch, but she knew the trays might have become contaminated as well.

The tables she could probably sell off for a few silvers a piece.

"What happened?" Nort asked.

"Whitecap blight. Took three trays yesterday and the rest today."

"Oh, my." Nort looked at his hands. "Dear, oh, dear. I believe I'm responsible for that."

"Don't be silly." Genever still wanted to give the goblin the benefit of the doubt, even though she suspected Trill was correct. "Could have come from anywhere."

"It might have, but I believe it came from me. You see, I've been spending so much time outdoors of late, and I think I accidentally came in contact with some blighted plants a few days ago." Nort rolled his eyes. "I've been a thoughtless goblin, yes, I have. Ms. Wells, I'm incredibly sorry."

The goblin's confession might have been a blow to Genever's state, but she shook her head at the confirmation that her gesture of kindness was, in fact, the cause of her current troubles. She truly had no one to blame but herself.

"No apology necessary, Nort."

"I politely disagree. I inflicted considerable consternation on you and capsized your project. I feel obligated to repay you in some way. Your kindness the other day was exactly the light of hope I needed. I was at my wit's end and feeling lost. That is, until I crossed paths with you. After you shared your croissant and your company with me, I found myself filled with renewed optimism."

"I'm glad to hear that," Genever replied. "But you truly don't need to worry over the flowers. I'll get my job back at the bakery and start saving up again."

"Saving? For what?"

"I had hoped to be accepted to Banneton. The money from this project would have covered my entrance fee at the school. But after they rejected me, I thought, oh, I know it sounds crazy, but I thought I'd open my own bakery. And the profits from Project Petunia would get me most of the way there." She looked around at the trays of dead and dying flowers. "Guess I'll just have to work a bit longer."

The goblin grew even more distressed. "Ms. Wells, I simply can't live with myself until I've rectified this oversight. If I may inquire, where are you currently residing?"

Sensing he would not give up, Genever relented and told him. Besides, if he had been telling the truth, the goblin was just as broke as she was. What could Nort possibly do to repay her? He would soon be gone from Oasis, and she'd likely never see him again.

Nort repeated the address out loud to confirm he had correctly memorized it. "Thank you. With your permission, I've business to attend to before the entire town shuts down for

Lantern Night. Please accept my sincerest apology and deepest regrets for my actions."

Genever dismissed him with a wave and well wishes for the holiday. She cleaned up the space as best she could, stacking trays on one side of the room and dragging tables to the other. She made several trips between the warehouse and her apartment until she'd stockpiled most of the remaining wood.

The late afternoon sky clouded over, and snow began falling when Genever made her final trip home. Her arms were tired, and her heart was heavy. She stoked the apartment's stove and made sourdough toast with butter—three, to be exact—before falling asleep to the distant sounds of holiday revelry.

For Genever, Lantern Night began with an annoyingly loud and rapid knocking on her door at what Trill would call a completely unreasonable hour of the morning. In this particular case, Genever was inclined to agree.

"I'm coming, I'm coming!"

Thankfully, the knocking subsided long enough for her to get dressed and rub most of the sleep from her eyes. She was still too fuzzy to give much thought as to who would be calling on her at such an early hour of the morning, but her visitor still surprised her.

When Genever opened the door, she found an elderly male gnome with gray hair and mutton chops holding a slim leather case. The gnome was dressed in a suit and sported a hat, which he removed.

"Ms. Genever Wells?"

"Yes."

"My name is Thedin C. Spanner. I've been hired to witness the transfer of deed of ownership of a bakery in Summerfrost

Vale to you." He glanced past Genever into her apartment. "May I come in? Or would you prefer to conduct our business elsewhere?"

"Um, inside. Yes. Fine. I'm sorry, did you say bakery?"

Genever was, fatigue aside, more than a little off balance. It wasn't every day she woke to a gnome lawyer trying to foist a bakery on her (though she wished it happened more often).

Thedin nodded and stepped inside, immediately removing papers from his leather case and placing them on the small table. "Indeed. If you'll just sign here, I'll take care of the rest. The papers of ownership will be waiting for you."

"Waiting? Where?"

The gnome adjusted his collar. "As I said, Summerfrost Vale. To be more precise, the bakery is located in a village known as," he looked down and consulted the papers. "Appleton."

"There must be some mistake. I've never been to Summerfrost Vale, and I don't know anyone who would give me a bakery."

There was more consultation of the paperwork before Spanner replied, "The seller is one Northington Bleveld. A goblin of your acquaintance, as I've been given to understand."

Nort? A bakery? This had to be more stuff and nonsense.

"If you mean Nort, yes, I know him. The goblin, I mean. But I still don't understand how—"

Thedin smiled at Genever, but it was a practiced smile and one she felt he used to hide other emotions he'd rather not publicly display. "Ms. Wells, I can assure you that I and my firm take particular care to vet our clients and our work. We hold ourselves to the highest standard of care. I have personally checked the paperwork on this and deemed it authentic."

"Oh, of course. I didn't mean to imply there was anything suspicious about this. Or that you were involved in anything illegal. Or, well, what I mean is, I'm sure it's all in order, but I still can't understand why—" She stopped talking. Thedin's smile had become even more fixed in place. "I'm sure it's fine."

"Wonderful." The gnome removed a bottle of ink and a quill from a coat pocket. He prepared the quill and held it out. "If you'll please initial here, here, and here, and then sign at the bottom."

Genever reviewed the paperwork as best she could. The contract was long, and the language was filled with lengthy and intimidating words like *hereto forthwith* and phrases that looked perfectly normal but didn't quite make sense after Genever read them.

She suspected lawyers were paid for their ability to use ten words when two would suffice and then twist those ten words into a puzzling pretzel whose meaning could only be deciphered by yet another lawyer.

Nevertheless, the papers did, indeed, seem to indicate Nort —or rather Northington—was transferring ownership of a bakery in Appleton to Genever, free and clear. There was no mention of payment, monetary or otherwise.

A bakery she could truly call her own! Could this be true?

Genever initialed the papers three times and signed them once and stepped back. Thedin used a silk blotter to dry the ink before filing the paperwork in his case.

"Mr. Bleveld asked me to deliver these to you once you had signed the deed transfer." The gnome handed Genever a sealed envelope and a small leather pouch that jingled with coins. The lawyer gathered his hat and said, "Good day, Ms. Wells, it was a pleasure meeting you. May your lantern last the night."

"And may your light shine bright, Mr. Spanner."

Genever opened the note.

Dear Ms. Wells,

By the time you read this, I shall be miles from Oasis and heading home. Fortune smiled on me, as my former business partner was apprehended trying to sneak out of Cozy Vales. While it will take months to unwind all the damage he's caused, the immediate benefit was the return of sufficient coins to speed the process of remedying his crimes (namely, allowing me to get home and straightening out my affairs).

However, I would be remiss if I didn't share some of my fortune with you, good lady, and not simply because today is Lantern Night. I wish you well on your baking endeavors, and, if fortune chooses to smile on us again, I hope to enjoy one of your creations at your new bakery.

Sincerely,

Northington Bleveld

P.S. Please give my regards to your friend, Trill.

Genever stood in her apartment with a note in one hand, a heavy pouch of coins in the other, and the feeling that her life was about to change forever. She only wished she knew whether her luck had taken a turn for the better or for the worse.

. . . And so concludes our cozy tale about a hearth witch whose blind generosity may have been rewarded with the key to unlocking her dream. However, her story is just beginning, dear reader. Will Genever venture to Appleton? Will she open a bakery? Will she meet Nort again? Was the goblin's gesture a noble one or simply a masterful connivance for reasons not yet revealed?

(Spoilers: yes, yes, yes, and you'll have to read Genever's next story to find out!).

If you'd like to read a short scene involving Genever learning about her hearth witch powers, discover more of her journey in Cozy Vales, and be the first to learn when her next story is published, sign up here: https://scottiswriting.com/cozy-vales-tales.

. . .

L.A. Scott is the pen name for author Scott Walker, who writes cozy and urban fantasy stories set in worlds he would love to visit and populated by people he would love to meet. Scott's love for storytelling has taken many forms over the years, but its current incarnation is writing cozy fiction. In addition to writing stories for the Cozy Vales shared fantasy world, Scott's first cozy urban fantasy series, Manhattan Magic, is now available, and you can read the first book for free. Learn more at scottiswriting.com/dwarves-and-daisies.

THE BALLAD OF THE CAT AND THE SILVER
REBECCA BUCHANAN

Listen to this tale that I
tell, the tale of the Cat and
the Silver. A vale star-high,
a poisoned spear, and a guard
quick-wingéd and quick-wittéd . . .

— from *The Ballad of the Cat and the Silver*,
as composed by Friederich of the Bog

"I beg your pardon, Master Toad, but did you just say . . .
ahem . . . did you just say that you want to follow *me*?"

Itaniph waited for the amphibian to answer. He could feel
his ears twitching, and his fur was standing on end. The
feathers on his left wing flexed nervously.

The little reddish-orange toad—Friederich, yes, that was
his name—lifted up on his hind legs, rising to his full three
inches in height. This brought him almost even with Itaniph's
nose. The toad removed his extravagant purple top hat,

wrapped as it was in layers of lavender and grape gauze; the rough-cut red jewel pinned to the front winked at Itaniph as the toad swept the hat around and bowed deeply.

"Yes, indeed, constable. It is just so." The toad sat back down and settled the hat on his head again. "I can see it. The manner in which the threads of time and history weave around you, ahead and behind. It is beautiful. You will do something worthy of song, and I wish to be present to witness and attest to the event." Friederich nodded firmly. "Yes, yes. Your name and your courage will be known throughout the queendom, and even beyond. Isn't that *wonderful?*"

Not the word Itaniph would have chosen.

He cleared his throat, his wings flexing in tandem. He shifted his front paws, aware of the thick bark beneath the pads of his feet.

Around them, citizens and visitors to Skypress Vale flitted, bopped, swooped, and dashed through the air, swinging and zipping between the massive trees: his fellow pegacats (alone and in kendels a dozen strong), plumes of pegasi, prides of gryphons, harpies, gargoyles, imps, dragons on the smaller end of the size scale. And guests from the valley below, some winged, others on carpets, trading and haggling. And flocks of all the usual birds, and butterflies alone or in roosts, and fat honeybees alone or in swarms.

Branches arched above and around and under them, filtering the high winter sunlight. Some of the branches were bare, others were thick with flowers of every color, and still others were covered in buildings of varying sizes and materials. More than a few of the larger branches bore the remains of old residences and businesses, bits of the buildings poking through from where they had been absorbed and surrounded by the endlessly growing and changing vale.

Itaniph sighed, one rear leg lifting unconsciously to scratch at his collar of office. He had no control over where the vale traveled. No one did. The mass of entangled skypress trees floated as the wind blew. He had awakened this morning to find the island leaving the golden-brown desert that was Pitaya Vale to crest the north-western slopes of the mountains that surrounded Ivy Vale.

He had visited many vales in his four years, but never Ivy. He was curious, of course, but it would also have been rude—and quite unprofessional—not to pay his respects to the local constable. Besides, there was always a chance that Skypress would still be overhead for Lantern Night three evenings hence. Their respective celebrations would have to be coordinated, as the last thing anyone wanted were kites and bags of live flame smacking into the trees. (That hadn't happened for a century, but the residents of Skypress Vale *still* talked about it.) Once they were clear of the mountains, he had left Ahna to meet with Maire Churchinien and the other Lantern Night organizers, and taken himself to the air, joining the flights of merchants, magicals, and artisans descending to Holly Town in the valley below.

Leaving Skypress, in hindsight, had been a terrible idea.

Because the bard toad had seen him, somehow, somewhere. Maybe when Itaniph was checking out the selection of woven ivy hammocks at a merchant's stall. Or perhaps when he was sampling mint and berry tea at the local Salt & Pickle Inn. Or maybe when he was paying his professional respects to Holly Town's constable and discussing Lantern Night activities. Regardless, the toad had looked *up* at just the right time, and seen . . . something. And so decided that an event in Itaniph's future was worthy of his musical skills.

An event that ... well ... bard toads did tend to favor the heroic. The adventurous, daring, narrow-escape, sure-to-lose-his-feathers-saving-the-day heroic.

"While I certainly appreciate your interest in me, Master

Toad, I do not anticipate anything particularly ... ahem ... *wonderful* happening in the short term. Or even the long term."

The toad cocked his head and blinked bright yellow eyes at Itaniph.

"Truthfully, nothing worthy of song has happened in Skypress Vale for the entirety of my term as constable."

"Indeed."

"Yes, quite." Itaniph nodded. "Nothing worthy at all. Uh, although, yes. There was that attempt by pirates from The Shoals to kidnap a plume of pegasi foals. And covert agents sent by Gravail did try to smuggle some live cuttings of skypress trees out of the vale. And, yes, somehow a carnivorous red dog found its way to the upper branches and started hunting the citizenry (we're still not sure how it got up here), but we took care of it quickly enough and dropped it in Bogbottom Vale when we passed overhead..."

The toad was smiling at him.

Itaniph scowled, ears flat. "All in a day's work," he muttered. "I promise, Constable, that you shall not even know I am here. I am very good at being unnoticeable. And quiet. Very unnoticeable and very quiet."

"Hrm."

"Booosssss! Hey, Boss!"

The call echoed down from above. Itaniph tilted his head, eyes rapidly searching the sky, the branches, the alternating patches of sunlight and darkness, the swooping and flitting crowds of winged residents and guests. A pegasus reared in mid-air, pulling back as a reddish streak darted in front of it. A gryphon swooped to avoid the same streak, hissing in agitation, and nearly collided with a visiting human sorcerer from Azure Spires; the magical shrieked, his flying carpet tumbling into a spin, before righting itself and dragging to a halt.

The sorcerer glared down over the side of his carpet.

REBECCA BUCHANAN

"Booosss!" the red streak yelled.

The pegacat snapped his tail, projecting his voice up. "Turn around. Apologize. Then report."

The red streak pulled a hard turn back up, darted to the sorcerer—"Apologies, sir! Very very sorry! Vale business! Very important!"—then swooped back down again. Within moments, the streak had resolved into Gobattie, her golden constable badge glimmering at her throat. Her frantic flight had left her dark hair a wild mess, nearly hiding her curling horns, and her red-tinted skin was flushed even brighter with exertion and excitement. Her feathery hummingbird-like wings continued to flap eagerly and her thin tail whipped back and forth, wrapping and unwrapping around her legs and waist over and over again.

And, now that she was mostly—but not quite completely—still, she was uncontrollably flitting in and out of visibility.

The toad lifted his impressive purple hat, stepping in before Itaniph could speak. "Friederich of the Bog, at your service. A pleasure to make your acquaintance. You will make a spectacular addition to the ballad. You are of imp and sprite descent, if I am not mistaken, yes?"

Gobattie snapped back into full view, nodding her head very hard and swooping in a tight circle to hover just above the amphibian. Barely twelve inches in height herself, she still dwarfed the bard toad. "Yep, yes, yes. And pixie and brownie, too."

Friederich's eyes widened. "Oh, that is *wonderful*."

There was that word again.

At least in Gobattie's case it was accurate.

Itaniph cleared his throat. "Deputy Gobattie, report."

She spun around twice, ending up just far enough from Itaniph's nose that he didn't have to cross his eyes to see her.

"Apologies, Boss. Ahna needs to speak to you right away, imme-diately, as soon as possible. Is he a bard toad?"

"Yes. Where is Ahna?"

"Old DeeDee, southern-most branches. Is the toad going to write a song about you?"

"He certainly seems to think so. Come along." Itaniph spread his wings and crouched, digging his paws into the solid bark as he prepared to leap into the air.

"I shall accompany you," Friederich announced, slapping his tall hat back onto his head.

"Oh, I don't—"

"Yes!" Gobattie exclaimed. "Can I carry you? Can I carry him, Boss? I can tell you all about the Boss while we fly. So many songs you could write!"

Itaniph tightened his jaw. With a heave of his rear legs, he sprang into the air. The wind caught his feathered and furred wings, lifting him higher, pushing him faster. He flapped hard once, and then again, legs pulled up against his belly, his tail twitching back and forth to help guide his path. He soared and swooped easily between the branches and trunks of the trees, and among the vale's many citizens (an angry harpy chasing a little dragon, a group of sprites hauling bags of honey), and visiting merchants and artisans and magicals on flying carpets.

Moments later, Gobattie came alongside him, the little toad clutched in her arms. He had one sticky-fingered hand lifted to hold his hat in place, listening with an enraptured expression as she told him all about the pirates, and their wicked plan to kidnap the foals, and their shadow-cloaked balloon that had dared to anchor to Skypress Vale on the night of the Horned Crescent Moons.

". . . AND THAT'S HOW WE RESCUED THE PEGASI FOALS! IT WAS ALL Boss's plan! Isn't he *wonderful?*"

"Quite astounding, Deputy Gobattie. I do thank you for sharing that tale with me. It will make an excellent addition to the ballad."

Itaniph tried not to roll his eyes as he veered around the massive trunk of Old DeeDee. No one knew exactly how Skypress Vale had come to be. Maybe it had been born along with the rest of the vales when founding queen Mishra had planted that magic golden acorn. Or maybe it had been floating around for centuries and then become trapped somehow within the borders of the new land.

No matter. He left such speculations to the historians and magicals. But it was generally agreed, given the tree's size and how its roots extended to the very edge of the floating mass of flora, that Old DeeDee had to be one of the foundational skypress trees; too much of the rest of the vale was entangled with it for the tree *not* to be ancient.

Itaniph flicked his wings and dove down, following that massive trunk deeper into the shadows, closer to the roots. They left the branches behind and, with them, most of the population of the vale. Down here, hidden among the roots, were the vast, sprawling bees' hives and the snarls of squirrels' nests. Usually the only people who came down here were . . . honey collectors.

Itaniph flipped around, lowering his rear legs towards a fat root. He flapped rapidly, slowing his descent, and settled onto the bark beside Ahna and the honey collectors. Gobattie and her passenger followed a moment later.

Or near to the half-sylph deputy, at least. As always, Ahna was hovering by an inch or so. Her bare feet dangled and her loose white trousers and blue and white vest rippled in the soft breeze that perpetually surrounded her. Even her long black hair, with its threads of white and blue, was always moving.

As a pegacat, Itaniph could fly. He could make use of the winds for gliding. But he wondered, sometimes, what it was like to actually *be* the wind.

He dipped his head in greeting, first to Ahna, then the honey collectors. "Deputy Constable. Jharral. Freneth."

The two sprites nodded in turn. Their expressions were a mixture of confusion and concern, their wings occasionally snapping in agitation; otherwise, they were still, arms wrapped around fat leather pouches of honey.

"Jharral and Freneth were down here collecting honey in hopes of selling some in Ivy Vale." Ahna paused. "Is that a bard toad?"

"Yes, but ignore him. He is very good at being very unnoticeable and very quiet. Proceed."

"Understood. Jharral and Freneth went to several of their usual hives, but the honey looked odd. Dark brown. Clumpy. The deeper and lower they went into the roots, the stranger the honey became."

Ahna waved a hand. The breeze caught the edges of Itaniph's whiskers and his nose twitched.

Still looking uncertain, Freneth came forward and opened her pouch.

Itaniph's nose twitch turned into a sneer and a near-gag. Beside him, Gobattie gasped and covered her mouth. Itaniph's ears flattened as he leaned forward and peered into the bag.

The honey stank. It reeked of rotting plant matter and something bitter and cold. It was also the wrong color—such a dark brown that it was nearly black—and too thick, with patches clumped together almost like tar.

"This is where we found the dead bees," the sprite whispered.

Itaniph hissed softly. Freneth hastily backpedaled, her wings folding tight against her back, her shoulders hunched.

"My apologies, Freneth. That was not directed at you. It is good that you brought this to our attention. Could the two of you do something for me?"

The sprites straightened, nodding firmly, talking over one another.

"Yes, absolutely!"

"Of course, Constable!"

"We'd be happy to!"

"Yes!"

"Excellent. First, I need you to tell us exactly where you found this honey and the dead bees. Then, I need you to fly to Maire Churchinien. Tell them—and only them—what you found. Tell them, too, that the deputies and I are investigating. When we have found something, we will report to the maire and the vale council. If we do not return by sunset, they should gather a search party, and make sure there are at least a few magicals in their number skilled in floral magic. Understood?"

"Yes!"

"Find the maire!"

"Search party!"

"Magic!"

"Sunset!"

"Very good. Now, describe *exactly* the location of this hive."

THE SPRITES' DIRECTIONS WERE DETAILED AND ACCURATE. THEY KNEW every root, every bump of bark, every intersection of tree trunks and the names of the trees. Once the sprites departed, their wings catching and rainbowing the sunlight, Itaniph turned and started walking *down*.

Down and down and down, following that fat root from Old DeeDee to another fat root from the tree known as Great Juphineith to another emerging from Twisted Geirgeis. Along that root, then down to another and another and another. Messy squirrel nests and a few bird nests clung to the roots and, here and there, hives; bees dodged in and out, legs sticky with the pollen of the hundreds of flowers that had learned to grow from the bark and dead branches of the skypress trees.

The sunlight faded quickly, becoming shafts of brilliance woven through shadows, and then was gone.

There were advantages to being a pegacat. Flight was only one of them. The ability to see in near total darkness had proven useful many times during Itaniph's career as constable —though not so much when they had been struggling to rescue the pegasi foals from the pirates.

The sky disappeared, too, and the wind. There was only the massive root system of the skypress trees. Moisture collected here, first in droplets along the ridges of the bark, then in a thin fog, and finally in full clouds. The only breeze was that generated by Ahna. Below, far below, beyond the bottom of the mass of entangled roots, he could just hear the howl of the dangerous winds that swirled in a great knot beneath the trees; even the rare crack of thunder as lightning arced between the clouds to ground in the lowest roots.

The constable's ears flattened in discomfort. The moisture clung to his fur, darkening the brindle pattern and forming thick tufts.

Perhaps being a pegacat had its disadvantages, too.

Itaniph glanced over at Gobattie, who was biting her lip, her eyes darting around. Her tail was wrapped tight around her waist. The bard toad was perched on her back, peering over and around her head, his yellow eyes shining, his tall hat sticking out at a jaunty angle. Itaniph had almost forgotten he was there. It would appear that Friederich *was* very good at being very unnoticeable and very quiet.

"There," Ahna said. She floated past him, the breeze barely tickling his matted fur. The roots were growing close and she had to twist sideways and duck to fit through. Itaniph followed, then Gobattie and the bard toad.

The bees had filled in the spaces between the roots with leaves and mud and honey, creating a hollow large enough for Ahna to float upright. It should have been filled with sound and movement and sweet scents. Instead, it was utterly still and silent. Tar-like honey oozed from the walls. The hive reeked of that same rotting plant smell.

And there were dead bees everywhere.

Itaniph stepped gingerly, his lips curled. Some of the bees were freshly dead, their bodies still thick with gold and black fuzz. Others were stiff and skeletal, legs curled in tight.

"Ahna. Gobattie." He flinched, his voice echoing too loudly. It seemed an insult in what was now a crypt. "Try to find the queen. If she is still alive, we might be able to save the hive."

"She's not," Gobattie whispered.

The deputy stood a few feet in front of him, her chin nearly touching her chest. She sighed, her shoulders sagging. Between one blink and the next, she disappeared. For a moment, Friederich the bard toad appeared to be floating in midair.

But then she moved and flickered back into visibility, her shoulders shaking as she cried.

Itaniph moved carefully around her, across the floor thick with bee carcasses. Ahna floated at his side, a gust of angry wind making her hair and clothing snap.

Gobattie had found the queen. She was larger than the other bees, but still smaller than she must have been in life. Her antennae and legs were curled in tight, her fuzz of gold and black nearly gone.

The bard toad sighed, a deep and heavy sound for such a little body. He lifted his gaudy purple hat from his head, pressing it to his chest. "This shall make for a very sad ballad. Yes, it shall. Very sad."

THERE WERE MULTIPLE HOLES SCATTERED ACROSS THE INNER SURFACE of the hollow for the bees to enter and exit. None were large enough for Itaniph or his deputies, and Ahna was not quite agitated or angry enough—yet—to shift into her full sylph form and escape as a breeze. The toad, however, was small enough. He crawled his way through a handful before he found one that opened onto another root wide enough for them to walk.

Between Itaniph's claws and Ahna's wind, directed in short controlled blasts, they were able to break a hole in the wall of the hollow. They crawled through and kept going down.

The bark beneath Itaniph's paws gradually turned as dark as the tar-like honey. It flaked and broke away in chunks, falling. The wood itself felt too soft; saturated and squishy.

Itaniph did not like it. No, he did not like it at all.

The cloud of moisture that had collected among the roots was so thick now that it seemed to Itaniph that he was walking through a rainstorm. It weighed down the ends of his whiskers and whirled around Ahna, caught by her wind. The cloud was too heavy even for Gobattie to fly, her hummingbird-like feathers dripping.

And then, suddenly, the cloud was gone.

Itaniph stumbled to a halt, blinking rapidly at the onslaught of sunlight. His fur stood on end, the wind whipping past his ears to strip the water from his body. In a matter of moments, he was dry again—and cold.

He peered over the edge of the root. It was barely wide enough for him to walk, not even four inches across. He stared straight down over the side, through the maelstrom of winds that curled and convulsed under the skypress trees, through quarter-mile of open air and right into Ivy Vale.

"Um, Boss?" Gobattie whispered. "Shouldn't we be . . . higher?"

The toad *rr-bb-tt*-ed and jumped from Gobattie's back to a nearby root, catching his hat before it could fly away.

Ahna scowled. "We'll never make it back over the mountains again if we stay this low. Skypress Vale will crash right into the mountainside, no matter which direction the wind blows us."

Itaniph blinked again and swallowed hard.

They were right. The vale was far, far too low.

He lifted a paw, examining the dark, tacky yet brittle bark that clung to his toes and the tips of his claws. "I doubt this is natural. The vale is at least as old as the queendom, and there is no mention anywhere in any of the Constables' Logs about anything like *this*."

Ahna pursed her lips, following the root as she floated past him. "It *could* be natural. We know how the trees live, and something about how they are seeded. And we know they definitely don't like fire. But we know nothing about how or when they die. What if they are nearing the end of their lifespan?"

Gobattie gasped, her eyes going wide. "Noooo . . ."

Itaniph scowled and shook his paw, flicking away the bits of bark. "I do not like that idea."

A pause, then Friederich spoke. "You may be correct, constable, that this is not natural."

Itaniph paused, raising one eyebrow as he turned his head to look for the bard toad. The little amphibian was perched on a narrow root above his head; so narrow, in fact, that it bent under Friederich's weight.

The toad lifted one sticky-fingered hand, pointing across the gap.

Itaniph squinted. Unable to see what the bard had spotted, he flexed his wings and leapt onto another root, then another. He twisted and slithered until he had come to rest just a little higher and to the left of Friederich.

Ahna, meanwhile, had just lifted herself up, wind pulling at her clothes and hair. She hovered, bobbing. Then her eyes widened and she sank back down beside Gobattie.

Itaniph felt his ears flatten against his skull.

There, perhaps thirty feet away, glittered something sharp and silver. And all around it, the roots had turned black. Great pits bled tar-like sap that dribbled into the wind. The storm beneath the vale caught that sap, rolled and hurled it, throwing it far and away, out into Ivy Vale.

"Oh dear," Gobattie whispered.

The constable paused, thinking, thinking, thinking hard. He couldn't see the sun from here, but he studied the angle of light hitting the too-close trees and buildings below. They must have been wandering through the root system for more than . . . four hours? Perhaps longer. It was already late afternoon.

"Gobattie, I need you to go back branch-side. I have no doubt that Maire Churchinien, or someone, would have noticed the vale *sinking*. Tell them everything we've found. Ahna and I will attempt to deal with . . . *that*, but the maire should be ready to evacuate the population. Understand?"

His deputy nodded, head bobbing rapidly. "Maire. Bees. Silver. Evacuation. Friederich should stay here with you."

"Agreed." The toad nodded.

Itaniph's ears flattened. "Uh, I really don't—"

"Song worthy! Give me a boost, Ahna!" Gobattie yelled and

then stepped off the edge of the root. She dropped fast. Ahna's hand flicked out and a breeze caught the little deputy, holding her steady in the midst of the maelstrom. Her wings snapped and she shot forward, angling down until she was free of the tumultuous winds.

Itaniph lost sight of her as she dipped sideways, her golden badge glinting, a reddish speck against the bright blue sky.

IT TOOK THEM ANOTHER TWENTY MINUTES TO MAKE THEIR WAY towards the sharp silvery *thing*. More than once, Ahna had to summon the wind and bend roots out of the way, creating a path for the three of them.

The closer they got to the sharp silvery spear, the greater the stench. And the more brittle the bark became, while, paradoxically, the wood of the roots grew squishier. They sagged and creaked and squelched simultaneously. It was an unnerving combination of sounds and sensations.

"Bard Friederich," Itaniph panted, hauling himself through a narrow opening, "I think it best if you find a comfortable place on my back. If the roots should give way beneath us, you are the only one who cannot fly."

The toad made a soft *ribb-tted* sound, his eyes widening. When Itaniph was clear of the opening, the bard gingerly hopped forward and leapt onto his back. He settled into the hollow between Itaniph's shoulder blades, one sticky-fingered hand pressed against the pegacat's collar of office.

Itaniph could barely feel him. It was no wonder that Gobattie had been able to carry him so easily. A kitten weighed more.

The silver spike was much larger than the toad. They were close enough now—about ten feet, across a gap of wind and sky

—that Itaniph could see it clearly, lodged in a wall of roots. It spiraled round and round like some unicorn horns, but was most definitely *not* a horn. Longer than his tail, it reflected back every bit of sunlight in glittering white rainbows.

Elsewhere, elsewhen, it would have been beautiful.

"Spider silk," Ahna hissed.

Itaniph's head reared back, and Friederich made a louder *ribb-tt-ed* sound.

Argentia. A fatal poison to every and all of the elven races, and there were rumors that it could do serious harm to others.

Apparently, it could do serious harm to skypress trees, as well.

Did that mean the skypress were of elven origin? Born of elven magic?

Bah. Another debate for magicals and historians.

Itaniph tightened his jaw and lowered his head. "Is the metal a threat to you, Bard Friederich?"

"No, constable. Fortunately, it is not."

"Then hold tight."

He spread his wings and jumped. The root beneath his feet dipped alarmingly at the thrust of weight, cracked, and broke. From the corner of his eye, Itaniph saw Ahna leap away, floating further back to a slightly more solid surface. The broken root fell, and was caught by the winds; within moments, it was a scattering of dust and clumps of pulp.

Itaniph flapped madly, feeling Ahna give him a boost when an errant wind tried to pull him down, too. And then he was safely, in a manner of speaking, on the other side of the gap, clinging to three different roots. His claws dug into the soft wood, and bark dust irritated his nose. He was sideways, peering down at the silvery spiral of argentia. The toad was making unhappy sounds behind his ears.

He glanced over at Ahna, still on the other side of the now-wider opening. She pursed her lips at his inquiring look, then spread her arms. Her hair danced wildly, the white and blue streaks mesmerizing as they wove in and out of the black strands. She stepped forward, into nothingness. She walked as she floated, trousers snapping, one step, two, three, four.

With the fifth step, she reached out and grabbed a root. She dug her toes into the rotten wall of twisting wood and her hair settled into gentler waves.

She gasped, drawing in deep, steadying breaths, then wrinkled her nose. Her toes and fingers flexed. "You've been walking on *this*? It's disgusting."

"Yes. Can you pull or pry this loose?" He dipped his head at the shard.

She frowned and peered closer. "Perhaps."

Ahna flicked the fingers of one hand, twisted her wrist, waved her arm up to the elbow, then the shoulder. With each successive blast of wind, harder and sharper, more of the mushy black bark and wood broke away. It came off in clumps and chunks, tipping out into the void or being thrown clear and then tumbling into the maelstrom below.

Itaniph frowned. Saving Skypress Vale was his first priority. His oath was to the people here. But there was a chance—great or small, he had no idea—that this rotted wood might be contaminated. It might present a threat to Ivy Vale below and the people who called it home, and even the people visiting from around the queendom.

He would need to alert the constable and maire below. They would need to find all of these globs of wood and clumps of bark and dribbles of tar-like sap and dispose of them. Somehow.

Ahna hissed. There was a loathsome sucking sound and the spiraled shard lurched free of the rotten, squishy wood. The deputy held it suspended for a long moment, sweat beading on her forehead. And then her hand dropped. Her knees gave out and she collapsed against the wall of roots. Her arms were shaking, and she was barely able to hold herself in place.

The silvery spear of argentia hung in the air.

And then it fell.

Itaniph jumped. He felt a minuscule weight flop into the back of his head, but then he was down, beneath the bottom roots of Skypress Vale. Wind screamed around him, yanking hard at his wings, his tail, his ears and whiskers. He could hear only wind and thunder. But he could feel the toad clinging to his scalp and collar.

The bard was mad. Absolutely mad.

Itaniph flapped frantically, spinning and arcing his body, tumbling, hunting for the shard. Lightning flashed in his periphery, and thunder assaulted his ears.

There. Far below, the shard glinted in the late afternoon light, corkscrewing and somersaulting end over end as the wind tossed it back and forth.

But still it fell, down and down towards Ivy Vale.

Itaniph kicked his wings, snapped his tail, angling towards the shard. His collar pulled tight against the front of his throat as the toad was thrown back. Somehow, the mad bard managed to keep his sticky-fingered grip.

He slanted his body down, flapping, then pulled his wings in tight. He dove, whiskers pressed flat against his face, fur rippling.

Closer to the shard. Closer.

Out of the maelstrom. They cleared the violent whirling beneath the roots and dove into open air. There was just normal wind here, screaming past him as he dove down and down and down.

Closer to the shard. Closer to the trees. Closer to the ground.

The argentia glinted, almost mocking.

Closer to the trees. Closer.

And then he caught it, his mouth opened wide to seize the shard between his teeth. It was cold and tasted bitter. He tried not to swallow, pulled his tongue back into his throat and away from the spider silk.

He could hear the toad now, yelling "Fabulous! Wonderful! Absolutely *wonderful!*"

Not the words Itaniph would have chosen.

He extended his legs, spread his wings, slapped his tail. His descent slowed, his body flattening out. He slowed further, flapping, feathers and fur and muscles straining, and curved into a controlled flight.

Not quite to the treetops, but terrifyingly close. Itaniph could see the humans and elves and fauns and centaurs and many others of Holly Town below. Some were pointing up, their expressions a mixture of concern and confusion. Others were clapping their hands and stamping their hooves, seemingly amused.

Another strong pull of his wings, and then a second. He swept wide and tipped his head back, looking up towards Skypress Vale. From down here, it was a big cloud with random flashes of lightning and, beyond that, the mammoth shadow that was the entangled mass of skypress trees.

Trees that were rapidly emptying. A plume of pegasi, solid white and solid black and a few dark reddish brown, their broad wings churning, were streaming over the sides of the floating vale. They had nets strung between them filled with foals whose wings were not strong enough yet for flight. There was a pride of gryphons, too, bundles clasped in their claws and aquiline beaks. And smaller forms that had to be pegacats and sprites and harpies.

Now the people below realized that something was wrong. Itaniph could hear their amusement turning to cries of fear.

THE BALLAD OF THE CAT AND THE SILVER

He arched his back and headed up. He wanted to yell at the toad to hold tight, but didn't dare loosen his grip on the shard of argentia—no matter how cold and bitter it tasted.

Up and up he flew, giving the plumes and prides and other evacuees as wide a berth as possible. A few of the passing gryphons and sprites threw questions at him, all of which he ignored. He spotted Jharral and Freneth, each carrying pixie-sized bags and pots of flower seeds. As he drew closer, he could see Churchinien coursing back and forth, swooping round and round the vale, diligently performing their job as maire and looking out for the citizens of Skypress.

"Boss! Booosssss! Hey, Boss!"

Itaniph turned his head, catching sight of Gobattie just as she streaked to a fluttering halt inches from his head. Her wings buzzed madly, and she fought to keep pace with Itaniph as the constable continued up and up.

Gobattie held out a black leather bag as long as her body, with a thong woven through the top. "Here! I brought this. I figured that silvery thing would be bad to touch. Maire Churchinien was already getting ready to evacuate! You were right. They noticed the vale sinking. Do you know what that is? Is that argentia? Eeeww. Where's Ahna? Do we need to send someone to get her?"

Itaniph spit the spiral shard into the pack. Grateful to be rid of the foul thing, he gagged and shook his head. "Good thinking with the bag. The maire is very observant. And yes to sending someone for Ahna. She was quite weak when I last saw her."

"Will do, Boss!" Gobattie drew the thong tight, closing the mouth of the pack and then looping it around his head. "Beg your pardon, Bard Friederich! You still have your hat! That's amazing!" And then she was away, a reddish blur. Itaniph could just make her out, heading for a small group of gryphons. He recognized a few of them as citizens he had temporarily deputized in the past.

The memory had him turning his head, looking down. The plume of pegasi had landed on the outskirts of Holly Town. Some of the residents were rushing over to help, lifting the foals and untangling them from the nets. The other evacuees were spreading out, landing on the opposite side of town or even further out in the woods.

"Constable Itaniph." The maire's voice was a deep rumble, drawing his attention. The gryphon slowed their flight, golden-brown and black wings as long as their body, allowing Itaniph to fly alongside. "Report."

"The cause of the damage to the skypress trees has been identified and removed. It appears to be a piece of argentia."

The maire's heavily feathered eyebrows jumped. "I was unaware that skypress were susceptible to argentia poisoning."

"Neither was I."

A second gryphon pulled up alongside them. Ahna sat perched on her back. *Solidly* on the gryphon's back. The fact that she was not floating was a testament to her exhaustion.

Itaniph grimaced and continued. "At this time, it is unclear if this was an accident or sabotage. I recommend a full investigation."

"Agreed." The maire let loose a loud, annoyed cry. A group of harpies who had been standing on an outer tree of the vale, arguing about something, squeaked in alarm. They hastily jumped over the edge, arms filled with sacks, nodding an apology to Churchinien. "Do you believe that the vale is out of danger now? Now that the poison has been removed?"

"From the argentia itself, I believe so. But I recommend that we send any magical we can find who is gifted in floral magic to the site of the contamination. The vale is still falling. The trees may heal themselves, but if the process can be accelerated so that the vale can lift itself back up, high enough to clear the mountains of Ivy Vale . . . "

"Agreed." The maire nodded. "Keep this argentia in your custody for now. Guard it carefully. Start collecting the magicals you need. Coordinate with the maire and constable in Holly Town as needed. Just in case the worst should come to pass, I will continue to oversee the evacuation." Another loud and even more aggravated cry, making Itaniph's fur stand on end. This time it was directed at a gargoyle who was struggling to fly with three massive iron trunks. "You there! I said essentials *only!*"

Itaniph veered down, Ahna and the second gryphon following. "Very well, then. You heard the maire. Let's go find some magicals . . ."

As it turned out, the flying carpet sorcerer whom Gobattie had almost sent tumbling was a specialist "in all that grows, whether underwater, underground, on the ground, or in the air."

His name was Markisin, and Itaniph hoped that the sorcerer was as knowledgeable and skilled as he claimed—along with the half-dozen other witches, warlocks, and druids they had managed to find who swore to have an ability for various strands of green magic.

They all crowded onto that flying carpet and Itaniph led them up to the rotted, squishy section at the bottom of the entangled root system. Up through the maelstrom, up through the hole in the cloud, to the stinking, flaking roots.

Markisin gaped, then grimaced, then made a thoughtful sound. He stood in the middle of the carpet, eyes narrowed, lips pursed. The other witches, warlocks, and druids huddled on their hands and knees, reacting to the height, smell, and sight of the decaying trees about as Itaniph had expected: terrified and/or curious and/or aghast.

They argued for an hour. The vale continued to fall, and yet still they argued. Itaniph scratched impatiently at the bark. The sun set beyond the rim of Ivy Vale. Ahna eventually regained her strength and floated to a nearby root, the gryphon who had carried her gratefully escaping the loud and lengthy discussion. Itaniph crouched nearby, hating the feel of the squishy root against his belly.

On top of Itaniph's head, the toad muttered to himself. "This part I shall leave *out* of the ballad. Magicals blah this, magicals blah that. It will just slow down the song."

After much waving of arms and citing of obscure, arcane texts and a few gardening manuals, the magicals settled on a solution.

"Cut it out," Markisin declared. "The original piece of argentia was larger. It has been broken down, absorbed by the roots of the skypress trees. The source has been removed, yes, but the poison will continue to work its way through the vale's interconnected vascular system."

Ahna crossed her arms. "You want us to *cut* a skypress tree? You want us to willfully *remove* part of the vale?"

Markisin nodded firmly once. "Yes. Pruning the poisoned roots is the only way to save the vale."

"That's assuming we don't prune the vale's ability to float in the process." Itaniph tightened his jaw. "No one truly understands how or why the skypress trees *work*."

The sorcerer shrugged. Those gathered around his feet looked away or raised their hands helplessly. "This is our solution. And it is the only one we can offer. Cut here and the vale might survive. Do not cut, and the vale surely *will* die."

AND SO THEY CUT. ALL NIGHT, THEY CUT. THE CITIZENS OF SKYPRESS Vale returned with saws and chisels and mallets, singly and in swarms. The few winged citizens of Ivy Vale joined them, carrying their own tools. The pegacats and sprites were small enough to fit among the roots, while the gargoyles and harpies worked along the outer edges. They hacked away, breaking and snapping every bit of rotted root they could find. The poisoned wood fell into the maelstrom, twisting and spinning. Those pieces that were not pulverized were caught by gryphons and dragons and carried off to be burned. Sylphs and others who could speak to the wind collected the fine dust and smaller clumps, herding the debris into bags carried between pairs of pegasi.

They worked by starlight and moonlight and magical light. A strange, frightening imitation of the Lantern Night they would soon be celebrating.

Hopefully.

And Itaniph worried. How much poison had fallen into Ivy Vale before they discovered the argentia? If the argentia had been there longer than they suspected, had any fallen into Pitaya Vale before they crossed the mountains? Would fire be enough to destroy it? If not, how much dust was now being carried by the wind, over the mountains and into other vales? Was it too little to matter? Or was the poison now being carried throughout the queendom?

He prayed to the Great Dam and the Wanderer, she who had created the pegacats and he who had taught them to fly, that his fears would come to nothing.

All night, they cut. They hacked and chopped and whittled

away at their home. Gradually, as the rot was cut away, the hole in the clouds grew smaller and smaller and finally closed.

And, with the rising of the sun, it was done.

ITANIPH'S EARS TWITCHED. THE ROCK BENEATH HIS PAWS WAS COLD. This close to the peaks of the mountains, frost and ice clung to the stone all year round. There were no trees this high, either. Itaniph had an unobstructed view of Skypress Vale as it slowly, slowly, slowly lifted and lifted and lifted. The clouds that swirled beneath the roots skimmed the tops of the trees as the wind pushed Skypress closer to the north-eastern border of Ivy Vale and, beyond that, Pearl Flower Vale.

Beside him, Ahna hovered silently while Gobattie clutched her hands and bounced, wings a blinding buzz. Friederich had started on her back, but quickly jumped clear. Itaniph only knew the toad was still around when he caught sight of the top of that purple hat over a small rock.

Bard toads did tend to favor the heroic. The adventurous, daring, narrow-escape, sure-to-lose-his-feathers-saving-the-day heroic.

Far below, the citizens of Skypress and Ivy waited anxiously side by side. They were smudges in the distance, clumped together in and around Holly Town, watching.

Maire Churchinien twisted their head from side to side. "The cloud *is* hiding the gap in the roots."

Itaniph's ears twitched again. The black bag with the spear of spider silk was a heavy weight around his neck. "The Royal Guard has a post in Pearl Flower Vale. I shall deliver the argentia to them and make a full report. I must say that I do find it curious that Skypress Vale cleared the northwestern mountains of Ivy easily, and then almost immediately began to experience problems."

"It's going up! It's working!" Gobattie squeaked and clapped her hands. "I knew it would work! I knew it! I knew it!"

Ahna drifted closer. "So either the argentia had been present for an unknown length of time and the poison finally reached a critical level, or the argentia was introduced *after* we arrived in Ivy Vale and the poison spread very, *very* quickly."

Itaniph did not like either option. No, he did not.

He would not decline an offer from the Royal Guard to assist with the investigation. He was almost certain that he would need it.

"It's working, Boss!"

Up and up and up. The trees thinned out and disappeared, exposing the bare rock of the mountain. The cloud, thunderous, with occasional flashes of lightning, swept closer, closer, shadowed by the tangle of skypress trees. Then overhead. He could feel the moisture and electricity on his whiskers. Thunder boomed. The massive form of the skypress trees blocked out the sun. It was even colder in the dark. Up and up and up—

And over the peaks of the mountains, with scant dozens of feet to spare, crossing the border into Pearl Flower Vale.

The sun returned, warming the stone beneath his paws. Itaniph heaved a sigh of relief, his head dropping, his wings sagging.

Gobattie cheered and whooped, spinning madly. Down in the valley, matching shouts and exclamations. Some of those distant smudges took to the air, arrowing towards home.

Ahna just smiled.

Maire Churchinien stretched, their claws scraping across the stone. "I shall see to our people's return. You, Constable Itaniph, have a delivery to make."

"Yes, Maire."

Itaniph's eyes narrowed as the bard toad jumped into view, the red jewel on his hat sparkling.

"And I shall accompany you."

"Shall you, Master Toad?"

"Yes indeed, Constable. Just so." The toad sat back down, settling the hat more squarely on his head. "I can see it. The threads of time and history have changed in their weaving around you, in their infinite pattern. You have accomplished something worthy of song, and a great ballad I shall make of it." Friederich nodded firmly. "Your name and your courage—yes, and those of your deputies and your maire and the people of Skypress Vale—shall be known throughout the queendom, and even beyond." His bright yellow eyes seemed almost to glow with delight. "Isn't that *wonderful?*"

REBECCA BUCHANAN IS THE EDITOR OF THE PAGAN LITERARY EZINE *Eternal Haunted Summer*, and is a regular contributor to *evOke: witchcraft*paganism*lifestyle*. She has published poems, short stories, and novelettes in a wide variety of venues, and has released several stand-alone novellas. The most recent are *Geek Witch and the Treacherous Tome of Deadly Danger* and *The Adventure of the Faerie Coffin: Being the First Morstan and Holmes Occult Detection*. A complete list of her publications can be found at *Eternal Haunted Summer*.

DORMANT

SELINA J. ECKERT

I settled onto the cold earth path in the middle of the greenhouse. The snow had piled up outside, but inside the glass walls, it was still mild. Not warm enough for plants to naturally grow on their own, at least not the plants we needed, but warm enough that I could leave my heavy cloak on the peg by the door. Spring and summer flowers were on the other side of the greenhouse, sleeping until the snow melted, but I sat in the winter section . . . the section that should have been the easiest to encourage right now. And yet the small patch of earth that had been assigned to me was still barren, unlike my family's flowerbeds. Lila's was full of tiny white snowdrops, Penny's had bright yellow winter jasmine, Weiland's was full of red winterberries, and Mom and Dad's had a mix of hellebores and poinsettias. While Mom didn't have magic of her own, since she was human, they always worked together and still somehow grew twice as many flowers as my siblings. All the family plots were ready for harvest, to be assembled into holiday wreaths and bouquets.

Except for mine.

They'd left me to grow red and white camellias. I loved

camellias, loved their full, lush blooms. And I couldn't grow them to save my life. Which, of course, my family knew. Yet they assured me it would be okay if I couldn't do it. That they would cover for me, and I could work the register again.

Just like always.

I sighed, disappointment with myself heavy in my chest. They always made sure I had something to do in the family business, tried to make me feel included, but even though they were nice about it, I could never measure up to their abilities. For once, I just wanted to work the innate plant magic that came easily to the rest of them. I wanted to experience the joy their magic brought them.

I wanted them to be proud of me, to contribute to the business as more than a clerk.

I reached a hand toward my empty plot, hovering it over the soil and trying to feel the seeds within, seeds I'd planted a full two weeks ago. There should have been *something* by now. With our innate magic, we didn't even need to wait. We could coax as many blooms as we wanted, when we wanted, as long as we gave the plants the nutrients they needed.

Well, the rest of my family, other than my mom, could. They could just touch a seed or the soil, infuse it with aether, and the plant would react. They could even communicate with the plants somehow. I didn't understand it, though, and I couldn't explain it, since I also couldn't forge that connection between plant and magic.

"Hey, Faren," came a voice from behind me. "No luck yet?"

I shifted to see Aster, who lived next door with her husband and young son. She was one of my closest friends in Honeyhive Vale, also in her mid-twenties, except she had her life way more together than I did. Aster's light lavender skin almost glowed from the light reflected by the snow outside, and the thorny horns on the sides of her head glimmered. She was one of the petalborn, common creatures in the vale with connections to the plants.

Like us.

Except I was probably the worst petalborn in existence, since I couldn't influence a single flower to do anything I asked. Maybe I just didn't have enough magic, like the human half of me was stronger. Unlike my siblings, I almost looked more human than petalborn, other than the pink cast to my light skin and hair and the honey gold shade of my eyes.

I sighed and leaned back from my plot. "Nothing."

Aster gave me a pitying half smile, then held a hand toward me. "Why don't you take a break? They're putting decorations up in the square, and it's really beautiful out."

I took her offered hand and let her pull me to my feet. Together, we walked to the door, and I grabbed my cloak before we stepped into the biting wind.

I winced as the cold hit my skin. Like Aster, I didn't care much for the cold, and this was the coldest it had been in Honeyhive Vale in years. The plants had gone dormant outside the greenhouses, and the bees and other pollinators were fast asleep. Yet the town was as busy as a hive preparing for the biggest day of the holiday season, the day we all lit our lanterns for the night to remember this past year and hoped for good luck in the coming year. With Lantern Night fast approaching, everyone was pitching in to decorate, just as Aster had said. The evergreen tree in the middle of town was most prominent, tiny candles stuck to many of its branches. There was no way they could be lit in this weather, but hopefully when it was actually time, the wind would die down. If not, we'd find other ways to share our light, like extra candles in the windows.

I looked around the square. There were small street booths in front of many of the shops, ready for the big party, each of them strung with paper decorations and wide swaths of winter florals.

If I didn't get those camellias growing, I'd just be the shop clerk again this year. Nothing magical about the season for me.

"Let it go," Aster said softly. "Just enjoy the winter."

I pulled my cloak closer around me, my thoughts mopey and my body already half frozen. "Just enjoy the winter?" I shivered. "Hardly."

Aster laughed lightly and grabbed my hand again, drawing me toward the café on the corner. "Let's get you a tea. Maybe that will help."

I tried to ignore the snow stinging my face as we crossed to the small café, but it was hard to focus on anything else. Mom was sure there would be a blizzard tonight, if the ache in her bad leg was any indication. She didn't need magic to tell us that, and she was never wrong about snowstorms.

Yet as soon as we stepped through the door, I felt my worries melt away, at least for a moment. A cheery fire crackled in a hearth to the side, and the tables were mostly empty. It was so quiet, I could actually hear myself over my racing thoughts.

"How about chamomile?" Aster asked, already a few steps ahead of me. "I think you could use it."

I rolled my eyes, grumpy that she was so intent on banishing my bad mood, but I followed her anyway. She ordered for both of us, then led me to the armchairs next to the hearth. Before long, Lavender, the café owner, appeared with a tray and set it on the table between our chairs. I exchanged a smile with her, and she turned back to the counter.

Aster wasted no time, already pouring chamomile tea into my delicate teacup from the bright white pot. She didn't need to ask before adding two huge dollops of honey and a splash of cream. Heavy on the honey and cream, just like my mom used to do when I was grouchy as a kid.

Aster was such a mother these days, to everyone, though I supposed that happened when she had a kid. It was hard to imagine me with a family of my own, let alone married. No one had ever interested me like that, though some had tried.

Aster gave my tea one good stir, then handed me the cup and saucer.

"Thanks," I said, trying to tamp down my grouchiness. It wasn't *her* fault I couldn't get the camellias to grow.

Aster prepared her own cup, then leaned back and studied me in a way that made me squirm, like she saw through me. She sipped before speaking. "Do you want help?"

I nearly choked on my tea. "What? No!"

"How are you going to grow the camellias, then? Doesn't your family need them in, like, two days?"

I waved my hand and took another sip of tea to buy me a little time. I didn't have an answer for her, but it didn't feel right to ask her to do my job for me. Even if it wasn't a critical job.

Maybe I should start considering other career paths...

Aster raised her eyebrows at me. "It doesn't sound like you have a plan."

Finally, I took a breath to gather myself and responded. "I appreciate the offer, but I can't ask you to clean up after me all the time. You've been doing it for years now. Lila knows I'm awful at it. My parents do too, and my other siblings. If I really can't do it, well, they've already said they can." I tried to hide the extra grumpiness that brought me. I didn't want them to do it for me, to fix it again.

I wanted to be able to do it.

"If you're so bad at it, what makes this time any different? They'll take care of it for you. I know they will, and so do you."

I sighed. "It *is* different." I bit my lip, studying the tea in my cup and struggling to get any more words out.

Aster waved a hand, encouraging me to continue. "How?"

I took a sip before answering, hoping the chamomile would calm my racing thoughts into something coherent. "Dad bought a booth in Capital City this year. In Commerce Corner. For three days!"

"So?" She sipped her drink. "That's not so different from your family's other sales."

My words came spilling out. "What if Queen Liana sees them? What if her favorite flowers are camellias, and I can't make enough for them to sell there? This is such an opportunity for them. I want to be more than a clerk for once. More than a burden. I want to actually help, not give them more work because I can't keep up."

If she heard me say it was more of an opportunity for them than me, she didn't comment on it.

Aster set her cup back on the saucer. "Is that what this is about? Capital City? You know the chances that the queen will see your flower booth, let alone buy an arrangement, are quite small, right?"

I sighed again. "Yes, I know. But I guess my heart won't accept it."

She chuckled. "Then maybe your heart should accept a little help."

I rolled my eyes. "You have your own work, and at some point, I need to figure out how to stand on my own two stems."

"If you say so." Aster leaned back in her chair. She didn't say anything else, merely sipped her tea and stared into the fire.

WE STAYED AT THE CAFÉ UNTIL ASTER HAD TO PICK UP HER SON FROM the schoolyard. After she left, I finished off the tea and returned the tray to Lavender. Then, I plodded out the door. I was still grumpy, just a little less so than when we'd arrived.

And I still had to solve the problem of the camellias.

I took my time strolling back through town, wracking my brain for any ideas, any possibilities. I looked at everyone around me, all the shops and street decorations, hoping for inspiration. We'd already tried talking to herbalists and other florists, visited the other petalborn families in town to get their opinions about my lack of magic. No one had any ideas how to help me. And tonight, nothing in the holiday decorations or faces of the town's citizens sparked any new ideas.

The snow was starting to pick up, along with the wind, and I shivered. I pulled the cloak tighter around me, feeling absolutely miserable. How did anyone stand this weather? Thank the gods it wasn't this cold all year! And now it was starting to get dark, and the bits of snow that were accumulating were going to turn to ice on the shoveled patches of stone.

This was hopeless. I should have just gone home, hunkered down in front of the fire, and called it a night. Admitted defeat to my family. Made them clean up my mess, just like always. And if I couldn't make the camellias work, what was I going to ever do to support myself? I had no other trade or skill.

Buttercups. Was I always going to be nothing but a burden to them?

Then I passed the potions shop, Nectar.

The potion on display was a carryover from the harvest season, a wheat-based concoction meant to enhance prosperity and . . . growth. Growth of finances, of businesses, of personal character. Not physical growth. But growth nonetheless.

Could it work? Could the growth be literal, rather than figurative, even though that's how people used it?

There was one way to find out.

I turned off the sidewalk, already covered with a fine layer of flurries, and pushed through the door into the potion shop. A small brass bell jingled as I stepped in, welcoming me with more cheer than I felt. At least it was warm in here, the shop heated by a small wood stove in the corner.

"Faren!" came a voice from behind the counter. "I was just about to close up. What can I do for you?"

"Elias!" I said. "Sorry, I can come back."

He waved a hand, coming around the counter. "Don't worry about it. It's good to see you!"

I hadn't seen Elias in a couple weeks, since I'd been so busy with the winter preparations at home, but he spent a lot of his free time with Aster and me on nice days. Like me, he was half petalborn and half human, only a couple months older than me, but his skin had more of a dove-gray cast, which was reflected in his gray eyes and silver hair. The silver gleamed in the diminishing daylight from the big window at the front of the store.

He didn't waste time, but wrapped me in a warm hug. I returned it, allowing myself to melt into his embrace. He was warm and smelled strongly of . . . cedar? The smell changed depending on what potion he was working on, but I was rather fond of this woodsy smell.

Elias pulled back. "So what brings you in? Does your mom need something? Lila?"

My family had been visiting Elias's family shop for years, usually with the same orders, all with the special friends and family discount.

Until today.

I held up a finger, turning toward the window. "Actually, they don't know I'm here."

"Oh?"

I nodded, then walked toward the wheat potion in the window. "How much are you charging for this one?"

"Wheat?" He rubbed his chin. "It's a common potion, so the usual price is fine. But what do you need it for?" His mouth quirked into a smile. "Trying to grow a sense of humor?"

"Har har." I rolled my eyes. "Just a . . . personal project."

"Mm-hmm. Because *that* doesn't sound suspicious at all."

I sighed. I should have expected the teasing from him. I dug into my coin purse and handed him the coins, then picked up the potion from the window. For a moment, my eyes bulged out of my head at the price tag hanging from the potion bottle. He was discounting to the friends price for *this*? It seemed like a bit more than a family and friends discount.

"Don't you want a little more for this?" I blurted, still staring at the potion. "It seems like a lot of money to lose."

He rubbed a hand over the back of his neck. "Yeah, don't worry about. Do you need instructions?" he said. "Or want me to wrap it?"

I held the potion between my hands. It was almost as cold as the air outside, but maybe that was because it had been sitting in the window, only inches from snow and ice.

"I think I'm good. I'm going right home, and I can just put it in here." I patted the pouch on my belt, where my coins jingled. I'd looped it over my belt before I'd left for the café.

"Are you sure? These potions can be tricky if you don't use them right."

"I'm sure." I sounded confident, I thought, though a twinge of guilt stabbed at my heart. Why had he discounted the potion so much for me? It was much more of a discount than he usually gave our family.

He nodded at my words, studying me with those icy eyes. I squirmed under the intense gaze. Was he upset I hadn't visited lately?

He pressed his lips together before speaking. "Are you okay, Faren?"

I blinked, my heart flopping in my chest. He could tell? "What do you mean?"

He crossed his arms, smiling softly. "I've known you our whole lives. I can tell when you're upset about something. You know you can trust me, right? If you need something, maybe I can help you."

Irritation flashed through my chest before dissipating. First Aster, now him? They all worried about me too much. "I'm fine. I just have a lot of work to do at home. You know?"

He nodded again. "Oh, I know. The winter season is upon us." He gestured out the window, where the snow was starting to collect in the corners of the glass. "Is it something with your magic?"

"Pollen dust, no!" My heart stuttered as the words came out sharper than I'd intended. Was I really that obvious? "I'm fine, Elias. But like you said, winter is upon us. We've been busy with holiday arrangements and preparing for sales in Capital City, and they're counting on me to finish up my chores still, so I really have to get going."

His eyes widened, just barely, but enough that I could see my words had cut him.

"Elias . . ."

"No, it's okay, Faren. I get it. It's a busy time, and you should definitely get home before it gets too bad out there."

I reached out to him, offering him a hug goodbye, but it lacked the warmth of his greeting. It was quick, almost businesslike, and I tried not to show my hurt or guilt. It was my own fault.

I'd make it up to him. As soon as I figured out these camellias.

"I'll come visit later this week, okay?" I said, hand on the door.

"Sure, Faren," he said. But he was walking back to the counter, not even looking at me now.

I sighed and tucked the bottle in my bag, then pushed back out into the cold.

The door fought me, the wind trying to push it closed again. Maybe even the wind knew I should apologize, but I really did need to get going. In the time I'd been inside there was already a layer of snow on the ground as deep as my first finger joint.

BY THE TIME I REACHED HOME, I WAS LUCKY I COULD STILL SEE WELL enough in the dusk that I didn't fall into a snowdrift. The lantern lighters hadn't been through to light the streetlights, probably because of the wind, or they simply assumed no one would be dumb enough to be caught out in the storm.

I let myself into the house, stamping the snow off my boots onto the tile floor of the entrance, and shook the flakes off my cloak before hanging it with everyone else's. It looked like the entire family was home, and the warm, savory scent of stew wafted on the air.

I followed my nose to the kitchen. I'd take a look at the camellias again after dinner.

The kitchen was a noisy hum of activity, everyone bustling about, talking and laughing while cooking. I crossed my arms, rubbing some feeling back into them, while I watched them with a smile. I felt warmer now that I was with them again. Even if I was embarrassed about my plant magic and wished for more, I knew they would always love me, always accept me, no matter what happened.

"Faren!" Mom said, noticing me in the doorway. "You're just in time. Give me a hand with these rolls?"

I nodded, still smiling, and joined her at the counter where she was rolling sweet buns for dessert. They would go in a cast iron crock in the hearth after everything else was done, while we were eating the main course. We rolled out the dough, then zigzagged honey across the surface, smoothing it out and sprinkling it with cinnamon before rolling the dough into a spiral. Mom took over slicing, and I rolled the next piece.

"All good, sweetheart?" she said, tapping my nose with a tiny spot of honey.

The honey warmed my skin, and I wiped it away with my finger, then stuck my finger in my mouth. "Yup. Couldn't be better."

Did that sound like the truth? Did she see through me?

Mom didn't say anything, though, and I breathed a sigh of relief. Soon enough, dinner was ready, and I tried my best to just enjoy my family's company while the bottle of wheat potion beckoned me from my coin purse.

AFTER DINNER, THE FAMILY WENT THEIR OWN WAYS, EITHER TO OTHER chores, to play games together, or to sit by the fire and read.

But I went straight to the greenhouse. No one else should be coming in tonight, so it was the perfect time to treat the camellias and hopefully solve my problems. If this worked, maybe I could get Elias to teach me how to make the wheat potion. Then, I could just use it whenever I was asked to grow plants at the last minute. My family would be proud of me, and no one needed to know that my magic was as weak as tea steeped for only a few seconds.

I lit the lantern by the door and stepped from the main house into the greenhouse. It was much darker than usual, and the only sound was a soft tinkling of snow piling on the roof.

The glass windows were all covered in a light layer of snow, which explained the dim light and muffled sound.

I followed the dark paths around the various beds of flowers, each peaking in a different season or used for different purposes, until I came to the winter patch. The others had already harvested their first set of blooms for the floral orders, and the next blooms were already budding. They would definitely be ready to harvest by morning.

And then there was my plot, barren and empty, the earth loose and wet where I'd buried the seeds and tried to coax them to grow.

I lowered myself to my knees on the brick path and set the lantern down next to me. Its cheery light threw a steady gold glow over everything, warming the cold space. Then, I reached into my coin purse and removed the bottle of wheat potion.

The bottle was just like all the other potion bottles from Elias: an inconspicuous brown color, corked and sealed with wax, its price tag still hanging off its side. The only indication of the contents was the imprint of a wheat head on the label and a list of the uses below it. This was meant for ingestion and personal growth, as he'd mentioned—and pried about—but that didn't mean it couldn't work to grow my plants.

Right?

I took a deep breath and broke the wax seal with my fingernail, then pried the cork off with a soft pop. The warm, earthy scent of bread wafted from the bottle, and I couldn't help smiling. That smell never failed to comfort me, and I found myself filling with hope that this could actually work. That I could actually contribute to the family business the way I was always meant to.

Something rustled in the plants behind me, and I froze, heart pounding. I turned slightly, keeping the bottle hidden by my body. A small topiary shaped like a cat pranced out of the poinsettias, padding up to me with a soft rustle of leaves.

One of the plant golems. This one was meant to chase the pests out of the greenhouse, so Weiland had created it in the shape of a cat.

It sat down next to me, just like any ordinary cat would, and tilted its plant head as if looking at me and asking what I was doing.

I released my breath. The golems couldn't talk, at least not this one. There was no need to hide what I was doing.

I rustled the leaves behind its ears, and it leaned into my hand. Satisfied, it wandered off, and I held the potion bottle up to my eyes again, examining the amber liquid inside.

Was this even a good idea? Would it be cheating somehow if I grew the camellias this way? But I didn't have any other way to do it, at least not before Lantern Night.

I took a deep breath as nerves knotted within me. The amount Elias had discounted the potion made me uneasy, but there was something more, too. It didn't feel quite right using it at all, but I didn't have any better ideas either.

It was now or never.

I turned my eyes back to the empty flowerbed. How much should I use? The plot was small, only big enough for a few plants. But the plants hadn't even sprouted. They'd need a lot more coaxing to not only sprout but grow enough to produce the beautiful full camellia blossoms we needed for the booth.

Best to use all of it, though my heart clenched at the amount of money I was literally pouring into the earth. Maybe I could add as much magic as I could access, just for an extra boost. It couldn't hurt much, right?

I carefully poured the potion out on the plot in a zigzag pattern, doing my best to cover the entire plot, especially where I knew I'd placed the seeds. I didn't want to waste a drop. As I spread it, I tried to reach for the aether, tried to add it to the liquid pouring over the soil. I thought I felt a spark . . . or maybe I just imagined it. I honestly wasn't sure. Then, to encourage the potion to spread and mix with the earth, I grabbed a watering can, already filled from the morning's work, and sprinkled the cool water over the top.

Then, there was nothing to do but wait.

After replacing the watering can with the other gardening tools, I settled down by the plot again and watched. Would it be minutes? Hours? When would I know it had worked?

I stared, unblinking, at the soil, waiting for what seemed to be an eternity. The golem wandered back to me, sitting by my side and watching the soil with me. Absently, I stroked its prickly leaves.

Nothing was happening.

I shivered, rubbing my arms. My knees were getting sore, and my legs were cramping from sitting on the ground so long. It must have been late by now, and finally, when my eyelids started to droop with exhaustion, I sighed.

Maybe it wasn't meant to be. I'd have to find another way.

I picked myself up off the ground, giving the golem one last pet, and grabbed the lantern. It was time for bed. Tomorrow, I'd have a fresh start, a new chance to find a solution to my problem.

Tonight, all I wanted was the warmth of my quilt.

I extinguished the lantern and left it just inside the door, then made my way down the hall to the room I shared with my sisters. They were already fast asleep in their beds, the room cast in sooty gray light from the snowstorm outside.

I quickly peeled off my dress, hiding the empty bottle in the chest at the foot of my bed, and pulled on my nightgown. I was fast enough that the cold only shocked my skin for a few cursed moments, then I dove into my bed and shivered until the heat from my body filled the pocket of air under the quilt.

As soon as the warmth began seeping back into my bones, sleep carried me away.

I WOKE SLOWLY THE NEXT MORNING, MY MIND FOGGY AND SLOW WITH the cobwebs of sleep. The house was quiet, muted in the way it only ever was during or after a huge storm. The room was bright with daylight, but the light was still that same silver-gray color it had been last night, meaning the sun hadn't come back yet.

Penny and Lila were still in bed, both snoring lightly, and I turned toward the window. How early was it? Usually I was the last to wake, yet all three of us were still here. And with how quiet the house was, Weiland and my parents must still have been sleeping, too.

Snow piled along the window, and outside everything was covered in a thick, fluffy blanket of white. Snow was still falling, though not as quickly as last night. Which meant we probably weren't going anywhere today.

I stuck a foot out from under the quilt and shuddered, still not quite awake and not ready to *be* awake. The air was ice cold, frigid with the storm outside. I pulled it back in quickly, dreading actually leaving the warmth and comfort of my bed, but my bladder didn't have much time left. Eventually, with a sigh, I hurried out of bed, used the small chamber pot, and dressed in warm layers of clothes. If I truly *was* the first person up, maybe that meant I could get the house warm before break-fast, even start some honey tea over the fire. Anything to banish the snowy cold from the corners of the house. I rushed into the living area and stoking the fire back to life. At least this room would be warm . . . soon.

Until then, I pulled a knitted afghan from the cushions in the corner. It was made of the warmest blue wool, the color of sky and lakes and bluebells, and it reminded me so much of the summer I wished it was right now. I shuffled over to the kitchen again, finally starting to feel some heat from the hearth, feeling a little more awake, and scooped water from the bucket by the door into the kettle. I hung it over the waking fire, hoping to have tea warm before anyone else woke up.

And then, as heat began settling back into my bones, I remembered what I had done last night.

Feeling more awake and slightly less grumpy about it, I hurried across the house to the greenhouse door, my heart in my throat. Did it work? My stomach clenched with anxiety and excitement.

And what was I going to do if it *did* work? I would need to figure out the potion situation quickly, find a way to keep myself in stock so I could keep up the growing. I winced, remembering how much that single potion was supposed to cost.

I shook my head, trying to clear my thoughts of money. I shouldn't have worried about it yet. I still needed to know if it had worked at all. Yet, despite my logical thoughts, the anxiety and eagerness pushed my steps faster.

I swung the door open. The greenhouse was dark, the glass completely covered by snow now, so I grabbed the lantern again and lit it quickly, anxious to see if the potion had done anything helpful. I stepped onto the cobbled path and shut the door softly behind me, my breath shallow as nerves grabbed me around my lungs—I didn't need anyone surprising me, and I didn't want to alert anyone if it hadn't worked. I swallowed, my stomach lurching again. I didn't want to give them false hope and then have to explain everything. It would break my heart to tell them how I'd failed again, even though they didn't know what I was doing exactly.

I shuffled between the stalks of the various plants and the sweet-smelling flowers that separated the house from my small patch of earth, craning my neck to try to see anything, but it was too gloomy with the snow covering all the glass. The plants around me blocked most of the light from reaching the far corners of the greenhouse.

Then I stepped into the winter garden. And right there, just as I had hoped, huge, full blooms of white and red camellias.

My heart flipped, and tears sprang to my eyes as I did a little dance for myself. I'd done it! I'd finally grown the flowers!

Well, sort of. But for now, sort of was good enough.

I set the lantern at my feet and took a step closer to the plot, reaching for the closest bloom. It sagged a little with its own weight, but I lifted it to my nose, inhaling the sweet scent and letting my eyes flutter closed as I just enjoyed this moment.

This one, rare moment where I'd done something right. Where I'd grown what my family needed. The flowers were here, and they were ready for harvesting.

And then my eyes flew open as I remembered I'd need to buy more potions from Elias. Expensive potions that I most certainly did not want him to keep discounting for me. How could I afford to keep this up? Unless I could somehow convince him to teach me how to make the potion myself, like I'd considered last night.

But then there was still the price of ingredients, and who knew—

"Faren? What are you doing out here?" Lila appeared behind me, rubbing her eyes.

I dropped the camellia bloom and stepped away, tucking

my hands behind my back like a kid caught with her hand in the cookie jar. "Nothing!"

But Lila's eyes had already found the flowers—it would have been hard to ignore, considering I was literally holding one like a kitten just a second ago.

"Not nothing," she said softly, eyes glued to the camellia and her voice full of awe. Like me, she reached out to touch it, to run her finger along the velvety petals. "You did it! You grew the flowers!"

Guilt dropped into my stomach like a stone, and I half smiled at her, a shaky expression. But she didn't notice, too preoccupied with studying my flowers.

And then the greenhouse door on the other side of the room opened again, and another person tumbled in. Then another. And another. I was completely surrounded by my entire family, all of them chattering excitedly, talking over each other to offer their congratulations. My stomach sank, guilt gnawing at my pride and excitement, tainting it.

Eventually, the chatter died down enough for Mom to raise her voice and say, "Why don't we harvest some blooms and have a snow day working party?"

A cheer went up among my siblings, and we got to work. I tried to hide my face, my skin flushed and my expression full of guilt, I was sure. Lila handed me a pair of small clippers and one of the big wicker baskets, and I set to work trimming off the blooms that were either ready or almost ready, along with a portion of the stem. The rest of my family did the same, filling their baskets to the brim before parading back into the house.

I was the last to finish the trimming, laying my clippers in the basket under the mound of flowers before following the others. I used to love these snow day parties, the family work parties where we did the arrangements that had been ordered while drinking tea and cocoa and baking delicious snacks, all in front of a roaring hearth. It was the only room that would be warm enough to be comfortable, and it was a fun way to get our work done before the business opened after the storm.

But today didn't feel the same. I never had this many of my own blooms before. I'd never cheated. And there was a part of me just waiting for my family to figure out what I'd done.

BECAUSE I'D ALREADY STOKED THE FIRE AND PUT A KETTLE ON FOR THE morning, it didn't take long for Mom and Penny to get breakfast going. The old clock in the hall said it was already mid-morning, so it was actually more like brunch. They set about preparing eggs on toast and putting the bits and bobs together for tea. The others began setting up the rough table in the center of the room for work by spreading out an old, green-stained cloth, their own clippers, and the vases we'd need.

I stepped into the living area just as the scent of toasting bread began to waft through the air, and I set my basket of camellias on the table. Instead of joining Dad, Weiland, and Lila at the table, I reached for the bowl of leftover sweet rolls from the night before, still sitting under a cheese cloth on the counter. I was craving all the sugar, probably because of my anxiety.

Mom slapped at my hand. "You'll spoil your breakfast!"

I tried giving her a smile, though even I could tell it was wobbly. "Snow day," I said around the icing and sticky bread. She rolled her eyes but accepted the excuse.

Lila appeared next to me, grabbing my hand and pulling me toward the flowers. "I'm so excited that you were finally able to grow the flowers! This can be a real family event now."

She was beaming ear to ear, and I transferred that wobbly smile to her. "Yeah, it's really great."

She paused, searching my eyes for a moment. "You okay?"

I blinked. "Oh, yeah, of course! Just hungry. And cold. You know."

She looked at me a few seconds longer, then continued dragging me to a chair at the table. She tasked me with trimming the ends of the first set of flowers, a big arrangement for the maire's home, then took over setting up the vase and filler. I handed her each of the flowers as I trimmed off the extra leaves, the end of the stem, and any thorns, and she poked them into the sandy white filler at the bottom of the glass vase. From a distance, it looked like snow, though I knew it was a type of sand that could hold on to plant magic longer than most other sands or soils. Once infused, it would keep the flowers alive and brilliant for weeks. It was the same sand that would sustain the blooms we were growing for Capital City.

Another thing I couldn't do: infuse the sand with magic.

I tried to focus on my task, helpfully snipping and suggesting placement for some of the flowers. It was fun spending time with Lila. I always loved time with my big sister. But this flower arranging? It wasn't really a fun activity by itself. Not to me, when all it did was remind me this was the closest I could come to petalborn magic.

Mom and Penny showed up twenty minutes later with heaping plates of toast, eggs, and jam, and we set the flowers aside long enough to dive into the quick meal. The eggs were perfect, crispy from the butter in the pan but with a runny yolk, exactly how I liked them, and the toast settled the nerves in my stomach. I slathered piece after piece in raspberry jam, eating until Mom gave me a funny sideways look.

Right. I didn't normally eat this much. My anxiety was definitely going to give me away if I didn't get it in check, and quick.

I finished the last piece of toast and got up to pour myself some tea. The world outside the kitchen window was still cold and dim, the snow falling like petals did in spring. When would it end? Would I be stuck here arranging flowers and keeping my potion-work a secret for days?

Gods, I hoped not.

I dropped a dollop of honey and a splash of cream in the tea, a simple black tea full of floral notes and bound to give me energy, then rejoined everyone at the table, sipping slowly in an effort to calm my nerves.

It wasn't working.

Still, I somehow managed to get through the next several hours without a hitch. Until Lila turned to me at the very end of our working session.

"Faren," she said, in front of the entire family, "do you want to infuse the sand? You're finally making flowers, so this feels like a big milestone!"

A chorus of "yes" and "you've got this" clamored against my eardrums, and my heart started to thud.

"Me?" I said. "Isn't that normally *your* job?"

But even as she opened her mouth to answer me, something crashed from the other side of the house. Every head swiveled in the direction of the sound. I blew out a breath of relief, saved from having to argue against using magic I definitely didn't have.

Unfortunately my relief was short-lived. Another crash sounded, and this time it was more than clear that it had come from the greenhouse.

Almost comically, we all rose from our places at the table and headed in the direction of the noise, like a herd of confused sheep or flower golems. Dad made his way to the front of the line, his clippers in hand, as if they would do much of anything if the source was actually dangerous.

He stopped in front of the door, turning to us just long

enough to put a finger to his lips. Then, he turned the knob and shoved the door open.

The greenhouse was quiet and dark, just as it had been earlier. I leaned around Weiland, trying to get a look inside. At first, all I could see were the towering, silhouetted fronds of the plants closest to the door.

Then, something that glowed like the snow at night caught my eye, something that immediately made my heart sink to my feet.

A camellia stood a head above all the other flowers and plants, its bright white bloom like a moon in the greenhouse.

My heart tremored, and sweat broke out on my skin. It had only been a few hours. No more flowers should have grown yet, if they would even keep growing at all! The potion couldn't have been that potent, could it?

I swallowed, wishing I'd brought my clippers like Dad had. Maybe he'd had the right idea after all.

No one else seemed to notice the camellia, but I was sure that would change. I tried to push my way ahead of the rest of my family, but Dad held out his arm when I got to him, holding me back. I pressed my lips together. What were they going to do when they saw the flowers? What was I going to *say*?

Dad turned his head away from me, scanning the greenhouse, and I took the chance to duck under his arm and bolt past him.

"Faren, no!" he hissed in a whisper.

But I was already gone, disappearing behind one of the larger shrubs. I wasn't out of trouble yet, though. I could hear the footsteps behind me, pursuing, even as I hurried around the various beds and plots to my own camellia plot.

I slid to a stop, catching my breath as my flowers came into view.

Not only had the flowers regrown, and regrown tall, but they were larger than they should have been, easily the size of my head. I could practically hear them still growing. And the source of the crashing sounds was also clear: several stacks of clay pots, knocked over and scattered across the floor in countless shards.

I looked back at my plot. Had they grown in the seconds I'd looked away? It seemed like the plants were now spilling over the edges of the wooden planter box, brushing the cobbles with their enormous leaves, creeping toward the planters around them.

The scuff of a foot only one path away made me jump. I only had seconds. I looked around, desperate for a pair of clippers, but it was no use. All the spare pairs had been taken inside for the flower arranging, and nothing but the broken pots and a few empty baskets remained here.

Even if I had the clippers, what did I expect to accomplish in only a few seconds? It wasn't like I'd be able to trim back the entire plant to the way it had been that morning.

Dad appeared first, and I turned in time to catch his wide eyes and awed exhale. "Whoa."

Whoa indeed. I turned back to the flowers, crossing my arms over my chest protectively. I was going to be in so much trouble.

One by one, the rest of my family slid to a stop in front of the planter, their eyes just as wide as Dad's, their surprise stealing whatever words they could have said.

I threw my hands up before dropping them to my sides. "Go ahead. Say it."

Mom was the first to break her silence. "Faren, I . . . you really need to practice your magic. Get some control."

What? She thought this was my own magic? That I just lacked *control*?

"I'll say," Weiland chipped in. "This is going to be a nightmare if you don't get it under control."

I blinked at the others in surprise, but then my gaze found Lila. She alone looked at me more than the flowers. As if she knew—or at least suspected—something the others didn't.

Lila continued pinning me with her stare and asked, "Why don't I stay back and help you? Then everyone else can finish the orders."

There was a murmur of agreement, a few words of encouragement directed at me, then the others filtered out of the greenhouse one by one.

After the door closed, the room fell into silence. Lila continued to watch me, her head slightly tilted. I shifted on my feet, rubbing one arm awkwardly. A rustle from my planter warned us both that the flowers were spreading again, growing longer, bigger. Invading the surrounding plots.

"Care to tell me what's going on?" she finally asked. I couldn't read the tone in her voice. I wasn't sure if she was going to be supportive or if she was just waiting for me to tell her how badly I'd screwed up.

I tucked a strand of hair behind my ear, not meeting her eyes. "Not really."

Her foot started tapping out a nervous rhythm. "I don't think this is your magic. Am I right?"

This time, my eyes shot up to hers. What had tipped her off? "You're . . . not wrong."

Lila sighed, reaching in her apron pocket for a pair of clippers. So she'd remembered hers, too. Approaching the plant, she trimmed off one of the largest blooms, giving herself plenty of stem. Almost as soon as she withdrew her hand, still holding the cut flower, a new flower began to sprout at the cut on the plant itself.

Lila sighed again. "Faren. What is this?"

I couldn't make myself form the words. So instead, I looked up at the snow-covered glass ceiling, dreading the words that were about to come out of my mouth . . . and the venture into the freezing storm that would follow. "I think we need to get Elias."

I CURSED UNDER MY BREATH AND PULLED MY CLOAK TIGHTER AROUND my face as we stepped into the snow, but it was my own fault. I knew that.

It didn't mean I had to like the consequences.

The wind bit into my face, but at least the snow seemed to have stopped. For now. The town was silent, everyone else smarter than Lila and me, nestled inside with their fires and their hot chocolates. None of the shops seemed to be open, which meant we'd probably have better luck going straight to Elias's house rather than the potion shop.

All the way on the other side of town.

I bit my lip under my scarf to keep from complaining. Lila would probably just remind me of my mistakes, which was valid.

What was Elias going to say? Especially after he'd asked me all those questions when I bought the potion yesterday. I could already feel my face flaming in embarrassment.

The center of town was silent in the snow with only the sounds of our footsteps crunching the fresh powder and our labored breaths as we trudged through the knee-high drifts. There was no echo, the sound muffled all around us. I shivered as slivers of ice settled into the tops of my boots.

We'd gotten more snow last night than we'd had in years. Of course today was the day I'd have to face it all.

I tried to focus on other things to distract myself from my

discomfort—and my fear over what was happening to my garden plot back home. The decorations were gorgeous and cozy, blanketed as they were with a layer of snow. Shining baubles poked out from amidst garlands of greenery and the ice, gleaming in the silver-spun daylight.

I shivered again. They were beautiful, but coated in ice and snow like that, they just made me feel colder.

I thought of something else. A nice, hot cup of tea. Or, better yet, hot chocolate! I could really use some of that hot chocolate. It would truly warm me up, physically and in spirit. And if I could just sit in front of the hearth, feet toward the cheery flames, snuggled into a blanket with a good book . . .

I got so distracted thinking about fires and hot chocolates and general coziness that I didn't even notice when I followed Lila off the sidewalk and down Elias's street. Suddenly, we were at his door. I blinked, reminding myself why we were here, and my heart sank to my very cold toes.

And then Lila raised her fist to the door, rapping her knuckles against the wood, and my heart leapt from my toes to my throat.

Maybe he wasn't home. Maybe he was taking advantage of a slow day to restock the shop. Or maybe he'd gone to visit—

The door swung open with a creak, and there he was, all sparkling eyes and bright smiles. He almost seemed *too* excited to see us. "Lila? Faren! What brings the two of you here?"

Lila glanced over her shoulder at me, but she must have decided I wasn't about to admit what I'd done. She still didn't really know why I needed Elias, though I was sure she suspected. Why else would I need to see the village potion master than to get a potion . . . or to fix a problem with a potion? Whatever she thought, she had to know Elias was somehow involved, even indirectly.

Elias must have noticed the trepidation in my averted eyes, and his face fell. "Is this . . . about that potion from yesterday?"

"Potion?" Lila said. "I knew it! I knew you couldn't have just figured it out overnight like that!"

"Figured what out?" Elias turned his eyes to her.

Lila crossed her arms and looked at me. "Care to explain yet?"

I took a deep breath. This wasn't going to be fun.

IT TOOK MUCH LESS TIME TO EXPLAIN WHAT HAD HAPPENED THAN I expected, though Elias wasn't very happy about the magic I'd tried to add to his potion. He was immediately ready to help, though, almost too eager, grabbing up potion supplies from inside then joining us on the snowy sidewalk. I couldn't think of any time I'd been more embarrassed, especially since Elias had sensed I was about to do something stupid yesterday and I'd brushed it off. I should've listened. He was an expert, after all.

As soon as he'd pulled on his warmest coat and slung his bag over his shoulder, we set off back for the house. Hopefully nothing much had changed in the time we'd been gone.

As soon as I thought it, I knew it wouldn't be true. The greenhouse slowly came back into view, and immediately I could sense something was off. The snow that had been piled on the glass roof had partially melted, and something writhed inside. Unfortunately, it was too dark through the glass to see much else through the glare of daylight.

The house was eerily silent. With so many of us, it had always been full of life and noise. Now, though, no sound emanated from inside. Even the windows were dark, which meant the fire had gone out.

Not good.

Lila and I traded a look, then stepped in front of Elias. Even though Elias had some plant magic, this was my mess, and I didn't want him to get hurt. And Lila could hopefully control whatever came our way.

I was using that word a lot: hopefully. It was a season of hope, what with the winter festivities, but this wasn't what anyone had in mind, I was sure.

"Stay behind me," Lila said, holding her arm out as if it would be enough to keep me back.

But I swallowed and nodded. Staying only a couple steps behind her, we approached the front door. Lila put her hand on the knob and leaned close, her ear almost touching the wood as she listened. I waited, holding my breath. After a moment, she pulled back, shook her head, then opened the door.

It was cold and quiet inside, just as we'd noticed on our approach. The family should have been in the main living area, still working on arrangements or holiday preparations, but they weren't.

Which could only mean they'd gone to investigate the greenhouse and something had happened.

Great.

We strode through the living spaces once, quickly, checking to make sure the house really was empty, then we made our way to the greenhouse. The closer we came to the door, the harder my heart pounded, every breath fighting the immense weight of guilt.

I'd done this. And if something happened to anyone in my family, it would be my fault.

Why couldn't I have just been honest? Why did I have to try to do this on my own? It wouldn't have been any different than previous years, anyway.

Something green and leafy poked out from under the greenhouse door, far too bright against the stone floor in the hallway. My eyes glued to the leaves, I reached for the basket on the table next to me, rooting around until I found something sharp and metal. A pair of clippers, finally!

Lila glanced back at Elias and me, then pulled open the door.

We were greeted by a wall of greenery that certainly hadn't been there when we'd left. I glanced at the clippers. So much for cutting it back. We'd need a sword or something bigger now.

Elias knelt in the hallway and dug around in his bag, coming up with a long, sheathed dagger.

"Why do you have that?" I asked, too surprised to keep my voice down.

He half shrugged a shoulder. "Sometimes I need to harvest plants, so I keep it with my potion supplies. I gotta be honest, though; I didn't think I'd need it today."

Me neither.

He rose to his feet and drew the knife out of its sheath, stepping up next to Lila. Lila's hands were up as she tried communicating with the plant, probably asking it to withdraw.

But the plant was ignoring her. It rustled a few leaves, but since we'd given it space into the main house, it had already spread several inches toward us.

Lila dropped her hands with a sigh. "Well, we tried to be nice. Elias, you might as well get us in there."

Dread weighed in my stomach like a stone as Elias slashed a path through the thick camellia leaves, blooms dropping to the ground like snowballs. I winced with every cut, tears burning my eyes as the plants fell. I couldn't communicate with the plants like the other petalborn could, but I could still hear them. Especially their pain at every slash of Elias's dagger. Clippers didn't hurt them like that.

I took a deep breath, trying to hold myself together long

enough to get through this. There would be plenty of time for remorse later. I was sure I'd be having nightmares about this day for the rest of my life, anyway.

Lila followed Elias, her eyes darting side to side and her hands up defensively. I came last, holding my useless clippers in front of me, though my hand shook. As afraid as I was and as badly as I wanted to find the others, I didn't want to be the one causing those plants to cry.

A flash of yellow caught my eye, and I tapped Lila on the shoulder. Elias stopped when we did, looking back in the direction I pointed.

Mom's shirt was yellow this morning, wasn't it?

Elias turned in Mom's direction with the knife, cutting the tendrils of camellia away more carefully as we approached. Mom seemed to be completely entangled in the stems, leaves, and blooms, and she wasn't moving. Next to her, closer to the floor, the topiary golem sat tangled up in the plant, looking up at me as we approached. I could feel the despair emanating from it, just like I could feel the pain of the camellias.

Another stem fell to the ground, leaving the path clear to them, and I stepped forward. Carefully, I clipped away the pieces of my flowers that covered Mom's face. Her eyes were closed, as if she were asleep, but they fluttered open once her face was free of the tangle.

"Faren?" she whispered. Her eyes raked over our group, coming to rest on Elias, and her face fell. "You didn't."

I flushed hotly and looked at my boots. "I did."

When I looked back up at her, she was rolling her eyes. "Just get us out of here, and we'll figure it out."

Thank goodness I was too old for punishments. Though, if she told me I'd have to do all the weeding and fertilizing for the next month, I wouldn't have been surprised.

I used the clippers to keep cutting away the pieces of

camellia from Mom and the golem, my hands shaking. Each cut was slower than it would have been if I wasn't so scared, but finally she was free, dropping back to the ground with a light thud. The golem dropped moments afterward, running back into the depths of the greenhouse. Mom dug in her apron pocket for her own pair of clippers, then settled into the ragtag line of would-be heroes as if she'd always been there.

The next person we found was Penny, fighting every tendril with the tenacity of a feral cat. She was all flashes of red and snapping stems, but the camellia fought back harder, holding her down.

We dove into the fray one after another, fighting back the plants, but each piece we cut or beat back only came back stronger, angrier, just as ferocious as Penny was. I snapped off a leaf, and the camellia responded by slapping me across the cheek. I touched my stinging skin as I fell back, half expecting to see blood.

This was nothing like the section of plant holding Mom, where she'd been so calm that the plant had seemed to mirror her attitude.

Wait, maybe that was it . . . maybe we just had to keep Penny calm, and then the plant would calm down too!

"Lila," I started, trying to get my sister's attention. I tugged her sleeve, but she shrugged me off. All three of them—plus Penny—were busy fighting the plant, too busy to listen to me.

I took a deep breath. My gut told me the answer to freeing Penny, but what good was it if no one would listen to me?

And why should they? I'd already lied and was wrong about what the potion, not to mention the magic I'd added to it, would do. Maybe this would be just the same.

I stood for several long seconds, unsure how to proceed, wringing my hands, when Lila finally noticed me.

"What are you doing just standing there?" she said,

swinging at a bloom that was headed straight for me. "Do you think that's going to save Penny?"

I bit my lip, then said, "Yes, actually."

She stopped moving. The bloom came back to thwack her in the head, and she cursed quietly under her breath before responding. "What do you mean?"

"Remember how calm Mom was? And how calm her plant was? It was so easy to cut her free. Maybe the plant is reacting to Penny's fighting."

Lila chewed her own lip, looking back at the three others fiercely fighting the camellia. After a moment, she said, "Anything is worth a try."

She stuck two fingers in her mouth and let loose the loudest, shrillest whistle I'd ever heard. I flinched, hands instinctively flying to my ears. I hated loud noises.

But it did the trick; Elias, Mom, and Penny all stopped flailing and looked back at us.

"What?" Penny snarled. "Get me out of here!"

I could hear the panic in her voice. Penny never did like small places after she'd fallen in a cave back in the woods on the south side of town. One day I still wanted to go back there, but I was sure Penny wouldn't.

Lila gestured for me to come forward, and I took a step closer, trying to raise my voice. It was hard to speak loudly when I was so embarrassed about all of this, but I did my best.

"Think about how we got Mom out," I said, looking to Mom and Elias. "She was practically sleeping . . . and so was the plant. Even when she woke up, she stayed calm. And so did the plant." I looked back at Penny. "What if the plant is fighting you so hard because *you're* fighting *it*?"

Penny blinked at me, then lowered her eyebrows, glowering. "So you want me to . . . what? Let it tie me up? Accept my fate?"

102

I held up my hands. "No, just stop fighting. Like swampy ground, right? The more you fight, the more it pulls. But if you stop fighting it . . ."

An expression of understanding flitted across Penny's face. "You float."

"Exactly."

I wrung my hands, waiting as she nodded, then closed her eyes and let herself fall back into the embrace of the plant. For a few agonizing moments, we couldn't see the flash of her red dress anymore, the plant completely consuming her.

But then the plant sagged and went still. Penny emerged from the tangle of stems and leaves, blooming like a flower herself.

The rest of us wasted no time, lunging forward to cut her out of the plant before it stopped being docile.

Finally she was free, landing on the path like Mom had, her eyes burning. "Whoever did this, I'm going to find them and I'm—"

"Me," I said, my voice small. "It was my mistake."

She blinked, staring at me, the fire going out of her eyes. "How did you manage to do *this*?"

I shook my head. "We'll talk later. After we find Dad and Weiland."

"Right. Of course. Well, they were closer to the winter plots. This stupid thing grabbed me before I realized what was happening, but they moved faster. We should look there."

Of course. The epicenter of this whole mess.

Elias took the lead again, slashing away with his knife to clear a path. We followed close on his heels, the path closing up behind us as quickly as we went. Penny and Mom were on their guard, flinching at every rustle of leaves, ready to strike if the plant tried to strike back. And several times, it tried. But their plant magic was strong, stronger even than Lila's, and between the three of them, they kept us unentangled.

"You really did a number, didn't you?" Elias said with a grunt. "This is going to take some work to fix."

I panted, pushing back another frond as gently as I could. I didn't want to cause it any more pain than I had to. "Can't we just fix it from here?"

Elias shook his head quickly. "No, if you put the potion in your plot, then we need to get to the root of the matter, as it were."

Of course we did.

It seemed to take ages, but finally we made it to the winter plots. And sure enough, just as Penny had suspected, both Dad and Weiland were suspended by the camellia, feet dangling off the ground. And just behind them, my plot, overflowing with stems and leaves and flowers that were much too big to be non-magical camellias.

Penny started to lunge forward, the fight already in her eyes, but I grabbed her arm before she could get too close. "Remember, the plant is responding to our actions!"

She forced herself to stop, but I could see her grinding her teeth with the effort. Instead of plunging into another fight, she yelled to Weiland and Dad about our discovery, urging them to hold still until we could get to them.

Mom, Lila, and Penny began making their way toward the rest of our trapped family, and I began to follow until Elias caught my sleeve.

"I need you," he said, and my stomach did a little flop at the words. "You're the one who added the potion, so I need you to help me counteract it."

"Oh. Right," I said, trying to keep my disappointment from my voice.

That was silly. Why was I disappointed? Why had his words

even affected me like that? I'd known Elias my entire life, and we'd been friends for most of it. Especially over the last couple years, as we made our forays into adulthood and strengthened lifelong friendships. I'd never really had any crushes on anyone, so why would I have one on Elias now?

I shook the thoughts out of my head. There would be time for that later. Right now, he was right. We needed to counteract what I'd done and stop this. I could practically hear him scolding me for altering his potion. That I should have known better.

That wiped the confusing thoughts about Elias right out of my head.

Elias cleared the path to the plot, and I held onto the back of his coat, trying to stay as close as possible. I couldn't do much with the flowers, but Elias was trained in potions, in how to mix the plants for various magical, medicinal, and everyday effects. *That* was his skill, his family's skill.

Once we reached the edge of the planter, we dropped to our knees, and Elias slid his bag around in front of him. He began pulling out the tools of his trade: small bags of herbs, a mortar and pestle, and a leather-bound book that held various recipes, remedies, and antidotes.

"I already know which potion you used," he mumbled, thumbing through the pages of the book until he came to the growth potion I'd bought yesterday. "The question is, how much did you use?" He glanced at me, then back at the book.

I took a breath. He was *not* going to like this answer. "All of it."

He froze, then blinked up at me. "I'm sorry, did you say you used the entire bottle of a very concentrated potion meant for a person to consume . . . on a handful of *seeds*?"

I bit my lip and nodded, unable to force any words out.

He shook his head. "When I asked if you needed help with instructions, the correct answer was yes."

"I know," I said, barely louder than a whisper. "I should have talked to you first. Been honest about what I was doing."

"Yes, you should have." His face softened. "Next time, okay? For now, let's just deal with this."

I nodded again, my face aflame.

He returned his attention to the book, turning one more page to what seemed to be a counter-potion to the growth potion I'd used. I couldn't read it all, and I didn't recognize all the ingredients, but he seemed to have everything he needed in the small herb bags. He pulled out small stems, seeds no larger than a grain of pollen, and the tiniest of flowers, dropping them into the mortar one after another. Then, he withdrew a small, carefully wrapped bottle of some kind of oil, adding it to the herby mix before crushing everything together.

As he crushed, he said, "This will be less of a potion and more of a paste, but it should still get the job done."

The paste in the mortar began to glow with a soft yellow light, like butter or the palest daffodils, and a bead of sweat rolled down his forehead. I resisted the urge to hand him a handkerchief, forcing myself to focus on what he was doing. I didn't want to break his concentration.

The light pulsed once, a bright, sunny yellow so contrary to the gray snow outside, and then it settled back into a dim, barely-there glow.

"It's done," Elias said, wiping his forehead. He handed the mortar to me. "You need to spread it wherever you put the potion."

I took the mortar, swallowing. "That's going to be a little difficult."

His shoulders sagged. "You spread it over the whole plot, didn't you?"

I shrugged, offering him an embarrassed smile.

He sighed. "All right. Just . . . I guess spread it evenly across the plot? We'll make more if we need to. But I'm adding this to your tab!"

I ducked my head, turning toward the plot. "As well you should."

I deserved way more of a consequence than the expenses of the antidote and Elias's specialty services.

I started to dip my fingers into the paste, but Elias caught my hand, passing me a small brass spoon instead. I swallowed, smiling at him apologetically, then used the spoon to scoop out some of the paste. It was sticky and didn't want to go where I told it, so I ended up mixing it into a nearby watering can—amazingly partially full—and began sprinkling the water over the tangle of stems and leaves. The paste thinned with the addition of the water and sank into the soil, the glow disappearing.

For several long moments, nothing happened. The greenhouse was full of the sound of rustling leaves and snipping clippers, hushed voices and scuffing feet, but we might as well not have put anything in the soil at all.

I looked up at Elias. "Why isn't it working?"

Elias ran a hand over his face. "It's got to be that magic you added."

"So what do we do?"

Elias didn't answer, and my heart hammered in my chest. The plants continued to writhe around me, and I simply watched them move, watched them expand as far as they could in the greenhouse.

Then one of the fronds touched the glass ceiling, the same ceiling covered in a thick layer of snow, where it hadn't melted away yet. The plant recoiled away from the frosty pane.

And I had an idea. Camellias were cold-weather plants, but

that didn't mean they wanted to be frozen. If it retreated from the cold, maybe I could cool it down a little. Maybe that could calm it enough for Elias's antidote to work.

I wouldn't even need magic. But it would mean accepting that I needed the cold season. In fact, I wouldn't have been able to do what I wanted if it wasn't winter.

Gods, I hated the cold. But for once I was grateful for it.

I shot to my feet and ran toward the nearest wall, diving through openings and leaping the sweeping stems until I reached a window. I unlocked it, throwing it upward. Snow tumbled inside, piling around my boots, and the bitter wind froze me to my core. I grabbed the biggest pots I could carry, shoving snow into them as quickly as I could. The leaves rustled behind me, and I glanced over my shoulder, catching my breath at how close the plant was coming to me.

As soon as the pots were full, I carefully made my way back to the plot where Elias stood, watching me from where I'd left him, a puzzled look on his face. I didn't bother explaining my plan, just dropped to my knees again and began piling the snow around the stems, surrounding the base of the plants.

Almost immediately, the plants stopped their writhing. For a few silent moments, nothing changed. Not even a leaf rustled.

Then, the plants seemed to sag, but not like they were wilting. More like they were falling asleep. The base of the stems began to glow with that soft yellow light. The light climbed slowly at first, then spread like a wildfire, engulfing the enormous camellia plants until the entire greenhouse was alight like the sun. I covered my eyes, trying to protect them from the immense light.

And then it was over.

The light on the other side of my eyelids receded, and I cracked one eye open. Sure enough, it was gone.

And the plant was retracting, as if growing in reverse, back toward the original plot. Dad and Weiland fell to the ground as it released them. Then the stems receded over the edges of the planter. Then into the soil.

Then it was gone, as if it had never been. As if I'd never used that potion. I fell to my backside, letting out a relieved breath. It was over.

And now came the hard part: explaining myself to my family.

I looked up at them. "Anyone else up for some hot chocolate?"

I POURED CHOCOLATE FROM THE KETTLE INTO THE LAST OF THE CUPS, bringing them over to the table where my entire family, plus Elias, waited for me. I'd already explained what happened, and no one had said a word since. I figured that was as good a time as any to supply the soul-warming concoction and maybe make them a little less mad at me, even if it wasn't as good as the Heart of the Vale a Taster's Guild member would have made.

For their part, they accepted the cups of steaming chocolate with small smiles or thanks, but it wasn't until I sat down with my own cup that Mom finally spoke.

She didn't meet my eyes, instead staring into the depths of the sweet drink in her hands. "I just don't understand why you didn't say something earlier. We all know you've struggled with flower magic. We would have understood. And we can still grow the camellias before we leave."

I took a deep breath. I knew this would be coming. "I . . . I'm not sure I completely understand myself." I sipped at my cup, immediately burning my tongue. I set the chocolate on the table in front of me so I didn't do it again. "All of you are just so

good at it. And it's the family business. I've never measured up."
I hugged myself.

Lila rolled her eyes. "You think just because you're not good at the family business that you're not still family?"

Penny snorted. "You don't get away from us that easily."

"Yeah, there are other jobs you can do," Weiland said, sipping his chocolate. His eyes lit with mischief. "Like spread all the fertilizer."

It was my turn to roll my eyes, but Dad's next words stopped me short, eerily echoing my thoughts just an hour earlier in the greenhouse.

"Actually," he said, "I think that's a great idea. How about fertilizer duty for at least a month? Then we reevaluate your abilities and what you can do."

I suppressed a groan. "Okay, I deserve that."

Lila shrugged a shoulder. "Or maybe in a month we start talking about a place of our own? You know, like we did when we were younger?"

A place of our own. I remembered. Lila and I had discussed it years ago, but it hadn't come up since our teens. We'd all become so preoccupied with the family business, it just didn't seem as important.

My heart did a flop. "Yeah? What would we do?"

What I didn't say: what would *I* do?

She shrugged again, studying her cup. "A tea shop? I can still do flower magic. Maybe we can focus on floral teas or something. You don't need flower magic to make tea."

She finally met my eyes, and I smiled at the warmth in them.

"Yeah, that's true," Penny said. "No one says you *have* to stick here with us forever. You'll still be one of us."

Mom and Dad exchanged a heavy look, their faces just a little sad. Then, Mom said, "It's true. Lila, you're the oldest, and you're still living in your childhood home. It would make sense for both of you to find your own way soon."

Neither of us responded, but my heart fluttered with the idea. They really weren't mad at me. But they wanted me to leave?

Except . . . Lila wanted to come with me. And Mom was obviously sad at the idea, even though she said she supported it. And it would only be to my own space, to find out who I really was, who I was meant to be.

Elias suddenly grinned. "You can always work with me, too. Potions are a decent living, and I could use a novice. Well, I guess technically my *mother* could use a novice." His eyes twinkled. "Or . . . you could marry me."

The table fell silent, then everyone burst into laughter. Except me and Elias. He seemed serious. For a moment, I wondered if he really did like me, if that was why he gave me such a good price on the potion, why he always seemed so happy to see me.

And then he *did* laugh. Maybe he was joking after all. Of course he would be happy to see me; we'd been friends practically forever.

I smiled with everyone else, but my head was brimming with the possibilities now. My family and friends weren't going anywhere, but I had my whole life ahead of me. And if I could stop trying to prove myself to everyone, maybe I could find what I was really good at.

It was time to wake up and leave this dormant phase of my life. I was ready to bloom.

SELINA J. ECKERT IS A BIOLOGIST-BY-DAY, WRITER-BY-NIGHT NATIVE OF Pennsylvania. She lives with her husband, dog, and two cats and spends her time writing, reading, creating art, and dreaming about fictional worlds. She has written two fairy-tale retelling short stories that were both finalists in Rooglewood Press short story contests and grew an entire series, Seasons of Magic, out of it. She now writes a lot of cozy fantasy, including her Pie-Jinks books. You can find out more about all her books and where she is online at www.selinajeckert.com/links.

BLIZZARDS AND BREWS
DEANNA AND ANGELA STUART

The gentle sway of the tea shop as it traveled always soothed Melsymar's nerves. The great tortoise Nyana, who carried the building on her back, had a smooth gait, and the shop itself was enspelled so even the uppermost floor didn't rock like the crow's nest of a ship, but there was still an ever so gentle rocking motion when they were on the road. Fifty years running the shop, and it could still lull Melsymar to sleep if he wasn't careful. Now was not the time for sleep, however. He had so much to do! So much to prepare for, and he was already running late!

The Skyglow Festival was tomorrow night, and it was always a grand event, drawing people from all over the queendom. Every year, the skies over the village of Welkinton in Painted Vale glowed and danced with brilliant lights. The festival marked the beginning of the season of Winter's Tide and launched a celebration that lasted two full weeks, culminating in a festival of lights on Lantern Night. It was a wonderful time of year, a time of kindness and warmth, of exchanging gifts, of music and merriment, and sharing delicious food. Above all, it was a time to be the light in the darkness, to hold a candle through the darkest time of the year, and to know that together, you'd make it back to the light.

It was Melsymar's favorite event, and the perfect one to be his last as proprietor of The Tinker's Tea. Which meant it had to *be* perfect. He laid the heavy, leather-bound ledger he had been reading on his lap and rubbed the sleep from his eyes with a sigh.

"You've checked that book three times already today," a silken voice purred from atop the mantlepiece. "Has something changed since you opened it last?"

The gnome looked up at his familiar sheepishly and was met with that aloof, judging expression common to all of the feline species. "I'm just making sure we have enough. I really do think we should have purchased more lavender and bergamot tea when we were in Oasis. It is always a favorite with the maire of Welkinton, you know." He stretched his legs toward the hearth to warm his cold toes. "And I *do* hope I purchased enough butter for Grainne's cardamom buns. We ran out last year, and she did not let me hear the end of it until Highsun."

Kittle stood up from where she had been curled and stretched, first her hind legs, then her fore, then each fuzzy little bat-like wing. The tip of her floofy tail twitched as she made her way to the end of the mantle and hopped down, spreading her wings to glide toward him. She landed gracefully—right atop his ledger.

"It will be fine. You worry too much. Even if it is not fine, it is not as if you will have to worry about it for much longer." She pressed a paw to his hand. "You are treating this like all of the other big events we've done. You're going to retire after this. Just relax and enjoy it. Even if you fail spectacularly—which you won't—you don't have to worry about Grainne's grumbling, or any snide comments about that one time you ran out of someone's favorite tea. Once you're done, you can just settle back with a good book and a cup of tea and say the very best of all phrases: 'Not my problem'."

He sighed and scratched his familiar behind her big, tufted ears. "Perhaps you're right. I just want this to be a day to remember. And if we do find our new proprietor, I want them to fall in love with the place as much as I did, to really care about it. I don't want to spend my retirement worried about how things are getting on, and if Nyana is being treated right."

"Mm. Well, that's fair." Kittle purred, looking back at him with gold eyes half-lidded. "But trust Nyana. You know she always finds the right person at the right time. Always has." She yawned and nudged his hand with her nose until he set the ledger aside to allow her to settle in on his lap. She was comically oversized for it, of course, but she didn't let that stop her. Grymalars were just a touch larger than the largest domestic cat, and though Melsymar was tall for a gnome, and solidly built, she still sprawled off both sides of him. She hadn't fully fit on his lap since she was a kitten. "It will work out."

"Hm." He wasn't convinced, but he had learned long ago not to argue with Kittle in situations like this. It was just that he had this tickling feeling in the back of his mind that something was going to go wrong, something he just wasn't seeing, and if he just double-checked *one more time* he would figure out what it was.

He looked out over the tearoom, going over his mental checklist again. He'd spent the last few days cleaning and the room practically glowed in the golden light of the flickerfire chandeliers. Each of the tables had been washed and covered with a fresh, crisp tablecloth, and he'd reorganized the room so patrons of any height wouldn't have difficulty finding a comfortable place to sit near their friends. The stones of the hearth that spread in front of the massive fireplace had been scrubbed, and the heavily carved woodwork of the mantlepiece had been polished until it gleamed. The long oaken counter had been similarly polished, and each of the high-backed stools along its length had been checked for wobbly legs. He'd even taken down, dusted, and refilled every single one of the one hundred and fifty jars of tea that graced the shelves behind the counter. Maybe . . .

Kittle cracked open one eye and looked up at him. "Not. Your. Prob—"

There was a sudden skitter to the swaying rhythm of the shop, a shuffling jolt from side to side that set the jars of tea to rattling and Kittle's fur to standing on end. As quickly as it started, it settled out again. Melsymar frowned, smoothing down Kittle's fur with a gentle hand. "You were saying?"

"Hmph." She hopped off of his lap and slunk over to the window, tail lashing irritably. At some point in the last few hours, the windows had frosted over. Which was odd, as it hadn't seemed quite cold enough for it earlier. Standing on her hind legs, Kittle pawed at the glass until she had scraped clear a spot large enough for her to see outside. Her ears flattened. "Ew. There is ice falling from the sky. Rude."

Melsymar's frown deepened, wiry brows furrowing in concern. "That's strange. I had scried the weather before we set out. It was supposed to be fair for the entire trip." It was rare for Bright Pass to have truly bad weather during the weeks leading up to the Skyglow Festival; a sprinkling of rain perhaps, or light snow—thick fog at worst. There was something that seemed gods-blessed about this particular pass, keeping it safe for festival-goers year after year.

"Yes, well, maybe next time you want an *accurate* scrying, you'll listen to me when I tell you your weatherweed is too old." Kittle sniffed and turned up her chin, looking pointedly away.

"The weatherweed was fine," he grumbled as he extricated himself from his comfy chair. And it had, in fact, been fine.

When he'd removed it from the enchanted pouch that kept it fresh, the seaweed frond had been dry and crisp, indicative of the dry, fair weather they were having. Besides, Melsymar had been a mage for over one hundred and twenty years. He knew quite well what it felt like when a spell went wrong, and his scrying most certainly had not.

He grumbled his way to the door and turned the lower knob—there were three, each at different heights for the comfort of a variety of patrons—and stepped carefully out onto the narrow porch that wrapped around the entire building. The weathered old boards shimmered with a thin glazing of ice, and the overhang had already begun to sprout icicles. That did not bode well. With a murmured word and a whisper of magic pulled from the aether, he melted himself a safe path across the porch and peeked his head through the bars of the bannister, squinting up at the sky. Steely grey clouds, pregnant with snow, loomed low overhead, and though it was near to sunset, only the palest traces of pink managed to make their way through. All around them, fat droplets of freezing rain hissed down from the sky, landing with slushy plops in the fallen leaves.

All in all, it was an absolutely miserable time to be outside, especially miserable for those with only the comfort of a tent between themselves and the elements when they made camp—as was the case for so many of the travelers on the road to the festival. Once again, he was grateful Nyana seemed impervious to temperature. Unlike her smaller, less magical cousins, she was just as comfortable in the snow as she was in the warmth of Turtle Bay. He hurried back inside and found Kittle curled up on the hearth, ears still half-flattened. "I think we will stop here for the night, just in case someone needs someplace dry and safe. It will put us a bit further behind, but I'd rather be late if it means getting a few people out of this cold."

"If they had any sense, they'd already be camping for the night," Kittle grumped, not bothering to open her eyes.

"Yes. Well. It is only about six hours to Welkinton if one is not on foot. I imagine there will be a number of people trying to push on before that snow hits. If we can save them the trouble, it will be worth it."

"Ugh. *Snow.*" Kittle's ears flattened fully in disgust.

Melsymar nodded his agreement. "Indeed. So strange. I cannot think of a year this pass has gotten snow before the festival. Truly."

With a focused thought, he reached out telepathically to his giant tortoise companion. *"Please stop here, my friend. Find a spot out of the wind where you will be comfortable. I think we will light the lanterns and offer shelter from the storm tonight."* He didn't expect an answering thought; it was rare that Nyana replied in words. Instead, he felt the warm impressions of approval, assent, and felt the rhythm change again as she made her way off the road and found a place to settle in.

Once she was settled, Melsymar set a large kettle of water on the hob and fetched himself his thickest wool cloak. Then he set about thawing the porch, lighting all the lanterns around its perimeter, and setting down the entry ramp. By the time he was finished, the rain had begun to turn to big, fluffy flakes of wet snow, and the porch had already begun to freeze again.

"Bother. So much for people pushing on before the snow hits," Melsymar grumbled to himself. "Well, this won't do at all."

He pulled his cloak tighter around himself and set about gathering up fist-sized stones from the area they'd settled in, using a fold of the cloak as a makeshift bag. When he'd gathered a few dozen, he made his way back up the ramp, placing the stones at intervals along the rails and marking them with sigils in chalk, repeating an incantation as he went. Aether hummed inside of him, building with every repetition. Warm, pulsing energy that pushed outward from his core with a gentle but tangible force, building until it felt like a constant pressure beneath his skin.

As he placed the final stone, he released his hold on the magic and it rushed out of him, pouring into the stone and cascading down into each of the others, setting the sigils aglow with golden light. Tiny motes of light, like dust caught in a sunbeam, glittered and danced in the air, forming an arch over the entry ramp. He watched with satisfaction as the drifting flakes hit the magical archway and stopped, hanging suspended for a moment before melting and running down the intangible barrier.

After a moment's consideration, he marked out the picketing area for the horses of their soon-to-be guests with the usual stakes and ropes, then repeated the process with more stones. The animals would be just as much in need of a warm and dry place to sleep as any of the people on the road, after all.

Pleased with his work, he smiled and brushed the chalk from his hands as he looked back at the shop. The golden light from its high windows mingled with the light from the lanterns, the stones, and the magical barrier, lighting up The Tinker's Tea like a beacon in the evening twilight. Snow had begun to settle on the roof, as well as the crest of the jaunty little tower that held his private rooms, coating it in a thin, shimmering layer that sparkled softly pink and gold.

Below, Nyana was safely tucked within her shell, only her nose peeking out from between her massive forelegs. A little puff of snow had piled up, adorably, on the very tip of her nose. He reached out his mind fondly to her and received an answering pulse of warmth as he headed back inside.

"That should hold it off well enough, I think." He hung his cloak on a peg near the door and let his breath out in a tired huff. As glad as he was to be able to provide shelter to the other travelers, he was not exactly prepared for guests at the moment. The kitchen staff was on holiday until the shop reached its destination—off to whatever realm they inhabited when they weren't cooking up delights for patrons and chasing Melsymar out of the kitchen with brandished cooking implements, or baleful glowers.

He'd been proprietor of The Tinker's Tea for fifty years and he still didn't know where exactly the ragtag bunch of hobs, goblins, and other folk, disappeared to when they weren't on duty, nor did he know the details of how they came to be a part of the shop. Grainne, the strange old hob who ran the kitchen with a (figurative) iron ladle, had been delighting people with her cooking for as long as anyone could remember. Every time the shop passed to a new proprietor, she would eventually appear and take over the kitchens, and was as much a fixture as Nyana herself.

Without Grainne and the rest of the staff, he wasn't certain what to do if he suddenly found himself with a full house. It wasn't that he was incapable in the kitchen. He was perfectly capable of making sandwiches, even serviceable soups, and the larder was plenty full for the coming event. But would that really do? It certainly wasn't up to their usual fare.

"You're worrying again." Kittle cracked an eye open. "You worry too much. It will be fine."

"I'm sure you're right. I would just rather have something better to feed to our guests than potato soup, and sandwiches on three-day-old bread."

"If they complain, they can take it up with the white stuff falling out of the sky." She closed her eyes again and wrapped her tail tighter around her body, covering her nose.

He chuckled. She did have a point, even if he wasn't one to agree with that sort of thing out loud. Soup it was.

He'd just begun to head back to the kitchen when he heard voices coming up the ramp and the door flew open. Two stout dwarves shouldering heavy packs tromped inside, laughing boisterously at some shared joke. They stamped the snow off their boots and looked around the shop with obvious approval.

"Lovely weather we're havin', isn't it, friend? Real glad yeh had those lanterns lit! Fella could get buried out there. Are yeh open for business?" the taller dwarf asked, pushing back the hood of his cloak to reveal a mop of dark curls, streaked with grey and accented with small braids and intricate bands of silver. His short, thick beard sparkled with melting snow.

"We are! Welcome to The Tinker's Tea. Settle in wherever you would like. May I bring you a warm drink to banish the chill? On the house." Melsymar held up a hand to ward off the objections already forming on their lips. "No, no. I wouldn't think of making an extra penny off of these circumstances."

The dwarves seated themselves at one of the low tables, throwing their cloaks over an empty chair and doffing their packs. The second dwarf smiled at Melsymar through a bushy red beard. "That is kind of you. I understand this is a tea shop, but if you have coffee, we would love some. Thank you." His accent was less pronounced than his companion's, his voice a gentle, soft-spoken bass.

"Of course! Right away. Make yourself at home." Melsymar bustled off to prepare the potent, bitter brew. It wasn't something his customers ordered often, but dwarves were known to have a particular love for the stuff, so he made a point to keep at least a small stock of the finest beans the queendom had to offer. "Do you know if there were others behind you?" he called over the counter.

"I don't rightly know. Snow's comin' down thick as fog now," the first dwarf replied, pulling his seat close to his companion's and settling in. "Couldn't see further than my arm until we saw yer lights. I'm hopin' anyone else had more sense than us and hunkered down."

"One can hope. Either way, our doors shall be open for all."

Although Melsymar didn't love the taste himself, the ritual of brewing coffee was quite enjoyable—especially with his gnomish-built, automatic brewing device. The graceful dance of the carefully balanced chambers, the unaided movement of water back and forth between them, the clinks, hisses, and cheerful burbles, all seemed like magic. In reality though, the clever contraption used heat, changing pressures, and a system of springs and counterweights—science! And even though Melsymar had long ago chosen the science of magic over the physical sciences that so many of his kin were fascinated by, he still found them interesting, and every bit as beautiful.

He hummed as he chose two large clay mugs that were glazed a shimmering indigo and placed them on a tray along with a small pot of cream, some honey, and a few pieces of buttery shortbread. A soft bubbling sound came from the brewer, and the rich smell of coffee wafted through the room. When it finished, Melsymar opened the spigot on the bottom of one of the chambers and released the brew into the waiting mugs, then brought them, steaming, over to the table. The dwarves had already produced a small wooden game board and some dice and were beginning a game of drakes. "Here you are, gentlemen."

The red-bearded dwarf took the mugs with a nod of thanks, then began pouring cream and generously spooning honey into one of them before setting it in front of his companion. His own mug he bravely took without any additions.

"Apologies that I cannot yet offer you something warm to eat. I was entirely unprepared to be entertaining customers tonight. Don't you worry though, I was just about to put on a pot of soup when you came in. I'll get right to—"

Before he could finish his sentence, the door swung open, slamming into the side of the shop with a bang that nearly jumped Melsymar out of his skin. A young human man stumbled in, clutching a swaddled bundle the size of a child to his chest, a young woman following close behind. She grabbed the door with both hands and leaned hard against the wind, wrenching it closed behind her.

"All the gods bless you, sir, for being a beacon in the storm!" the young man exclaimed.

The bundle in his arms squirmed and began to squall loudly, "Down, Papa! Down!"

"Hush now. Just a minute dear. Let's find a place to sit first." The young woman led them over to a low table by a sofa that was close enough to the fireplace for extra warmth, but far enough away that it would not be too tempting for little hands, and then unshouldered a pack nearly as large as she was.

"Happy to be of service," Melsymar said. "Cocoa for the three of you? I was about to get some soup started, but let me get you settled in first."

"That would be perfect, thank you," she replied, pulling off her cloak and taking the child into her arms. There was something about her that was familiar, the young man as well, but Melsymar couldn't quite put his finger on it.

Kittle watched the scene curiously from her spot on the hearth. She would emphatically deny it, but Melsymar knew she loved children, and she had quite the way with them. On many occasions, she had settled a cranky or overly adventurous child with a purr and a snuggle, or some entirely undignified feline antics.

While Melsymar made up the cocoa, the family settled in and draped their cloaks on the back of the sofa to dry. The dwarves welcomed them cheerfully, the more boisterous of the two introducing himself as Ivar, and the other as his husband,

Duncan. The young couple were Tania and Lorn, and again Melsymar was certain he should know why they seemed so familiar.

He brought the mugs of cocoa over, and the child, an impish looking little girl with ringlets of strawberry blonde hair, smiled at Melsymar when he set the tray on the table in front of them.

"Hi. I'm Molly, and I'm free." She proudly held up four fingers, frowned a moment, then used her other hand to tuck her pinky down. "What's your name?"

"Nice to meet you Molly, I'm Melsymar."

"Mel-smar." She squinted at him thoughtfully. "How old are you? Are you free too?"

"Molly!" her mother chided, cold-reddened cheeks turning an even brighter shade of crimson. "I'm sorry. She hasn't met many gnomes."

"Quite all right." Melsymar chuckled. It wasn't the first time a human child had been confused by their similarities in height. "I am one hundred and eighty-six, Miss Molly."

"Wooow!" Molly gawked. "You're old!"

"Molly!" This time it was Lorn. "Come here and have your cocoa." He gave Melsymar an apologetic look.

Molly shot her father an impish grin, more amused at being in trouble than remorseful. "Okay, Papa! Fank you, Mel-smar!"

"You're welcome. Now, if you're all settled, I'm going to make that soup. Just ring the bell on the counter if you need anything."

As he headed back to the counter, an amused voice purred in his mind. "*You **are** pretty old.*"

He shot Kittle a sidelong glance and chuckled. "*My dear, I was not much older than those two when I found you, your eyes barely open. If I am old, so are you.*"

"*Hmph. Grymalars do not get old.*"

"*Mhm. Right. I had forgotten.*" He shook his head, amused, as he raised his hand to push open the kitchen door. "*Anyway, there is nothing wrong with—*" A prickling sense of *wrongness* crawled across the connection with his familiar and down his spine like hundreds of tiny, icy, spiders.

From her perch on the hearth, Kittle let out a low growl, and Melsymar glanced over to see her crouched low, ears flat, her fur beginning to puff up as she glowered at the door. He followed her gaze, listening, but he could hear nothing over the blowing gale outside and the quiet conversation of the common room. "*What—*"

The door suddenly flew wide, once again slamming against the wall outside with a force that threatened to take it off its hinges. A chill wind brought a swirl of snow into the room and revealed a pale, dark-haired woman, woefully underdressed for the cold.

Startled as the rest of them, Molly began to cry.

"Oh dregs! Rancid dregs!" the woman cursed, struggling to pull the door closed behind her.

The wind whipped her long hair around her, making it seem like a living thing, and for just a moment, Melsymar could have sworn he saw a ghostly flicker of blue light behind her eyes, just as she managed to finally best the wind and pull the door shut.

She turned and gave the room a sheepish smile. "Sorry."

Melsymar reached out to the shop's wards, mentally tracing the lines of aether like a spider testing a web. Nothing seemed disturbed or untoward. If something or someone with ill-intent had attempted to enter the shop, the resulting alarm would have been immediate and impossible to ignore. There weren't any obvious attempts to bypass it either. With a questioning glance toward his floofing feline companion, he came around the counter to get a better look at their new guest.

"Quite all right, dear. You are not the first tonight and likely will not be the last." If there had been a cold light behind her eyes, all traces of it were gone now. Her skin, however, was worryingly pale, the tips of her fingers a dark purple-blue. The edges of his wariness melted into concern. "Oh dear. Oh my." Melsymar hurried over and offered her a hand. "Come, come. Let's get you settled in by the fire. You look like you nearly caught your death of cold."

"*What are you doing?*" Kittle snapped.

"*The same thing I'd hope she'd do for us, were our situations reversed. Don't worry, I already checked the wards. You can check them yourself if it makes you feel better. She hasn't disturbed them.*"

The woman's hand was icy, no trace whatsoever of warmth, and yet she seemed completely undisturbed by the fact. She allowed Melsymar to lead her over to one of the armchairs by the fire, looking mildly amused as Kittle fled for the top of the grandfather clock nearby. She thanked him as she settled in and unbuttoned the light coat she was wearing. Jewelry flashed on her fingers and at her neckline in the light of the fireplace, and Melsymar recognized more than one arcane sigil worked into them.

Interesting.

"Let me go gather you some blankets and get you something warm to drink. You poor dear. Would you like tea, or cocoa perhaps?"

She glanced over her shoulder as if looking for someone, and then turned back to smile at Melsymar warmly. "Tea would be lovely, thank you. Queen's Blend, if you have it. Don't worry about the blankets, though. I'm fine."

"Oh, it's no trouble at all." He patted her hand and headed back to the counter to start her tea. Though the rest of the patrons had gone back to their cups, and even Molly had calmed down, a hushed wariness had settled over the room.

"*Melsymar . . . She is not alone.*" Kittle hissed in his mind.

"*What do you mean?*" All cats had a sort of second sight, and

Kittle was no different. If she said she saw something he could not, he believed her.

"There are spirits with her. A creepy librarian lady, and an armored man with a sword and a silly mustache."

"Hm. Well, that is interesting. I noticed some sigils on the jewelry she is wearing as well. I find it odd that a practitioner would be in such a state though, unless they were a novice or more exhausted than she seemed." Finished with the tea tray, he headed to the small closet near the pantry to retrieve a warm woolen blanket. *"Are you certain they are spirits?"*

The reply came with the sandpaper brush of indignation, *"Of course I am certain. What else do you think I would mistake for spirits? Hmph."*

With his hands hidden under the blanket, Melsymar made a small gesture and murmured the brief incantation that would allow him to share the sight of his familiar. His eyes changed from their natural mossy green to golden, his pupils stretching to slits.

Sitting by the dark-haired woman were two other patrons. In the way Kittle saw the world, they seemed solid as any other flesh and blood being, though a strange, misty sort of an aura floated about them. In the second armchair, sitting prim and proper, was a white-haired, matronly woman with a stern, yet kindly look about her. At her feet was a pack filled with books, one of which was already open on her lap. On the floor between the two women sat an older gentleman with steely grey hair and a long, droopy mustache, his feet stretched out to the fire. He wore light armor as easily as one would wear their favorite shirt and had a rapier lying beside him as he lounged.

"Well, it's a bloody fine thing we found this place when we did." The gentleman looked over his shoulder at the dark-haired woman, and while she met his gaze, her reply did not come aloud. He laughed. "Oh yes. That famous sense of direction of which you seem to be possessed."

The other spirit tutted at him, giving him a disapproving look over her spectacles. "Now, now, Ambrose, you be nice to 'er. It's not 'er fault she sees things a little different."

Melsymar allowed the spell to drop, and the spirits vanished from his sight, leaving the woman alone once again. *"Hm. I see. Well, keep an eye on them. They don't particularly look threatening at the moment, but one can never be too careful, I suppose. What about her? Her hands were so cold I almost expected to see the same aura about her, but she otherwise seems as mortal as anyone else here."*

"I don't know." Kittle crouched down on top of the clock and peered out from one of the holes in the decorative woodwork. She was much too large to be fully hidden, and the sight was so adorably silly that Melsymar had to be very careful the sense of fond amusement didn't find its way down their connection. *"She feels alive and not-alive—but not dead. It is strange, and I don't like it. Don't worry. I will keep a very close eye on them."*

"Thank you. Don't you worry either. If any of them try anything, I have full confidence in the wards, in Nyana, and in ourselves. It will be just fine."

Melsymar made his way back over to the woman, and set the tea tray on the table before offering her the blanket. She took it with a patient smile, though she only laid it loosely upon her lap. "Here you are. Now, don't trouble yourself. Let me pour your cup and let's get those hands thawed out. I am not much of a healer, but I know a few things. Once we get you warmed up, I can take a further look if you like."

She smiled that patient smile again and allowed him to pour her first cup. "Thank you. You are too kind." When he was finished pouring, she took the cup and cradled it in her hands for a moment, inhaling the scent of the tea with a blissful expression. "You know, there is just something about warm tea. One could almost say it was . . . " She took a deep sip, eyes closing in pleasure. As she did, the color slowly came back to her hands, her cheeks, and within seconds, she looked healthy and hale again. She grinned down at Melsymar. "Magic."

Relieved at the transformation, he barked a laugh. "Indeed it is, madam. Indeed it is. Potent magic at that, it would seem." He was absolutely burning with curiosity now. That kind of healing magic was not the easiest to do, especially without a gesture or an incantation. And yet, a mage with that kind of skill should have been able to keep themselves from getting frostbitten like that in the first place. Perhaps the spell had been stored in one of her pieces of jewelry, or perhaps she was a different kind of magical. A druid? Maybe a warlock? So many questions he wanted to ask, and introductions hadn't even been made!

"Excuse my manners. In the hurry to get you settled in, I neglected to introduce myself. I am Melsymar. Welcome to The Tinker's Tea. May I ask your name?"

"Of course. Myrshai Llyshana Althaewyn, but just Myrshai will do. Pleased to meet you."

"The pleasure is mine. It's always lovely to meet a fellow magical. If you don't mind me asking, where is it that you studied mag—"

Again the door opened, a gust of bitter wind quickly sweeping in a small drift of snow. A tall leporia strode in, carrying an unconscious young man in their arms as if he weighed nothing. The leporiae were people who shared physical traits with rabbits and hares. This particular leporia was a longears, one of the hare-like, and their silvery-white fur marked them as one of their moontouched. They pushed the door closed behind them with a large, unshod foot and scanned

- BLIZZARDS AND BREWS

the room. "Is there a healer among you? He needs attention, quickly."

"Oh dear! Yes. Come, bring him over here." Melsymar scurried around, gathering up pillows from the various armchairs and creating a makeshift bed a small distance from the hearth.

Myrshai quickly stood and came to Melsymar's side with her blanket at the ready, and without discussion, they began removing the young man's snowy outer clothing as soon as the leporia laid him down upon the pillows. Together, they quickly wrapped him in the blanket, and Melsymar hurried off to gather more.

The young man looked to be in grave shape. His skin was pale and clammy and ever so cold, his breathing slow and shallow. They needed to get him warmed up carefully, then they could assess what other healing he might need. He gathered up an armload of blankets and turned to find the dwarves behind him.

"How can we help?" Duncan asked.

He pushed the blankets into their arms. "Oh, thank you. Take these over and help get him wrapped up as quickly as possible, please. I'm going to fill some hot water bottles."

When Melsymar returned with the bottles a few moments later, he found the dwarves staring awkwardly at Myrshai, the blankets still in their arms.

She was digging through her pack, eyes glimmering with a silvery blue light. "I know!" she grumbled. "Yes! I know where it is. Just a moment." Strewn around her were a number of rather curious items: black candles, an ivory handled athame, a pair of leather-bound tomes, and pouches of pungent smelling herbs.

"Blankets!" Melsymar barked. There was no time for gawking or hesitation when a man's life was at stake.

The dwarves startled guiltily and set to work wrapping the young man, while Melsymar set the hot water bottles along the man's torso between the swaddling. Myrshai came over shortly thereafter with a small jar of noxious smelling unguent and began applying it to the bits of skin that had taken the most damage from exposure. Once she was finished, she sat cross-legged at his head and gently took it between her hands, closing her glimmering eyes. She whispered an incantation, concentration knotting her brow, and this time Melsymar could feel the flow of the aether as she gathered it.

The room was silent as she worked, the tension and worry palpable. Even Molly was quiet, watching Myrshai with huge eyes, more curious than frightened. After a long moment, Myrshai opened her eyes, the glimmer now gone. "He'll be all right if we keep him warm. Voithra hasn't wholly claimed him yet."

Everyone let out a collective breath of relief. If the death goddess had not yet placed her motherly kiss upon his forehead, there was hope.

Duncan clapped Myrshai on the shoulder. "Well done, lass!"

She eyed the dwarf sidelong until he sheepishly removed his hand, then smiled at him and murmured something that might have been thanks.

Melsymar looked up at the leporia and found them watching quietly, whiskers twitching, long, black-tipped ears perked forward intently. It wasn't often he'd chanced to meet one of the longears, and in all his years, he could only count one other moontouched. Their more rabbit-like cousins were common enough in the cities and villages around the queendom, but the longears preferred the wilds. Melsymar hadn't been in their company since his adventuring days.

Back then, he'd traveled with a wiry old moontouched named Sele, the most extraordinary tracker and wilderness guide he'd ever known. He'd heard the stories about the moontouched when he first started adventuring. That they had a special affinity for the stars and moons that meant they never became lost. That they owed their particular androgyny to their connection to the moons as well. Some said that they changed gender along with the phases of the moons—male when Freydon was full, female when Freya was. Others said they could change at will. Still others postulated that they inhabited a third space, either both genders in balance, or one unique to themselves.

Sele had most definitely proven the first part true. They'd never lost a trail, no matter the weather or the terrain. Even when they couldn't see the sky, Sele always knew which way to go. They said it was because the pull of the moons was a constant presence to the moontouched, just like it was to the oceans and their tides.

As to their gender, well, Melsymar hadn't been gauche enough to ask. And honestly, it didn't matter to him which legend was true, or if all of them were.

"Thank you, friend. That young man owes you his life. Come, let's get a warm drink in you. My treat. Would you like cocoa or tea? Coffee perhaps?"

Their ears perked up and swiveled to Melsymar. "Oh, I shouldn't stay long. There will be others who need to be guided in . . . " Their nose twitched as they scented the air. "But maaaybe a small cup of cocoa wouldn't hurt."

With a smile, he led the leporia over to the counter. "It most certainly will not. In fact, it will fortify you against the cold." Melsymar filled a mug that was shaped like an acorn, glazed with deep browns and brushed with gold. The cocoa was thick, almost thick enough to spoon, and smelled richly of chocolate. He slid the mug across the counter. "Did you know him?"

The leporia shook their head. "No. But I am a warden on this part of the mountain. Generally, I keep travelers from wandering off the road too far and getting themselves in trouble with the local wildlife." They sipped the cocoa, and their ears relaxed partway down. When they looked back up at Melsymar, the fur on their upper lip had a little cocoa mustache. "Once the storm started, I started patrolling the road for wandering furless. He'd wandered off the road once it had gotten dark."

"I'm glad you were there. I've known other members of the Wardens in the past. You won't find better wilderness guides in all the queendom. Uncanny knack for knowing the weather as well." Melsymar leaned against the counter. "Tell me, did you feel the storm coming?"

One side of their whiskers twitched upward in amusement. "Did you *not?*"

"No, though that's of no surprise. I'm terrible at forecasting the weather on my own. I had cast a spell to augur it, however, and saw nothing untoward."

The leporia thumped a foot on the floor thoughtfully. "Hm. That's weird. It did come quickly, but I smelled snow on the wind first thing in the morning. Maybe you should find a spell that improves your nose instead. Much more reliable." They finished the mug of cocoa and licked the chocolate from their fur. "Still. It is strangely early. I've never seen snow before the lights before."

"That was my thought as well. Hm. Well, would you like to stay for some soup, or do you wish to get back to it?"

"I think I will head out. Thank you. No time to dawdle. I'll be back if I find any other stragglers."

"Thank you. Ah, and what should I tell our friend is the name of his rescuer, when he comes to?" Melsymar asked, taking the mug to the sink.

"Oh. Um. It's Kuu. You don't need to, though. It's all right. I just hope he'll be ok." With that, they pulled their coat back on, wrapped a long fuzzy scarf up over their nose and headed back out into the storm.

Melsymar watched them go and briefly considered asking Nyana to head back out onto the road to assist in the search. They could certainly cover more ground that way, but with visibility what it was, it would probably be too risky. They were in a mountain pass after all, and tortoises couldn't fly. And while Nyana had never stepped on anyone before, he'd also never asked her to travel in these sorts of conditions. He hated just sitting here and waiting as it got worse, but it was better for everyone not to risk it. He had faith in the skills of the Wardens. If anyone could find the other travelers, it would be one of them.

The mood in the room was tense, despite Myrshai's insistence that the young man was no longer on death's door, and it had grown so hushed that the crackling of the fire and the howl of the wind outside seemed deafening. In the silence, Molly crept over and stared at the young man, then up at Myrshai, then back at the man, wide-eyed and curious. The strange mage smiled down at the little girl reassuringly and checked her patient's pulse again, closing her eyes as she counted the beats. When she opened them again, Molly was still staring.

"Boo!" Myrshai whispered teasingly and lurched slightly toward her.

Molly gasped and jumped back, startling everyone in the room except for Kittle, then collapsed into a peal of squealing giggles.

Kittle gave them a look of disgust, tail flicking. "*Saw that coming.*"

"Mhm." Melsymar chuckled. "*I see that poofy tail.*"

Kittle wrapped her tail around her paws and did not deign to respond.

When the giggle fit passed, Molly moved to sit close to

Myrshai, mirroring the woman's position. She looked down at the young man for a moment and then back up at Myrshai. "Why'd you do that?"

"Hmm? Startle you? You were staring."

"No, silly. Why'd you do this?" She put her hand on the man's throat where Myrshai had taken his pulse.

"Oh! To feel his heartbeat. I'm just checking how fast he's getting better."

"Oh. Ok. Can I help?"

Myrshai tilted her head and studied the girl for a moment, then scooted closer. "Here. Put your fingers here." She guided Molly's fingers to the man's throat again and gently held them there. "Do you feel that?"

Eyes squinted in concentration, Molly sat very still for a moment, then gasped. "Yes!"

"That's life energy."

"Wooow." Molly looked down at her hand in awe.

"You have it too. Put your fingers here." Myrshai leaned over and touched her fingers to the girl's neck.

"Your hands are cold!" Molly shrieked, but she did as she was asked. After a few seconds, she grinned at Myrshai. "But mine's much faster!"

"Yes. You're younger, and he's cold. That makes his heart slower."

"Oh," Molly nodded seriously, as if that made all the sense in the world to her. "Are you a healer?"

"Mm," the mage's response was neither confirmation nor denial. "How about you go see if you can go find your mommy's and daddy's heartbeat?"

"Ok!" She ran over to her mom and leapt up onto her lap. Tania shot Myrshai an apologetic look, and the mage smiled back, shaking her head.

A groan came from the bundle of blankets on the floor and

the young man began to stir, murmuring something about hammers. His eyes fluttered open, and he drowsily turned his head, looking around the room in confusion. "Where . . . Wha—?"

Myrshai laid a hand on his shoulder. "Shh, now. Rest. You were found in the storm and brought to a safe place. You're safe."

He looked up at her, bewildered, and shivered. "C-cold."

"I know. We're warming you up, but we have to take it slow." She smoothed his hair. "Don't worry. You'll be okay."

"M-my t-tools. D-did the b-bear bring my t-tools?"

It was Myrshai's turn to look bewildered. "Bear?"

"I think he means Kuu." Melsymar said. "They were a leporia, sir, that brought you in. And sadly, they didn't have your tools."

The man groaned and tried to sit up on his elbows. "I n-need—"

"Yeh need t'rest, boy," Ivar chided. "Tools are replaceable."

Sighing, the man flopped back on the pillows and burrowed under the blankets. Within a few seconds, he was asleep again.

Melsymar breathed a sigh of relief. Now that the worst was past, it was time to get the young man settled into a proper room. The tea shop did, in fact, have a few rooms for rent, though how many, like most things, varied with the whim of the shop. At times, they'd have enough rooms to house an entire performing troupe, others, perhaps a single room for a weary traveler. It was a strange sort of magic that Melsymar dearly hoped to study further during his retirement.

He checked the drawer that held the room keys—that was the quickest way to know what, precisely, was available—and to his surprise, he found it full to the brim! A key clattered out to the floor. It was heavy and iron, the head shaped like a horseshoe twined in delicate vinework. Inside the horseshoe was a bold number one made of polished brass.

"Could a few of you please help me? Now that he's stable, we really should move him somewhere more comfortable. I have a room ready, but I need some strong arms to carry him there."

"Of course!" Tania was the first to volunteer.

Between herself, her husband, and Ivar, they managed to get the man onto another blanket, and lifted him carefully. Melsymar led them down a hallway off the main room to the very first door on the right. He never knew what to expect when opening the door to a room. They were always comfortable and well appointed, but often they were somehow also tailored to the person staying there and what they needed at the time.

The door opened easily into a small, simply furnished room with a woodstove in the corner, already cheerfully warm. An iron pot of water and warm spices simmered on top of it, filling the room with the scent of cinnamon, cloves, and ginger. The bed was just large enough for the young man, and incredibly plush, with piles of woolen blankets and down pillows. They settled the young man in bed, and Tania offered to take the first watch.

WITH EVERYTHING SETTLED AND THEIR CHARGE QUIETLY SNORING away, perhaps now Melsymar could get that soup started. The wind outside was truly starting to howl now, the snow hissing against the windows with each gust, setting the panes to rattling in their frames. Wherever Grainne and the rest of the staff were, he hoped it was someplace warmer than this! He pushed open the door and waited a moment, entirely expecting another emergency, and was pleasantly surprised when one did not suddenly materialize.

The kitchen was larger than one would expect, judging by the size of the building. Like the rest of the shop, it seemed happy to ignore boring constraints like spacial dimensions and predictable layouts. At least it was still in the same configuration that it had been for the past few months. Melsymar wasn't sure he could handle another surprise right this moment, and it was not entirely uncommon to come into the kitchen, or into the tearoom itself, and find the space completely reorganized or redecorated.

He huffed out a sigh and set to gathering together the ingredients for a simple, hearty potato soup. Scrubbing and chopping vegetables was a soothing, mindless sort of chore, but it also left him with too much time to think. This was not how he had envisioned his retirement going. While he was very glad The Tinker's Tea could be a refuge for travelers in this awful weather, and while most of his worry was on the safety of people who might be stuck out in the storm tonight, a small part of him also worried at whether the storm would stop in time for them to make it to the festival, and whether he'd make it to his own retirement party.

Melsymar had hoped to spend his last few days as the proprietor of the shop celebrating with old friends, serving up delights to customers, and basking in the clank and clatter, bubble and bustle, of a busy shop. Most importantly, he'd hoped that amongst the festival goers, he'd find a worthy successor to take over the shop.

For the last year he'd been watching for just the right person, someone with the right spark of wonder, the right adventurous spirit, someone who the shop just sang to, the way it had to him. So far, no one had been quite right.

It wasn't as if he hadn't tried. He'd taken a number of people on for a time to see how they'd work out. There was Lellan, a kindly silver elf with an encyclopedic knowledge of teas from all over the world. She could pair the right tea with anything, from cinnamon scones to a terrible mood. She was brilliant. However, she'd also been a little too quick to argue with customers when they made what she considered a poor choice, even going so far as to serve them her preference instead on more than one occasion. (He'd written her a letter of recommendation to The Guild of Worshipful Tea Masters, and encouraged her to seek membership there, instead. She was a perfect fit.)

And then there had been Mikel, a charismatic dwarf who had an incredible work ethic and made some of the most incredible herbal blends that Melsymar had ever tasted. He also suggested installing taps, and serving ale and spirits as well, and that just would not do. There was Ina, who was always late. Evi, who was always early. Vigol, who was much too loud. Cassie, who was just too . . . tall.

Kittle had chided him for being too picky, but he felt he was being perfectly logical. It was a very important decision, after all. The shop, in all its iterations, had been an important part of Cozy Vales for generations. He couldn't leave it to just anyone. Besides, it wasn't only his pickiness; Nyana hadn't bonded with any of them, either.

Melsymar chopped through the last of the onions with a satisfying thunk, and deposited them into a large pot with the rest of the vegetables. He'd just have to hope they'd make it to the festival on time, and the right person would be there. Nyana seemed content that this was the right place to be, so he'd just have to trust her.

He bent down to feed some wood into the stove and nearly hit his head when he heard a scandalized tut behind him.

"Just *what* do you think you are doing?" Grainne demanded, entirely unconcerned with the possibility that she could have startled him to death by just materializing without warning like that. The hob glared up at him, her black eyes narrowed until they were just barely visible through the intricate webwork of lines and wrinkles on her aged face. Even at half his height, she was intimidating.

"Ma'am." He inclined his head. "I'm sorry, but we have guests, and I didn't want to bother you. I thought I'd just pop in here and make a pot of soup. I wasn't going to touch anything else." If there was one unforgivable sin, it was moving something in her kitchen. Only the shop itself could do that without risking her ire, and even it seemed to ask somehow. He should have known touching her stove would summon her.

"Hmmph," she grumbled. "Fine. Get out. I'll finish it."

"Thank you, ma'am. Of course. All the vegetables are chopped. I just was about to—"

"Out!" She shooed him toward the door. "I said I will finish it."

He scurried out of the kitchen, knowing better than to comment further. Kittle was waiting for him in the hall.

"Oh, good. I was just going to fetch you. Things have gotten a bit . . . busy since you left."

He eyed her warily. "Exactly how busy?"

Kittle's tail lashed. "Nearly a full house."

"Oh, cups and kettles!" he cursed. "Well, we have Grainne now. Though I don't think any of the kitchen or serving staff followed her back. We'll just have to make do."

"She chased you out of the kitchen again, didn't she?"

Melsymar did not answer that. Instead, he set off for the main room at a brisk clip, mentally preparing to handle the rush.

A WALL OF NOISE HIT MELSYMAR WHEN HE OPENED THE DOOR TO THE common room. Cups clattered, chairs scraped, and a multitude of voices spoke over each other all at once. All manner of people were crowded around the tables, shaking off the cold. Despite the situation, the atmosphere was light, and the laughter and good cheer made the cacophony a little more bearable.

"Melsymar!" a familiar voice called above the din, one he hadn't heard in ages. "So good of you to leave the lights burning for us!" The voice belonged to a wiry gnome about the same age as Melsymar, with a stylish swoosh of blonde hair, and a long mustache that was waxed and coiled up at the ends into impeccable curls.

"Yerril! I haven't seen you since . . . Oh heavens, the dirigible incident!"

"Incident! Pah! We got her home in one piece." Yerril caught Melsymar up in a rough embrace.

"Barely," Melsymar laughed.

"I'll never forget the look on the gryphon's face once the fowl beast," — Yerril had a terribly unfortunate tendency toward puns; he most definitely meant fowl with a 'w' — "realized we weren't a lady gryphon. I thought he was going to tear us apart for sure!"

"Yes, well." Melsymar tugged down his waistcoat and glanced around the room uncomfortably. "If you hadn't insisted on the feathers, and flying so close—"

"Ah, it was the perfect cover." Yerril waved him off. "Anyhow, congratulations on your retirement! I do hope we make it to Welkinton in time for your party. I was looking forward to raising a few glasses of frostwine in your honor."

"Oh, thank you." Melsymar sighed. "I do hope so. I haven't even begun to get this place decorated." He drew himself up, putting on an air of cheer he didn't quite feel. "But, it's all right. If my retirement party is to turn into a rescue mission, I am entirely content to be of service. What better way to spend a day?"

"A rescue mission indeed. How can I help? For old times' sake."

Under Melsymar's direction, they worked together to get cocoa and tea to the newcomers, and make sure their needs were provided for as best they could. Grainne provided everyone with a hearty and delicious herbed potato soup, and, miraculously, also managed to produce piles of roast turkey sandwiches on crusty, fresh bread. How she had found the time to make bread, much less roast a turkey, Melsymar could not fathom. People swapped stories about their misadventures in the storm, more than one person sharing a tale about a strange leporia who appeared out of the snow like a ghost and led them to safety.

The night ticked on and the storm blew harder, giving no signs of letting up. As people began to tire, Melsymar handed out keys, and indeed there was a key for each person there. Myrshai politely declined hers, opting instead to take watch over their sleeping patient and promising to sleep in the morning.

When everyone had made their way to the comfort of their beds, Melsymar flopped into the armchair by the fire with a groan of exhaustion. What a day it had been! And with the storm as it was, he didn't dare go to bed, just in case others found their way in. He laid his head back and closed his eyes, soaking in the crackle of the fire and the blissful quiet of the empty tearoom. It wouldn't hurt to doze for a few moments here, would it?

Kittle hopped up onto the chair and curled up across his lap, purring comfortingly. "Go ahead and get some rest. I'll watch for customers and wake you if anyone comes in. It's okay."

"I'll be all right. I'm just going to close my eyes for a few moments." Melsymar yawned.

"Of course you will." She nuzzled her head under his hand and curled closer, a warm and soothing weight. He began running his fingers through her soft fur, and before he knew it, he was fast asleep.

A FRIGID BLAST OF AIR STARTLED MELSYMAR AWAKE.

"Who—What—?" He leapt from his chair and whirled toward the door, dumping Kittle unceremoniously from his lap and sending her desperately flapping for the other side of the room.

"Sorry! Sorry." Kuu leaned on the door frame, ears drooping from exhaustion. Dawn's light was barely coloring the sky behind them, and still the snow continued to blow. "I didn't mean to startle you, but there's a situation. I need your help, you and whoever else might be willing to brave the storm. There's a caravan stuck a few miles from here. The snow on the slopes above them is unstable, and I'm afraid if they stay there long, there will be an avalanche."

"Oh heavens! All right. You just come in here and thaw out for a moment and I will gather the forces. Oh dear." Melsymar started toward the rooms, then paused, wringing his hands. Waking everyone one at a time and explaining things would take too long, and they needed to get moving. If he was to have time to get everyone prepared, there was not a second to waste. He hated waking *everyone*, but there was no helping it.

Behind the front counter, set into an alcove in the back wall, was a small magical apparatus that allowed him to be heard in all parts of the tea shop at once, no matter how many rooms the shop decided to add. It was made of bronze, inset with a grid of multicolored crystals. He bound a bit of aether to his will and tapped the crystal bell on top of the device. It rang all throughout the tea house, brilliant and clarion. As the note faded, he leaned in and spoke into the mouthpiece, which was oddly, and appropriately, shaped like an open mouth.

"Excuse me, everyone." He cleared his throat. "I apologize for the rude awakening, but we have a bit of a situation. There is a caravan in need of help. It is mired in the snow a few miles from here, and our friend Kuu thinks there is potential for an avalanche over that part of the pass. If there are any of you possessed of the skills and equipment to be out in this weather, your help would be greatly appreciated. This be a dangerous trip, and no one will think ill of you if the risk is more than you are willing to take. It is entirely understandable. The same goes for those who are inexperienced or unequipped. I would hate for any harm to come to any of you. If you are willing and able, however, please meet in the common room as soon as possible, and Kuu will apprise you of the situation before we start out. Thank you." With that, he rang the bell again, and went upstairs to gather a few things.

When he returned, a number of people were gathered in the common room in various states of ready and alertness. He was relieved to see Myrshai there, as well as Yerril, and Ivar and Duncan. When they noticed him, all conversation ceased and they turned to him, looking for direction. It had been a long time since he'd led an adventuring party, and even then he'd only done so when others were unable. The weight that settled on his shoulders was familiar, but that didn't make it much easier to bear. He took a deep breath. One of the most important parts of these situations was to project confidence, even if you didn't feel it.

"All right, friends. I trust Kuu has explained the situation?" There were nods all around. "Good. Then I won't waste time rehashing it or questioning your certainty. You would not be here if you did not think you could handle it, or that the risks were worth it. With Kuu's guidance and all of your skill, we will just nip out there, get them unstuck, and be home in time for breakfast." He gave them a reassuring smile. "Now, if you would all please remove your shoes and place them in a ring right here."

"Excuse me, what?" someone asked, incredulous.

Melsymar was already drawing a circle on the hardwood floor in chalk, inscribing the proper sigils around the shoes as they were set down. "Well, I don't have enough of these for everyone." He gestured to the snowshoes hanging from the pack on his back. "This spell will make it possible for you to walk on top of the snow as if you were wearing a set of these. We will make much better time if we're not struggling through drifts."

The rest of the group rushed to add their shoes to the circle, and he made quick work of the remainder of the inscriptions. Kittle supervised, weaving around the circle, occasionally wiping at a bit of chalk to straighten up a line. When he finished, he let go of the aether he'd been gathering and the soles of each pair of shoes began to glow softly blue.

"There. Now, gather up your shoes and let us make a plan as we go. I trust Kuu's skills as a warden implicitly. As long as we stay together, I know they will get us there and back. But, in case someone gets separated from the group, I would like to leave a trail of lights along the way, to guide people back to the shop. I can set up mag—"

Yerril hopped to his feet, eyes alight. "Save your magic, Melsymar. I have just the thing! Oh, this is perfect! I have a new invention I whipped up just for the festival. I grabbed one just in case, but I have heaps of them on my cart!" From his bag, he pulled two halves of a crystal sphere. Each half was filled with a different liquid, one yellow, the other blue. He placed the flat sides atop one another and twisted them until they screwed together. On the last twist, there was a sharp crack as the dividing pieces gave way, sending the liquids swirling into one another. As they mixed, the orbs began to glow with a brilliant green light.

"Wonderful, my friend! I will leave the lighting to you. Everyone take a few globes, and Yerril will show you how to place them as we go. I will save my magic for the wagons. I should have enough in me to make them all ride more lightly on the snow, but we will still need to dig them out manually. I cannot do both."

"Leave that to us." Duncan grinned. "Ivar and I can lead the digging team."

"Perfect. Those of you who are strong of back, please attend Duncan and Ivar when we arrive. Who has skill in healing? I have a very little, but I will be otherwise occupied unless absolutely needed." He looked to Myrshai questioningly.

"Think of that as your last option, but probably not your worst," she replied with a small shrug. When no one else spoke up, she sighed. "If they're beyond my practical abilities, I should be able to keep them alive, but it is likely they'll find the experience a bit . . . unnerving."

Melsymar raised an eyebrow, but didn't question her further. Now was not the time. "Alive is good. All right, let's get going then."

They filed out into the night, stopping briefly to fill their packs with multicolored orbs from Yerril's cart and gather what shovels and digging implements could be found. Kuu took up the lead, guiding them through the storm, and Yerril brought up the rear, placing an orb every time they reached the point where the last one could only barely be seen.

Ahead of Melsymar, Myrshai seemed distracted, waving

dismissively, as if she were having a conversation with someone. He itched to bring up his augmented sight and see what the conversation was about, but he didn't dare use more magic than he had to. Besides, eavesdropping was rude. Instead, he fell into step beside her, giving her a questioning look. Her skin had once again taken on that deathly pallor, and she seemed too engrossed in whatever unseen conversation she was having to notice his presence.

He cleared his throat. "Trouble?"

She started. "Hm? I'm sorry, what?"

"Trouble? You seem distracted."

"No. Nothing. I'm sorry. Was there some way I could help?"

He shook his head. "Oh, no. I just thought perhaps your friends were telling you how horrible an idea this was, or something along those lines."

She hesitated, looking down at him warily.

"I saw them earlier when you came in." Melsymar smiled up at her reassuringly. "Well, Kittle did first, and I shared her sight for a time. It's all right."

"Ah." She chuckled. "No. No trouble. I was just trying to convince Sir Ambrose that we were not going to go attack the avalanche single handedly." She shot an amused glance at the seemingly empty space beside her.

Melsymar laughed. "Ah. I see." They walked in companionable silence for a while before he ventured, "That pallor, if you'll indulge my curiosity, what spell is it? I presume it helps you weather the cold?"

"Well, I'm certainly not feeling the temperature anymore, no." She was quiet for a moment, obviously struggling to find just the right words. "The spell is . . . Well, it's . . . It is temporarily relieving the inconveniences of living flesh, so to speak." She sighed. "You'll have to forgive me. I wasn't trained in any of the formal colleges, so I don't always have the correct terms."

His eyebrows raised. "So essentially it's a living death? But you can dismiss it at will?"

"Mhm. Close enough."

"Truly? How fascinating. Does your heart still beat?"

She held out a wrist. Melsymar took it and placed his fingers on the pulse point. It was icy cold and entirely still, no hint of a heartbeat. He blinked in surprise.

"*How fascinating!* So essentially you're putting yourself in a sort of stasis so that you do not have to deal with the body's response to hypothermia?"

"Mhm. Exactly."

"But that leaves you more prone to things like frostbite, hence your fingers earlier."

"Yes." She reached up and touched one of the necklaces at her throat. "That's what this is for." Myrshai studied him for a moment, a hint of that wariness still behind her eyes. "Do you find it unsettling?"

He chuckled. "Perhaps a little, if I am to be honest, but it's also brilliant. What a novel use for necromancy!"

"Well, that's a dirty word." She smirked. "To most people, at least."

"Ah." He waved her off. "Magic is a tool. Like so much else, it is the application that matters. To disregard an entire school of magic and its legitimate uses, simply because someone can do ill with it, or because it is '*creepy*', is foolhardy at best."

Myrshai smiled, and this time it made it all the way to her eyes.

"May I ask you though," he continued, "why use such a complicated spell when an aura of warmth or the like would suffice?"

"Simple. I can't." Her smile took on a hint of bitterness. "I am what other mages like to derisively call, a natural talent."

"Ah! Let them choke on their derision." He snorted. "To be so connected to the aether that a type of magic just comes naturally to you like that, that is a rare and wonderful thing. It is *not* inferior to formal magic. Hmph! Natural talents have been some of the most powerful magicals there have ever been."

"Maybe so, but it's also extremely limiting." She shrugged and looked at him sidelong, a hint of a smirk playing on her lips. "Thank you, though. I almost think I could like you."

A sharp whistle from the head of their line interrupted their conversation. The group came to a halt and Kuu gathered them up. "The caravan is right up ahead. Tread carefully through here and stay close. No climbing. Stay on the road. If you hear a cracking sound or something that sounds like a drum, alert everyone and start moving as quickly as possible back along the road. Understood?"

There were nods and murmurs of assent from all around.

"Good." Kuu reached into their pack and pulled out one of the orbs, activating it with a sharp crack before holding it aloft. This one shone brightly golden, like a tiny sun. "Shall we then?" Without waiting for further response, they led the group down the road, light held high.

As they got closer to the caravan, snippets of conversation rode the howling wind toward them. The words were unintelligible at first, eerie whoops and fragments of whispers that would have chilled the blood if it hadn't been so cold already—and if they hadn't been listening for those very sounds. Eventually, the fragmentary sounds coalesced into a man's shout.

"Ravar! I see a light! I told you I heard a whistle! Hello! Over here! We need help!"

A rougher voice responded. "Are ye daft, boy? Who knows

what could be out here. Don't go callin' the attentions of evil spirits!"

"Hail the caravan!" Melsymar called out. "We're here to help, and we're neither evil, nor spirits!" With a glance at Myrshai—and then beside her, to where her spirit friends would presumably be—he murmured, "Not most of us, anyway."

Cheers broke out as the news passed along the caravan, and when they finally reached it, they were met with a large group of exhausted but hopeful caravaners and merchants.

The owner of the gruff voice, a stout older man with a huge, bushy, black beard that was made nearly white by a thick crusting of snow and ice, caught up the first person he saw into a big bear hug—which would have been Kuu had they not deftly hopped aside. "I just knew someone would come for us. Didn't I tell ye, Beryn?" He looked back at a young man, who rolled his eyes in response.

Beryn hopped down from where he'd been keeping watch atop one of the wagons. "We are so glad to see you, friends. I know this probably looks pretty stupid, trying to move in the storm like this." He dug a toe into the snow. "I promise you though, it's not. It's just, we heard rumbling on the mountain where we camped, and decided to risk moving early. The going was, well . . . harder than we expected." He gestured back toward the wagons wallowed deep into the snow, and the exhausted-looking oxen and horses that had been pulling them.

Kuu had been right to be worried. A steep slope angled up the mountainside on one side of the road. A few yards off of the other side, it ended in a sheer cliff, high enough that the tree-tops below just barely peeked up over the edge. If there was an avalanche here, it would sweep them right off the cliff, and there was nowhere to run.

"We'll get ya dug out, lad. Don't worry," Ivar reassured him.

He waved for the group of diggers to follow as he headed toward the wagons. "All right folks. Let's get to it."

Myrshai approached Beryn, patiently ignoring the wary look he gave her as he took her in from head to toe. "Are there any injured, and do you have a healer?"

"One broken arm from a tipped wagon, a few strained backs and shoulders, but nothing serious. Thank the gods." Beryn hooked a thumb over his shoulder. "Second wagon back. His name is Errol. We don't have a healer, but someone did know how to splint it."

"Thank you." She nodded and headed off toward the wagon, muttering under her breath.

When she was safely out of earshot, Revar grumbled, "Strange one, that one."

"Perhaps," replied Melsymar. "But she is capable and trustworthy. Don't you worry about her."

He headed over to the first wagon and set to work laying the enchantments while the dwarves led the digging team around him. It took more oomph to allow a wagon to glide atop the snow than it took to enchant shoes to walk upon it, and he found himself beginning to sweat as the aether coursed through him. Once the first enchantment was laid, setting its wheels thrumming with blue-white magic, the dwarves swung a large block and pulley up over an overhanging branch and gave a great heave-ho while the caravaners drove their weary team forward.

With a creaking of ropes, and the crunch of icy snow, the first wagon was free! Cheers went up and people clapped each other on the back, hope rekindled. Melsymar found himself grinning like an idiot. The exhilaration of working with others under this sort of pressure was something he had completely forgotten in his fifty years at The Tinker's Tea, and if he were to be honest, he'd kind of missed it.

They headed to the next wagon and found Myrshai standing beside it, speaking quietly with the two spirits he'd seen earlier, only this time, they seemed quite solid. The gentleman held the reins of a large, dappled grey horse, wearing tack befitting a cavalier. The older woman was digging in Myrshai's satchel as she muttered to herself.

Myrshai gave Melsymar a wary smile. "Melsymar, allow me to introduce my friends. This is Tilliana Blackwood, herbalist and healer, and this is Sir Ambrose Montroy, cavalier, personal guardian, and pain in my rear."

Sir Ambrose bowed with a "harumph" that was more amused than irritated. "A pleasure to meet you, sir."

"The pleasure is mine!" Melsymar bowed in return, burningly curious how she had managed to manifest the spirits so solidly. Sadly, there was no time to indulge that curiosity.

"Tilly is going to tend to the injured, and Ambrose is going to help with the pulling and digging. I was thinking, these animals are so tired. I'm not sure all of them will be capable of pulling the wagons all the way back." She dropped her voice for Melsymar's ears only and turned from the group. "I could find some spirits, mountain goats, elk, maybe other beasts of burden, and task them with aiding the pulling. They won't be visible unless someone is particularly sensitive. The horses may spook, but the oxen should be fine. Would you like me to try?"

"That is a wonderful idea. Absolutely. By all means, do what you do best." He patted her icy arm and added with a chuckle, "Within reason, of course."

"Of course." She smirked.

For the next hour they worked their way down the line, Myrshai summoning the spirits of creatures to aid them, Melsymar enchanting the wagons, and the rest of the group digging, hauling, and pushing. Sir Ambrose led the party in a number of jaunty working songs as they toiled, his voice a beautiful, rich baritone, and the whole atmosphere lightened.

About halfway down the line, Melsymar was almost certain he heard a crack from off in the distance. No one else seemed to hear anything, but it was enough to make the hairs on the back of his neck stand on end. Before he could say anything, there came another crack, and then a thundering boom in quick succession, and Kuu cried out, "Avalanche!"

There was no time to move before the torrent of snow came rushing toward them. Reflexively, Melsymar reached out and pulled at all the aether his mind could grasp. The energy surging through him was almost more than he could handle. It was a burning frisson down every nerve, and a building pressure in his head so strong he began to see sparks in his vision. He was made for meticulous detail work, for handling large amounts of aether through the insulation of careful inscriptions and incantations. It had been many, many years since he'd wrestled magic into a spell in response to an emergency, and he deeply hoped he could still handle it.

He called to mind a shield spell, and pushed the aether outward, forming it into a domed wall of force that started at the slope above them and arced down to the cliff on the other side of the pass. He pushed it forward toward the head of the caravan, but there was no way he was going to manage to cover both ends in time.

"Myrshai!" He gasped, jerking his head toward the back of the caravan.

"Yes! I'm working on it!" She stood back to back with him, eyes glinting with that silvery-blue light. From the scabbard at her hip, she pulled the ivory-handled knife and drew it across the back of her arm. Blood flashed, bright crimson in the trampled snow. As the drops fell, she cried out an incantation, but

Melsymar was too busy, the river of snow too loud, to make out the words.

And then the snow hit, battering his shield with staggering force. Sparks of aether flew everywhere it impacted, bright even in the mid-morning light. From Myrshai's side came the sudden wild trumpeting of elk, a screaming cry that would have chilled his blood if it hadn't been on fire with aether. He glanced over to see the air above them filled with the ghostly figures of wild creatures. Elk and deer, bear, scores of raccoons and squirrels, birds, more animals than he could name, raced through the air above them, glowing with the same silvery-blue light that reflected from Myrshai's eyes. They crashed into the snow, driving it away in waves, then circled back, seemingly unharmed, to do it again.

Back to back, he and the necromancer stood, panting and straining to hold the line. Through the massive flow of aether around them, it became hard to tell where he ended and Myrshai began. At once Melsymar felt the heat of the aether he wielded, wild, rushing, and electric, and the searingly cold, yet strangely languid, almost peaceful, pulses of aether she so expertly directed. One of them started to tremble, or maybe it was both of them; he couldn't tell. His vision swam, and fine snow began to blow in erratic bursts against his face, escaping through or around his shield. He wasn't going to be able to hold it for much longer . . .

And then, as suddenly as it had begun, the torrent of snow ended, and all went silent.

Both mages fell to their knees in the snow, gasping and spent. When Melsymar finally gathered his scrambled wits and looked up, he found the entire group gathered around them, gawking in awed silence. Sir Ambrose and Tilly knelt to either side of Myrshai, the cavalier carefully holding her upright, the old healer patting her arm soothingly.

"Is everyone all right?" he wheezed.

When no one else immediately spoke up, Kuu echoed the question. "All accounted for over here. Is everyone else all right?"

A murmur passed through the crowd, then a gruff voice came from the other end of the caravan. "All accounted for!" A cheer went up, a little wild around the edges, and everyone hugged their neighbor or clapped them on the back, laughing in grateful disbelief that they actually made it through.

Sir Ambrose helped Myrshai to her feet and offered Melsymar a hand up as well. He accepted it gratefully. Then the group descended upon them, offering Melsymar, Kuu, and Myrshai their gratitude. When Kuu and Myrshai began to look as if the press of people was becoming more terrifying than the avalanche had been, Melsymar raised a hand to quiet the crowd.

"Well! That was . . . something, wasn't it? I devoutly hope none of us ever have to experience *that* again. Come! Let's get these last few wagons freed and start back. Hot tea and warm rooms await."

The next hour was spent freeing the last of the wagons and moving their contents to the ones that had been enchanted, so that they would be easier to pull. Myrshai and Melsymar were relegated to one of the carts to rest while the remainder of the work was done, and honestly, neither one of them truly objected.

It was early afternoon by the time they returned to the tea shop, and the snow had finally begun to slow. To Melsymar's satisfaction, his enchantments still held. The Tinker's Tea shone like a beacon, even in the grey afternoon light.

Once the animals were unhitched and the helpful spirits set

free, there was laughter and celebration as they made their way up the ramp and into the tearoom. When they opened the door, they were met with a raucous cheer.

"To Melsymar! Our light in the darkness! Happy retirement!"

Melsymar stood frozen in the doorway, blinking in stunned surprise. While the rescue party had been away, those who had stayed behind had decorated the whole tea shop. Evergreen boughs festooned the walls, decorated with strings of brightly colored beads and glittering baubles. Colorful candles were set on every table, ready to be lit at last light. The main counter practically groaned under the weight of all sorts of delightful food, from roasted goose and platters of roasted and herbed vegetables, to pies and cakes, and glittering candied fruits. The smells of spiced cider and mulled wine wafted from simmering pots on the stove.

And sitting in the middle of it all, chest puffed out proudly, eyes half-squinted in smug contentment, sat Kittle. "Surprise," she purred.

"I—" Melsymar swallowed hard, the room blurring through happy tears. "Oh! My friends, you didn't need to go to so much trouble for me. Oh my. Thank you so very much. It is too much."

"It is not nearly enough," came a quiet voice from beside the fire. The young man Kuu had rescued the day before was sitting in one of the armchairs, wrapped in a blanket. He looked tired, but so much better. "It's the least we could do. Thank *you* for being here for us."

Melsymar sniffled and dipped his head in acccptance of the gratitude, moved beyond words. He drew a handkerchief, embroidered with teacups and cogs, from his pocket and dabbed at his eyes.

"The food is getting cold while you all argue over who to

thank," Grainne grumbled from atop a stool behind the counter. "Come and eat."

He laughed. "Yes, of course. Let's."

In a whirlwind of merriment, everyone descended upon the tables of food, laughing and talking over one another. Everyone insisted the group from the caravan and their rescuers went first, of course, and ushered them to the head of the line.

At the peak of the chaos, Melsymar sent his thoughts to Kittle, though even doing that usually effortless bit of magic made his head throb. *"Was this your doing?"*

"Oh, you do know how much I enjoy basking in due credit, but this one I have to share." She made her way over to him and rubbed up against his hip before extending a wing toward the young man by the fire. *"He insisted he was going to do something to show you his thanks. When that couple with the kid came out for breakfast, they agreed. So, I organized. Grainne insisted on a feast— so the food wouldn't go bad if we get stuck here, of course."*

"Of course." Melsymar reached out and scratched her ears. *"Thank you, my friend."*

Kittle simply rumbled a deep purr in response, looking terribly pleased with herself.

Sir Ambrose's clear baritone sounded from somewhere on the edges of the crowd, singing out a festive Winter's Tide carol. He had, at some point, procured himself a lute and was playing it beautifully. Others joined him in song, a few even pulling out their own instruments to play along. People danced and made merry between plates of food and mugs of good drink.

It wasn't just a celebration of his retirement or a thanks for being there in the storm. It was a celebration of life and light. A celebration of bonds forged in adversity. The joy of people who came through hardship, who weathered a storm and great peril and came out the other side, grateful to be alive. It was beautiful, and Melsymar's heart was full.

Someone tapped their fork against the side of their mug, calling for attention. "Ho! Ho! Can I get yer attention?" Ravar hopped up on one of the chairs and raised his mug. "To Melsymar, and to all of ye who came out today. If it weren't for yer bravery, we wouldn't be here right now!"

"Hear, hear!" came the answering cheer. "To Melsymar and company!"

When Ravar sat, Lorn stood up, his daughter on his shoulders. "I wanna say somefin', too!" Molly shouted. It took a moment for the cheers to die down, so she tried again. "Helloo! I'm sayin' somethin!" When the chatter died down and she realized all eyes were on her, she shrank a little, smiling shyly. "I um. I wanna say fank you, Mel-sa-mar," she pronounced each syllable carefully, obviously having practiced. "Fank you for my mommy meeting my daddy."

Lorn beamed proudly and explained, "We met at the Skyglow Festival five years ago, right here. We married the following festival."

"*That's* where I remembered you from! Oh, that is wonderful! I remember that night clearly now. You were both so nervous to talk to each other, and the shop was entirely full that night—"

"So you asked us if we could share a table." Tania grinned.

"So I did, so I did. Well, I am incredibly happy things worked out. Belated congratulations!"

More and more people stood up, toasting Melsymar for times he and The Tinker's Tea had been there for them. Yerril shared stories of their adventures that were maybe not the best for public consumption, but stirred that pull in Melsymar to get out there again. He had missed those days, and after the past two days, he had to admit, he was starting to miss them even more. And then they were toasting Myrshai, Kuu, and Duncan and Ivar, and then their friends and loved ones, round and round.

Somewhere during the merriment, night had fallen, and the skies had finally cleared. Hours ago, they had lit the candles, bathing the room in their warm glow. Melsymar was well into his second mug of mulled wine when the colors in the room seemed to shift, first toward green, then purple, then back to green again, then back to gold. He blinked, wondering precisely what mulling spices Grainne used. And then a yowl came from the window. Kittle was on the sill, tail thrashing excitedly.

Melsymar went to her side and peered out. The sky was luminous with dancing lights of all colors, streaming in great ribbons overhead. He let out a whoop. "Bundle up, everyone! It seems we'll be able to enjoy the lights after all!"

And so they brought the merriment outside, bundling up in their coats and wrapping up close in extra blankets with friends and loved ones. Impervious to the cold, Sir Ambrose and Tilly continued to play music for the group, this time a little softer, mirroring the awe-inspiring dance of the lights.

Caught up as Melsymar was in the show, he almost didn't notice the quiet presence behind him. He glanced up and saw Myrshai standing there, watching the sky with an enigmatic smile.

"Well, that's something," she murmured.

"It is, isn't it? One of my favorite sights in all the queendom."

They stood in companionable silence for a while until she spoke up again. "Congratulations on your retirement."

"Why, thank you."

"Where are you headed from here?"

"Welkinton, most likely. From there?" He shrugged. "I'm not yet certain, but the road is calling to me. And yourself?"

"Oh, possibly to Welkinton and then south before it snows.

Good money to be made this time of year for one with my skill set."

"Oh?" He turned to look up at her, curious.

She smirked, eyes sparkling. "Oh yes. There's always some rich idiot or another having nightmares from a guilty conscience. Of course, more often than not it's a bit of undigested beef or some bad cheese, but they pay me to deal with it anyway. Normally I just tell them to do some charity work, and the ghosts will leave them alone."

He laughed. "Sounds interesting."

She shrugged. "It pays. Anyway, I will be leaving out tomorrow morning before everyone gets up. I'm not fond of overly long goodbyes, so don't go getting sappy on me."

"I wouldn't dream of it. But I do hope our paths cross again. It was good to have you at my back tonight. Made me nostalgic for my adventuring days."

"Well, you're not dead yet." She grinned and glanced over her shoulder at Sir Ambrose. "Though I suppose even if you were . . ."

He snorted. "Perish the thought." Melsymar offered her a hand, which she clasped firmly. "Good luck with your misers."

"Enjoy your time off."

IT WAS NEARLY DAWN BEFORE EVERYONE FOUND THEIR BEDS, AND Melsymar made his way up to his room at the top of the shop. His heart was lighter than it had been in months. Instead of nervousness at his impending retirement and all the little details that still needed to be figured out, he felt peace. He felt hopeful.

Over the course of the last fifty years, the shop had always found its way to exactly where it needed to be. If he hadn't found his successor yet, it was simply because the time was not yet right for them. But the time was right for him. He yawned and stretched, picking up one of his favorite books of magic theory, and settling into bed. The wine still warmed his limbs, and his belly was comfortably full. Perfection.

Whatever came, he was ready for the next adventure.

<small>THANK YOU FOR READING, AND THE HAPPIEST OF WINTER'S TIDES TO</small> you and yours!

Rest assured, Melsymar, Kittle, Myrshai, and friends will be returning soon. We have two series currently in the works for you. One takes us on an adventure all across Cozy Vales and introduces us to the new proprietors of The Tinker's Tea. The other follows a younger Myrshai, newly out on her own, and starts with the story of how she met a certain dashing knight and kindly herbalist.

We cannot wait to share these stories, and to further explore Cozy Vales with you! Come follow us on Facebook to see what we're up to, say hello, and enjoy a cup of tea with the rest of the cozy community.

https://www.facebook.com/DAStuartFantasy

SOUR AT THE SALT AND PICKLE
CASSANDRA STIRLING

"A re we there yet?" a grumpy voice inquired from within the miniature, wooden house on the seat beside me. "Nearly, Frangi."

A jolt rattled my bones as the carriage hit a rut in the road, and I caught the open book on my lap before it fell. I shifted my weight to the other hip, but the odds of finding a soft spot after three days of sitting on the same bench were nil.

A shock of pink and white hair followed by a celery green nose poked out of the house's tiny, front door. "Good. Too much time playing with my shinies will lessen their luster. What good are they then?"

The dwarf sitting across from me tucked his wrists closer to his body. I cleared my throat, and Frangi closed the door with a disgruntled click.

"I apologize again, Mr. Brownblaze, for the incident this morning. Frangipani's treasure leans toward simple wooden items and stone buttons. I have no idea why she wanted your gemstone cufflinks." After the ensuing scuffle that rocked the carriage hard enough to alert Sully, the coachman, and his threat to leave us stranded on the side of the road miles from anywhere, I convinced Frangi to remain in her home for the trip's duration.

"They're the most interesting things we've seen so far," Frangi said.

I fiddled with the earrings at the pointed tip of my ear and pushed the curtain aside to look out. Dilapidated shacks dotted the roadside, their wooden structures breaking the unending waves of grain in our view since we crossed into Soursalt Vale this morning. "I'm bored, too, but once we reach the inn, you'll have plenty to look at."

"If I may make a suggestion, Ms. Nevyn? You'll be less bored if you challenge your mind. A book filled with history or philosophy will take you further than reading a popular mystery." The dwarf gestured to the tome laying open on my lap.

"I like Ms. Vaughn's mysteries. They give me time to daydream. Besides, I've read plenty of challenging books," I said.

"I apologize for assuming otherwise." The gentleness in his voice took the edge off my blossoming anger. And then he had to ruin it. "Daydreaming is all well and good, but cultivating your mind is how you stay sharp well into your elder years."

"Thank you for your advice. I'll keep that in mind." If my magic ran that way, frost would've formed on the inside of the carriage windows.

"Very well." He bent his head back to the text before him.

I followed suit, but after reading the same sentence three times, I closed the book with a sigh and stowed it in my satchel. My fingers brushed Lindie's letter, giving me formal permission to occupy her cottage, and I fought the urge to squirm. One more night of riding until the quiet of Pokeberry, with its lush gardens and quaint cottages, and it would be a welcome respite from the Capital City's chaos.

After what felt like an eternity, the carriage halted in front

of a rambling building with a sign proclaiming it as The Salt &
Pickle Inn. I scrambled to get out of the coach's cramped
confines with Frangi's house dangling from my wrist. A breeze
warmer than what usually funneled down the city's streets at
this time of year stirred my hair. A twinge of nostalgia for frosty
cheeks and hot cocoa from a Taster's Guild's chocolate maker
ripped my breath away.

I could've waited to leave town after the remaining week of
Winter's Tide and the penultimate Lantern Night festivities,
but I knew myself too well. Staying for the holiday would've
turned into staying for a friend's birthday, a book reading, or
any event until I remained. Forever stuck there like a dried
flower, forgotten in a dusty tome on a shelf. Uninspired and
unable to create unique designs.

Pushing down the fear threatening to overtake me, I studied
my resting spot and its decaying leaves mingling with the
road's dust. The inn leaned to the left, as if it sought safety
under an elderly oak's towering but bare branches. Lit torches
guarded an archway festooned with holly and ivy, and wreaths
hung drunkenly from each. Their red ribbons seemed tattered,
as if victims of the local cat.

It wasn't home, but it would do for one night.

A porter barreled out of the doorway, and his white, billowy
shirt escaped his vest. He slid to a stop with bangs darker than
tree bark flopping to cover his eyes. "You made it."

The warmth in his voice surprised me. "Do you often lose
coaches on the road to Croesfford?"

"Only lost the one, but that was Farmer Murphy's fault. And
the other incident with Crosby. Never during Winter's Tide,
though, because there aren't that many carriages running."

Cursing my magic's choice to show itself, I tamped down on
my nerves. "That's not exactly comforting."

He brushed the hair out of his face, and a flush crept up the green-tinged cheeks, clashing with the lighter tusks jutting from both sides of his mouth. "Sorry, miss. The roads are quite safe if you're heading north."

Relief rushed through me. "Good."

"Welcome to the—watch out!"

The porter lunged and pushed me out of the way, his knees buckling as he caught the trunk aimed at my head. "Careful, Sully. You almost crushed her."

"It's her own fault. Why she needs all that is beyond me," Sully said from atop the coach.

"*She* is standing right here, and you almost killed me," I said over my pounding heart.

"Too bad it was almost," Sully muttered under his breath.

"I heard that."

Sully tugged on his ear; his bushy eyebrows lowered. After a moment, he scowled. "I meant you to."

I glared at him and then swept inside before he launched another piece of luggage at me. Or my magic caused yet more unwanted and uncomfortable confessions.

The entryway opened onto the main floor and weathered stairs led to the rooms above. Long benches and tables ran down the middle of the dining area, ending at a blackened stone fireplace. A scattering of cozier tables with chairs covered in faded green cloth nestled under the windows. The seats were already half-full.

"Popular place," I said.

"It's the best inn within forty miles. Wait until you try the food," the porter said.

It was the *only* inn within forty miles. Besides, the last innkeeper claimed his bread was remarkable. And it was.

165

For breaking teeth.

An orc woman stepped out from behind the bar, her pitch-black hair coiled in braids near her ears, and a tarnished ring hung from her right tusk. "Welcome to The Salt & Pickle, the original inn that started them all. May your lantern last through the night. I'm Matilda Motts and I run this place. This here is my nephew, Chester," she jerked her chin to the porter, "who can help you with anything you may need."

"Thank you. I'm Kithaela Nevyn. May your light shine bright," I said with a dip of my head to both.

"Are you staying the one night, or are you planning on enjoying the festivities over the next few days? We sing the songs and pass the mulled wine at midnight, and tomorrow is the feats of strength. It's sure to be entertaining."

"Just the one night. We're back on the coach in the morning."

Mrs. Motts nodded. "She's in The Gherkin, Chester."

"Good, good. I'll meet you there, miss," Chester said as he climbed the stairs.

"That'll be one hundred coppers and includes breakfast, served at seven sharp, but not dinner," Matilda said.

"Can I come out now?" Frangi asked.

"Yes," I replied.

"About time." Frangi climbed up my skirt, to her favorite perch on my shoulder.

"Is it extra for my companion?" I asked.

Mrs. Motts frowned in scrutiny. "I didn't think pixies strayed from their clans."

"Not clans, pleasures. We don't, and I haven't. My pleasure is here, with Kit," Frangi said, punching me in the neck as she stretched. "We're on an adventure."

Laughter tugged at the innkeeper's lips, but she pointed a

meaty finger at Frangi. "No tricks with the food or ale, or you're out. Got it?"

That left too much wiggle room for me. "Also, no tricks to the cat or people who are larger than you."

"That leaves no one!"

"Those are the rules, Frangi, or you'll stay in the room all night." I craned my head to give her a stern look—tricky to do since Frangi stood six inches tall and liked to tuck herself behind my ear.

"No extra if you pay for her food, but any damage she causes comes out of your pocket."

Tallying the coins I'd spent thus far on Frangi's antics, I gulped. "That's generous of you. Thank you, Mrs. Motts."

"Matilda. Mrs. Motts was my mother-in-law." She jerked her chin to the stairs. "Off you go then."

Frangi kept up a stream of patter as I climbed the stairs, and her hair tickled my neck. One statement gave me pause. "No swinging from the chandelier," I said.

"That wasn't in the rules."

"It is now."

"You ruin all my fun."

Chester stood before a cracked open door, and a voice inside spoke low enough that I couldn't make out the words. He turned at our arrival, and the door banged shut. He blinked, and the confusion on his face smeared away to politeness.

What was that all about?

"Your room is here, miss. I placed your trunk at the end of the bed and stoked the fire." Chester waved at the nearby door and absentmindedly rubbed his shoulder.

Quashing the curiosity streaming through me, I strolled toward him. "I'm sorry my bag was so heavy."

"It's alright, miss. It's not that bad. I've got a little arthritis in the joint is all, which is rare for one as young as me. But it flares up like clockwork in winter. It doesn't matter how much I move it, or how much I carry. The ache settles deep in my bones." He slapped his palm over his mouth, his tusks peeking out over his fingers. "I apologize again, miss. First rambling about the roads, and now this. I have no idea why I told you all that."

"It's my fault. I can't control my elven magic for truth saying because my human half gets in the way. It causes unending embarrassment. No harm, no dark, right?" At his nod, the knot in my neck eased. "Have you tried the remedy Fen prescribed for that issue? Nerium Oil?"

"Fen?"

"The queen's healer?"

"Oh, *that* Fen."

Frangi laughed. "You've never heard of him. That's alright. I've never heard of, where are we again?"

"Croessfford," I murmured.

"Chester!" Matilda's bellow rushed up the stairs and almost knocked me over.

"Thanks, miss. I'll give that remedy a go." He handed me the key to my room, bowed, and thundered back down the stairs.

Frangi climbed down before the door clicked shut behind me and streaked under the bed. She bounced off the amber-washed walls as if she had wings like a sprite and poked her head into corners and crevices. The first inn we stayed at contained a treasure trove of lost items to add to her collection, but it also required a bath afterward.

And some screaming from me when a spider almost larger than Frangi's head crawled down her leg.

I shuddered and examined the corners of the room, but no webs decorated their shadowed depths. Cinders crackled in the fireplace, and the kettle hanging over it brought a smile to my face. A cup of tea would smooth away my jitters.

Frangi flopped on the bed. "Nothing good to find."

"There's still the common area downstairs. You'll find plenty there."

"Where are we going again?"

"You know where. You're choosing not to remember."

"Am not. Will it be as fun as Capital City?"

I grimaced. My hasty decision to move left little time for discussion. "Probably not. It'll be more like Wallesly, where we first met."

"Why didn't we go there then?"

"I'm not moving back with my parents, for one. Two, they aren't there right now. Dad is joining Mom in Turtle Bay for the holidays, so going home makes little sense. Besides, aren't you excited for a new place to explore?"

"What will it have?"

"A new home, and maybe new people to meet." I nibbled my lower lip. It wouldn't be fair to lie. "And plenty of quiet for me to work."

"Quiet is boring."

"For you, yes, but not for me. I haven't been able to think in the city, let alone create anything new. The colors jumbled together, and the sounds clashed like a cat trapped in a barrel."

"I liked living there. Tildare was going to show me how to scale the queen's house without getting caught." She plucked the maroon threads holding the quilt's patches together.

"Frangi, I'm sorry. I never asked if you wanted to come along. You had plans too, and I just didn't think. You could've stayed."

"Without you?"

"Yes. There was nothing shiny for me to find but plenty for you."

"Don't you want me with you?" Her lower lip quivered.

"I'll always want you with me. Always and forever." I made

a circle around my heart and then held out my pinky. "We're a team. I should've given you the choice, and I didn't."

She gripped my finger with all ten of hers. "It's alright. You make fun choices."

I wasn't so sure about that. "You can have all the fun you want in Moonseed Vale."

"You promise?" A wide grin showed the pointy ends of her front teeth.

"Yes."

Frangi whooped.

I hid my grimace by crouching down to unlock my trunk. I'd worry about that promise after I laid other concerns to rest. With any luck, it wouldn't be until spring before I'd need to address it.

The door creaked open behind me, and I whirled. Frangi climbed up the footboard and brandished her needle sword. A woman with wisps of blonde hair framing her face squeaked to a stop, and water sloshed out of the basin in her hands, much like the color from her face.

"I thought you were downstairs," she stammered.

"Did you?" My tone was drier than the dust on my shoes.

"I knocked."

"A pixie fart is louder than your knock," Frangi said.

"I apologize, miss. I'm Danys, and I've come with fresh water for your basin." She curtsied, but the clenched muscle in her cheek told a different tale.

I nodded at the full bowl on the table. "What's wrong with the water we already have?"

"It's from this morning, and the dust from the road can settle in it. You can't keep it out, no matter how tight the windows are," Danys said, her tone daring me to call her bluff.

"Very well."

She set the new basin down and removed the old one to the

hallway before returning to mop up the spillage. Frangi leaned on her sword, watching the woman's every move.

"Where is it you hail from, miss?" Danys asked, with a flick of a glance at my satchel.

"Capital City."

"Really? What's it like to live there?"

I sat on my trunk and crossed my legs. "Hectic. Noisy. You can find anything you want or nothing at all. Ne'er-do-wells do both now and again, although the queen's guards handle them."

Danys busied herself with rearranging the table. "It sounds wonderful. I can't wait to see it in person."

"When are you planning to go?"

"I'd love to be there for Lantern Night. I've heard tales of flickering candlelight in windows, and all the tarts and pies. I have grand plans to take it all in. There's much more to the queendom than this meager village, and I want to experience it. Besides, it will solve—oh, listen to me prattle on." She slapped her cloth on the table to clear invisible dust. "Do you need anything else, miss?"

"No, thank you."

"Best come downstairs quick then. The tables are filling up for tonight's Winter's Tide celebration, and you won't want to wait."

"I will once I've washed up. Thank you for your time." I followed her to the door, the click of the lock not as satisfying as I'd hoped.

"She's looking for something to take," Frangi said.

"Indeed."

AN HOUR LATER, I TUGGED ON MY TRUNK'S LOCK TO ENSURE IT HELD. Glancing in the mirror over the washbasin, I tucked a few stray brown and blonde curls back into the bun at the nape of my neck, reassigning hairpins to keep the heavy mass tidy. A hairpin wrestled free and slipped down my blouse. After fishing it out, I straightened my corset and pinched my cheeks to give them a bit more color.

"Ready for some food and exploration?"

"Yes!" Frangi swished by me, and I stepped into the hall and locked the door. I paused midway down the stairs to survey the common room below. It had more bodies jammed into it than when I'd arrived, and the clamor had grown to rival an early Friday night in the city.

Danys strode toward a woman in a faded cotton dress, the woman's drab skirt coated in dust. "What are you doing here?"

"You know why," the woman replied, the wrinkles scoring either side of her nose darkening as her nostrils flared in disgust. Danys grabbed the woman's arm and yanked her into a corner created by the stairs.

If I peeked over the railing, I could hear everything. After a quick glance around, I crushed the twinge of guilt that arose when I did so.

The woman leaned in until their noses almost kissed, her eyes flicking to the side as a man in a stained cotton shirt and breeches wandered past. "It's a holiday, isn't it?"

"Not for me. Later maybe." Danys's head shook enough to stir the air between them. After a moment, she scowled. "Who's tending the farm? The cabbages need harvesting."

"One day isn't going to hurt it. I'll deal with it tomorrow, along with all the rest of your mess." Bitterness darker than fireplace stones drenched her tone.

Danys jerked back. "You said you were alright with handling it."

A shout broke through the pocket of intensity surrounding the women, and they glanced at the bar.

"I need another beer," a man yelled, his fists thumping each word into the worn surface.

"You know he's not good for you, D," the woman said.

"I know, Briony."

She tapped her knuckles against Danys's heart. "Do what you have to do to be happy."

"No matter what?" Danys stalked away, her braid brushing each hip like a pendulum.

Briony watched her go, and then she sauntered to the bar to hoist herself on a stool. She bumped the waiting man's shoulder, who turned to her with a scowl as Matilda placed a pint before him.

A roar rattled the windows, and I jumped. An orc at a corner table leaned over the card-strewn surface at the man opposite him. Gleeful smirks lit the crowd's faces as they awaited an inevitable eruption.

Matilda wandered over to that side of the bar quicker than her easy stride conveyed. "Oy, Garlin. It's too early for that. Drink your beer."

Garlin bared his teeth at her. Matilda placed her hands on the bar and held his stare. With a sigh, Garlin sat back against his chair and crossed his arms.

My entertainment over, I descended the stairs and snagged an open table under a window. A cool breeze ruffled my hair, and I shut it, the hinges moving without a protesting squeak.

"Our winters are mild, but their tempers are not, so you'll want to open it soon enough once they get going," Danys said when she approached the table.

"You mean they haven't yet?"

"No."

"I'll keep that in mind."

"It's your last rites. What can I get you?" Danys asked as she shifted her weight, the steaming bowls atop the tray she held not spilling any of their precious cargo.

"I'll have that," I said, nodding to the stew, "and half a loaf of bread, a saucer, a cup of milk, and elderberry mead."

"Coming right up." She almost ran into the fastidious dwarf from the coach.

Mr. Brownblaze sat at the chair of the table next to mine and said, "Mrs. Mattherson, I'll take my usual as well, please."

After a wary glance for Frangi, I rummaged around my satchel and pulled out two sheets of paper and a pencil that I always carried with me. Nothing new came to mind for my latest book cover design, so I sketched the scene I'd just witnessed instead. I fumbled with capturing the banister with my depiction's angle veering too far to the right. I moved to correct it when the glimmer of an idea formed. My pencil hovered over the page, and tension tightened my chest.

"Excuse me, but may I join you? It is so hard to dine alone, especially when traveling," a soft voice asked.

My breath blew out of me in a gust, and I scowled up at the figure.

An orc hesitated at the table's edge. Ribbons of dark hair floated around her face with the rest pulled back into a braided design at her crown. The ruffles on her coral blouse fluttered as she clasped her hands at chest-level to create a cascade effect that rippled into her yellow skirts.

Decorum overrode my irritation, and I waved her to the chair opposite me. "Of course."

"Thank you. I'm Ms. Cletts," she said, extending her hand, palm down.

"Ms. Nevyn." Unsure how to shake something angled to be kissed, I gave her fingers a firm-yet-gentle squeeze.

"Please, don't let me interrupt you." She gestured to the drawing and sat with her back to the room.

Playing a game as old as time, I smiled with no warmth and tucked it away. "It's quite alright. I've finished capturing what I wanted to for now."

"What brings you to Croesfford?"

"A coach." When she didn't so much as twitch at my poor attempt to lighten the mood, I said, "I'm passing through on my way to Pokeberry Village. I leave tomorrow."

She clapped her hands, and a warm smile took the edge off her formality. "That's marvelous. I, too, journey to Pokeberry tomorrow."

My face strained to hold my smile in place. Why was I cursed with company I didn't want? The silence lengthened between us, and the background noise dimmed to a roar as I worked through a response. When Ms. Cletts's knuckles whitened, I knew I'd taken too long trying to be tactful.

"Excellent. You can fill me in and let me know where Lindie took a few liberties in describing the town," I said.

"Do you mean Lindie Marston?"

"Yes. I'm staying at her house while she takes over my room in the city."

Her cheeks lightened with pleasure. "Her cottage is down the road from mine. She's a good friend, and now her friend can be mine as well."

A disquieting pang twisted in my gut as the solitude I longed for slipped from my fingers before I'd even arrived in my new home. Maybe she'd forget it once I settled in. Frangi zipped across the long table, giggling as she dodged fists, tableware, and serving utensils.

Or maybe the quiet I sought was a myth I told myself to feel better about my lack of progress.

"That's good to hear. I was worried the village wouldn't be friendly," I said.

Ms. Cletts frowned. "Did Lindie give you that impression?"

"No. I grew up in a small town where everyone knew everyone else. It took Mr. Grady ten years to no longer be called the new person in town because someone else moved there."

"I see. Small villages can be like that, but I like to think we're different in Pokeberry. Why, four years ago, a woodworker joined the community, and he, well, he's a different fiddle altogether. I know had he tried, we would've welcomed him."

"I'm sure you would." My cheeks hurt from holding them in place. I'd forgotten what small-town life could be like. Every move scrutinized, every behavior either chastised or gossiped about.

"No, it's true. All you need to do is try, and you'll fit right in. And I can help. In the spirit of a new friendship, you may call me Vivane."

The thawing of her formal manners mirrored the tension easing between us. "You can call me Kithaela or Kit, which is what my friends call me."

A yawn interrupted whatever she planned to say next. She covered her mouth with a white handkerchief. "Please excuse me. The supply wagon I rode on had a stop on the way, requiring an earlier-than-normal start."

"Of course." The handkerchief's border of intricate daisies snagged my gaze. "That's lovely needlework. Did you design it yourself?"

Her words disappeared into the background as inspiration struck faster than a pixie changing topics. I whipped my drawing paper out, the pencil whisking along the page as I captured the idea before it ran away.

"Are you drawing my handkerchief's border?" Vivane asked.

I finished the rough sketch and glanced up to find her studying it. My hand covered it, and she straightened. Heat crept up my cheeks. "Sorry, it's still rough."

"Please, don't apologize. I've sacrificed many an initial design to the fire over the years."

A smile warmer than any I'd had in recent days curled my lips. "Thank you for understanding. It's hard to keep the muse alive, especially if someone sees it before it's ready. Or worse, they add a suggestion."

"I know what you mean. People have good intentions, but not well-thought-out ideas. Mrs. Jenkins once recommended I add a barn to a scroll stitch design with hearts, and it put me off the piece for months."

"Well, if you ever want to sell your work, then you'll fetch a pretty copper in the city. I know at least three people who would kill for your design and precise needlework once the word got out."

"I never thought someone would want to buy my little hobby. It's something I do to keep my hands busy." She ran her fingers over the threading. After a moment, she said, "No, I think not, but thank you for the compliment. Do you sew?"

I squelched the desire to press her further. Besides, I'd have plenty of time to explore the topic in the tranquility of Pokeberry. My breath whooshed out of me as the thought anchored itself into my bones.

I was an idiot.

I didn't want to live isolated from everyone. I wanted a fresh perspective and a new environment. Enthusiasm for a new friend surged through me, and I said, "Only on leather and specific types of cloth. I create book covers, which require working with leather and other materials. Speaking of books, Lindie mentioned a bookstore in town. Is it any good?"

"I should hope so. It's my family's business after all."

A flicker of dismay dimmed my excitement. Maybe I was cursed after all. Lindie had very little to say about the bookstore besides a scathing review of the owner. Why would she say that if she and Vivane were friends?

My need for business triumphed over my confusion, and I pressed on with the conversation. "Would you be open to displaying a few of my covers in the windows? The bookstores who've done so in the past had successful sales."

"I would, but we'll have to see if my Uncle Bixby agrees. He runs the shop for me and makes all the decisions concerning it. Apparently, I don't have the head for business." She wrinkled her nose, her gaze skittering away from mine. "We have an extensive selection of books, and I'm sure we can talk my uncle around."

Danys set my order down with a thump. "What can I get you, Ms. Cletts?"

"Stew and a small glass of mead, please, Danys."

"Coming right up."

Vivane snapped her napkin open to dab a drop of spilled milk before spreading it on her lap, every movement precise and dainty. At the next table over, Mr. Brownblaze mimicked her movements, but he tucked his napkin in the top of his vest and laid a familiar book on the table.

Hemmed in on all sides, I followed their lead, my movements stiff with disuse. If nothing else, at least Mom wouldn't be able to fault my table manners the next time I visited.

The bread crust shattered as I tore off a piece. I laid it in the saucer and poured the milk over it by using my knuckle to test the sogginess. Pleased with the texture, I dug out a vial of lavender honey from my purse to spread over the top.

I gathered my stew and paused with the spoon midway to the bowl, and then, my gaze locked with Vivane's. She said, "Please, eat, while it's hot."

"Thank you." The meat's flavor mingled with the salty broth and an unknown-to-me herb. The taste exploded on my tongue. I tucked in, eating with more enthusiasm than proper table manners required. Vivane shifted in her seat and turned to peer out the window.

"Is that food for me?" Frangi asked, sauntering to her saucer.

"It is," I said between slurps. "Vivane, this is my friend and companion, Frangipani."

Frangi sat cross-legged near the saucer and shoved a hunk of bread in her mouth. "It's Frangi. Who are you?"

"Don't talk with your mouth full. Ms. Cletts lives in Poke-berry and joins us in the carriage tomorrow," I said.

The clatter of a chair hitting the stone floor captured Frangi's attention. She hopped to her feet with crumbs spilling out of her lap. "Did you see that? The drunk one is going to get pounded flatter than a flower under your foot."

I glanced over to the corner, and Danys's words about tempers echoed in my head.

"You cheated, Igor," a thin, red-haired man declared.

Igor surged to his feet and swayed by catching the table to stay upright. "I did not, Avanoff. You're sore you lost."

With his face redder than hot coals, Avanoff shoved the table. A tankard of beer tipped over, splashing across the surface, and dripping to the floor.

"I wasn't done with that." Igor launched himself at Avanoff. They smashed into the fireplace, and Igor pinned Avanoff against the blackened stones. "I am not a cheat."

Avanoff pushed Igor away. "I saw you. You palmed a card and presented a queen."

Garlin slapped a card on the table. "You mean this queen?"

Both men glared at Avanoff, who blanched. "I swear I saw him lay it down."

"If I knew how to cheat, I wouldn't owe that mug a cent," Igor said.

"If you had any smarts at all, you wouldn't owe me anything," Garlin said.

Igor staggered toward him, a grimace crossing his face.

Danys stepped between them. "That's enough, boys. You'll spill your beer."

"He already did." Garlin roared with laughter.

"Aw, why'd she stop it? It was just getting good." Frangi veered to the edge of the table and crouched down. "Oh, look, a shiny!"

Before I could stop her, she scrambled off the table and disappeared. I gave Vivane an apologetic glance, but her gaze hadn't left the corner table. "Vivane, are you alright?"

She shook her head and smiled, the politeness in it sharp enough to cut. "Yes, fine."

I frowned. "Some people shouldn't drink."

"Especially that one."

"Do you know him?"

She set her napkin down and stood. "Excuse me for a moment. I must use the facilities."

A heavy sensation swirled within me, and it wasn't from the stew. Vivane painted a different picture with her actions than she shared with words. What harm would it do to confess to knowing him?

Across the room, Danys tugged up her corset, grabbed the tankard Matilda brought to the end of the bar, and danced around the orc, dipping out of sight behind him. She placed the beer in front of Igor, not spilling a drop.

"Sit down, have a drink, and stop betting money we can't afford to lose."

A chant rose as Igor swiped the drink and guzzled it. He slammed the cup on the table to a cheer and wiped his mouth on the back of his arm. A burp erupted, lasting longer than the fight, which he cut off with a frown. Laughter broke out as insults littered the air. Igor waved them off, one hand clutching his stomach and stumbled to the hall leading to the back of the inn.

Danys watched him go. When a patron at a nearby table touched her hand, she stirred to life. She cleared their table, and her abrupt movements clattered along to the noise of chinking silverware. When her hands were full, she disappeared into the kitchen and returned with a full tray, and of course, headed in my direction.

She placed Vivane's dinner on the table and scooped up my bowl. "Anything else?"

"We'll bring this to our room, if that's okay," I replied and pointed to the half-eaten sopping bread and honey mixture.

"Matilda will charge you if you don't return the saucer. She's a miserly old codger. She blamed me for the missing silver."

Not a muscle twitched on my face, although it was close. "Not a problem. I'll bring it down in the morning when I arrive for breakfast."

"Don't be late or you'll miss it. She's also stingy with her promises. Now why did I tell you that?" Danys asked as she swished away.

Vivane returned to the common area, her eyes focused on our table. She sat down, her posture stiffer than the beams holding up the ceiling. "The patrons in this place leave little to be desired, no matter how clean it is. While I've enjoyed our conversation, I think I might eat in my room."

"If you don't mind waiting a moment, I'd also like to visit the facilities, but I'd rather not take everything with me." I waved at Frangi's dinner.

"Of course," she replied with a prim smile.

The brisk air shocked me awake as I stepped into the dim moonlit courtyard at the back of the inn. Clouds crept over the twin moons, and the shadows stretched toward me. I could make out the privy in the far corner and I hastened toward it.

"I don't feel so good," said a muffled voice from within it.

I halted. "Excuse me, what did you say?"

"I don't." An odd gurgle and a thump followed, along with the last of the light, leaving me in murky darkness.

"Are you alright in there? Sir?"

Spikes of unease trickled down my spine. I inched forward, the distance between me and the privy seeming to have doubled as tension thickened the air around me. I gasped when my fingers brushed the wood, my heart jerking in my chest. I tapped my way down to the handle. "I'm opening the door now unless you tell me to stop. Please, tell me to stop."

Nothing but the wind replied.

Nerves twisted in my belly. I took a deep breath and yanked on the door. A heavy object smashed against my legs, and my backside hit the dirt. My breath shuddered in my chest, my lungs aching as I gasped out pent up air.

A creak shattered the still darkness and I scrambled to my knees. I crawled forward, my fingertips shying away when they touched warm skin.

"Sir?" The word skipped over my lips in time with my heartbeat.

The clouds cleared, the silvery moonlight slithering down to chase away the shadows.

And glisten in the whites of Igor's unblinking eyes.

Fear gripped me in its icy hands, and my stomach rebelled as a pungent odor wafted toward me. Sitting back on my heels, I covered my face and forced my breathing to slow. Once the fluttering panic subsided, I braced myself and lowered my hands.

Igor lay with his bottom half in the privy, his arms outstretched, and a strip of white fabric clutched in his hands. Vomit trickled down his cheek, soaked his shirt, and pooled around his shoulder. I leaned forward and hovered my palm over his mouth. When no warmth reached it, I surged to my feet and sought the safety of the inn.

Matilda stood near the end of the bar, and I rocked to a halt before her. "We have a situation."

"Did your pixie misbehave?" she asked.

"I wish it were that simple. Igor's dead."

"Where?"

I jerked my head and strode back outside.

Matilda nudged me out of the way and crouched down. She placed her ear on his chest and then sat back on her haunches. "Well, I'll be an ogre's aunt. He's definitely dead. Was this how you found him?"

"No. He fell on me."

The intensity of her gaze cut through my shock. "Did he now?"

"Yes. Watch out for the vomit near your left knee."

"I've stepped in more vomit than a healer. It doesn't bother me."

I licked my parched lips and regretted it as soon as I tasted the sourness lingering on the air. "Could someone have done this to him?"

"Maybe, maybe not. He had quite a bit to drink tonight, no more than normal. But I don't like the look of him."

"He's pale."

"Aye. Paler than when Uldrig came to tell him his pa died. Only the constable and healer will know for sure." She drew a powerful breath, and I braced myself. "Chester!"

Heavy footfalls preceded him, and he skidded to a stop when he caught sight of the tableau. "What's happened? Is he dead?"

"Yes. Fetch Uldrig and Temver. We need to get them here before Danys finds out."

Chester nodded and barreled back inside.

"I'll stand guard, but I'm guessing Constable Uldrig will want to talk to you about what you found," Matilda said.

"Of course. What about the other guests?"

"What about them?"

"If he was killed, the constable will want to talk to them. How do we stop them from leaving?" An image of the layout of the common area and the few faces I'd paid attention to over the course of the night filled my head. My fingers itched with the need to capture it.

"The ones I don't know are staying here, so they'll not be hard to find. The rest are locals." She gave me a pointed look, and I shivered.

"Matilda, you better get back in here. They're getting rowdy again," Danys said at the door. She caught sight of Igor and rushed forward. "Igor!"

Matilda met her halfway and wrapped her in a bear hug, saying, "You can't help him anymore."

"No. That wasn't supposed to happen. I never should've given him that last drink." Sobs muffled Danys's words, and she sagged in Matilda's grip.

"There's no cause to think like that. This wasn't your fault," Matilda said with a gentle voice.

I jumped as Frangi climbed up and hid her face behind my ear.

"What's going on?" Frangi asked.

Matilda pointed a meaty finger at us. "You and you. Back inside."

"I can help," I protested weakly.

"No, you can't. Get going."

After a last look, I retraced my steps, moving aside to let a dwarf in an all-black constable's uniform pass.

"What're you doing here? Get back to your table," the dwarf said, his tone more aggressive than Avanoff's during the fight.

"I'm going, I'm going."

A chorus of voices lifted in a bawdy song, the contrast of the common room's revelry jarring. My steps slowed, my curiosity whipping up along with the nerves zipping through me. I put my hand up for Frangi and moved her in front of my face. "Go back outside. Stay hidden but listen carefully. Can you do that?"

"I can be the best spy."

I winced. "Great. When the dwarf leaves, find me. Remember everything."

"This is the best inn ever!" Frangi streaked outside, a shimmering of purple dust the only evidence she'd been there.

Dodging swaying patrons, I threaded my way through the tables, slid into my seat, and drained my mead. I slammed the glass down and grimaced at the echo of the dead man's actions.

"Are you feeling well, Kit? Your pallor is concerning," Vivane asked.

"I'm fine, but Igor's not. He's dead."

Her eyes widened. "What do you mean?"

"Dead. As in never drinking again. Never gambling again. Never singing again. Dead." Brown splotches appeared on her cheeks in time with a dull throb blooming behind my eyes.

"I don't understand. How did he die?"

"I don't know, but it doesn't look good. The constable's there now." My brow furrowed as a multitude of questions clamored for my attention. "You visited the privy before me. Did you notice anything? Or run into him?"

Vivane dropped her gaze. "I noticed nothing."

"Where's the patient?" a sharp voice asked. The song wheezed out like the bellows of a blacksmith, and a rustling of whispers followed.

The speaker, a tylluan covered in brown and white feathers, blinked his round eyes, and cocked his head as he scanned the room. A red woolen scarf slipped off his shoulder and he pushed it back, his other hand clasping a black leather bag.

"Temver, through here," Matilda yelled.

He trotted down the hall but paused to let Chester and Danys pass. Chester led the weeping woman to a nearby chair. A woman rushed over and grabbed Danys's arm, but Danys shrugged her off.

I knew the woman, but how?

Vivane turned to the commotion and caught Chester's gaze. A blush spread across his cheeks, and he fidgeted with his cuffs. My eyebrows rose at the answering heat spreading across Vivane's face, and one curious event from the evening dropped into place.

"Vivane, does your room border mine?"

"I'm not sure. Why do you ask?"

"How well do you know Chester?" The question dropped between us like a history book in a quiet study, and I winced.

"I don't think that is any of your business." Icicles dripped from her tone, and she turned to face the window.

I sighed. That went about as well as could be expected, given I'd been as subtle as a hungry pixie.

I shook my head, wishing my magic smoothed my tongue instead of everyone else's, and pulled out my drawing supplies. At least this way, I couldn't offend anyone else while hunting down answers. I'd almost finished capturing the fight scene when the conversation around me dwindled. Constable Uldrig ambled into the room, with his gaze bouncing from table to table. Matilda loomed behind him and cast a shadow over his features.

I folded my drawings in neat squares and put them away, fear hammering away in my chest. Uldrig threw a comment over his shoulder, and Matilda answered him with a nod at me.

The constable crooked his finger at me. "Kithaela Nevyn. I'd like a word. Follow me."

Dread dripped down my spine. I'd done nothing wrong, so why was I so scared?

I FOLLOWED HIM DOWN THE HALL AND INTO THE KITCHEN. HE WOVE around the cook tending to a copper pot bigger than her body and stepped into an office tucked into the back corner. A battered desk covered with ledgers dominated the room.

"Sit," Uldrig commanded. I perched on the edge of a chair facing the desk and clasped my hands to hide their shaking. The dwarf set a thick ledger on the desk chair and climbed on top of it. He picked up a quill and hovered it over the paper before him. "Address?"

"That's tricky."

"What's tricky about it? You either have one or you don't."

"I've got a room in Capital City, but I am on my way to a cottage in Pokeberry Village."

"Pokeberry Village? Is that in Moonseed Vale?" If he had antennae, they would have been quivering even harder than his quill.

"Yes. Why do you ask?"

"I'll ask the questions. What's the address in Pokeberry?"

"Jessamine Cottage, Ivy Lane."

"Have you visited Moonseed or Pokeberry before?"

"No."

"Yet you have a house there?"

"It belongs to a friend." The scratch of his quill made me nauseous.

"Did your friend give you anything to bring on your journey?"

"No."

"What about your companion?"

My brow furrowed. "Frangi? No, besides a new button."

"What are you talking about?"

"My companion collects buttons." At his glazed look, I continued, "She's a pixie."

He grunted. "Not that one. The other one."

"I only have the one."

He glared at me. "Then who is the orc eating dinner with you?"

"Oh. You mean Vivane Cletts."

Ink spattered the page, and he blotted it with the frayed cuff of his uniform. "I just said so. Tell me about her."

"There's not a lot to tell. We met this evening when she asked to sit with me."

"What did you talk about?"

"Embroidery. Pokeberry Village. The bookstore."

"Nothing else?"

"No." Acid churned my stomach.

He shoved his beard into his mouth. After a moment, he said around the ratty ends, "How did you find the deceased?"

"I needed to use the privy, but when I approached, I heard him inside."

"Did he say anything?"

"Just that he felt unwell."

"How did he end up on the ground then?" His quill feather vibrated in anticipation.

"When he didn't respond, I opened the door, and he fell out."

His eyebrows crawled up his forehead. "Interesting. How well did you know the deceased?"

"I've never met him before." The silence thickened around us, and stress stretched my nerves taut. When I couldn't take it any longer, I said, "I'm passing through. How could I possibly have known Igor before?"

"Very well." He made one last note on the page. "You may go."

"That's it? You don't want to know what I saw in the common area?"

"No."

"But a lot happened. He fought with Avanoff and owed money to Garlin—"

"I don't want to hear about that," he said, cutting me off. "Go back to your table and send your companion in."

"Vivane or Frangi?"

"The orc."

"Fine." Before I reached the door, it opened, and the tylluan popped his head in.

"There you are, Uldrig. Hello, my dear." The tylluan blinked, the brown tufts on the side of his head wiggling with the movement.

"I didn't say to enter, Temver," Uldrig said.

"Sorry, old thing. I wanted to let you know I'm done with the body, and it's being moved to my office. It doesn't look like a natural death." Temver's beak opened to show a black tongue.

"Temver, stop smiling at my suspect," Uldrig sputtered.

My jaw dropped. "What? I didn't even know him."

"You knew him enough to find him and know his name."

"Because of the fight. The one you aren't letting me tell you about."

Uldrig waved his hand. "That's enough. Go away."

Temver raised his tufts. "Quite."

"Not you, Temver, her," Uldrig said, pointing at me.

"For the official record, I did not kill him." I swept past the healer, my head held high. Anger licked my heels as I made my way back to the table. How dare Uldrig think I could kill someone? He couldn't find his way out of a brown sack, let alone discover who killed Igor. I sat down and crossed my arms.

"It didn't go well?" Vivane asked.

"No. That idiotic constable had the gall to say I could've done it, and why is he so focused on Moonseed?"

"He asked about Moonseed?"

"Several times. He even asked if Lindie gave me something."

"Did she?"

"No." I nibbled on my lip, my thoughts pinging from one thing to another like a pixie exploring a room. "He wants to see you next."

"Me? Why?"

"No idea." At her flinch, I softened my tone. "I'm sure it's nothing. Walk through the kitchen to the office at the back. That's where you'll find him."

I watched Vivane weave her way through the room, and my fingers drummed the table. After a moment, I pulled out all the paper I had and sketched out the rest of the night. When I finished dredging my memory for the details, I slumped back against my chair. I needed more information. I searched the room for Frangi, and my irritation grew the longer she failed to turn up. She'd better not be chasing the cat right now.

Just when I'd given up, Frangi climbed on the table, breathlessly announcing, "I have so much to tell you. Oh, food!"

"What did you hear?"

"The bird guy, does he fly? Where are his wings? I see the feathers, but nothing to flap besides his beak."

"Frangi, focus."

She blinked. "Bird guy said poison."

"Did he say anything else?"

Frangi burped. "He said the stars were pretty."

I sighed heavy enough to stir her hair.

Frangi stood and put her hands on her hips. "What? I know things. The dead guy had debts. The other orc threatened to pull his legs off, and the honey in the kitchen is too near the fire. They also said Moonseed a lot. Like a lot a lot."

"Why focus on that vale? Because Lindie said nothing like that about it."

"Lindie said nothing about a lot of things," Frangi grumbled.

"I'm beginning to agree with you. All I know is about the lack of men, the grumpy blacksmith, and the miserly bookstore owner. Who happens to be Vivane's uncle."

"Who?"

I pointed at Vivane's glass. "Our dinner companion. She's being questioned right now. I hope she's okay."

"Why do you care?"

"She's nice. Also, she's keeping secrets that could help me figure out who did it. Preferably before the constable pins it on me."

Frangi scowled. "I won't let him."

"You may not have a choice. Why won't Vivane tell me what she knows?"

"I saw her talking to the dead guy. She looked upset."

My jaw dropped. "You saw Vivane talking to Igor?"

"Yes."

"No wonder she's cagey."

A wisp of thought blossomed, and I scrambled for my drawing supplies. Before I could grasp its tail and smash it onto the page, it fled to wherever lost ideas congregated. I banged my forehead on the table as exhaustion washed over me. Maybe it was time to return to our room.

"The orc is coming back. She looks like an over-ripe apple," Frangi said around a yawn.

My head popped up, and I tucked my drawings under my thigh. Guilt crawled across my skin, but until Vivane started talking, I couldn't trust her. I almost reversed my decision when I saw her red-rimmed eyes.

She sat and gulped down her remaining mead.

"I'd ask if you were alright, but I have a feeling you'd say no."

"They think I had a hand in it. They found something of mine near Igor. And the things they implied!" Vivane sniffed into her finger.

A missing piece fell into place, and I fought to keep my expression neutral. "Someone killed Igor, Vivane. They must follow the evidence as they see it. Did the, er, something at the scene belong to you?"

"Yes."

"Was it your handkerchief?"

Her eyes widened. "How did you know?"

"I saw it in his hand. How did it get there?"

"I have no idea." Her frosty tone reverberated with echoes of our previous conversation, and I bit back my response.

I needed to trust someone. If not her, then who?

"Vivane, I apologize for my earlier question. It is none of my business how you know Chester," I said, sincerity laced in my voice.

Her expression softened. "It's quite alright, Kit. You were not wrong in your supposition, but I don't wish to discuss it further."

Before I could respond, Uldrig clomped down the stairs. My

stomach dropped at the look of triumph on his face. He marched toward our table. "Ms. Nevyn. Ms. Clutts."

"Cletts," Vivane and I said at the same time.

Frangi awoke with a snort. "What's going on?"

"The Constable's putting on a show," I said.

Uldrig laid a few items on the table, his nose just breaching the surface. "This is not a show. It is a murder inquiry."

The crowd whispered, passing the word like a Lantern Night candle from table to table.

"Can you verify these are yours, Ms. Nevyn?"

I snatched up a familiar item. "Where did you get this?"

"Put that back," Uldrig demanded.

I ignored him. "Vivane, is this yours?"

"No."

Fiery rage blurred my vision. "You searched my room. Did Matilda give you permission to do so?"

He cast a guilty glance at Matilda. "It is within the purview of my duties."

"Is it though?" Mr. Brownblaze asked.

Uldrig swung around and the two exchanged glances, the older dwarf staring down at the constable with an unreadable expression. Uldrig's shoulders drooped, and he fiddled with the buttons on his uniform.

The interruption took the edge off my temper and my mind spun to life. I snapped my fingers to bring Uldrig around to face me. "This was in the locked trunk in my room. Which means you had to break the lock to find it. Is that what you're saying happened, Constable?"

His mouth moved below the table, no doubt chewing on his disgusting beard. "It is within my rights to do what I feel is necessary."

A patronizing smile slid across my face. "According to the

statutes of law and order, you cannot search a person's locked possessions without either a warrant from the court of jurisdiction or express permission, which I did not give you. Thus, any evidence you've taken from my trunk is irrelevant to your inquiry."

"The young lady is correct, Constable," Mr. Brownblaze said. "The law is quite clear. It is also clear you did not follow it."

"Your honor, I appreciate your input in this matter, but it has not yet come to a place where you are involved."

I covered my mouth to hide the shock at Brownblaze's identity as a magistrate. Although given our interaction, it made more sense than the businessman I thought him to be.

"The law is the law, Constable Uldrig. You would be wise to follow it regardless of where in the process the case takes you. Ms. Nevyn is correct as to her evidence, and you would be well-served to gather a stronger finding before arresting anyone."

"Thank you, sir." Fatigue and despondency tugged Uldrig's words.

Pity marred my victory. I tried to let it go, but it wouldn't let me. "Constable, this is tea. If you smelled it or gave it to the cook, she'd be able to identify it."

Vivane pointed at the cloth. "That is my handkerchief."

"How did it get in the victim's hand?" Uldrig asked.

"I must have dropped it."

At the suspicious look on Uldrig's face, I said, "He was vomiting. He must have picked it up to wipe his face."

Uldrig fastened his beady eyes on mine. "A likely story. How do I know you've not been here before, Ms. Nevyn, met Ms. Clutts and formed a friendship? You then agreed to meet up and put an end to Igor."

Vivane gasped. "That is not true."

"No, it isn't. I already told you, I met Vivane for the first time tonight when she asked to sit at my table."

Uldrig opened his mouth to speak, but the magistrate broke in. "No need to confirm it, Constable. I can attest to all that she stated as I was present for the entire exchange."

"They could be faking it, sir."

"Yes, or they could be telling the truth. Who else have you questioned in this matter?"

"Danys, the victim's wife, and Matilda."

"Far be it from me to tell you how to run your investigation, but why haven't you spoken to any of the victim's friends? The one he owed money to, or the person with whom he fought?" Brownblaze kept his tone gentle, but the twinkle in his eye told a different story.

"Who was that?" Uldrig asked.

"Garlin and Avanoff," I replied, biting the words out between stiff lips.

Uldrig glared at me and pointed a finger at the corner table. "Very well. Garlin, a word."

Garlin stood, and every eye in the room followed them out of the main hall. That had been too close for comfort.

GLANCES FLICKED IN OUR DIRECTION, AND I STARED THEM DOWN UNTIL they looked away. All except for the magistrate's soft look of approval. "Thank you, your honor, for coming to our rescue."

"You seem well-informed, my dear. Do you have any legal training?"

"No, but I recently covered a treatise on the rights of criminals and couldn't help but read it." At his raised eyebrows, I rushed to explain. "Knowing what is in the book helps me design the covers more appropriately."

"Was it *The Rights Forgotten*?" At my nod, he continued, "I have a copy in my collection. The leatherwork is detailed and gives the book the gravitas it deserves. An excellent job, Ms. Nevyn."

"Thank you, sir. It is one of my favorite designs. I've had so few recently, but that one designed itself."

"Indeed." With a tip of his head, the magistrate turned back to his book. His words from this morning echoed in my thoughts.

Maybe I should read challenging books more often.

"I'm glad I read it before all of this. Otherwise, things could've gone quite differently," I said to Vivane.

"I am, too. Thank you for sticking up for me. I only wished I had done the same for you, although I told that reprehensible constable nothing."

I jumped on the opening she provided. "We're not out of the woods yet. You could help by telling me what you're not telling me, and I don't mean about Chester."

She fiddled with her glass. "I suppose I owe you that much. I knew Igor. My uncle had arranged for us to marry, but after I made inquiries, I called it off. Much to Uncle Bixby's dismay."

"What did you find out?" I leaned over the table.

"I don't want to speak ill of the dead."

"We need to know why someone wanted him dead and we could find it in his past." She fidgeted and I pressed my point. "You and I are in Uldrig's sights. We need to figure out who did it. And soon."

Vivane sighed. "He had debts, and he had the gall to intimate we could get a lien on my shop to pay them off. He couldn't stay away from gambling any more than he could from drink."

"Frangi mentioned he owed Garlin."

"See? I know useful things," Frangi said.

"Yes, you do." The idea of Garlin killing him hung there,

196

sparkling for a moment until it withered faster than the inspiration for my designs.

As if I'd conjured him, Garlin returned to the dining area, and every eye followed his progress. He tapped Avanoff on the shoulder and whispered something to him. Paler than one of the new twin moons, Avanoff stumbled toward the kitchen.

The woman comforting Danys whispered something to her, who frowned and shook her head. The woman stood up and followed Avanoff down the hall.

"That's where I know her from."

"Who?" Frangi asked.

"The woman. Briony, I think her name is. She was talking to Danys when I first came downstairs. What do you know about his wife, Vivane?"

"Not much, I'm afraid. They married a short time after our arrangement was called off."

I drummed my fingertips on the table. "Interesting but not exactly helpful. We need to know when he was poisoned."

The color leeched out of Vivane's face, leaving a smear of green behind. "He was poisoned? Are you sure?"

"Yes," I said with a certainty I didn't feel, even with Frangi's contribution.

"Oh, that's good. That's very good." Vivane covered her face with her hands.

Frangi and I exchanged a glance. "Why is poison good, Vivane?"

She lowered her hands and leaned forward. "Then, it couldn't have been my fault."

"Did something happen when you ran into him in the hall?" I asked.

"You knew?"

Frangi rolled her eyes. "Of course, we did."

"Why didn't you tell me?" I jumped in, cutting Frangi off

and squashing the worms of guilt burrowing in my stomach. My magic's propensity to encourage secrets to be told was bad enough, but telling Frangi to spy took that to a whole new low.

Even if it kept me safe.

"You were so nice to me, and I didn't want you to think I couldn't control myself."

Understanding dawned. Vivane was a gentlewoman. How she controlled her natural orc aggression fascinated me, but that was not a thread I needed to pursue right now. "What happened?"

"I had reentered the inn and he cornered me, saying he didn't feel well. I pushed him away, harder than I intended, and he bumped into the wall."

"He was alive when I went outside after you, so it definitely wasn't your fault."

The air rushed out of her. "I'm so glad. I would never wish harm on anyone, including him."

"We've still got holes, though. Where the poison came from, how he was given it, and when. Oh, and why Uldrig was so keen on Moonseed," I said. I shuffled through my drawings, studying every detail but nothing jumped out at me.

"I think I know the answer to one of those questions," Vivane said, the words dripping from her month like honey from a pot.

"Which one?"

"The Uldrig one. Moonseed is known for its medicinal plants, potions, and poultices. And it's poisons."

My jaw dropped. "What?"

"You didn't know?"

"Obviously not."

"If it came from Moonseed, I think I know how it may have come to town," Vivane said, excitement flushing her face. "As I mentioned earlier, the supply wagon I arrived on carried herbs and medicines to Croesfford for our healer, Mr. Doeth. We made a stop right before arriving at the inn."

"Within Soursalt Vale?"

"Yes, just outside of town. It must have been urgent, too, because the recipient seemed quite keen on getting it, not even letting me knock before the door opened."

"What was in it?"

"I didn't want to pry."

The hope rising inside me dried up faster than my inspiration, and I buried my head in my hands. "Back to step one again."

"Maybe Mr. Doeth's manifest mentioned what it was."

I sat up. "There's a manifest? Can you get it?"

She nodded and slipped out of the booth. "I'll be right back."

Now we were getting somewhere.

VIVANE'S SKIRTS HAD DISAPPEARED WHEN BRIONY RETURNED TO THE common area. She slid in the seat next to Danys and nodded. More tears slipped down Danys's face, and she laid her head in her arms. A muffled sob arose from her, and Briony put her hand on Danys's shoulder.

"Work may help you keep your mind off things, lass," Matilda said from behind the bar.

"Of course, you think like that," Danys replied, her voice thick with resentment.

"I'll do it for her," Briony said as she climbed to her feet.

Danys peeked up from her arms. "So, you can hold that against me as well, Briony?"

"I never have. I'm trying to help."

"Go on then, but I'm not sharing my pay."

Briony's lips whitened. "I'm not asking you to."

I fiddled with my empty glass, my thoughts jumping more than Frangi did when she attempted to catch a moth. "There are too many nuances between these people to unravel them all. How do I untangle them?"

"Dunno. I tug on one end until something happens," Frangi replied, scratching dried milk on her face.

I tapped my chin, my gaze following Briony around the room. When she turned my way, I waved her over. "That's a good idea. And I know where to start."

"What do you want?" Briony asked.

"I'll have another glass of mead." She made to leave, so I rushed on, "I'm sure Danys appreciates your support."

Briony sniffed. "Thank you. At least someone sees what I do."

I gathered as much emotion as I could to activate my magic, a sour taste filling my mouth at the manipulation. But I couldn't see any other way to get what I needed. "It must have been a shock, especially after the fight Igor had with Avanoff."

An expression passed over Briony's face too quick for me to catch. "That? That weren't nothing. A regular Friday night around here. You'd know that if you weren't outsiders." She pivoted on her heel and walked away.

My eyebrows rose at the venom in her tone. "That was odd."

"She's not very nice," Frangi said.

"No, she isn't."

A commotion near the bar caught my attention as Avanoff returned to the dining area, his hands trembling. He leaned down and whispered something in Danys's ear. She sat up, almost hitting her head on his. Briony set a drink down with a thump and made straight for them.

"Frangi, be the best spy again and eavesdrop on that conversation." I jerked my head toward the trio by the bar.

She raised both fists in the air. "Yes!"

I scooped her up and set her on the floor. She streaked away faster than a breath. I only hoped she'd be quick enough to catch what they said.

Danys stabbed Briony in the chest with a rigid finger. Avanoff's mouth dropped open, and he grabbed Briony's arm, spinning her to face him.

"Order's up, Briony," Matilda said, interrupting their argument.

Her face pinched, Briony yanked her arm free and moved to the bar, oozing hostility. Danys shook her head at Avanoff and sank back into her chair. After flicking a glance between the two women, Avanoff staggered back to the table and sat with his head in his hands.

My knee bounced, shaking the table hard enough to spill Frangi's milk. I mopped it up and then scanned the room for Frangi, leaning over to peer under the tables. A pair of knobby gray legs thinner than a walking stick got in the way and I jerked upright.

Temver stood next to Brownblaze's table, a sheaf of paper in his hands. "Your honor, here is a copy of my report on the death of Igor Mattherson."

Brownblaze scowled. "This is not the proper procedure, Mr. Temver, but put it there."

"Very good. To save you time, the cause of death is poison. I am still identifying which one, but I have it narrowed down to three. I shall know more by morning."

The color drained from Danys's face, and Briony whirled around, her fingers tangled in her corset strings. Temver leaned forward and whispered. "Just between us, the victim ingested it within no earlier than twenty to thirty minutes before death."

Brownblaze caught my eye, and I whipped my head around

to gaze unseeing out the window. He said, "Now isn't the time to discuss such matters."

"Right, right. I'll deliver this to Uldrig and be on my way. Such an exciting night." Temver bowed and bustled away.

"It's only exciting if you aren't either the victim or the murderer, you old fool," Brownblaze said.

A glass slammed down on our table, and I jerked around, my heart fluttering in my chest.

"You have some nerve, sitting here drinking when we all know you killed Igor," Briony snarled.

Anger curled in my chest. "I had nothing to do with his death."

"Sure, you didn't." Briony sneered. The conversation in the tavern ceased as patrons leaned over each other to hear. "Convenient, isn't it, how both her and her friend followed him outside and were the last to see him alive? And how they keep backing each other up?"

The eye of every patron fixed me in place. My gaze skittered from one to the other, until it landed on Danys, who frowned at my accuser instead. Feeling the pressure on my chest easing, I lifted my chin. "I did not murder Igor. It's the truth, whether you want to believe it or not. Besides, it would be best to leave the judgment to the actual magistrate who is sitting right here."

"Quite right, good folk of Croesfford. It does no good speculating. The crime will be solved, and the perpetrator punished," Brownblaze said, peering at the crowd from under his bushy eyebrows until they looked away.

Briony opened her mouth to protest, but Matilda forestalled her. "Briony, leave it."

"Enjoy your drink while you still can," Briony said.

I needed to solve this before everyone turned on us. One more outburst from Briony, and they just might.

Vivane skipped down the stairs, her skirts swirling to a stop when she almost ran over Briony. Confusion passed over Vivane's face and she took a step back. Briony's mouth opened and then shut with snap. She whirled around and disappeared down the hall. Vivane watched her for a moment and then hurried to the table.

Another piece of the puzzle fell into place. Only one more to go. Anticipation sizzled through me for the note in Vivane's hands. I had to stop myself from snatching it from her when she arrived at the table.

"You'll never guess who I saw." She placed the note between us.

"Who?" I picked it up and turned it this way and that, but Mr. Doeth's scrawl had loops where I expected lines.

"The very person I visited this morning. Here, in the common area."

"Is her name Briony? Mousy brown hair and clothing?" I frowned, bringing the paper closer. Was that an a or an o?

"How did you know?"

"Educated guess. Can you read this?" I pointed to a scribbled line.

"Yes. It's instructions for a sleeping tincture."

"That couldn't have killed him. At least I don't think so, unless taking the whole thing could." The budding excitement fizzled out as fast as it had come, and my shoulders slumped. "It doesn't matter. That's not enough to shake Uldrig."

"Will this help? There's a second instruction for Nerium Oil," Vivane said.

I straightened. "You delivered two medicines?"

"Yes."

"Nerium Oil is for arthritis. Do you know what's in it?"

"Not everything, but I know it has oleander in it because Mr. Doeth mentioned it once, how deadly," Vivane's voice trailed off and she paled. "Is it my fault?"

The conversation had flipped so many times, I struggled to keep up. "For what?"

After a furtive glance at the magistrate, who hadn't even twitched an eyebrow in our direction, Vivane leaned forward and whispered, "Did I supply the poison that killed Igor?"

"Not unless you poured it down his throat. Did you?"

She shook her head, her fingers worrying at the paper.

"Then it wasn't your fault. Mr. Doeth made the oil, and you delivered it. That's it." A tug on my skirts signaled Frangi climbing up on the table. "What did you hear?"

"The man said, 'I've done nothing wrong.' A woman said, 'but we meant to'," Frangi replied.

"Which woman?" I asked.

She shrugged. "Couldn't see from under the table."

"Did they say anything else?"

"The other woman said she'd never forgive her, or something like that. Can I have some mead?"

"No. I don't feel like peeling you off the ceiling," I said.

"That only happened one time," Frangi replied.

"How did you end up on the ceiling?" Vivane asked.

I ignored their patter and laid each of my drawings out on the table in sequential order. Whatever I needed to know was here. I picked up each one and scrutinized it. When I reached the last one, the final piece clicked together and the paper fell from my fingers. "I know how it was done. I need to talk to Uldrig."

"How?" Vivane asked at the same time Frangi asked, "Who?"

I'd only gone a few steps toward the kitchen when Uldrig

appeared with Temver and Chester hovering nearby. "Constable. I need a word."

Uldrig rocked back on his heels. "I knew you'd confess."

"I didn't do it. Can we talk in Matilda's office?" I threaded as much urgency in my tone as I could.

He pinned me with a malevolent gaze. "I don't have enough evidence to arrest you, Ms. Nevyn, but I know you're up to your eyeballs in it."

"What are you talking about?"

"You know very well what I mean." He shoved past me and headed for Vivane. "Ms. Clutts, I'm arresting you for the death of Igor Mattherson. You do not have to say anything unless you wish to do so, but anything you say will be taken down and given in evidence."

I raced across the room to get between them.

"I didn't do this," Vivane said, her breath stirring my hair.

"No, she didn't. Constable, you have to listen to me," I said.

"No, I don't. If you want her to take the fall for you, that's your business but arresting her is mine. Move out of the way and allow me to do my job."

"You couldn't do your job if I made you signs," Frangi yelled from the table.

A chuckle erupted from the next table over and gathered steam into a full belly laughter. Magistrate Brownblaze slapped the table with his hand, tears leaking out of his eyes, not caring that every eye was on him. His laughter wound down as fast as it arrived, and he wiped his face with his napkin. "I apologize. That hit the right sentiment for me. Carry on, Constable. You were relaying the evidence you had against the accused."

"I was?"

The magistrate peered out from under his eyebrows. "You were."

Uldrig cleared his throat. "Ms. Clutts had a history with the deceased and had an altercation with him moments before he died."

"He was alive after that, which you know from my statement, Constable," I said.

"You could've lied," Uldrig retorted.

Brownblaze cleared his throat. "Evidence only, Constable."

"Your honor, this is quite unusual." Uldrig stepped up to the magistrate's table while fiddling with the button straining against his stomach.

"Perhaps, but it is within the bounds of the law, or rather, there is no law to prevent it. Humor me, please."

Uldrig sighed. "Very well. Ms. Clutts arrived this morning from Moonseed with the medicinal supply wagon. It would not have been hard for her to take whatever she needed with no one noticing."

"I did no such thing," Vivane said, her color high.

"We've already taken stock, old thing. All items were accounted for," Temver said from his position near the bar.

"She could've asked for it from her healer in Moonseed," Uldrig said through gritted teeth.

I jumped in before Uldrig could pursue that line of questions. "It doesn't matter whether she had something from the healer or nothing. She had no opportunity to give it to Igor."

"Sure, she did. After the altercation in the hall—"

I cut him off. "Igor drank his beer in one gulp and slammed his tankard on the table in front of everyone here. He then stumbled down the hall. Vivane and I never got near his table. When would we have given it to him?"

"And Ms. Clutts' property at the scene?"

"She already told you; she dropped it. Besides, the poison wasn't on the handkerchief, so it's irrelevant."

Uldrig chewed furiously on his beard. "If you know so much, then tell me who did it."

I raised my arm and pointed.

HEADS WHIPPED TO FOLLOW MY FINGER, WHISPERS IGNITING FASTER than cinders. Those sitting nearby the person I identified scooched their chairs away. I had a feeling it was less an accusation than the desire to get a better seat at the show.

Her chair squeaked as she pushed it back and stood. Danys lifted her chin and crossed her arms. "That's rich. I had nothing to do with this, you spiteful cow."

"But you planned to."

The color left Danys' face.

"That's not enough for an arrest. You'd know that if you were the constable on this case. Move out of my way," Uldrig said.

"I would like to hear Ms. Nevyn out, Constable," Magistrate Brownblaze said, his voice ringing with authority.

Uldrig's shoulders slumped. "Yes, sir."

I paced between the tables, my thoughts gathering like gossip at a sewing circle. "I grew up in a small community, and the commonality between all small towns is that everyone talks about everyone else's business. Croesfford is no different. Throughout the night, I learned that Igor had a gambling problem and owed at least one individual money. That same person threatened to pull him limb from limb."

All eyes turned to the corner table, where Garlin sat with his arms crossed.

"There's nothing wrong with a threat if it gets me what I want. Besides, killing him doesn't get me my money," Garlin said.

"Exactly, which is why I dismissed you as the killer. Second, I learned that someone was taking the silver from the inn, and based on an encounter when I first arrived, I would bet Garlin a silver that several customers had complained of missing items as well." I glanced at Matilda.

"We've had a small problem, but nothing I didn't make right," she said begrudgingly.

"Igor could have been the thief, but it's doubtful. He wore loose clothing and had no way of smuggling items out without being detected. He also didn't have access to the locked guest rooms, but his wife did. It was during my first conversation with you, Danys, that you mentioned moving to the city. But how could you do that with no money and a never-ending coin hog like Igor? Simple. By stealing."

"I knew it," Matilda said.

"You can't prove a thing," Danys said, keeping her gaze on mine.

"I won't have to. I can prove something more dire than theft. The biggest obstacle in solving who killed Igor was not why, but how. How did the killer slip him the poison, especially when Igor remained surrounded by most of the people in this room? Once I figured that out, the rest was easy. Danys, you were desperate to leave this 'meager village,' I believe you called it, so you decided to do something drastic. But you needed help and that help came in the form of a fight."

"That fight was real," Avanoff stammered as he stumbled to his feet.

Garlin rubbed his nose. "Was it? I thought it odd you called out the queen when I'd played it two hands prior."

"Indeed. The fight with Avanoff needed to accomplish one thing: spill Igor's beer so that Danys could bring him a new one. With one small addition from the bottle in her corset."

Avanoff looked around like a cornered mouse and then pointed at Danys. "You said it would make him sleep. A funny prank for the holiday. He wasn't supposed to die."

Whispers rustled around the room, the patrons' gazes swinging from him to Danys. She backed up, her hands clenched on her stays. She swallowed and shook her head. "No, he wasn't. I don't know what went wrong."

A frisson of relief slipped through me at her admission. The reveal of the killer depended on too many uncontrollable factors, and it could still go wrong. "What you put in his beer after the fight didn't kill him, Danys. We all saw Igor drain it and then stumble outside. Less than five minutes later, he was dead. The poison that killed him wasn't instantaneous, it took at least twenty minutes to take effect. Right, Mr. Temver?"

"Or thirty. It's not an exact science yet," Temver replied.

Danys's eyes widened. "You mean I didn't kill him?"

"No."

"Oh, thank goodness." She sagged to the floor, her shoulders shaking, and Briony rushed to comfort her.

"If she didn't do it, who did?" Uldrig asked as he pulled at his beard.

"It was a conversation I overheard that gave me the final clue, added to what Vivane told me. She delivered two medicines this morning at the behest of Pokeberry Village's healer, Mr. Doeth. But the house she delivered them to is within the bounds of Soursalt Vale and should have been served by Mr. Temver."

"There have been times when I am out of a specific ingredient. What was the medicine?" Temver asked.

"A sleeping tincture and Nerium Oil."

Temver cocked his head to one side. "I have plenty of those available."

"Exactly. So why ask for them from another vale? Because you don't want anyone to know you purchased them." I resumed my pacing. "The case hinges on who had a reason to want Igor out of the picture, someone who had nothing left to lose. Danys was that person, except she loved Igor too much to kill him. Her plan was to give him the sleeping tincture and slip away before he came to. But the killer didn't want to knock him out, which is why they needed a common remedy that wouldn't raise suspicion. Nerium Oil, which contains the poisonous oleander, is used topically to relieve the symptoms of arthritis. Something Chester and I discussed when I first arrived."

Heads swiveled to where Chester stood, and he backed up, his hands splayed out before him. "All we did was talk. I've never heard of it before Ms. Nevyn mentioned it."

"No, Chester had nothing to do with it either," I said before Uldrig could open his mouth. "The killer stuck to the plan and brought Danys the sleeping tincture after it was delivered this morning. But they had another agenda. One that hinged on either getting away with it or Danys being accused. After the handoff, the killer walked to the bar and bumped into Igor while he fetched a refill. A fight started in the corner and when everyone's eyes were on it, she tipped it in his beer."

Danys's eyes widened, and she climbed to her feet. "You didn't."

"Don't listen to her, D. She's wrong," Briony said as she stood.

"No, she's not. You weren't supposed to be here. 'Can't I enjoy the holiday?'" Danys sneered as she mimicked Briony's words.

Briony stiffened and glanced around the room.

My heart thumped hard against my chest. I had nothing else to lay on the table, all my cards out like the queen from earlier. If she didn't take the bait, it was over. My skin itched with the tension, and I struggled to remain silent.

When Briony's shoulders drooped, I blew out a breath and my head dropped.

"Fine. I poisoned Igor. I told myself I wouldn't do it if I

didn't have a chance. And then I did, and it was only too easy," Briony said.

"Why? He didn't need to die," Danys said, her voice as befuddled as a drunk pixie.

"He would've followed you. Or you would've only gotten as far as the next town and come running back. I would've done anything to save you from this place. God knows I can't leave, but you can. You have your whole life ahead of you and I didn't want you to waste one more holiday on that man."

The women stared at each other, hurt and confusion crossing Danys's face. The air condensed around them, drawing in the townsfolk who hung on every moment.

A log shifted on the fire, and a hiss pierced the silence. Danys wrenched her gaze away and watched the sparks crackle and sizzle as they roamed free of the flame.

"D," Briony said, tugging on Danys's arm.

Danys pulled away. "Is she right? Were you planning on pinning his death on me?"

"Of course not. I was going to get rid of the bottles before that could happen."

"When? You spent all this time consoling me and not once did you ask for the bottle back."

Briony shook her head. "Because it didn't matter. Even if someone saw you do it, it's not a crime putting your husband to sleep so that he doesn't drink anymore."

Danys pointed a rigid finger at me. "She accused me, and you said nothing. You didn't do this for me, you did this for you!"

"What? Why?"

"If Igor isn't around, you can run the farm the way you want, especially since I'll not be around. How did I not see it before? This was all your idea, and I fell for it."

Briony snickered. "Yes, you did, you ungrateful cow. I spent my days toiling on your property while that lout spent all our coin. You dreamed of leaving it behind, but what you'd leave behind is me, with him still driving it into the ground. No change, no help, no relief from the misery and backbreaking work. And for what? I couldn't even take a break for the holiday without you lording it over me."

"If you actually worked, you'd be able to take a break. But not you. No. You have excuse upon excuse. 'It's cold,' 'my fingers hurt,' 'I'm tired.' If you have nothing to show for it, it's your own fault," Danys shot back.

Briony gasped and rushed Danys. The two of them went down, screaming and pulling each other's hair. Chester waded in, dodging elbows and arms, but couldn't get one to let go of the other. Matilda reappeared from the back with a pot. She heaved its contents at them, and the women pulled apart, gasping, and covered in dirty dishwater.

Uldrig stepped in, his chest puffed out and his spine rigid. "Briony Abbott, I'm arresting you for the death of Igor Mattherson. You do not have to say anything unless you wish to do so, but anything you say will be taken down and given in evidence. Danys Mattherson and Avanoff Cerrid, I'm arresting you on suspicion of drugging Igor Mattherson. You do not have to say anything unless you wish to do so, but anything you say will be taken down and given in evidence."

Chester pulled the women to their feet and held them apart as they tried to kick each other, marching them out of the tavern. Uldrig grabbed Avanoff's arm and led him through the quiet tables. The chatter in the inn returned with a roar as people moved from one table to the next to gossip.

I plopped down in my chair, relief dripping from me like the water dripping from the two sisters. "Vivane, there is one more thing I need to know."

"What?"

"Will it be this exciting in Pokeberry?"

I TILTED MY HEAD BACK AND BELTED OUT THE LAST LINE OF MY favorite Lantern Night song, the cool night air rich with frivolity. Frangi tightened her grip on my ear, her tinny voice raised along with mine.

The street in front of The Salt & Pickle overflowed with merrymakers, some leaning on each other and laughing, others huddled in pockets. Chester wandered through the crowd, delivering goblets to all. When he reached Vivane, he leaned in and said something that caused her to cover her mouth and look down.

A grin blossomed on my face. I had a feeling everything would work out all right there.

Magistrate Brownblaze nudged my elbow and held out a goblet of wine. "My compliments, Ms. Nevyn."

We clinked glasses. "Thank you for allowing me to speak tonight. If it hadn't been for you, we would be confined and awaiting trial before you."

He chuckled. "That's why I did it. I hate wasting time during the holidays on the wrongly accused. Besides, I haven't quite enjoyed myself in years as much as I did tonight, so I have you, and your companion, to thank for it. Have you ever considered employment in the law? I have a vacancy for a clerk, and I think you'd be good at it."

"Thank you for your kind offer. I have my own path to take, one that until this evening I questioned. But now I know I've made the right decision, and I want to see where it leads."

"I wish you luck, my dear. I'm sure you'll do great things in Pokeberry Village."

"I hope so." I smiled and sipped my wine, the spices fanning the flames of excitement within me.

I had a feeling everything was going to work out all right for me too.

CASSANDRA STIRLING IS A DEVELOPMENT EDITOR, BOOK LOVER, AND author of urban fantasy, cozy mystery, and cozy fantasy mystery. You can find out more about her work, and get the latest updates on her new series, *The Pokeberry Village Mysteries*, featuring Kit, Frangi, and Vivane, on her website, https://cassan dracstirling.com/cozy-vales. The first book of the series, *Bereft at The Belladonna*, is publishing in Spring 2024.

FLAGONS AND DRAGONS
K M JACKWAYS

Mistletoe Vale is a land of rolling hills dotted with lakes. It ranges from alpine in the north to temperate lowlands in the south. The flora is mostly evergreen, and garlands grow over every building. Most of the population lives in Faerton, a town surrounded by forest.

"**M**ama, I found something!" The cry came from up ahead.

Flora stretched her back out with a sigh. Their walks took them further each day, as she taught her son, Hedric, about the trees and plants of Mistletoe Vale and their uses in cooking and spells. This was usually done from the ground, talking to his legs while he sat in a tree, his feet dangling from a honeypine branch. With one last glance back at Faerton, spread over the side of the hill, she followed where he'd disappeared into a stand of trees beside the dirt road, down a path they hadn't followed before.

When Flora pushed through the leaves, she saw it. The 'something' was an old inn sitting in the middle of a field of red flowers, the road leading up to it long overgrown. The building was two storeys of wattle and daub, with one half completely covered in vines; not only the mistletoe and bright white shimmerbell that curled gently around most buildings in Mistletoe Vale, but also ivy and creeping crowfoot. The front porch was slumped towards the ground, and the two chimneys were more birds' nests than stone. It normally wouldn't bear looking at twice.

Flora wanted to be practical, so when she came upon that empty inn, her mind *definitely* didn't fill in freshly painted white walls, gently smoking chimneys, an open door, and horses tied up outside. Perhaps a grove of trees alongside, bursting with cocoa pods. It didn't imagine a cauldron, boiling with sweet smells, and a community of rosy-cheeked souls discussing their art and telling stories around the fire, while she served hot drinks behind the bar.

The vivid image took her by surprise, hitting her like her pestle crushing cacao beans. Perhaps that had been the dream, once. Her dream.

FLORA COOPFORD GREW UP IN A HOUSEHOLD WHERE HER PARENTS HAD always made barrels and her grandparents had always made barrels. She wasn't allowed to forget that they also made pails. Her mother, Roseneath, was an ogre and her father, a human, was named Malcolm, but everyone called him Tubs. They were practical, hard-working people.

At sixteen, Flora had left home for Capital City to join the Tasters' Guild. It was a bold move for a half-ogre from Mistletoe Vale, but she'd insisted, and her parents had let her go, gently prodded by her aunt Ludette, who thought all magical ability should be encouraged.

She'd relished the chance to work with cocoa beans and learn from some of the best artisan chocolate makers in the queendom to create something special. The purpose of the guild was to perfect the art of not just hot chocolate making, but a very special kind of hot chocolate, Heart of the Vale. It was a sought-after drink that lifted the spirits, calmed the nerves, and soothed minor ailments.

In the guild, nothing mattered but the art of taste and the wielding of magic. Flora had crushed, sniffed, stirred, and tested her way through her apprenticeship to become a guilder. She had found her purpose; to serve Heart of the Vale to folk who needed it. But she'd put that dream on the shelf, along with her pestle and mortar. Hadn't she?

"COME ON, HEDRIC! WE CAN'T GO IN," SHE CALLED, BUT HE'D already disappeared up the steps of the inn.

Flora lifted her skirts and ran to catch up, stepping over branches that were leaning against the wall, almost as if they were forcing their way in. She pushed the door open to let some light into the musty-smelling place, but it stuck halfway. She paused, letting her senses explore. No guard creature or magical wards that she could see.

The first thing she noticed in the gloom was a pile of cream donuts covered in a sprinkling of sugar, sitting on a table. Hedric was reaching towards them, his chubby fingers outstretched.

"Don't," she said, stepping inside.

One of the donuts bared its teeth, making Hedric jump back. The pastry-like creatures took flight and settled some-where near the rafters, sending down dust clouds that spiraled in the thin ray of sunlight.

"They're just bats, see?" Flora said, pointing up. "Fuzz bats. They won't hurt you." The bats were often found in barns and workshops around the vale. Many an unsuspecting visitor had fallen for their sweet appearance. "They'll be more frightened of you than you are of them."

Now that Flora was inside, she couldn't help but be intrigued by the place. Who had let it get into such a state of disrepair? She pulled some sacking across from where it covered the window, letting light spill in.

"Yes, Mama," Hedric said. He was already heading towards a corner of the large room, where a long bar and stove were almost hidden under planks of honeypine, and she followed. There was a barrel on its side, that she recognised as a Coopford, in the old style, from long before she started in the family business.

"We really should leave," she murmured, running her hand over the smooth edge of the bar, making tracks in the dust. Flagons of steaming chocolate lined up in her mind. She could almost smell the sweet, rich aroma. She closed her eyes for just a second, letting herself live the daydream.

As she thought about how she would arrange the inn just so, a jolt of recognition came to her. She understood how the inn felt. It was once a thriving place, where stories were told, where mouths were kissed, where jigs were jigged. It was an inn filled with warmth, song, laughter, and love . . .

"A house needs a hearth, and a hearth needs a home," came a rasping voice from somewhere near the floor, interrupting her thoughts.

"What was that?" Flora asked. "That voice." The flash of *inn sight*, as she privately called it, could wait 'til later.

Hedric lifted up a blackened pot. Inside was what looked like a pile of red and purple coins. She realised it was a tiny, scaled creature, all curled up tight, its wings tucked around its body.

"I know what this is," Hedric said, puffing out his chest. "I read about it in *The Wilde and Woody Queendom*. It's a myvern."

"Is it really?" Flora was impressed. Hedric's thirst for knowledge was only matched by his thirst for adventure. Just like his father.

SHE REMEMBERED THE LOOK OF SURPRISE ON HER PARENTS' FACES, when she had turned up on the doorstep at almost twenty-five years' old, reaching under layers of fabric to show them baby Hedric in his sling. He had batted his fists around like a warrior, despite the cherubic expression on his face.

She sat her parents down, prepared them a Heart of the Vale and watched while they sipped it. She saw their faces calm and their brows smooth. She knew her chocolate was healing their ills and raising their mood.

"I'm going to raise him here in Mistletoe Vale," she said, gesturing to baby Hedric, now on her mother's knee. Roseneath was patting him absently on the back, with a well-practised hand.

"That's fine, Flora," her father said. "Of course you can live with us. But it's not very practical and that's exactly what we would expect from you."

It wasn't easy with four mouths to feed and everyone needed to pitch in. Flora rolled up her sleeves and worked hard. The Coopford barrels were known for miles around as the sturdiest and most barrelsome barrels. The orders came rolling in, and the barrels went rolling out. But Flora thought they made a dull, hollow sound.

Once, she went to her parents and showed them the markings she had burned into the side of a barrel, a delicate flame design, inspired by the three fires of Winter's Tide.

"We can use it for the best brews," she said. "Do you like it?"

"That's all well and good," said her father with a shake of his head, "but we can't take up all our time making things look pretty."

Roseneath sighed. "If you want to create something, help me with the bread," she said, tying her hair up in a practical bun. Tubs came up behind his wife and slid his arms around her waist, the top of his grey head just visible over her shoulder. "There are two of you to think of, now."

HEDRIC PUT THE POT DOWN AND HELD UP HIS HANDS, WHICH WERE covered in soot. Then he reached in to poke the little dragon. "They should have two legs."

"Maybe just leave her," Flora said. The old tales said that myverns were mostly females, although Flora had not seen one before.

"You were right when you said you shouldn't be here," came another voice, quiet but authoritative.

Flora stepped closer to the little dragon, which now seemed to be warning them to leave. It lifted its tiny head, lazily, showing whiskers and a mouth full of teeth.

"Up here," came the voice from behind and above her, amused.

Of *course* it wasn't the creature in the pot speaking. She quickly regained her composure. Flora Coopford was a hearth witch and a member of the esteemed Tasters' Guild. But she was on someone else's property here, so it paid to be cautious. She looked up to see where the voice was coming from.

"Er, I'm sorry," she said. "My son . . . "

"Is climbing up the wall," came the low voice.

This wasn't strictly true. Hedric, having gone halfway up the stairs, had discovered he could get closer to the fuzz bats by standing on the delicate balustrade. He leaned out towards the enticing puffy creatures.

"Hedric, love," Flora said, her heart galloping along as her motherly instincts kicked their heels in. "Get down from there."

He must have heard the warning note in his mother's voice as he did what he was told, sliding down the stairs on his bottom, saying 'bump' each time. The bottom step split in two with a loud crack when he landed on it.

Flora stared at it in dismay. She held her hand out to her son. "We're leaving," she said, hoping no one had heard the breaking noise.

"Yes, you should." The man stepped out of the darkness on a landing on the stairs and bowed low to her. Perhaps he had heard it after all. She made out only a short beard, a long, straight nose, and the suggestion of broad shoulders beneath the cloak. "Unless, of course, you'd like to live here?" His voice lifted hopefully.

"Yes!" Hedric yelled.

Flora blinked. "No, I will not be doing that," she said, slowly. Live in a crumbling old inn? With her child? *Guzzling gorgons,* she thought.

"Please, Mama."

"No, Hedric. That's just plain strange."

The man seemed to crumple. "Of course it is. Forgive me, please. It's only that I've been listening to that flaming dragon for too long." He waved towards the corner of the room. The creature in question squeaked indignantly.

"You've probably noticed that she speaks only in prophecies? 'The curse breaks after she moves in.' That's what she told me. So, I thought I'd ask, on the off chance."

"It's not a dragon," Hedric muttered.

Curse? Alright, I'll bite, Flora thought, still focused on the man. "What curse?"

"Minor misfortune," he said. "Sword's never sharp, potions have unintended side effects, baking doesn't rise, deals tend to somehow always come out in the other party's favour . . . and this sort of thing," he gestured at the bottom step that had broken under Hedric's slight frame.

The words were matter-of-fact enough, but Flora thought there was a depth of feeling behind them. Was it he who was cursed? Or the inn?

"Do you live here?" Hedric asked.

"You don't need to answer," she said, despite her curiosity. It never hurt to be well-mannered when inside a stranger's home. "By the way, I'm Flora. Flora Coopford."

He waved her protestations away. "I'm Wes. I don't live here, but I inherited this place, and I would very much like to turn it into an alehouse."

"An alehouse. That would be perfectly fine," Flora said, not quite able to say that it was a good idea, since her dream was already vanishing from her mind. Somehow, she felt that wasn't quite what the inn *wanted* to be. "Are the prophecies always true, then?"

"It seems so."

"Well, why did you think that she meant me?" she asked abruptly, wishing he would come down the stairs so she could see him better.

"Because you're the first person to come to the inn in a long while. But I can see I was mistaken." He inclined his head.

"All right. Well, goodbye."

Flora grabbed Hedric's hand and tugged at the door, which stuck halfway open. No matter how hard she pulled, it wouldn't budge, so she had to squeeze through sideways. If this was what it was like experiencing the curse for ten minutes, it must be horrible to live with.

"Stranger than a bean maiden with no basket," she murmured to Hedric, after they went down the steps and started across the field.

"I like him," he said.

"Do you? Why?"

"He's got a big house," Hedric said, and ran off towards the trees.

"He does," she sighed, with a last look back at the building.

It struck her again. Without being able to explain it, Flora *knew* how the inn felt. She knew it as well as she knew the curve of her son's cheek. The inn was uncomfortable. It was tired and it was in pain, a niggling ache that stopped it from resting and made it snappy with visitors. The inn wanted to be welcoming and friendly, full of life. If it was a person, Flora would offer it a warming Heart of the Vale to sip until it felt like itself again.

Flora's eyes flicked over the outside walls, all covered in vines. She noticed straight away what the problem was. A branch had fallen from the old apple tree and was wedged across the corner of the building.

That can't be comfortable, she thought, approaching the wall to see the damage. *Perhaps I can help.*

She drew on hearth magic that she hadn't used in a long time—comfort, homeliness and the energy to make things right. As she watched, the building creaked and the outside wall moved, less than an inch, but it was enough. The branch fell. Something that sounded very much like a sigh escaped from the shutters.

"Hey!" Wes stuck his head out the door, mainly because he couldn't fit his whole body easily through the gap. He had dark eyes and jet black hair and features that Flora thought she really should be able to place. He called to her, "You're a magical? Did you just bond with my inn?"

"I think I might have," Flora replied. She was a witch, after all. "I don't know if I did anything, really. I'm mostly just a barrel-maker and a mother these days." The familiar dizzy feeling came over her from drawing on the aether and she put her hand out for balance. Perhaps she had used more magic than she thought.

"Well, that sounds like a lot for anybody to be getting on with," Wes said, before sheepishly continuing, "I have to admit that the branch has been lying there for the past few months. The curse, you see."

"It was causing her pain," Flora said, patting the smooth wall, "but it's better now."

She heard Hedric's voice from the forest, calling 'Look at me' and wondered how far up the tree she would find him this time.

"I've got to go. Good luck with the curse." Flora was surprised to find that she meant it. As she turned away, she thought she heard the inn calling, "*Come back to me.*"

IT WAS SIX DAYS LATER AND THE EVENING BEFORE LANTERN NIGHT when there was a knock at the door. The Coopfords' cottage was at the end of a row of similar thatched-roof houses, covered in vines, facing the village square. Noisy markets, petanque games, and town meetings that usually went on three hours longer than expected, all took place in Faerton's square. The Exchange, the library that travelled the queendom, was often found there, too.

A row of three bonfires burned night and day in the square for the two-week holiday season of Winter's Tide leading up to

Lantern Night. This was the time of year when Faerton came to life.

People opened their houses to their friends and neighbours and tried out their new recipes. They sang songs and told stories until late at night. Some exchanged gifts of crafts or poetry. The Coopfords and their neighbours had just sat down at the table and Roseneath was ladling mutton stew into bowls.

When she heard the rap at the door, Flora expected to see her favourite aunt, Ludette, bustling in. People said they were alike, with their curves and wavy red hair. Their innate way with hearth magic. And their lateness, but she didn't admit to that one so readily.

Flora yawned and rubbed her eyes. She'd woken, early, from a dream where she worked with the inn as she mended the floorboards and wiped down the bannisters. Another one. They always slipped away, leaving her feeling like she'd missed something.

"Flora," her mother called, "Master Moongrove is at the door." She raised her eyebrows at her daughter as she came back to the table.

The spoon stopped halfway to Flora's mouth and stew dripped into her bowl. All eyes turned to her.

"Moongrove? The maire's son?" asked Stef Chandler, who lived in the next cottage. "Flickering light! No one's seen him for years."

Stef's wife nudged him and he put his hand over his mouth.

Still confused, Flora pushed her chair back.

"Hello there," came a low voice.

The same man that Flora had seen at the empty inn stepped into the room. He was an orchard elf, she realized. His long dark hair was glistening with snowflakes. Weslin Moongrove, by all the gods. He hadn't been seen around town for eight years, yet it turned out that she had met him twice in the space of a week.

"Not official business," Weslin said, lifting his hat to those gathered at the table, where all the adults were staring with their mouths open. Hedric reached for an extra slice of bread while he thought no one was watching him.

"Can I have a word?" Weslin's eyes found Flora's.

Wiping her hands on her dress, she led him into the sitting room.

"Have a seat," she offered, "You could have told me your surname last time," she couldn't resist adding.

"That was on purpose," he said with a laugh. He looked younger today than her first impression of him. His face was unlined and there were only one or two greys streaked through his beard. He sat down but leaned towards her. "Since we last talked, many things have changed. I know how to get rid of the curse."

"That's great. But how? Did you get someone to move in?" For some reason, this thought made her feel cold, although she was sitting close to the fire. She wiggled her toes in their thick, woollen socks.

"That's just it!" Wes reached out to pet their family cat, who arched her back and twirled around his boots. "Remember the prophecy? I initially thought that flaming dragon meant that you had to move the inn."

"After she moves *inn*," Flora said, frowning. "I don't like that. It's not exactly grammatical."

"But you did. You moved it, just a little bit." He grinned at her and she noticed that his eyes were almost the colour of her Heart of the Vale mixture at the point where she added her magic, a purple-brown. The exact shade was hard to pin down.

"No curse," she said softly.

"But the curse isn't–"

"Do you want to join us for dinner?" Tubs asked from the

226

doorway, looking back and forth between them. "Sorry to interrupt, but Roseneath's stew waits for no one."

Wes nodded. "Yes. I'd love to, thank you."

After a few moments of chair shuffling, so that there was room for Wes at the table—then more shuffling so that Hedric could sit next to him—they were all sitting comfortably. Flora eyed Wes. He certainly looked like a load had been taken off him.

"So, you make barrels?" Wes asked, dipping his spoon into the bowl of stew that was set in front of him and looking up at her parents. "Is it a profitable trade?"

Flora wondered if he'd like the simple, but tasty, fare. She broke off a large hunk of the sourdough bread her mother had pulled from the oven an hour ago. Now, *this* was magical. Not for the first time, she wondered if her mother had a touch of ability.

"And pails," Tubs answered, reaching for a bottle on the high shelf. "We've got the best barrels and pails from here to Turtle Bay. We do all right for ourselves. Mountain mead?"

"Yes, please."

"How do you two know each other?" Her father asked, almost as if they'd all planned to find out why Weslin was here. But Wes just smiled comfortably.

"You may know of the old Faerton Alehouse? Or you may not be old enough? We met there. My mother used to run it but it's been empty for a long time."

Tubs nodded. "Ah yes, I remember it from when I was knee high to a pixie. It's out near Lake Chalice. Used to be a great spot in the right season."

"I've been trying to do it up a bit."

Roseneath was leaning forward in her chair, looking intently at Wes. Her ogre heritage made her an imposing figure, but her ready smile softened her appearance. "For dessert," she said, "we've got scones with medlar jelly. And a drink of Heart of the Vale, of course."

"Heart of the Vale? I didn't know we had anyone here in the vale who could make it. It's been years since I've had one."

"It's Flora's specialty." There was a hint of pride in her mother's voice.

"She does make the very best. It's just a hobby, of course," Tubs added, quickly. "Magical stuff will never beat good old hard work."

Wes turned to look at her with those dark eyes. Flora let her hair fall over her face in case it was showing any impractical thoughts. When she'd finished her dinner, she ducked into the little kitchen and melted the chocolate in her cauldron, adding a little cream and the spices that she had long ago sworn to keep secret. She tasted it, then added a little more of everything, to make sure there was enough for their extra guest. She stirred it with a wooden spoon, pouring her magic in slowly, gradually. Drawing on the aether to pull in comfort and life, she swirled the dark mixture until it was brimming with comfort and heal- ing. She heated the cups, giving warmth from her hands.

"Here you are." She placed a flagon in front of each guest, then leaned back in her own chair, reciting the customary words of the guild members, her heart swelling with pride at her creation.

Hale and heart,
Bless the sweet art
They clinked their mugs together.

Wes took a long drink. After a moment, he held up his cup. "A hobby, you say? This is as good as any I've had."

Roseneath smiled, but her eyes flicked to her daughter, uneasy. "We do support her making it but she's busy enough as it is."

"A good hobby," Tubs said, nodding. "But you couldn't

make a business out of it. It's not something people need every day."

"Aren't I lucky?" Stef commented after a while, lifting and lowering his leg, slowly. "This knee's been stiff since the start of autumn. And see? It's moving like a mermaid in water now."

Flora felt a warm glow as she watched the small group enjoy the benefits of the drink she had made.

After dinner, her father said, "Show him the barrels, love."

Flora rolled her eyes. "He doesn't need—"

"Nonsense. Barrels put all this food on the table."

"I'd love to see your barrels," Wes said, with a look that made the heat flash into her cheeks.

After putting on her cloak, Flora went out the side door out to the workshop. It had the familiar mistle oak smell of the timber they worked with, mixed with the smoky, sweet tang of the honeypine they burned to forge the iron bands.

"These are the half-finished ones."

Wes followed her around, asking questions about the process. Flora moved the barrels around, lifting them easily. She laughed when Wes tried to move one, but almost fell over it.

"I'll just admire them from afar," he said.

"And these ones are all done. My pa will take them to Capital City."

Wes was quiet, but Flora was getting more and more frustrated. It was obvious there was another reason for the visit.

"All right. Out with it." She went up the step and back into the warm house, but paused in the doorway, with her hands on her hips. "What are you doing here, Master Moongrove? No one's seen you for years. And now you've turned up at my house?"

From her vantage point two steps up, their eyes were at the same height. The others were singing a loud rendition of *When I*

Danced on Lantern Night in the sitting room. Hedric was eating another scone.

"You did the same thing to me, not so long ago," he said, then spread his hands. "I apologise, Flora. I asked around town where the Coopfords lived, because I need to talk to you. I must break the curse and I think you are the key." Wes ran his fingers over his short beard. "I wondered if you might help. What did the dragon tell you?"

Flora paused.

"A house needs a hearth, and a hearth needs a home," chirped Hedric from the table behind them, looking down at his plate.

"Did it now?" Wes asked, rubbing his chin, thoughtfully.

"Yes," Flora said, surprised that Hedric remembered. "But it doesn't mean anything, really." She went inside and sat down in the kitchen chair.

"Wait a minute." Wes paced up and down the little kitchen. "You can't discount prophecies. Let's think about this," he said, seemingly having a conversation with himself. "But I haven't fully completed my quest. Because the inn doesn't belong to me yet."

Flora blinked. "Quest?"

"Walk with me, if you will?" Wes gestured to the front door.

She nodded. "We're going for a short stroll," she called to the others, who exchanged significant looks. She knew they must be burning with curiosity.

"I'm coming, too," Hedric called, scraping the chair legs as he got down from the table and trotted to the door. Flora knew better than to tell him not to come. She waited for him to put on his cloak, hat, and boots, before opening the door to the chill.

Faerton was putting on its best show. The mountains behind the town were iced in white. Lights glowed in the honeypine trees. Snow-dusted roofs made the houses look like sugared candies. People had hung bright wooden ornaments in their windows and golden ribbons streamed between lamp-posts and fluttered from the upper floors of buildings. They walked through town and stopped beside the closest of the three bonfires in the square.

Hedric stopped too, standing calmly for once, hushed by the leaping flames. His eyes were as round as the two moons in the sky behind them. Flora put out her arm to him, drawing him gently to her.

"I was so disappointed when I realized that I was still cursed," Wes said, staring at the fire. "And I couldn't even drown my sorrows as the wine glasses were all broken. Then it hit me. Your purpose. I saw you bond with the inn, remember?"

She nodded. "That was a surprise. As soon as I saw it, I knew it wanted to tell me something. It did seem very similar to what other witches say it feels like to bond with a familiar, like a cat or crow. But who bonds with an inn?"

Wes shrugged. "But that familiar bond goes both ways, apparently. The windows are firmly stuck shut. They will not open, although there's no paint sticking them closed. It's like a toddler having a tantrum."

"Oh, dear," she said.

"Listen, what if 'hearth' means a hearth witch? A hearth witch needs their own home? And the inn needs its hearth witch, I'm sure of it."

"But you didn't know about that before you came," she argued, somewhat lamely.

"You're right. But I felt that you were important as soon as I met you. And there's something else. One of my powers is finding the spark in others," said Wes, turning to look at her, "recognising and nurturing inspiration. I don't often use it. It's been many years since I've done so."

Flora warmed her hands in front of the fire. "Everybody says you went missing for years. They say—"

"I know what they say. I'm the son of the maire. When I was cursed, I felt like I was letting everyone down. If I went to a town meeting, the speaker's papers would fly away in the wind. Horses that were tied up would break free and get into the apple stand. Everything turned into a jumbled-up mess. In the end, I shut myself away. It was simpler."

"Who cursed you?" Flora asked.

Wes took a deep breath. "I'm not sure if you're familiar with The Last Will and Testament of any elves? They're . . . different. If you are bequeathed something, there's always a catch somewhere."

Flora gasped. Although her parents were stuck in their ways, she was sure they'd always support her. "Your mother left you the inn and added a dollop of curse on the side?"

"I've asked my father why. Apparently, elven notaries encourage people to think about what the person they're giving the object to needs to do. Once they achieve that, they receive their inheritance."

"It's my personal quest, if you will. It was never specified exactly what I had to do, but it was enchanted into the contract. I'm sure that my mother never thought I'd take so long to do it. She probably thought it would take me a month or two. But there were many clues. She loved puzzles."

He turned to her. "It would make sense if my mother wanted me to inspire someone. She always got such joy from me using it to help people when I was young. Now that I've seen your talent for making Heart of the Vale, I think my mother wanted me to find your spark. I saw you really shine tonight," Wes said, "and before you say anything, it was not when you were showing me the flaming barrels."

"Flaming barrels," Hedric echoed.

Flora laughed despite herself. She remembered the first time she had made Heart of the Vale without any assistance in the guild. Her mentor had told her then that her gift would heal many hearts. Flora's own had filled up to bursting in that moment, as if her chest were being water-tested like one of their new barrels.

"Come on, love." As Flora turned to walk back through the square, the beginnings of a tiny flame that had long been smothered began to warm her chest, even in the cold. She felt the truth of Weslin's words as if they were tattooed on her skin. She was meant to practise magic.

It wasn't until they got back to the house that Wes spoke again. He paused outside the open door, while Hedric ran inside, stomping snow onto the floorboards.

"I'd like to ask you a question. Please think carefully about it," Wes said, opening the door for her. "Would you like to serve Heart of the Vale at my inn?"

That was a very large question. But as soon as the words were out of his mouth, she knew that it was what she wanted. More than that, she knew that it was what the inn wanted.

But it paid to be careful with elvish bargains. "What are the conditions? That I supply free barrels for the ale? That I pay you a portion of the profits? What?"

"None of those," he replied. "Only that you fulfil your dream and your purpose. Let's try it out for six months."

"Why do you keep using that word? Purpose?"

"Because I'm here to find that one thing that brings colour to your vision and breath to your lungs. But I need your help. I can't fully claim the inn until you do your part."

"Would you be living there too, then?"

Wes shook his head, "My father has asked me to go to Capital City to meet with their maire. He wants me to grow up a little once the curse is gone. Step into his shoes."

It would be a long journey, probably ten days' ride. "I'll make a jar of Heart of the Vale for you to take," she said.

The sides of his mouth turned up, but he just said, "I'd like that. So, what do you say? It's entirely up to you. If you say no, I'll not ask again."

Flora didn't say anything. Her eyes flicked to the pestle and mortar on the shelf. Her mind was already spinning, thinking of how she could tweak the recipe for a unique twist and how she could make her vision of the inn come to life.

IT WASN'T UNTIL THE NEXT NIGHT THAT FLORA JOINED HER PARENTS IN the sitting room. The lanterns had floated off into the sky above the square for their Lantern Night celebrations. Hedric had gone to bed, tired but happy, and the cat was sprawled over Roseneath's knee.

Flora sat down. "You know how Lantern Night is a time of new beginnings?" she said, voice hesitant but growing stronger, "I'm going to make a new start, serving Heart of the Vale at Weslin's inn."

Her father opened his mouth, doubtless to say that it wasn't really practical.

Roseneath got in first. "When you first went off to the guild, I just knew that you'd be a happy pumpkin, working on your magic. But sometimes life gets in the way, love."

"We've got a perfectly good business here," her father agreed. "Nobody pays silvers for a dream."

Flora took a large breath. Sometimes, you had to find out what you didn't want to do, to find out what you *did* want to do. "I can't thank you both enough for supporting me and Hedric," she said, firmly. "Living here and working with the family business was exactly what I needed when I arrived here. But as someone wise once said to me, a hearth witch needs a home of her own. Barrels will never make my heart sing."

She didn't add that she wasn't given much choice about it, after bonding with an inn that was both bossy and stubborn.

Roseneath let out a sigh. "'Tis plain to see that making Heart of the Vale is your calling," she said. "We'll get an apprentice. We'll manage without you, won't we, Tubs?"

Her father made a grunting noise as something sharp jabbed him in the ribs.

Flora smiled gratefully at her mother's unexpected support and turned to her father. "Pa, I've learnt a lot from you about business. I'd never be able to try this if I hadn't worked in the workshop."

"It's only that we're worried about you, Flora," said Tubs. "And the lad, too. Are you sure this is a good idea?"

"I'm sure I can make this work," she said. "The inn used to be a thriving business, didn't it? It can be once again. People will come to the lake in the summer and I can sell Heart of the Vale in winter."

"Who made the new deal with the blacksmith?" cut in Roseneath. "She can do this."

"It was Flora. I'll give her that."

Her mother nodded. "You've got the talent, Flora. Go. We'll be here if you need us."

Flora didn't need to be asked twice. She felt that word pulsing in her veins as she began making plans. Purpose.

A FEW DAYS LATER, FLORA ARRIVED BACK AT THE EDGE OF THE FIELD, looking at the snow-covered inn. Hedric popped his head up out of the half-barrel in the family cart. She held tight to the horse's leading rope and let a smile creep across her face as she felt the inn call her home.

The snow lay chill around her, but the air was crisp with possibility.

K M JACKWAYS IS AN AUTHOR AND MOTHER OF TWO FROM NEW Zealand. She has been publishing weird and witchy stories with characters who struggle and succeed since 2020. Her short fiction has appeared in places like takahē and The Best Small Fictions. You can find updates on books featuring Flora, Hedric, and Wes at www.kimjackways.com or on Facebook at https://facebook.com/kmjackways.

A Dress with Pockets
G Clatworthy

Perched at the northernmost tip of the queendom, Juniper Vale is a hub of trade, much like Turtle Bay to the south. Additionally, this vale borders not one but two other lands, the Republic of Wistram and the Celestial Clouds kingdom.

This confluence of geography has elevated Juniper Vale into one of the biggest jewels in the queendom's crown. A sizable amount of mercantile goods flow through Juniper Vale, but so do people, information, and exotic items.

The large trading town—practically a city—of Oasis nestles up against the northern mountain range separating Juniper Vale from Wistram and Celestial Clouds. A large and heavily travelled road—well maintained by the vale and regularly patrolled by the royal guard—connects Oasis to the rest of the queendom.

—Intara's Guide to Cozy Vales

"I s there anything else I can help you with?" Crimson asked as she tied off the beige string with a twist. Her small hands made quick work of the knot, and she kept her rainbow flecked eyes averted as Guilder Senda, her mentor, had taught her. No one trusted a teg, and while Crimson didn't have the wings of her mother's species, her eyes shared her ancestry clearer than a badge pinned to her apron.

Rochella, the dwarvish ATOZ trading company representative, took the package and handed over a bag of coins. The dwarf smiled up at the young woman. "Everything's here. A pleasure doing business with you." She paused. "Unless . . ."

"Yes?"

"Do you have anything new? Our clients in the capital are always looking for new trends, especially for their Lantern Night festivities."

New. That wasn't what Senda's Emporium was known for. Crimson met the dwarf's gaze. "Only what's in the shop."

Disappointment flashed over the ATOZ representative's face.

"Except . . ." Crimson bit her lip. "I've been working on something."

"Well, get on with it. You're not my only stop today."

"Sorry." Crimson pulled back the screen that divided the shop front from the workshop at the back, the place where creations in glorious fabric came to life through hard work, blood, sweat, and tears. All at the same time. "This is a new design."

Rochella cocked her head to one side and studied the dress adorning the mannequin. She plucked at the bright fabric, then frowned. "What's that?"

"Pockets. You can put things in them instead of needing to carry a separate bag."

238

The representative sucked on her lip. "Well, it's certainly different."

Crimson's heart plummeted to her striped socks. What had she been thinking? Of course, a seasoned representative of the largest trade organisation in the queendom wouldn't be interested in her dress. She was just an apprentice for now, anyway. Crimson hugged her arms around her midriff, making herself smaller as she waited for the inevitable 'No.'

"All right. I'll take it. It's new enough, and I like the idea of these pockets. I've heard of them before but not seen them in this vale. Same price as the regular stock?"

Crimson nodded, lightheaded at the dwarf's decision.

"Come on, then. I've got to get on, and the market's causing havoc with the roads."

"Yes, of course, yes." Crimson unlaced the dress and wrapped it in the tan paper that was Senda's trademark while Rochella counted out the coins.

As the ATOZ representative left, Crimson did a twirl of joy. She had sold her first dress. Twirling wasn't enough. She broke into an impromptu jig just as Namu, the other apprentice and her mentor's son, walked in.

"What's this about, Sonny? Have you finally started dancing with the mice? They're about the right height for you." He joined in her dance with an amused tilt to his lips.

Crimson laughed, ignoring the standard jibe at her height; Namu wasn't tall, and she barely came up to his shoulder. She clapped her hands together. "I sold my first dress!"

"That's fantastic! Which one?"

"The one with pockets."

"I never would have thought that would sell. But this is why we'll make a great team. You out back doing the sewing with that cunning teggish eye for detail you have and me in the shop selling."

Crimson smiled. Once they were both guild members, they could start making their plans a reality and branch out from Guilder Senda's traditional designs. She longed for the freedom to follow her heart. Maybe she'd put pockets on all her dresses. Once she had a stake in the shop with Namu, maybe she'd finally feel that she belonged here instead of being just a charity case; an orphan taken in by a respected guilder.

Namu's forehead creased. "Wait a moment, wasn't that your Lantern Night offering? What are you going to show the guild?"

All celebration fled from her mind. "Stitches! How could I be so stupid?" Crimson screwed her eyes shut, grinding the heels of her palms into them to prevent the hot tears from flowing.

"Hey, stop that." Namu took her in his arms and tucked a stray strand of reddish-brown hair behind her ear. Crimson stopped breathing. "The presentation's not for a week. You've got time to make another one and I know you can stitch like a demon when you need to. Remember the rush order for Lady Snootypants last summer?"

Crimson let out a laugh at their shared nickname for one of the more demanding customers they worked with.

"I'll have to beg some fabric off Guilder Senda . . ."

THAT EVENING, ALL THREE OF THE SENDA FAMILY, PLUS CRIMSON, their orphan apprentice, sat around the kitchen table in front of a roaring stove, ready for dinner. The shop had longer hours during the Winter's Tide season to take advantage of the holiday shoppers, and Crimson stretched out her feet under the table, enjoying the warmth of the fire after a long day behind the counter.

Marie, Guilder Senda's wife, dished out a hearty winter

stew while Senda poured them all a glass of ruby red wine. He was careful to give the apprentices a smaller measure, and Crimson didn't say anything when he added an extra glug to his son, Namu's, glass.

"Crimson sold her first dress today." Namu raised his glass, a huge smile on his face.

"Nonsense. She's sold clothing here in the shop for years." Senda continued cutting his meat.

Crimson shot Namu a smile. It was nice that he'd tried to share her success and get some rare words of praise from his dad—her mentor—but it was more likely that the sky would turn green.

"No, she sold one of her own designs," Namu persisted.

This caught Senda's interest. He leaned back in his chair and gave Crimson a level gaze. "Did she now?"

Crimson forced herself not to squirm. She nodded.

"And what dress did you sell?"

"The one with pockets," Crimson said, lowering her eyes. Her voice was barely louder than a whisper, but he still heard.

Senda banged his palm on the table. "Are you mad? Have you gone quite insane?"

"Dear . . ." Marie cautioned her husband.

"I'm sorry, Guilder Senda," Crimson said.

"No, really. I want to know what on earth possessed you to do such a thing."

"Rochella said she wanted something new . . ."

"And you thought that you would just give her your dress with pockets? I knew we should have delayed your guild offering for another year. I've said it before and I'll say it again, you can't trust a teg—"

Crimson hung her head. Try as she might, she always let her mentor down, whether it was experimenting with a new pattern or doing something stupid like selling her Lantern

Night offering. It was as if her entire being conspired against her fitting in with Guilder Senda's family.

"Senda." Marie's tone was sharper.

Her husband took a breath, and when he next spoke, his voice held the controlled tones of a teacher running through their lessons. "Where do we make the most profit in this business?"

"Accessories," Crimson mumbled.

"Pardon?"

"Accessories," she repeated.

"Accessories. Exactly. Accessories like bags, where our margin is . . ." Senda snapped his fingers.

"Fifty percent," Crimson said, her head bowed with shame. The profit for each item was burned into her brain from years of lectures about wastage and pricing.

"Correct. Compared to our clothing, where the average margin is only twenty percent on everyday wear. So, what do you think will happen to our profits when people don't need bags, when they can carry around everything they might need in *pockets*?" He spat out the word.

Crimson hung her head. "Sorry, I just thought–"

"No. You didn't think. Typical teg behaviour, never thinking about consequences. Just like your mother. And worse than that, you've sold something that wasn't in our range for this season. Now people are going to associate your novelty dress with this store. You've tarnished my reputation."

She gulped, her mouth dry.

Senda took a deep drink of his wine and drummed his fingers on the table. His hand stopped moving. "What are you presenting to the guild? That was your offering, wasn't it? Or have you decided you're too good for the guild, as well as my name?"

Crimson cringed. Senda had been kind to take her in as a

child and apprentice her to his business, but was it so bad that she wanted to keep her mother's surname? Brouderer wasn't a teggish name, as far as she knew, and all she had of her past was her last name, a few blurry memories of smiles, iridescent wings, and a sewing box. Sometimes it seemed like she'd have to change every part of herself to belong here in Senda's shop.

"Senda!" Marie snapped. "That's enough. It's done. She didn't want to sabotage you. She's sorry, that's clear from the poor girl's face."

"Hmph. And you, Namu? I trust you haven't gone mad and sold your guild presentation, too?"

"No, Dad." Namu shot Crimson a look of sympathy.

"At least I can rely on my son to uphold our family name. I have high hopes for you, my boy. Thank the Artisan that I have someone I can trust with my business and my legacy. You'll make a fine guilder."

Namu stared down at his food.

"Senda! Enough!" Marie banged her hand on the table, and Senda huffed but said nothing more.

They ate the rest of the meal in silence, and Crimson slunk up to bed straight after, shame at her own stupidity and pride filling her.

Namu would never do anything like this. Maybe it was her teg side rebelling against the rules; they were well known for being tricksters and living outside normal society. Guilder Senda had told her that enough times. She'd have to work harder to quash her instincts if she wanted to fit in and become successful here in Juniper Vale. If only there was a way to get the dress back. She turned and plumped up the pillow before burying her head in the downy softness. It took her a long time to fall asleep that night.

The next morning was her weekly trip to the market. She

half thought that Senda wouldn't let her go, but he was nowhere to be seen when she crept downstairs.

Marie bustled around the kitchen, heating a kettle of water on the stove for the morning tea. She placed a steaming bowl of thick porridge on the table and motioned for Crimson to sit.

Crimson slipped into the chair, head down, making herself as small as possible as she spooned amber honey onto her breakfast. There was something about the contrast of the golden colour against the greyish white of the porridge that lightened her soul before she swirled it in.

"We need more of the herringbone if you can get it, and red and green are always popular colours for this time of year."

"Mistress Marie . . ."

"Just Marie, as you well know. You don't need to butter me up like a piece of toast." Marie joined her at the table.

Crimson took a deep breath. "I need more fabric for a dress. I'll pay you back–"

"Nonsense. We provide for our apprentices, and didn't you get money for your sale?"

"I put it in the till."

"Well, then." Marie marched over to the money box and retrieved a large handful of coins. "Here, you can use this to cover your fabric as well as what we need for the shop. You have the best eye for colour. Must be the teg half of you. Do you want Namu to help with the carrying? He's asleep, but he should be down soon."

Crimson shook her head as she finished her porridge. She loved her buying trips, and the Winter's Tide Market was in full swing this close to Lantern Night.

"Take this for The Thicket. We need to make sure we show enough thanks to make sure the little dears continue to choose to stay in Oasis." Marie handed her a small box of candied fruits. "They're responsible for good fortune here in the town, you know."

"As you say." Crimson smiled at Marie's superstition, commonly held by Oasis' residents, and raced out into the freezing streets.

THE SMELL OF BAKING BREAD MIXED WITH THE FRESH AIR AS CRIMSON paused at the large collection of oak trees that made up The Thicket neighbourhood near the centre of Oasis. Each huge tree trunk sported around a dozen small, carved doors, many decorated with tiny but elaborate wreaths during the holiday season.

Crimson laid her offering on the table set up for the purpose. Everyone in Oasis made sure their smaller neighbours were well cared for during the cold winters. A tiny sprite waved thank you as he strung a garland of painted acorns among the lower branches.

Crimson hurried on to the main square that held the market. At this time of year, it was larger than usual as traders crowded the streets hoping for sales in the run up to Lantern Night.

"Books for every occasion," a dumpy man with a thick beard called out. "Roll up to Dewey's library and as a special Lantern Night treat, we've got some books for sale too."

She paused at the travelling Exchange library parked up on the outskirts of the market and already open for the day. The Exchanges were sponsored by Queen Liana herself and well-known for their comprehensive collections of books, of both the magical and ordinary varieties. Two unicorns grazed beside the enormous curved wooden cart, ignoring their feed, and nibbling on the weeds that sprouted between the cobblestones.

It was tempting to pop inside, especially when the cheery librarian gave her a wave.

"Any fantasy books?" Crimson asked, unable to stop herself.

"A shelf-full. What's your poison?"

Crimson shook her head. What was she thinking? She didn't have time to read. She had to get back to the shop and make a dress fit for the guild in a week. But she hadn't yet found a Lantern Night present for Marie. "What's your best-selling murder mystery?"

He showed her a selection of books for sale, and Crimson picked the one with a knife on the cover. The more murder the better, in Marie's view. Only in books, of course.

"We're here until after Lantern Night if you want anything else. There's always time for a book." The librarian turned to hail another potential customer. Crimson continued into the main thoroughfares of the sprawling market.

For the Winter's Tide Market, the usual tables had been replaced with sturdy stalls in the shape of small houses, complete with pitched roofs. A sprinkling of snow coated the tops of the stands, and Crimson tugged her cloak closer against the cold.

She passed the stalls of twinkling lanterns decorated with stars and planets, some of them glowing with coloured magical candles to show off their patterns. Shoppers stopped, enchanted by the sparkling colours which would be even more beautiful when dusk fell, seeming to hold the very magic of Lantern Night in their glistening orbs.

Other traders sold gifts, and the zesty scent of orange and cinnamon tugged at Crimson's stomach as she passed a stall selling Lantern Night wreaths made of dried fruits next to one offering sweet fudge. There was a tray of samples at that stall, and Crimson couldn't resist. With a smile, she took a small corner piece and salivated at the buttery sweetness of the caramel fudge, making a note to come back later if she had time. These gift stalls wouldn't sell out, but if she was late to the fabric stalls, she'd have less to choose from.

There weren't many customers in the streets this early, and those that were about scurried to work, perhaps pausing to purchase a pastry on the way. The shoppers who came for trinkets and gifts would come later in the day. The warm, chocolatey aroma of Heart of the Vale–the special drink that only members of the Tasters' Guild could perfect–filled the air as she passed a stall selling the coveted brew, and she took in a deep breath as she felt all her cares melt away for a short time.

A shout came from the end of the street where two guards argued with a carter who tried to drive his vehicle through the market.

Despite the porridge filling her belly, she slowed as she passed the bakers' stalls selling crumbling pastries in all flavours and crusty bread. She waved to her friend, Ayla. The elf had a rosy flush to her face from the cold, and her pointed ears were tucked into a knitted hat as she served customers. Crimson caught sight of Rochella buying a chunky pie from Ayla's stall. If she could convince the dwarf to give her back the dress, she would have time to get a fantasy book after all.

Crimson pasted a bright smile on her face and stepped up beside Rochella. "Lovely morning."

The dwarf smiled and nodded as she paid, then turned to go.

Crimson took a deep breath, determined not to let this opportunity pass. "I don't know if you remember, but I sold you a dress yesterday."

"I buy a lot of stock round here."

"It had pockets . . ."

"Oh yes, I'll let you know if we want more. Now, I've got breakfast to eat." She licked her lips.

"No, I need it back. Please, I'll refund you." Crimson's hand went to her money purse, which hung from her belt.

The dwarf's eyes narrowed. "That's not how we do business."

"But I need it. It was a mistake; I should never have sold it."

"Here's some advice for you; if you don't want someone to buy something from you, don't offer to sell it to them. You've made the sale now. We were both happy with the price. The deal is done. Now, I'd like to eat before this goes cold." With that, Rochella stomped off about her business.

"What was that about?"

Crimson looked up into her friend Ayla's perfect elvish face. She sighed. "Nothing."

"Didn't look like nothing. Do you want me to give her a burned pie next time she comes?"

Crimson laughed. "No, it's all right. I made a mistake. How's business?"

"Good. Dad let me expand into Lantern Night cakes. Want one?"

"I've got to get to the fabric stalls." Regret filled Crimson's face. Ayla's baking was so good, it had transformed their small bakery into a mainstay of Oasis, and they'd moved to a more central location last year, just opposite the Moonlit Mug Café.

"Here, take one for later, before they all go." Ayla had the easy confidence of someone who knew her stock would be gone before mid-morning.

"Thanks." Crimson rummaged in her purse.

"On the house for my best friend."

"I don't know how you make so much when you give things away for free."

Ayla shrugged. "Maybe it's an elf thing. When you live for so long, you learn that friendships are more important than money."

"You're not that much older than me . . . are you?"

Ayla winked, avoiding the question as always. "But I will live for hundreds of years. Automatic wisdom."

"I'm not sure that's how it works . . ." Crimson trailed off as a group of customers surrounded the stall–apprentice blacksmiths from the look of the sturdy leather aprons wrapped over their shirts.

Her friend switched to sales mode in an instant, and Crimson waved goodbye, placed the wrapped cake in her bag, and headed for the fabric merchants.

She walked down the row, her eyes picking out the fabrics that she needed with practised ease, making her plan. She was a familiar face in this part of the market and returned the greetings of the cloth merchants with relish. They shared her love of fabrics, the subtle differences between shades of colours that others would simply call green, the twist and twill of the weave, the feel of the cloth between her fingers as she considered which material would drape better for a particular garment.

There were two traders who she did the most business with. The first had the herringbone fabric that Marie had asked for. After some bargaining, Crimson arranged for the entire bolt to be delivered to the shop later that day. It was a sound investment. Senda loved the subtle interplay of the pine green against the off-white in the distinctive pattern. It made for sophisticated clothing for both men and women and matched the small sample she had with her perfectly. Crimson also chose a length of plain linen in a weak tea colour that was perfect for undershirts and simple nightwear, always best sellers.

Satisfied with the practical purchases, Crimson headed for her second trader of choice: Bright, a kobold with the best fabrics in the market.

"I need some more of the blue, the one the same colour as evening just after dusk, please."

Bright's eyes gleamed, and the small kobold sifted through the thick bolts of fabric. "I know just the shade you mean. Here."

"Fourteen feet, please. No, better make it sixteen."

"Of course, and anything else?"

Crimson allowed herself time to peruse the fabrics. Bright prided herself on the very best quality and had some lovely pieces. Crimson allowed her fingers to trail over the velvets, soft as rabbits' fur, and shimmering silks that slipped through her hands as if they were water. She had the material she needed to remake the dress, so this was an indulgence.

Marie gave her a small allowance for these wild purchases, trusting Crimson to select quality fabrics for the small number of luxury garments and accessories they sold. She picked out holly berry reds and deep greens that reminded her of mistletoe, perfect for the season.

A bright yellow caught her eye. Although that was too tame a description for the vibrancy of the fabric half hidden under a heap of bolts. It was sunshine yellow with a hint of golden shimmer as Crimson pulled it from its hiding place.

"Ah, saffron sunshine. It's a bold choice."

"It's beautiful." Crimson tilted the fabric, studying the nap and weave as she felt the weight of it. The same weight as the material she'd bought for her dress. Just looking at the colour brought a smile to her face. "How much is it?"

"For you," the kobold tilted her head, "a silver for the lot."

"A silver?"

"I bought it in Saffron Vale and haven't been able to shift it. Glad I only bought a small roll of the stuff. Doesn't seem to do so well. It's too bold for most folks."

She shouldn't. It was too much. Too vibrant. It didn't belong in the tradition of Senda's Emporium. And yet . . . she had to have it, even if it didn't fit in.

"Are you sure?"

"You'd be doing me a favour. Do you want it on the roll?"

"Folded, please. And separate from the rest." She could imagine what her mentor would say if she walked home carrying a roll of this gorgeous sunshine over her shoulder. Better to hide it in her bag until she could figure out what to use it for.

A fleeting thought crossed Crimson's mind that she shouldn't have to hide something that made her happy, but she pushed that away. She had to focus on getting into the guild. And that meant making sure her mentor was happy to sponsor her, not following her heart.

With her purchases for the morning done, Crimson hurried back to the shop.

"DO YOU WANT ME TO CLEAR YOU A SPACE IN THE WORKROOM?" MARIE asked as she tidied up her sewing pins, the workday finished.

"No, I don't want to cause any trouble. I'll work upstairs," Crimson replied, eager to get on with remaking her dress. "Are you sure you don't want me to sweep?"

"Away with you. I've handled a brush since before you were born." Marie shooed her out with the broom, and Crimson giggled as she headed up the stairs.

In her room, she swept the floor and laid out the blue fabric. It was brighter than the fashionable navy blue, more of a berry colour, but it was full of promise. Crimson took her time laying the pre-cut pattern pieces on the fabric, making sure the nap flowed in the same direction.

A dangerous idea said that she could deliberately cut it so the nap went in the opposite direction to create subtle stripes, but she squashed that thought down. When she was a guilder,

251

there would be plenty of time for experimentation. Until then, she had to fit in with Guilder Senda's expectations and quell the creative voice that got her into trouble. She needed his sponsorship to get into the guild. No one else would back a teg, not even a half teg, as Senda had told her over and over.

She retrieved her mother's sewing box and opened it up. Inside were all her tools; the specially sharpened fabric scissors, pins of all sizes gleaming in the soft candlelight, spools of threads organised like a rainbow. Crimson ran her fingers over the threads, passing over her mother's favourite green and tracing the blues that ranged from navy to duck egg.

The possibilities spread out before her as she selected her thread. It was tempting to go for a contrast colour, but for today, she would stick to tried and tested methods so as not to antagonise her mentor. Perhaps she would finish the cuffs and collar with embroidered edging in a different colour. If there was time. Stitches, she had so much to do.

Snapping out of her daydream, Crimson set to work pinning the pattern pieces together.

"WHAT DO YOU THINK?" CRIMSON FUSSED OVER HER DRESS, NOW hung on the display mannequin in the Guildhall alongside all the apprentices' Lantern Night offerings.

"It looks great. Only you would have thought of embroidering the cuffs in yellow with that blue. And only you could get away with it. Dad always said your mum could make a sack and people would buy it thanks to teggish cunning. Or was it because tegs can talk people into anything? Anyway, you've got a gift." Namu reached out and lifted a cuff to study it more closely. "Not that this looks like a sack."

"You don't think it looks rushed?" Crimson asked, ignoring

252

the pang at the insult to her mother; she was so used to the offhand comments, they almost didn't hurt anymore. She didn't know any tegs – they were rare in the queendom – but the widely held view was that they were trouble, and one should never bargain with them or trust them in any sort of exchange. She studied the embroidery. It *was* rushed. It had been a last-minute addition, her way to show some more skill and add some colour to the blue fabric.

"With that neat stitching? It looks great." Namu leaned in conspiratorially. "I don't know about you, but my stomach feels like two trolls are having a fight with my intestines. How can I be this nervous when it's not even presentation day?"

"It's because you care."

He raked his hand through his hair. "I do. It's all I want. If I don't get in . . . I can't even think about it. What would Dad say?"

"Guilder Senda would love you no matter what; he's your father."

"But if I let him down–"

"You're going to get in." Crimson cut off his doubts. "No one can deny your skill."

Namu smiled. "Nor yours. Only you would think of contrast embroidery on the cuffs. Only . . ."

"What?"

"Nothing. It looks great."

"Come on, if there's something wrong, tell me now."

"Nothing wrong, it just . . . it doesn't look like you."

"It's a dress." Crimson frowned. "How would it look like me?"

"I mean, it doesn't sparkle the way you sparkle. You have such a love for bright colours and a genius for putting them together. The embroidery is so subtle, it's like something Dad could have done, but it's not a piece with original Sonny flair.

Still, it's great, you'll do fine. I'm being silly. Better go, Dad looks like he's found a loose thread in my garment."

Crimson pursed her lips as she studied the dress. Namu was right. It was a safe piece, something that wouldn't look out of place in Senda's shop, except for the tiny flash of colour at the cuffs. It wasn't from her heart. And, clear as a pin, she knew she wanted the guild to accept the true, whole her, not the watered-down version of herself that Senda wanted. But what could she do now to show the guild who she was?

She rooted around in her bag for her portable sewing kit; maybe there was something in there that would give her inspiration. Crimson pulled out a piece of fabric and stared at it. It was the sunshine yellow material she couldn't stay away from at the market. She'd bought it because it was beautiful, for no other reason, but it matched the flashes of yellow on the cuff and there was just enough fabric. If she cut it carefully . . .

"Crimson, are you coming home with us?" Senda called from where he stood admiring his son's work.

"I'll be home soon. I just want to make some final adjustments."

Senda nodded, the barest glimmer of a smile tugging at his lips. "I was just like you at my first showing, worrying if I had done enough. I want you to make sure it's the best you can do; it's my reputation on the line, after all. Come on, Namu. We'll see you at home, Crimson."

On their way out, Namu gave her an encouraging smile. She grinned back, glad he'd said something, so she had the chance to show who Crimson Brouderer was and make her impact with the guild.

THE REVEALING OF APPRENTICE WORKS HAPPENED ON LANTERN NIGHT, an opportunity for guilders to study the clothing ahead of opening the doors to the public the next day. It was a calculated move to bring members of the town into the Guildhall, showcase their wares, and maybe set some new trends for the next year.

Crimson waved to apprentices she knew from past guild events and hurried over to join them by the food table. She took a drink of chilled lemonade and scanned the room. Guilder Senda worked his way through the crowd, greeting every guilder with a handshake and a smile. Crimson thanked the Artisan she was apprenticed to such a respected guilder. Ayla glided over.

"You look like someone stuck a pin in you."

"Thanks for your support, Ayla, so glad I invited you."

Namu appeared at Crimson's side and linked his arm through hers. "How are you feeling, Sonny?"

"Nervous. You?"

"Same. I heard they're only letting five people in this year. Did you stick with the original design?"

Crimson bit her lip and looked round. "I may have altered it last night."

"I admire how you stick to your style."

"I'm worried it's a bit much."

"How could they not love it?" Ayla asked, downing her drink.

Crimson smiled and helped herself to a sticky bun oozing with sweet honey icing, the midwinter spices filling her nose as she ate to calm her nerves.

Dean Tamworth, overseer of the Juniper Vale chapter of the Dressmakers' Guild, stepped up to the dais and clapped his hands for attention.

"Here comes the boredom for the night," Namu said.

Crimson choked on her bun and elbowed him in the stomach. Others nearby looked over at her with disapproval in their stares. Once she'd recovered, Namu left her to talk with his father as Tamworth droned on about the guild's history and reputation and welcomed some new apprentices to the guild. The fresh-faced twenty-somethings gathered close to their sponsors and shuffled nervously as all eyes turned to them, assessing them and wondering who would have what it took to become a fully-fledged member at a future Lantern Night presentation.

"But now, onto the main event for the evening. Those at the end of their apprenticeships have worked hard to produce their showpieces, designed to show both their tailoring skills and their design flair and I am sure they have all done their sponsors proud. After all, each of the apprentices' offerings here in Oasis will reflect not only on themselves but on their sponsors' reputations. We only have five spots open this year, so I encourage you all to study the designs well ahead of our guild vote for membership. Apprentices, to your places."

Crimson scurried over to stand behind her design, licking her sticky fingers to clean up the remains of the icing before she took a corner of the chestnut brown cloth in her hands. It was rough spun wool, coarse against her palm but also worn from the many previous apprentices who had undertaken the same ritual.

Her stomach swirled as she clutched the fabric, waiting for the dean's signal.

"Three, two, one. Reveal!"

She tugged at the cloth. It snagged on the mannequin before she managed to get it all the way off. A few gasps came from those closest to her. Crimson stood, screwing up her hands in the brown cloth as the crowd turned in her direction, drifting towards her as nudges and whispers travelled out from those nearest like ripples in a pond.

Guilder Senda strode over from his spot next to Namu, a forced smile stretching over his face. He hooked his hand into the crook of her arm and steered her behind the mannequin as the whispers rose in volume like the humming of hundreds of confused bees.

"What were you thinking?" Senda hissed through a strained smile.

"I–"

"Pockets! Again with the pockets! And that colour! Such a bright yellow against that beautiful blue. Why did you have to make it so obvious? Have I taught you nothing? You have to blend in to be successful." He drew his hand over his eyes.

Crimson stayed silent and kept her face towards the floor, her hands still winding the brown cloth. It had been a risk, but fashion took risks, and her dress was memorable at least, not like some of the other bland offerings that copied the latest plain styles and didn't innovate.

Senda inhaled and exhaled. "I'll have to withdraw it from consideration."

"What?" It was too much. Her design was unique, but it didn't warrant taking away the possibility of getting into the guild, the membership she had worked years for. "Please, Guilder Senda . . ."

"It's the only way. I cannot allow that," he shuddered, "*monstrosity* to be associated with my name. I cannot sponsor it for consideration. Why did you change it? Yesterday, it was perfect, something I was happy with."

"But I wasn't. It reflected you, not me," Crimson whispered, wondering how she dared say anything.

"Yes, it is a reflection on me. I have been too lenient with you. I have allowed you your fancies instead of telling you the truth of the world. People shun things that are different, people that are different, then they turn on them. You move too fast. You're too different."

"But—"

Senda dug into his pocket and pulled out a pair of fabric scissors. With a determined snip, he cut into the collar of her dress, ruining her neat stitching. "The decision is made. I will withdraw your offering from the ballot." He turned on his heels and strode off.

Crimson bit her knuckles, then ran outside, gasping in the frigid midwinter air. She sank to the ground, the frozen stone hard and cold through the skirts of her dress. Magical lanterns floated overhead from early releases, taking the hopes and wishes for the new year with them.

"Sonny?" Namu shouted for her.

"Over here," she croaked.

He joined her on the ground and placed an arm around her shoulders. "Quite a view you've got here." His tone was conversational, light-hearted.

"I'm imagining those lights are my dreams, floating away."

"Oh, Sonny, I'm so sorry."

Crimson wiped away a hot tear. "It's not your fault," she mumbled against his shoulder. He was warm and solid. No matter what, she was lucky to have him in her life.

Namu squirmed in her arms. "I should never have talked you into adding those pockets."

"It was my decision."

"I am so sorry," he said again.

"Stop apologising for something you had no control over."

"I didn't think he'd withdraw your offering."

"It was up to him."

"Yeah, but," Namu pulled her closer. "I shouldn't have talked to Dad."

Crimson sniffed. "What do you mean?"

He shifted against her. "I may have said some stuff to Dad about his reputation when you revealed your dress . . . but I didn't think he'd go so far."

Crimson stiffened. Namu was the reason for Senda's reaction. He had taken away her dreams when he knew how much being part of the guild meant to her. Crimson broke free from his embrace and shoved herself to her feet, scrambling away from him. She couldn't talk to him, couldn't look at him. She needed to get away.

"Sonny." Namu tugged at her sleeve.

She stopped walking away and spun to face him. "You don't get to call me that."

"I messed up. I got scared when I found out they had fewer places this year, and you're so talented; you can do anything, go anywhere. But I need this. The shop is all I have."

"You want me out, too?" Was there no one who thought she belonged here?

"No! Look, I'll talk to Dad, and once I'm in, I can talk to the guild—"

"No. I don't need any more of your help. You've ruined my life. You know that, don't you? I mean, you do know you've cut my dreams to ribbons."

"No! That wasn't me. Dad—"

White hot anger flooded her body, and her hands trembled as she clenched them into fists. "All I wanted was to get into the guild. And now," she swallowed the lump in her throat, "now, I'm a laughingstock. There is no second chance for the Dressmakers' Guild, not without a sponsor, and who's going to sponsor a failed apprentice? You saw how they looked at me. You know how much sway your dad has in the guild. What am I going to do now?"

"I'm sorry, I just . . ." He raked his hand through his hair and huffed out a breath. "I knew you'd get one of the spots if I didn't do anything. And I had to get in. I couldn't risk it. You don't understand the pressure I'm under with the family business."

Crimson took a deep breath. "You know, I even thought we could work together in the future, shake up Senda's Emporium a bit, change some of the colour combinations, attract some new customers, just like we always talked about."

"Maybe we still can. I'll talk to Dad; you can still work at the shop."

"As what? A piece worker on piece rates? Or a shop girl ringing up the tills while you design?"

"If you want," he nodded eagerly, missing the venom in her words. "We can still be together, just like we always planned. Just like we wanted." Namu reached for her arm.

Crimson stepped away. "What I need is to get away from you."

Crimson turned and strode away, the anger giving way to tears which streamed down her cheeks, chilling her skin as the wind caught the moisture. Good. Her heart needed to freeze so she didn't go back and seek comfort in his arms.

"Sonny, please."

"Leave me alone." She sped up, pushing her way through the crowds that lined the main streets doing some late-night shopping for the festivities, until she found a quieter spot where she leaned against a wall, panting as sobs wracked her body. She felt as though the tears would carry her away on a tide of sorrow, wash her right through the streets and to the midden heap that sat on the outskirts of town.

A hand touched her shoulder, and she jumped, startled at the invasion of her private grief. Blinking away the tears, she looked up into the kindly face of Dewey, the dwarvish librarian she had met at the Winter's Tide Market. He handed her a handkerchief edged in embroidery.

She took it and dabbed at her eyes and nose, seeing her surroundings more clearly. She had wandered to the edge of the market, to the quiet street where the travelling library stood, unassuming and ready to serve books to those who needed them.

"Go on, girl, give it a proper blow."

Crimson cleared her nose. "Thank you."

"No problem. You keep it."

She gazed down at the dirty handkerchief in her palm. The bright fabric was poppy red with buttercup yellow embroidery in the shape of small flowers. "Did you make this yourself?"

"No. My sewing's limited to mending books and maybe a bit of leatherwork. My wife, Jarissa, did the embroidery."

"She's very talented."

"Aye, she is." He paused, then leaned against the wall next to her. "I know it's none of my business, but if you need someone to talk to, librarians are very good at listening."

Crimson sighed. How to explain to a stranger that her ordered life was now chaos, her once clear future was now a dirty puddle of confusion, and the person she'd believed she could trust had cut her dreams from her? "I don't feel I belong here anymore."

That was about the core of it. Without a clear path and unable to rely on her childhood partner in crime, she was lost in Juniper Vale. She had expected guild membership to bring acceptance of herself but instead she felt more disconnected from Senda's family than ever. And no one in Juniper Vale would sponsor a second attempt at guild membership while Guilder Senda had a vote, and she wasn't sure she could stand staying with someone who had betrayed her. But she had nowhere else to go.

The librarian thought on this for a long while, stroking his beard, and staring out over the bustling marketplace where a troupe of acrobats juggled oversized acorns. Crimson fidgeted with the handkerchief.

"Come with me," said Dewey, pushing himself up from the wall and heading for his caravan.

Crimson followed him, not knowing what else to do. At the library, he pulled out two folding chairs from a storage compartment concealed in the base of the cart and set them up under a canopy that jutted from the back of the library.

"Ma," he called to the inside of the caravan, "pour a cup of tea for our young guest. She's having a bad evening."

That was an understatement. Crimson tried to smile at the woman who bustled into view, a steaming cup of tea balanced in her hands. The male librarian patted the padded chair he had set up under the caravan's canopy and Crimson sank into it, accepting the cup and saucer with grateful hands.

She sipped the hot beverage, savouring its warmth and the spicy sweet taste of honey, lemon, and ginger.

"Something to eat?" the librarian's wife asked.

"Thank you, but there's really no need."

"Maybe not, but that's never stopped me," the woman said with a grin. She disappeared back inside and reappeared with a plate of warm biscuits cut in the holiday shapes of lanterns and stars. How big was the library inside that there was a stove as well as all the books? Maybe there was magic involved.

Crimson accepted a biscuit and watched as both librarians dipped theirs in the tea before taking a bite. She copied them, savouring the spiced biscuits and the sweet honey.

"This is really good."

The woman smiled at the compliment.

Pride beamed from the old man's face, and he reached over to squeeze his wife's hand. "My Jarissa makes the best Lantern Night biscuits on the road."

"Give over, Dewey," Jarissa said, but she smiled at the compliment.

There was so much love between them, it gave Crimson some hope. The world couldn't be so dark and empty of dreams if this couple could be so in love. As she thought that, lanterns climbed into the sky and a cheer sounded from the main square. The early lanterns swarmed the sky like a thousand enormous fireflies welcoming the new year.

Crimson looked away, unable to take in so much hope when hers were dashed. Instead, she studied the handkerchief. "Is this your embroidery?"

Jarissa smiled. "Aye. The roads are long, and I sew for a hobby."

"It's exquisite. Where did you get such vibrant thread?"

"Ah, I think I still have some." She got up and retreated inside the library.

Crimson wondered if she should make conversation, but Dewey seemed content to stare out at the sky where lanterns still bobbed among the stars, taking hopes for next year with them.

"Here we go." Jarissa pressed the spool of thread into Crimson's hand. Even in the dim light, the colour sang; a yellow so bright it was as if the summer sun or the dandelion flowers that grew in the alley by the shop sat in her hand.

"It's amazing."

"That's Saffron Vale for you. Home of the brightest colours in the queendom."

Crimson handed it back, but Jarissa pressed her hand closed around the thread. "A gift, for Lantern Night."

Crimson stammered her thanks and stared at the thread.

"What's that story, Ma, the one about that bird?"

"You'll have to be more specific, Pa." There was a hint of laughter in Jarissa's voice.

"The bird they caged but couldn't keep."

"Ah, the Firebird's Song."

"That's the one." The man settled back in his chair. "Tell it for us, will you?"

Jarissa nodded and began speaking in a singsong voice that pulled Crimson forward in her chair. "Once upon a time, there was a queen. She was a kind ruler who wanted the best for her queendom. One day she was walking in her garden when she heard the most beautiful singing. She followed the sound to a stream where she found a young firebird in a willow tree.

"She sat there for a time, listening to the sweet music, tears of joy running down her beautiful face. 'Oh, firebird,' she said, 'will you join me in my palace? I will give you every comfort and you can belong in my court.'

"Well, the firebird agreed, thinking that the comforts and privileges of the court was what she wanted. And so, she stepped into a cage of solid gold and sat upon a silken cushion and sang for the queen, her flames glowing bright in her happiness.

"But, as her days became monotonous, her song turned from one of joy to one of sadness and then the firebird found she could not sing at all, and her flames dulled. The queen was worried for the firebird and sent for the best healers in the land. But they could find nothing wrong with the bird. The queen then spoke to the small bird and asked her what ailed her."

"You'd think she'd ask the bird first before calling in the healers," Dewey said, shaking his head.

"Do you want me to tell the story?" Jarissa asked. Dewey reached for her hand, kissed it, and motioned for her to continue.

"The bird replied, 'I do not wish to be ungrateful, for you have given me everything I ever wanted; a comfortable life, a fabulous place to live, but I cannot sing here in the palace, for all my inspiration lies outside in the garden where I was free.'

"The queen smiled and unlocked the cage. 'Then go, little firebird, return to your home and live the life you choose. and maybe I shall hear your voice as I wander in the garden and know you are happy once more.'

"And the very next day as the queen walked in the garden, she heard the joyous song of the firebird and spotted a flash of magical fiery plumage among the willow branches."

Dewey took a long sip of his tea as his wife brought the story to a close. "It's a metaphor, of course, that what we might want isn't always what we need."

"No need to labour the point, Pa."

"You should read the story; it's much better written down." Dewey walked the couple of steps into the library and returned with a slim volume of tales from across the queendom. "Here, you can borrow this until we leave. Now, if you've finished your tea, I'll walk you home."

"May your lantern last through the night," Jarissa said as they left.

"And may your light shine bright," Crimson replied with the standard holiday greeting, clutching the book to her chest.

As they wound through the streets back to Senda's Emporium, Crimson found her mind couldn't contain her swirling thoughts.

"If there's anything we can do, you find us at the market. We're here 'til the third morrow after Lantern Night and we always have space to take travellers with us on the road. The library's bigger than you think."

Crimson thanked him again and went inside. The Senda family sat around a table laden with half-eaten platters of food for the traditional Lantern Night feast. Her stomach clenched. She had no appetite, not even for the rich fruit cake or the sugared plums that lay like frost-covered jewels on the best plates.

Senda got to his feet. "There you are. We've been worried."

Crimson took in the family feast. They hadn't waited for her to begin. Why had she ever felt like she could belong here?

"You're back now, that's all that matters," said Marie with a nervous glance at her husband.

"Yes, well. Now we can light the lanterns."

Crimson swallowed. She didn't feel much like wishing joy to the world with the holiday ritual. But her mind raced with the possibility of new beginnings, and the lanterns were a celebration of new year's hopes as well as last year's memories.

With a sigh, she fought down the squirming feeling in her stomach and joined the family at the table. Namu looked down at his lantern and twisted his candle in his hands. Senda drank his wine, letting his wife organise the lights.

"Here's yours." Marie handed her a fat candle made from pearly beeswax. No expense was spared for the holiday when the lantern had to burn all through the longest night to guarantee good luck. No one was more superstitious than a guilder.

Senda coughed and held a taper to the thick, stumpy candle they lit every Lantern Night. It was so bobbled with runs of previous years' wax that it resembled a sagging tree stump, but it was tradition. No floating lanterns in this house. They did things the old-fashioned way.

"With this light, we hold on to the memories of the past and look forward with hope for the new year. May this lantern last through the night."

Each of them repeated the ritual words and lit their own candles from the central family light before placing them in their individual lanterns. As Crimson held her wick to the candle, it sputtered and almost went out.

"Careful! You'll put out the family light and then we'll have bad luck for the year. And I think we've already had enough misfortune for one Lantern Night, don't you?" Senda glared at Crimson.

Marie held out Crimson's lantern to her with a sharp look at her husband. Crimson held her breath and finished her turn. She placed her candle in the lantern she used every year, faded paint flaking from its metal surface and then moved to the stairs.

"Are you not joining the feast?" Senda asked.

"Leave her go," Marie said. "I'll put a plate in the pantry if you get hungry later."

Upstairs, Crimson carefully placed her lantern on the table, watching the flame flicker. All she needed was bad luck for the entire year if it went out now. The candle's flame wobbled but stayed lit.

She reached for her mother's sewing box and opened it, the colourful threads arranged like a rainbow of possibilities. Crimson placed her new spool of dandelion yellow in the rainbow then paused. Something about the shimmer by the lantern reminded her of the thread she'd loved as a child.

With shaking fingers, she lifted the tray from the box and placed it carefully on the bed before reaching for the thread wound tight against the delicate wooden bobbin. It was a vibrant green, the colour of the fresh moss that gathered around the fountain, a totally different colour from the yellow in her hand and yet . . . they both had the same quality.

She turned the bobbin over in her fingers, so familiar to her. Everything else in her mother's sewing box she had used or replaced without a second thought; needles, threads, pins. But this, she had kept.

"Everything has its time," her mother used to say as they sorted through fabrics and threads. "Each colour its perfect complement."

It was one of the few things she remembered about her mother. That and green was her mother's favourite colour. She had loved the variety of shades and said it drew her closer to nature. Crimson could never bring herself to use up this thread, so it sat in the box as a reminder of her mother.

"Oh, Mum, what would you do?" she whispered to the empty room.

There was no answer. Her mother's radiant smile or bright laugh couldn't cross from beyond the grave. Crimson brought the green thread to her lips and murmured the Lantern Night words. "May your lantern shine bright, wherever you are."

As she turned the spool of thread over and over in her fingers, she saw the small flower carved into the end of the wood; a crocus. Her heart raced as if she'd discovered a rare treasure, and she unwound the yellow thread that Jarissa had given her. There, half hidden by the strands that wound around the spool, was a tiny crocus.

Thoughtful, she placed them both back in the box, tucking them against the faded lining and returning the top tray to its place before closing it up.

It was said that strange things could happen on the longest night of the year, but this was just a coincidence. Two threads given to her that had both come from Saffron Vale? Odd, perhaps, but a coincidence, that was all.

Crimson settled back and began to read the book Dewey had given her.

A cough pulled her from her book. Namu stood in the doorway.

"Sonny, I mean, Crimson. I really am sorry." She stayed silent. "I got you something. I didn't know if you wanted a Lantern Night present from me, but . . . I'll just leave it here."

Namu's footsteps retreated, squeaking along the old floorboards. Crimson waited until he'd left the room before she got up.

A package wrapped in stencilled paper with a sparkling yellow bow lay on the floor in the doorway to her small attic room. She tiptoed over to it, making her way around the edge of the room so the telltale floorboards didn't creak and give away her curiosity.

The box was light and formed a perfect cube. For a fleeting second, she wondered if he'd wrapped up a pile of twigs again. Typical joke present. With a sigh, she unwrapped the delicate paper, revealing a plain box inside. A piece of paper fluttered to the floor.

She picked it up with trembling fingers.

I'm sorry.

Crimson opened the box and stared at the bright loaf of cake that sat in the centre. No cake would make up for what Namu had done. She wasn't sure what she'd expected, but a cake didn't even come close to the apology she wanted. Or the life she'd wanted, surrounded by the comforts and support of the guild, selling her own creations in Senda's Emporium. She realised now that it would never have happened. Senda would never stray from tried and tested designs.

The librarian's story fluttered across her thoughts. That was what she wanted, but she couldn't have it. And would she be happy confined to following Senda's designs and colour choices until he retired? Or would she feel trapped like the firebird, her flames burning lower and lower as she fought to make her voice heard and keep her inspiration?

A golden sticker glinted in the lantern's light, and she idly closed the lid to read it; *Saffron cake from Saffron Vale.*

Everything pointed to Saffron Vale this Lantern Night. And when there were clear signs on such a magical night, there was only one thing to do. Crimson made her choice.

CRIMSON STOOD BY THE TRAVELLING LIBRARY. THE WINTER'S TIDE Market was over, and she'd decided to go. She rocked on her heels as she weighed her decision again.

"You don't have to go, you know," Namu said, pleading with his eyes and soft voice.

"I think we both know that I do."

"I am sorry."

"I know." She believed he was sorry. But his betrayal cut her deep. He'd snatched away her guild membership, her life ambition and all the careful plans she'd made.

He leaned in, as if for an embrace. Crimson pulled back. She couldn't do it. The sting of his actions was too deep. Instead, she held out her hand. Namu shook it, pain etching his face. A pang of sympathy plucked at her heart, and she almost pulled him into a hug, as if they were friends and he hadn't destroyed her simple dreams.

Crimson inhaled. There was something she had to say. "Good luck, Guilder Namu." It was like stabbing herself through the heart with the sharp fabric scissors.

Namu shrank back like she'd struck him and released her hand.

"So, you're really going." Senda's voice didn't contain any emotion.

Crimson nodded, not trusting herself to speak. They had too much history. He wasn't a bad mentor or a cruel man, but he had a life he wanted to protect, content to travel in his groove of tried and tested designs and serve the customers who wanted that. And she couldn't conform to his ideals.

He hugged her, stiff and unbending as his attitude and Crimson felt something pressed into her pocket.

"What's this?"

Senda coughed. "It's usual when an apprentice leaves their mentor to present them with a gift of money to help them set up their own shop."

"But I didn't–"

"I know. You didn't make it into the guild, but it is still traditional."

Crimson blanched. She hadn't got membership because of him. But she took a breath and said, "Thank you for all your lessons, Guilder Senda."

A cough sounded, and Dewey shuffled his feet. "We're leaving. Got to get through the pass before it closes."

Crimson broke away and stepped back. "So, this is goodbye."

Senda nodded. Behind him, Namu gave a small half smile. She returned it. Even if he had sabotaged her, that misdeed had led to her decision to leave. And despite butterflies flapping in her stomach at the unknown, this was what she needed; to follow her own path. So, she waved at him and forced a smile onto her cold lips.

Marie pulled her into a hug, breaking through her conflicting thoughts about Namu. Crimson wrapped her arms around the older woman and swallowed the sob that threatened to break free.

Marie pressed a leatherbound design book into her hand. "Here, a late Lantern Night gift for you."

"Thank you," she said even as her chest heated. A design book was another traditional present from mentor to apprentice, filled with copies of the mentor's patterns and other useful information. A symbolic representation of the knowledge gained during the apprenticeship. Crimson flicked through the pages. "It's empty."

"Sometimes you have to follow your heart and draw your own designs."

"Thank you," Crimson whispered, pulling Marie into another hug, and planting a kiss on her soft cheek. Both women's eyes filled with tears.

"We do have to go," Dewey said, twisting his cap in his hands.

Crimson stepped onto the library cart and sat on the backboard, clutching her design book to her chest with one hand and savouring the quiet of being alone while Dewey and his wife sat up front, driving the unicorns . The travelling library set off at a slow pace, barely faster than a walk as the unicorns pulled the heavy load onto the main road leading away from Oasis. Her eyes prickled with hot tears, and she allowed them to fall down her cheeks, dripping onto her sturdy emerald travelling cloak.

Only when the family was a distant speck on the horizon, and the town merged with the mountain range behind it, did she turn and peek around the railing, facing forward. A rare gap in the dove grey winter clouds opened and a shaft of light shone through, illuminating the way forward with the buttery light of the season.

Crimson scrubbed the tears from her face. It was time to look forward. She opened the book Marie had given her.

It was time to draw her own designs.

G CLATWORTHY STARTED WRITING DURING THE 2020 LOCKDOWN (HER first book was called *The Girl Who Lost Her Listening Ears*, which tells you all you need to know about lockdown!). She soon switched to fantasy, and she loves mixing the magical with the mundane, especially if it involves dragons! She lives in Wiltshire, UK with her family and two cats. When she's not writing, she enjoys playing board games, drinking tea and eating chocolate. You can become one of her book wyrms by signing up for her mailing list at www.gemmaclatworthy.com for free stories and you can find her on facebook at www.facebook.com/gemmaclatworthy and instagram at www.instagram.com/gemmaclatworthy.

G CLATWORTHY ALSO WRITES CHILDREN'S BOOKS AS GEMMA Clatworthy.

NOTE: THIS STORY IS IN UK ENGLISH.

THE BEST THIEF IN CAPITAL VALE

NATHANIEL WEBB

I t was winter, and midnight, and Hunter Myff was working alone when he heard a thump high above his head.

He ignored it. Rustic Reads, Capital City's premier bookshop, was an oldish sort of a building, and a very large one, four stories tall with a footprint the better part of a city block. That meant creaks, groans, thuds, taps, and yes, even thumps were nothing unusual in the shop.

The smallest sounds tended to be mice, who sometimes chewed the books. The largest heralded the toppling of one of the many stacks that populated every corner of Rustic Reads and lined its hallways like a second set of walls. Medium sounds could be anything, but were never anything important.

The thump in question was a medium sound, so Hunter carried on with the crucial job he had set himself: organizing the books behind the café counter by color and height.

On principle, Hunter disapproved of having a café inside a bookstore. For one thing, it exposed the books to the dangers of drips, drops, splashes, splooshes, and—Artisan forfend—spills. For another, some customers, regulars even, came in, bought their drinks, and bustled off without so much as riffling through a book. That seemed inappropriate for a bookshop.

And then there were the shelves behind the counter. The shelves behind the counter had a knack for getting jumbled. Customers would ask to see one book or another and a busy barista would grab it without memorizing where to put it back, or a barista would borrow a book for themselves, or one barista would take a book down and another barista would use the vacant spot for a dirty mug or spoon. Hunter had opinions about baristas. The word "shambles" was often involved.

Nevertheless, the customers seemed to like the café, and Hunter's boss certainly did, so he considered it his duty to keep its little bookshelf in order. After all, it was undeniable that for every few buy-a-drink-and-leave customers, one would spot an interesting title behind a barista's head, ask to see it, and wind up buying it. At least, this was how Hunter reconstructed events when he saw a coffee purchase and a book purchase right next to each other in the financial records, as he pored over them each night, checking for arithmetic errors.

Hunter squinted through his glasses and tugged two novels from the shelves, one bound in lime cotton and the other in leather of a sort of faded jade that made Hunter think of dragons. He had never seen a dragon, but then again, he'd never asked a barista to please stop putting dirty spoons on the bookshelf, so Hunter Myff's List of Undone Things was still fairly extensive. He whistled softly as he examined the green covers, and—

There was another thump.

This one was also well above Hunter's head, but it sounded closer, that was to say, lower down. If the first had been a fourth-floor thump, for instance, this one was a third-floor thump. It was still, however, medium in volume, so Hunter ignored it and slipped the lime-green novel onto the shelf, then the jade one.

His whistling returned, adopting a satisfied little melody as he moved along the bookshelf. Every now and then he paused to buff a bit of dust away with the sleeve of his cardigan. He owned seven cardigans: six brown, which he wore to work, and one navy blue, which he wore at home on his night off. He also owned seven pairs of corduroy pants and one pair of reading glasses.

The whistling faltered. Hunter glanced back at the two green books. They were wrong! Clearly it should go jade, then lime. With a narrow-shouldered shrug, Hunter moved back and swapped them. The medium thump had distracted him, that was all. There was no accounting for thumps.

The sorting went smoothly for some time after that, uninterrupted by either mystery noises or errors in Hunter's color judgment. After perhaps twenty-five gratifying minutes, Hunter stood on the far side of the café counter with his hands on his hips, surveying his handiwork. He fairly glowed with satisfaction. Yes, the shelf looked far nicer this way. He had done an important thing, and it was barely past midnight. There were hours left in his shift, plenty of time for more sorting and cleaning before Rustic Reads opened for its single busiest day of the year: the first day of Winter's Tide. Why people waited to do their gift-shopping until the holiday week before Lantern Night, Hunter couldn't imagine, but as he personally had nobody to shop for, the question was academic.

He'd be gone by opening time, of course. He didn't like to be present when customers arrived. It had happened once, by accident, and had been very awkward for everyone involved, what with Hunter's thoughts getting jumbled at the prospect of talking face-to-face with a stranger, and his mumbling and foot-shuffling and insufficient conversational undertakings.

Lesson learned. Nowadays he stuck around only until his boss showed up, which he supposed she liked because it proved he had, in fact, come to work. Then he hurried home to read before bed.

Hunter felt he had earned a break. Working as he did without an immediate overseer, he tried to be conscientious about granting himself minimal breaks and keeping them to a ten-minute maximum. Often by eight minutes he felt antsy anyway and wanted to get back to cleaning and sorting. But at the moment, he—

There was a clang. It was undoubtedly closer (i.e., lower) than the second thump, and much clangier, a sort of metal-on-metal sound like a knight dueling a plumber. It was a second-story clang if Hunter Myff had ever heard one.

It was still medium, though.

Hunter sat in one of the overstuffed armchairs by the front window. From here, he could relax by counting the pile of gift-wrapped books that stood near the door, awaiting tomorrow. One, two, three, five, eight, thirteen, twenty-one—Hunter could feel his tension over the matter of the green novels drain away . . . then slowly return, as he neared the top of the pile and the end of his count. Seventy-six, seventy-seven, seventy-eight! Seventy-eight gifts!

It wasn't possible!

Hunter leapt from the chair in alarm and set himself to a sober and focused recount. This was no time for casual relax-ation counting, this was a crisis. But he had, unfortunately, been right the first time. There were seventy-eight books in the pile, each one beautifully gift-wrapped and ready to be handed (by someone else) to an orphan as soon as Rustic Reads opened its doors in the morning. The Rustic Reads Giveaway was no less than a Capital City tradition, the first, best act of Winter's Tide.

Last year, however, there had been eighty-six gifts. Every one of them had been claimed, each by a different orphan. And that meant that if the same number of orphans showed up this year, at least eight—it hardly bore thinking about—would go bookless.

Hunter fretted. He paced. He chewed his fingernails, which was hard, because he always kept them neatly trimmed. He—

There was a very loud, rather resonant thump from the wall by the stairs to the second floor. It was sudden, it was close, and moreover, it was definitely not medium in volume. It could hardly be ignored. Yet there was this matter of the inadequate gift pile to be considered, and—

"Um, hello?" said the wall. "Is anyone there?"

To his List of Undone Things, below *see a dragon* and *scold a barista*, Hunter added *talk to a wall*. Then he mentally crossed it off.

"Yes, I am," he called, moving warily toward the stairs.

"Oh, thank the Artisan," said the wall. It had a female voice, fairly humanish sounding, and it belatedly occurred to Hunter that it might not be the wall talking to him, but rather a female human person behind or inside it. He sighed and added *talk to a wall* back to his List.

"Are you . . . " Hunter cleared his throat. He hadn't talked to anyone in hours. Days, if he didn't count saying hello and goodbye to his boss. "Are you, er, stuck?"

"Yes," said the voice.

"In the wall?"

"Yes."

"Or behind it?"

"No."

"I see," said Hunter. He had reached the stairs, and he sat on them near the wall. From it came a sound sort of like a person huffing in frustration. Then quiet, until at length

Hunter thought of another question to ask: "How did you get stuck?"

"There's not a lot of space between the walls in this building," said the voice. "I doubt it's up to fire code. Also, I hate to break it to you, but I think you have mice."

"Yes, we have mice. They sometimes chew the books, and they're responsible for the smallest sounds at night."

There was a pause, as if the voice was considering that. "What's responsible for the biggest sounds?"

"Lately? You."

To Hunter's surprise, the voice in the wall laughed. Quite a lot, actually. But unlike most laughter Hunter had heard in his life, which resembled alarming sounds like geese honking or off-key trumpets, this laughter reminded him of the little bells that hung from sleighs in winter. It was interesting, he thought, that the voice could make a sound like multiple bells. Most people only sounded like one thing at a time.

"Don't you want to know why I'm in your wall?" the voice asked when she was done laughing.

"Would you like to tell me?" said Hunter. "I'm a good listener, as long as you don't need me to say anything in reply."

The voice sighed. "Sure. Well, you've probably guessed already. That's right: I'm a thief. I just so happen to be the worst thief in Capital Vale."

"Hmm," said Hunter. He noticed a spot of ink on his shirt-cuff and rubbed at it with a thumb.

"You really aren't much of a conversationalist, are you, Bookworm?"

"I'm afraid not," Hunter said. But it was curious—normally he couldn't keep up his end of a conversation because people jumbled his thoughts. This time his thoughts were clear, he had simply gotten lost in them. Specifically, he had been thinking how much he liked the voice. It sounded both kind and intelligent . . . which, Hunter had to admit, was an unlikely combination for a thief who'd gotten herself trapped inside a wall.

"That's a shame," said the voice. "You should talk more. You sound nice. Are you nice?"

"I've never really thought about it," said Hunter. "The philosophers I've read generally measure kindness by how one deals with other people, and I don't deal with other people." He pondered for a moment, then stood up. "But I suppose I shouldn't be nice to a thief. In fact, if you would please do me a favor and stay trapped in the wall a little longer, I think I should probably go fetch a constable."

"Sorry, Bookworm, no promises. You understand. In fact," the voice added, "I'm very nearly unstuck and I'll be out of this wall any second, so you really can't leave me now."

"Because you'll escape if I do?"

"Exactly."

"What if you escape while I'm sitting here?"

"Then you leg it for the constables while I wiggle my way to freedom. I bet you can run faster than I can shimmy between walls, don't you?"

"I think so," said Hunter. He wasn't as confident about talking to the constables, but he could cross that bridge if and when he had to. Probably. "And if you don't manage to get unstuck, my boss will be here in the morning. She'll know what to do about you."

There was another extensive pause. At length, the voice said, "Well, what should we talk about?"

"Talk about?" echoed Hunter, who had been staring somewhat distractedly at the pile of gift-wrapped books, wondering again what he was going to do about its inadequate number.

"You weren't just planning to sit here in silence, were you?"

"Of course not," said Hunter, who'd intended to do something a lot like that.

"Let me put it this way," said the voice. "You've got the worst thief in Capital Vale right here in front of you. Literally a captive audience. If you think about it, this is really the chance of a lifetime. You could ask me anything, anything at all, and I'd have no choice but to answer."

"That doesn't follow," said Hunter. "You're inside a wall, not under a truth spell."

"Yes, but I'm very bored."

"Oh."

"So? Ask away. Anything you like. Worst thief. Go."

"Hmm," said Hunter. "Hm. Well . . . hmm." He picked some lint off the sleeve of his cardigan. "Is there . . . ah! Aha! I'd like to know—"

"Finally."

"Is there anything interesting on the inside of the wall?"

The voice sighed. "Forget it. I have a question for you. Where do you think treasure chests come from?"

"I—what?" Hunter looked up from his sleeve and stared curiously at the wall. "Obviously someone makes them."

"Sure, but who? Who sits down at her workbench in the morning and says, *I'm going to make a nice big iron-banded oak chest today, I sure hope a crazy wizard fills it with coins and loses it underground*?"

Hunter tapped his lower lip thoughtfully. "A carpenter?"

"Between fixing Mrs. Broomwhistle's credenza and banging together some chairs for the local tavern? No, constructing a good treasure chest seems like a specialized skill to me."

"Well . . . " Hunter sat up a little straighter. "I doubt if only one person is involved. I'll grant you that a good carpenter would be needed to make tight joins, but fitting the iron bands, that's more like a cooper's work. And neither of them could install the lock, not if it's to be done properly. Locksmithing, now there's a specialized skill."

The voice gave a little whistle. "You make a good point, Bookworm. You think they have assembly lines, or—"

"Why are you a thief?" asked Hunter so suddenly he surprised himself. Quite literally: he actually gave a little jump, sitting there on the stairs. Certainly the voice was caught off guard, because she stopped mid-sentence and had to clear her throat before she replied.

"What do you mean?"

"Well, I suppose I mean what I said." Hunter picked at his sleeve, embarrassed by his outburst. "I just thought—you seem intelligent, aside from the wall situation, and you seem kind, aside from the robbery situation, so I was just wondering."

"A better question might be why I'm the worst thief in Capital Vale."

"No," Hunter said, "I just want to know why you're a thief at all."

There was a long stretch of silence, but for once, Hunter was comfortable with it. He understood that he wasn't expected to fill it, and moreover, he suspected that if he let the silence linger, the voice in the wall might eventually be forced to break it by answering his question.

He was right.

"It's the family business," she said. "I'm just lucky I'm so good at it—"

"Present circumstances notwithstanding."

"Granted. I mean I'm usually good at it, which is lucky, since it's hard to find a carpenter to take you on as an apprentice when your dad's a thief. I *wanted* to make treasure chests for a living, but they all thought I was a double agent."

Hunter stared at the wall. The voice had laughter in it, and Hunter knew that meant she was making a joke. But for reasons he couldn't explain, he felt the laugh was false and the words were true, rather than the other way around.

"Voice," he said, "did you—"

"Oh! Oh!" the voice shouted. "There's a mouse!"

Hunter leapt to his feet. "In the wall?"

"Yes, in the wall, I'm not just offering you a friendly warning!"

"You're a thief who's afraid of mice?"

"I'm not afraid, I'm stuck and it's nibbling on my toes."

Hunter's eyes narrowed. "Aren't you wearing shoes?"

The voice sighed. "No. Barefoot is best for this sort of second-story work."

"Technically it was fourth-story work."

"Are you going to do something about this mouse or not!"

"Yes! Right." Hunter cast a hasty glance around, looking for anything that might be useful against a mouse he couldn't see. None of the bookstore cats was nearby . . . His gaze fell on a rather old and patchy broom leaning forlornly against a stack of books in a corner. Lacking any better options, Hunter snatched it up.

He returned to the wall and strained his ears, but he couldn't hear any nibbling sounds over the voice saying "Oh! Oh! My toes!" in an increasingly higher pitch. So he shrugged and began thwacking the wall with the flat of the broom, hoping to scare the mouse away. With each hit, the stacks jumped and dust puffed down in little clouds from the ceiling. He hoped to hear the sound of scurrying—away from the voice, ideally—but now there was the thwacking of the broom to contend with, so he had no way to be sure the mouse had gone, and he just kept thwacking until he realized the voice was laughing and shouting, "Enough! Enough! Bookworm, stop, it's gone!"

Hunter stopped thwacking the wall and set the broom on his foot, bristles up. His cardigan was powdered with ceiling dust, but he was smiling. He felt pretty sure the voice's laughter was of a different, more genuine sort than when she had made that joke about apprenticing with a carpenter. It was certainly going on longer.

"He ran away at the first hit," she was saying through gales of laughter. Or maybe *peals* was the better word, Hunter thought, since he was reminded of bells again. "You were really going for it, huh? He was off like lightning, but you just kept on smacking! You're a madman! Oh . . . " The voice sighed. "I haven't laughed like that in . . . well. I'm lucky you're working tonight."

"I'm glad I could help," said Hunter. He added *save a thief from a mouse* to his List of Undone Things, then mentally crossed it off.

"Why are you?" the voice asked softly.

Hunter hesitated. It was a fair question, so he gave it some consideration, and found that the answer surprised him a little. "I suppose because I like you."

"No, not—" The voice made a sort of mix between a laugh and a cough. "I meant why are you working? It's the night before Winter's Tide."

"Technically, it's already Winter's Tide. It's after midnight."

"You should be home with your family," continued the voice, as though Hunter hadn't made an excellent point. "Or out with friends or something. Oh, do you own this joint? But it's a big shopping day tomorrow, and you'll be handing out all those gifts to the orphans. Shouldn't you be resting up?"

"I always work nights," said Hunter. "I tidy up, organize the shelves, do the sums, and all that sort of thing. It's very satisfying."

"It sounds lonely."

"I have a lot of time to think."

"About how lonely you are?"

"About—" Hunter hesitated. He didn't think about being

284

lonely, he thought about *not* being lonely, which surely wasn't the same thing at all. "I think about the city."

"Capital City?" said the voice. "What about it?"

"Well . . . do you know the orphans? I just think someone ought to do something for them."

"Loads of folk do things for them. There's the Queen's Fund, the Roofer's Guild Charity, Bacon Week . . . between the Shoe Drive, the Boot Drive, and Sandal Day, those kids probably go barefoot less than I do. Not to mention that big stack of gifts by the door."

"Yes," Hunter said slowly, thinking again of how much sparser that stack of gifts was than last year's. "But I mean something special. Like, I don't know, just to pick a random example, perhaps someone ought to write them stories."

"Stories?"

"As an example."

"Bookworm, are you a writer? Do you work a lonely overnight job so you have time to write stories for orphans, but you haven't got the guts to show them to anyone?"

Hunter rubbed his shirt-cuff and said, "Mm." There was a pause, during which he expected the voice to laugh, but she didn't. Then they both started to speak at the same time, but Hunter was a bit quicker. He said, "Are you sure you want to be a thief? You don't seem very enthusiastic about it. For example, you haven't actually done anything to get yourself unstuck from the wall in the whole time we've been chatting."

"Well," said the voice, "it's hard to find a carpenter to apprentice under—"

"When your father is a thief," Hunter said. "You said that already. Would you rather be a carpenter?"

"You're a good listener."

"Oh, listening's easy." Hunter gazed out over all the books

that lined the walls and filled the corners of Rustic Reads. "It's like reading, but with your ears. It's talking I have no talent for."

"Sure you do."

"No, any time I try to talk to someone, my thoughts get all jumbled."

"You don't sound jumbled to me."

Hunter opened his mouth to disagree, but found that he couldn't. It was true: the conversation had gone on for some time now, and he still didn't feel jumbled. The voice in the wall was remarkably easy to talk to. Perhaps it was because she was just a voice in the wall, as faceless as a character in a book. But Hunter was beginning to wonder if there was, in fact, some other reason.

"Bookworm," said the voice.

"Yes?" said Hunter.

"Don't you think it's rude, me calling you Bookworm all the time? I never even asked if you minded."

"I don't mind."

"I know, but I should have asked."

"I called you Voice once."

"I don't think I caught that."

"Well, I did."

"I guess . . . if we're going to be chatting, it seems like we ought to know each other's names, don't you think?"

Hunter took off his glasses and examined them in the thin golden glow of the bookshop's turned-down lanterns. He buffed the lenses with his sleeve, breathed on them, and inspected them again. There were an awful lot of scratches and bits of dust on them.

"I'm Dez," said the voice. "What's your name?"

"Hunter," he replied without meaning to. He suspected he ought to feel foolish about telling a thief his name, but when he searched inside his head and chest for guilt or shame, he couldn't find any. All the space was taken up by a warm sort of glow that Hunter tentatively identified as companionship.

"Hunter," said Dez. "I like that for you."

"Really? I never thought it fit. I'm not a hunter, for one thing. I don't even look good in green."

"That's why I like it!" Dez laughed. "I like ill-fitting names. Why shouldn't a bookworm be called Hunter or a barbarian be called Norbert? Or a famous beauty be called Murgatroyd Mudd, who was an aunt of mine? Nobody's ever what they seem, anyway."

"Well—"

"And who says you don't look good in green?"

"The mirror?" ventured Hunter.

"I'm going to go out on a limb here and guess that you don't have a magic talking mirror. Do you like green?"

Hunter looked at his brown cardigan. He had worn his navy blue one to work once, but it had made him anxious. "Green is just more of a dragon color, that's all."

"I wouldn't know," said Dez. "I've never seen a dragon." She sighed. "Someday, maybe. Well, Hunter, can I ask you a favor?"

"Possibly," said Hunter. The little hairs on the back of his neck rose, fuzzing against the collar of his cardigan and making him tickle. What sort of favor would a midnight thief ask?

"Turns out, in addition to narrow, the spaces between your walls are pretty hot and pretty dry. There's a real desert vibe happening back here. If I squint, I think I can see a mirage."

"That's not how mirages work."

"Irregardless," said Dez, which made Hunter wince. "Would it be maybe possible for you to get me some water? It really does look like I'll be here a while."

Hunter blinked. "Some water?"

"You know—the wet stuff."

"But how would I give it to you?"

"Well . . . " Dez gave a creaky little groan. "If I tilt my head back just wrong, I can see a crack of light above my head. I'm betting there's a loose floorboard up on the second floor there. You could pull it up easily, I'm sure, and hand a cup down. Or at least pour it into my mouth."

"You could choke!" said Hunter, alarmed.

"I'm choking now—" Dez's voice was raspy. "All this sand —my lips are cracking, my throat—I probably couldn't even hit an E-flat right now—oh, the relentless beating of the sun! Hunter, I think I see a scorpion!"

Hunter laughed. "All right, there's no need for melodrama. I'll just go to the cistern—no, I'd better get you fresh water from the well, it'll be clean and cold. Then I'll see about finding that loose floorboard."

"Hurry, Hunter," whispered Dez. "Scorpions . . . my opera career . . . "

THE NIGHT WAS BLACK, SPOTTED WITH THE LITTLE AMBER FLAMES OF distant torches and the cold white glint of the stars, even farther away. Hunter braced his hands on the lip of the well and drew a long, deep breath of midwinter air. It stung his throat, but in a strangely pleasant way. And that wasn't the only discomfort he found himself enjoying: his face was sore, but from all the smiling and laughing he'd been doing. It was hard to remember another night quite like this.

He winched up the bucket and drew off a cup of water for Dez, filling it to the brim, then trotted back to Rustic Reads and through the rear door. He was careful not to spill a drop: after all, there was Dez's opera career to consider. Hunter laughed at the thought, and a little water sloshed out onto his hand. Strangely, it didn't bother him.

He took the back stairs to the second floor and wove his way through the narrow, book-stacked halls to the little alcove he suspected was just above where Dez was stuck. After setting the cup carefully on a nearby shelf, he knelt and squinted along the floorboards. Sure enough, there was a gap about a half-inch wide between two of them, and the board nearest to hand looked loose. Hunter wedged two fingers into the gap and—

Froze.

There was light up here, enough to spill down into Dez's little space between the walls. That meant that as soon as he moved the floorboard, her face would be revealed. If she engaged him in further conversation, it wouldn't be through a wall, but face to face. And that . . .

Hunter made himself think it: he didn't like talking to people face to face. It jumbled him, and if there was one thing Hunter Myff disliked, it was messy bookshelves, but if there were two things, they were messy bookshelves and being jumbled.

Hunter stood, grabbed the water cup, and took a sip. It was as cool and clean as he'd hoped, and it seemed to soothe the anxiety buzzing in his chest, at least a little. But this went beyond the usual anxiety, Hunter realized as he stopped himself from gulping down the rest of the water in one greedy swig.

He wasn't anxious about talking to someone. Well, yes he was, but he was most afraid to break this strange spell that had arisen between him and Dez. She was the first person he'd been able to talk with, really talk with, in more years than he could recall. If seeing her face ruined that, as it had with everyone else in Capital City—if he got jumbled with Dez—eight missing gifts would be nothing in comparison.

"Bookworm?" came a voice from beneath his feet.

"I'm here," Hunter said. "I have water. I just—"

289

"Can't find the loose board? We've all been there. You're probably standing on it."

"No, I . . . "

"My brother once spent thirty minutes looking for a trip-wire. Turned out he'd knelt on it right when he got down to look. He only found out when he stood up to stretch and got a sleeping dart in the knee."

A brother. The concept hit Hunter like—well, like a splash of cold water to the face. Here in the quiet solitude of Rustic Reads, in the depths of one of winter's longest nights, it was easy to forget anyone existed aside from him and Dez. But of course that wasn't true. Of course she had a whole life to get back to, one that had no room for a jumbled-up midnight bookworm.

There was no sense waiting, then. Hunter knelt, set down the cup, and pried up the loose floorboard.

In the thin golden light of the hallway lamp, he saw two wide, green eyes staring up at him. A smile—a grin, even—flashed in the murk of the space between the walls. Slowly a face resolved in the shadows: a round face wearing a look of surprise, black hair pulled tight into a workmanlike bun, freckles spattered across the bridge of her nose in a decidedly asymmetrical way.

"Hiya," said Dez.

She was beautiful.

"Hmm—hm?" said Hunter. He was trying to remember how to respond to a polite but casual greeting. "Mm-hmm."

Dez's thick eyebrows pulled together. "You all right, Hunter?"

"Wow! Yes! Right all right." Hunter snatched up the water cup and thrust it toward Dez's upturned face. "Well, here we are, then. There we be. There you be, I mean. You go. I'll go. I should go. Enjoy in good health!"

Hunter leapt to his feet, wondering frantically when was the last time someone under the age of one hundred said "enjoy in good health." A swift kick was all it took to reset the floor-board, then he was off and away down the hall, with Dez's muffled voice calling out behind and beneath him.

"Hunter, wait!" A quick and messy sound of gulping. "Oh, that is *good*. Hunter! Did I do something wrong?" Hunter rounded a corner. The voice was growing faint. "Aside from breaking into your shop, I mean . . . and getting stuck in a wall . . ."

He could barely hear her now.

"Hunter . . . ?" she was saying. "Hunter, wait."

But he didn't.

It was winter, and midnight, and Hunter Myff was getting snowed on.

He ignored it. A little snow was nothing, not now, not after he'd made every possible error in the space of one night. He had talked to a thief. He had gone and fetched her water as if he were back in Huffton-Under-Tibbs, serving drinks to booming-voiced and boisterous patrons at his mother's inn, praying no one would try to make small talk with him. He had mixed up lime green and jade!

And now he had left work without permission.

Yes, he was going to fetch a constable at long last. Yes, it was the right thing to do. And yes, his boss would surely approve. No, none of that made him feel any better.

He had read all about thieves. All about burglars, confidence people, hucksters, and scam artists. He knew how they won over honest folks like Hunter. A trickster started small with some innocuous connection—like swapping names. This put the mark at ease and lowered their guard in preparation for the next stage of the game: a minor request. A cup of water, perhaps. No harm in that, surely?

And when *that* was done and delivered and the world hadn't come crashing down around the mark's ears, they were as trained as a show pony into believing that giving the trickster whatever they requested was as harmless as pumpkin pie. Then it was safe to ask for big favors, like help escaping from inside a wall.

Hunter huffed out a cloudy white breath. Snow had piled up on his shoulders in powdery little mounds, and he moved to brush them off, only to discover that he had left his gloves back at Rustic Reads in his hurry to reach the constables' station before Dez, rejuvenated by the water he had so foolishly brought her, made good her escape. To think he had almost fallen for her tricks. Him! Who'd read all about such tactics in any number of books. Naturally, Dez was the first con artist he had ever encountered in person, but he should have identified the signs from the first.

There probably wasn't even a mouse.

A teenage boy with pointed ears sticking out from under a peaked cap, hurrying down the street with his hands in his pockets, gave Hunter a hasty smile that suggested commiseration—perhaps he thought Hunter was a fellow errand-runner, making last-minute preparations for Winter's Tide in the morning. Hunter smiled back as they passed each other. He was nearing the constables' station now. It was just around the next corner, and—

At the corner, Hunter came skidding to a halt on the snow-dusted sidewalk. A streetlamp burned above his head, shedding wavering golden light in a pool around him.

He had very nearly missed it, it had come and gone so naturally. But that was what made it so extraordinary: the very ordinariness of it! That anonymous boy had smiled at Hunter as though he was any friendly stranger, and Hunter, rather than jumbling up, had simply smiled back.

Dez had smiled at him, too, when he brought her the water. And if Hunter had believed in the sincerity of the errand boy's smile, then why not the sincerity of Dez's?

He tilted his head up and stared at the wobbling glow of the streetlamp. The snow was falling harder now, in fat flakes that tumbled on an uncertain breeze. Each time a particular snowflake caught his eye, he tried to guess its fate—and each time, he failed. Some flitted past the light and back out into the dark. Some stuck to the lamp and melted. And some, caught on a fluke of the air, hung, glittering, seemingly forever.

"No," Hunter said, on a breath that clouded in the night. He shook his head as though clearing out a bad dream. What presumption, to think he could suddenly understand faces and voices after one strange night of thumps and phantom mice! No, it was his lot in life to get jumbled around people, smile or no smile. And besides, his hands were cold. He stuck them in the pockets of his cardigan and set off around the corner. Soon he came in view of the constables' station, where a wan light glowing in one window suggested a lone officer keeping the midnight watch.

Anxiety hollowed out Hunter's belly. The prospect of explaining it all to a constable—telling the whole story, from the thumping to the voice to the cup of water—was already jumbling him. He moved forward, forced himself to put a hand on the doorknob, but the hollow feeling was spreading up into his chest and down into his legs. He drew a shaky breath. If only he could understand faces the way he understood words, like in the books he read.

Or the words Dez had spoken to him when she was just a voice in the wall.

Hunter took his hand off the doorknob.

THE MOMENT HE STEPPED THROUGH THE DOOR OF RUSTIC READS, Hunter shucked off his snow-damp cardigan and let it fall to the floor. He felt a little guilty—he promised himself he would hang it up and mop the floor soon—but right now, he was a bookworm on a mission. He strode to the wall by the stairs, took a deep breath, and knocked softly.

"Dez," he said, "I'm sorry I ran away. I should have trusted what you said. The truth is, I actually like you quite a lot, and I find that rather frightening, because not only have I never liked a thief, I've never really liked anyone. And when I'm frightened, I get jumbled. You'll have to take my word on that, but I can assure you I've amassed a great deal of evidence on the matter. Well, anyhow, what I want to say is that I think I can get over being frightened of liking you, and it's my belief that if I'm not frightened, I won't be jumbled either."

"Um, hello?" said a voice behind him.

Hunter jumped, but only slightly. He recognized the voice, and when it laughed, he recognized the sound of sleigh bells on a clear winter night. He turned and saw Dez, her round face bestowed asymmetrically with freckles, sitting cross-legged on an overstuffed armchair beside the teetering pile of gift-wrapped books. She still held the cup of water.

"Ta-da," she said.

"You escaped."

"Well, yes." Dez took a sip of water. "While you were off doing whatever you found more entertaining than chatting with me, I wriggled my way to sweet freedom. Astonishing what you can achieve when properly hydrated. My opera career thanks you, too."

Hunter leaned against the wall, feeling somewhat light-headed. "But why didn't you *escape* escape? I was going to fetch a constable."

"You were?" Dez, eyes widening, half rose from her chair.

"I didn't!" Hunter said hastily. "I was going to, but I didn't."

Dez sat back. "Oh, that's all right, then. Well, to answer your question, I didn't leave because my job wasn't done."

All at once, Hunter felt his legs give out beneath him. It was a good thing he was leaning on the wall, he thought as he slid down it and onto the steps, feeling as though the sudden, stony weight of his heart was dragging him down. "I knew it," he said. "You were using me all along, and now you're going to hit me over the head with a sock full of copper pieces and tie me to a chair and steal all the rare folios. I've read all about your sort. I'll go along with it. I don't want a lump on the head."

Dez stood, and to Hunter's surprise, heaved a sigh that sounded rather sorrowful. "That wasn't the idea at all," she said, "but if that's what you think of me, I'll show myself out."

"What *was* the idea?"

She cocked an eyebrow. "You really want to know?"

"Well, of course. I exist in a constant state of misunder-standing people. I would love nothing more than for you to explain what's actually going on in your thoughts."

"All right, Bookworm." With a smile quirking her lips, Dez sat. She took a long swig of her water, set the cup on the floor, and looked Hunter in the eye. He didn't look away. "I told you more than once I was the worst thief in Capital Vale."

"I assume because you got stuck in my wall."

"Don't interrupt. And no, not because I got stuck in your wall, because I wasn't here to steal anything at all." Dez gestured at the seventy-eight gift-wrapped books beside her— and Hunter felt his heart leap. There was no way that pile held a mere seventy-eight books. "I broke into Rustic Reads to leave

295

some things behind. I don't know if anyone but me would ever notice, but I counted—"

"The pile was smaller than last year's!" Hunter yelped. "This year there were seventy-eight books, but last year there were eighty-six."

"You noticed!"

"I'm sorry for interrupting you."

Dez laughed her laugh like bells. "Who cares? You thought about the orphans."

"Of course I did. It's the first day of Winter's Tide." Hunter's face felt hot, but not in a jumbled way. In a way he couldn't quite identify, a way that felt dangerously, deliriously good. "The Rustic Reads Giveaway is my favorite holiday tradition."

"Mine too." Dez's voice was suddenly soft. "You were right, by the way. About me. I never wanted to be a thief. I wanted to be a carpenter—to make things, not wreck them. But everyone judges you when they hear half your story. You're the first person who ever stuck around to hear the other half."

Hunter smiled a small, confused smile. "Of course. Who would only read half a book?"

Dez slipped from her chair and, strangely, began shuffling toward Hunter on her knees. Soon she knelt before him, so that with him seated on the bottom step, their faces were equal in height. And, Hunter thought, quite close.

"There's another reason I stuck around." Her voice was even softer now.

Hunter found himself speaking quietly as well. "There is?"

"I really wanted to meet you in person." Dez reached out, slowly, and put her hand on his cheek.

"Dez—"

"How long was I trapped in that wall?" she asked.

Hunter thought for a moment. "About an hour and a half, all together."

"Then I think you might be the best thief in Capital Vale."

Hunter raised his own hand and laid it on hers. When they touched, she smiled, the same smile she'd shown him when he brought her the cup of water. And he knew, without hesitation and without jumbling, that her smile promised something he had never dared add to Hunter Myff's List of Undone Things. Something that had always seemed even more impossible than seeing a dragon.

"And why is that?" he asked.

"It only took you ninety minutes to steal my heart."

Nathaniel Webb is writer and musician from Maine. He's best known as the author of *Bard City Blues*, a cozy fantasy novel of love and music, and the founder of Wyngraf, a publishing house dedicated to cozy fantasy fiction. For news, giveaways, and over a dozen free stories by Nathaniel and others, join our lovely little mailing list at https://read.wyngraf.com.

https://www.wyngraf.com

https://www.nathanielwebb.com

THE ALCHEMIST'S SURPRISE
BONNIE AXTON

Mabel's hand shook slightly as it hovered just above the surface of the flickerfire lamp she was working on. A swirl of elaborate cut-out designs on the brass sides would allow light to spill out. Inside was a crystal that should light up and produce a soft, heatless glow if she got it right. Once finished, the lamps were easy to light with the touch of a wand, but she would be activating the crystal for the first time. Mabel closed her eyes and imagined the crystal in her mind's eye as she tried to trickle aether in a small, steady flow. Sweat beaded on her forehead. Even through her closed eyelids, she could see a light shine in front of her. It was working! Then she felt the aether pulse and flow faster. It was too much. The magic fizzed and crackled in the air, making all the hairs on Mabel's body stand on end. Her eyes snapped open.

"Oh, gods, no, no, no!" Mabel stepped back, grabbed the magic-dampening blanket from its hook, and threw it over the lamp, which was now so bright it hurt to look at it. There was a boom. The blanket puffed up momentarily, and acrid black smoke started seeping out from underneath. Mabel wiped a hand across her damp forehead. That was close. Her eyebrows had only just grown back after the last time she had blown something up. She lifted the blanket to see the damage. The brass flickerfire lamp was bent and twisted beyond recognition, the crystal inside shattered. The wood of the workbench underneath was blackened from the explosion. It smelled of sulfur and soot.

"Ugh, it stinks in here now. What did you have to do that for?" Mabel's workroom partner, Brianna, complained. The willowy elf was perched on a stool at the workbench on the other side of the room. She was holding a sleeve over her nose and making a show of looking disgusted.

"I was so close to finishing that one. I was sure I had it right this time," Mabel said, putting the blanket back on its hook. Various alchemical experiments had scarred and burned the thick oak worktop many times in the past. Mabel judged it would be no worse for wear after this latest insult. She might even treat it to some linseed oil later to apologize for the explosion.

"I don't know why you bother. You're not getting any better, and I'm tired of all the noise and mess. Why don't you just move on to non-magical projects?" Brianna said, her voice muffled by her sleeve.

"Perhaps I should," Mabel said. She kept her voice level, but Brianna's words had spoken to her secret fear, the little voice that whispered she would never succeed.

She put on a pair of heatproof gloves and swept the scraps of brass into one of the workroom's metal bins, perhaps a little more roughly than necessary. Brianna was right. Mabel could spend the rest of her apprenticeship working on perfectly acceptable, non-magical projects and become accepted into the guild if her masterpiece was good enough. But Mabel wanted more than that. Years ago, during her novice days, she remembered her teacher shaking his head after one of her magical disasters. "You'll never be a truly great alchemist if you can't control the aether, Mabel," he had told her. She had been upset at the time, but nestled within his disappointment was a glimmer of hope—that she had the potential for greatness. Mabel had worked tirelessly to improve. Even so, all these years later, her control over the aether was still shockingly bad. It was so awful that some kind of self-preservation instinct had kicked in and led to her developing an incredible sensitivity to the aether, stronger than anyone she knew in her guild. Mabel could tell when the usual magical instability started tipping into dangerous territory. It was the only reason she still had all her fingers.

"Have you had any new ideas for your masterpiece then?" Brianna asked in a suspiciously innocent voice.

The question made Mabel's stomach sink. Brianna knew very well that Mabel had been struggling with inspiration. All the ideas she had tried had turned out to be impossible. Now, she was having trouble thinking of anything at all.

"No, but I've still got two years left until I have to submit it. I'm sure I'll think of something soon. You must be excited, with your masterpiece so close to being ready now. I wish you would tell me what it is."

Brianna finally lowered her sleeve from her face, and her mouth twisted into a grimace of distaste.

"You know I don't want anyone using my ideas. I'm not telling a soul until I present it," she said.

Mabel tried not to be offended at the implication that she might copy someone's work. However desperate she became, she would never stoop so low. She began to wipe down the worktop. Brianna had been grating some gek root into a bowl. It smelled heavily of cat wee and was, in Mabel's opinion, a lot more unpleasant than her exploded flickerfire lamp. Brianna pushed the bowl away from her.

"Well, I can't stay in here now. I'll never be able to concentrate with the smell of the smoke. The least you can do is finish my gek brew once you have cleaned up."

Mabel's jaw clenched, and she stopped wiping the table. When she first came to the Whispering Vials Alchemists' Guild in Capital City, she was nervous, new, and desperate to make friends and get along with people. Brianna began by asking her to help with small things, this and that, and she had been happy to do it. When Brianna had asked the younger girl to share a workroom, Mabel had been flattered. But the more she did, the more she was asked to do. It had come to a point where it was affecting her own work badly, and her mentor, Alden Wisefoot, had taken Mabel aside for a word about it. Now every request from Brianna grated on Mabel's nerves.

"I told you, Brianna, I've got to stick to my own work. I'll open a window. It'll be all right in five minutes."

"I can't bear to stay in here that long. My head's already starting to ache. Sometimes I think humans don't have any sense of smell at all." Brianna pushed her stool back from the bench and removed her protective work robe, revealing a shimmering dress that seemed to change color in the light. Beneath Mabel's own work robe was a practical warm blouse and a long pleated black skirt. If a person were to look very closely, they might spot patches of tiny stitches here and there. They could be from that time when something corrosive had eaten its way through Mabel's work robe and into the clothes below. Or perhaps that small fire with the sparks that wouldn't go out. Mabel had become very good at mending clothes. Her small stipend didn't stretch to replacing clothes that had become damaged, and it happened a lot. At any time, the fabric might get burned, stained, or permanently tainted by strange smells. Those kinds of accidents never seemed to happen to her elegant workroom partner, though.

Brianna undid the ornate clasp holding her silver hair up and opened the door.

"Please, Mabel. It will put me so behind if it's not ready for tomorrow. I'll see you in the morning." The door banged closed behind her.

Mabel finished cleaning up and, to her shame, found herself grating the last of the foul-smelling gek root into a bowl. Her skin would smell of it for days. She brooded about selfish work-room partners as she used a funnel to put the root into a round glass bottle. Mabel was so absorbed in pouring the correct amount of undiluted alcohol onto the grated root that she didn't hear the door open.

"Mabel, I thought you were working on the flickerfire box today?"

Mabel gave a guilty start, and poured a large glug of liquid into the bottle, spilling some on the worktop, too. Her mentor stepped into the room, his silver-tipped cane tapping on the stone floor.

"I have been, but, well—I'm only helping Brianna because I filled the room with smoke." Mabel wiped up the alcohol from the table and stoppered the bottle.

Alden massaged his forehead and gave her an exasperated smile.

"You need to stand fast, Mabel. I could intervene, but you need to do this for yourself. I know you have it in you." Mabel knew Alden was right. She was twenty-one years old and a full apprentice working on guilder membership, not a novice to be bossed about by others.

"I have been trying to say no, but somehow I seem to end up doing it anyway."

She had hardly finished speaking when Delton, one of the older elven students, creaked the door open and looked around.

"Brianna gone?" he asked.

"Just a short while ago," Mabel replied. Delton looked disappointed, but came in and put some folded paper packages on the table.

"Can you tell her I dropped these off? She said she needed them for tomorrow."

"I will. See you later, Delton."

Delton grinned, nodded, and hurried off.

Alden raised a gray eyebrow. "There's another one who needs to learn to say no." He picked up the gek brew and swirled it around in its bottle. "Double the alcohol required, I'd say. Brianna will get a surprise when she pours that into her mix tomorrow, and you won't be here to worry about her losing her temper over it either."

"I won't?" Mabel felt a hint of fear. She looked over at the metal workroom bin that was still slightly smoking.

Alden must have read her expression. He smiled gently and sat down on the stool next to her.

"It's nothing to worry about. I need to travel quickly, and I very much hope you'll agree to come with me. Look at this." He slid a cream-colored envelope across the table. Mabel opened it and unfolded the note. All bunched up at the top, in a firm script, was written:

Alden, I need your advice on something. Please come to see me without delay. Remember the old days in Rumbelow's class?

Yours in good faith and friendship,

Thorne Emberwald

Mabel turned the note over to see if anything else was written on the back, but it was blank.

"Who is Thorne Emberwald?" She asked.

"My old workroom partner from, oh, too many years ago. He lives in Turtle Bay Vale now and has a shop near the Trading Square. I mean to travel tomorrow morning. Getting to Turtle Bay by the Stone River will take a week and a half."

"What does the part about Rumbelow's class mean?"

"I've been wondering about that part of the message, too. Rumbelow took us on for extra tuition on the art of magical transfusion. He was a fearsome master, and we were always getting in trouble. Thorne set fire to his hat by accident once. We used to pass notes to each other, stick Rumbelow's scrolls to the desk, frogs in the drawer, that sort of thing. It's not something I'm proud of," Alden said. He smiled wistfully, his eyes crinkling in fond remembrance. "Perhaps he wants my advice on a matter of transfusion? I wish he had said plainly what the problem was."

"I'm really grateful that you have asked me, but don't you want to take one of the more senior apprentices on a trip like this?"

"I can't help but notice that you have been struggling for some while," Alden said, not unkindly, but Mabel winced and started picking at her sleeve. "My friend Thorne is a talented alchemist. It will be very instructive for you to meet with him and visit his shop. Also, we will have a lot of time in a coach with little to do. I'll bring books, and we'll have ample time to discuss your difficulties. Not only that, but travel is good for the mind, and excellent for inspiration. Of all my apprentices, you would have the most to gain from this trip."

Mabel's cheeks flushed. Being reminded of her shortcomings was deeply uncomfortable, but it was such a great opportunity. A journey, and to Turtle Bay too. Mabel had always wanted to travel the vales but had committed herself to apprenticeship, which meant long hours of work and study. New places, fresh sights, and an interesting alchemist's shop to look around. With a start, she realized they would also be there for Lantern Night. The winter solstice holiday was celebrated across the queendom and was her favorite festival of the year. Every vale celebrated Lantern Night in its own way, and Turtle

Bay was famous for its breathtaking solstice sunsets and a lantern parade that wove through the streets like a river of stars. Mabel felt excitement rising up through her blood like little bubbles in a shaken potion.

"Thank you so much! Of course, I'll come. Do we really leave tomorrow?"

"Wonderful. Yes, indeed. Meet me first bell before breakfast tomorrow at the front door." Alden stiffly rose from the stool, putting his weight on his cane. "Good night, Mabel."

Mabel sat absolutely still for a while, her mind racing with the changed direction her life would take for the next month or two, and then she stood up in a rush. Packing! What should she take? There wasn't even enough time to make a list! She hung her work robe on the hook next to Brianna's and let the door bang behind her as she hurried out.

THE DECEMBER AIR WAS CRISP, THE SKY WAS HEAVY, AND A FEW SNOW flakes fell gently, melting on the ground and not settling. Mabel dragged her traveling trunk down the stone steps at the front of the Whispering Vials Guild House, a green leather satchel on her shoulder. She turned back to look at the thick stone building covered with red and gold ivy that had been her home for the last year. There was no time to linger, a large black coach was already waiting. Four very fine horses shifted impatiently in their harnesses, misty clouds of hot breath coming from their nostrils. A dwarf in a thick leather cloak jumped down from the front of the coach to greet her.

"Good morning, Miss Willowstone. I'm Grimer, and you have the pleasure of traveling in my coach to Turtle Bay and back again. Your companion is already aboard. As soon as you're settled, we'll be ready to leave."

"Thank you. Those are beautiful horses!"

"They are indeed," Grimer smiled widely. Mabel reached down to grab her trunk handle.

"No need, miss," Grimer assured her, easily lifting the trunk and carrying it to the back of the carriage.

As Mabel pulled open the carriage door, she was struck by the contrast between the coach's plain exterior and its opulent interior. Intricate carvings of leaves, pinecones, and woodland creatures decorated the rich, cherry wood panels. She tentatively touched the thick leather padding on the seats; it was smooth under her fingers. Heavy velvet curtains were pulled back from the windows with elegant ties, and the scent of wood polish and leather filled the air. Her mentor was seated on the far side. His enchanted silver-tipped walking cane hung from a hook, and he had neatly placed his polished black boots by the opposite door. Alden had been making himself comfortable, with a pair of slippers and a checkered blanket around his shoulders. His eyes brightened at her arrival as he looked up from the book in his lap.

"This coach is wonderful," she said, closing the door behind her.

"It's a long journey. I thought we would travel in comfort. I'm too old to be rattled about in a bone shaker for a week and a half. Make yourself at home."

Mabel took off her scarf. The interior was so warm and cozy. Alden pointed to a gnomish-made box fixed to the roof of the carriage. She held her hand up and could feel the heat radiating out of it.

"How does it work?" Mabel said, shrugging out of her coat. She wished she had brought some slippers too now.

"I'll explain as we go. I've also brought plenty of books so we can continue your lessons." He patted a pile of leather-bound volumes on the seat next to him. "First, though, we need something to eat, as we were up too early for breakfast. Open that cabinet and let's see what we've got." Mabel realized that the carved wooden panel in front of her was actually a set of doors, and the two carved oak leaves were handles. Inside were shelves stocked with pastries, oatcakes, bread rolls, butter, glass bottles of water, and a stone bottle that was warm to the touch.

"Tea," Alden smiled. "Perhaps you could pour us some?" Mabel reached down to the lower shelves where some homely earthenware round mugs and plates were stacked. She jerked, as the carriage started moving, but the motion was smooth as soon as they were underway, and she had no problem pouring two mugs of tea. Her heart was light as she looked out the window, watching the city slide by. After she'd had another mug of tea and some bread, the road widened, and the buildings were less crowded. Mabel thought they must have joined the Stone River, the longest road in the queendom. The road wound its way from the northernmost tip of Juniper Vale, through Capital Vale in the center, and down to Turtle Bay in the south, carrying goods and people just like a trade river.

"I was a child the last time I traveled this road," Mabel said. She instantly regretted the words as memories flooded her mind. An eleven-year-old girl in a black mourning dress, traveling with relatives she hardly knew to a new home away from everything familiar. She quickly buried those thoughts, stamped down on the soil, and put a rock on top for good measure.

"I've journeyed along the Stone River many times." Alden said. "I try to visit my friend Thorne regularly, but I also have family in Azure Spires and like to visit Juniper Vale when the opportunity arises, so I travel north almost as much as south. Plenty of inns are along the way, so we will have somewhere to sleep every night. It should be quite a comfortable journey."

At around noon, they heard Grimer calling to the horses, and the carriage stopped outside The Fencing Hen inn.

"Oh, thank goodness," Mabel exclaimed. She pulled the door open and leaped out of the carriage. Grimer was getting down from his seat as she called out, "Privy?"

"There's one out back, that way," he pointed. Mabel promised herself she would not drink so much tea on the next leg of their journey as she ran to the rear of the inn.

The initial excitement of travel wore off quickly over the next few days. Alden and Mabel kept the little cupboard stocked with food, and sometimes they would eat lunch and dinner in the carriage. They studied books in the morning and spent the afternoon talking. Sometimes Alden would doze off, his alchemist's cap sinking over his eyes.

One morning Alden put away the books and took out a wooden box.

"I have a gift for you," he said, handing it over.

"Thank you." Mabel took the box, puzzlement mixing with surprise. "But, it's not Lantern Night yet?"

"It will help you with your studies. Go on, open it."

Mabel unlatched the little brass catch on the front of the box and pushed the lid open, revealing layers of crumpled brown paper. A thick glass bauble the size of an apple was nestled safely in the middle. She lifted it out, feeling the weight heavy in her hand. Inside was a copper rod that ran from one end of the glass ball to the other. In the center of the rod was a wheel of twisted copper blades. It reminded Mabel of the water wheels she loved as a child in Medlar Vale. When she turned it upside down, the wheel wobbled on its axis.

"It's fascinating." Mabel held it up and shook it. Nothing happened. "What is it?"

"I've been thinking about your difficulties controlling the aether. We have tried all the usual things, so now it's time to try something unusual! I had Guilder Tanin make it for me. It is the only one in the world, so take good care of it."

"I don't understand. What does it do?"

"Try to channel the aether into it, just a little, as you would for any level one project."

Mabel cradled the globe as she concentrated and channeled the aether. As she did so, the wheel inside rotated. It made a quiet 'tick ... tick ...' noise as it went around.

"This is amazing. Truly, Alden, thank you."

"I want you to practice with it. Try to keep the wheel at a steady pace. Seeing what is happening with your eyes, hearing it with your ears, might help you keep control. Try to keep the ticking at the rate of a heartbeat."

Mabel tried to keep the rate steady, concentrating harder and harder, but as so many times before, she felt the aether pulse and surge. She gripped the bauble tighter, brow creasing as she fought for control. The wheel inside spun faster, becoming a blur, and the ticking went from a slow heartbeat to a galloping horse. Then the flow of magic stuttered, and the wheel stopped. She looked up at Alden, her face crumpled.

"I can't do it."

"I didn't expect you to, not straight away. But unlike a flicker-fire box, this globe won't explode." Alden tapped it gently with his forefinger. "You can get it wrong as many times as you need until you start getting it right. Have a practice with it every day, and let's see if it makes any difference."

Mabel felt her shoulders relax. Permission to fail was a gift even more valuable than the unique bauble in her hands. She turned to face the other window, hand curled around the globe, ready to try again.

THE STONE RIVER WOUND ITS WAY THROUGH MANY VALES. THE DAYS passed, one much like another, but the food changed from place to place. Mabel enjoyed looking through the packed lunches given by innkeepers each morning. The basket from the Prancing Goose contained interesting cheeses and bread baked with nuts and peppers, while the Queen's Heart Inn gave them a bundle wrapped in cloth containing cured meat with savory biscuits and herb butter. They were well into Winter's Tide now, the two-week holiday leading up to Lantern Night. Decorations were going up in the inns they visited, and seasonal spices were baked into cakes and sprinkled on drinks. The evening meals they ate were often foods Mabel hadn't tried before. Some were sweet, with fruit in the main course, others spiced with unfamiliar flavors. Several times at night, Mabel heard her mentor's cane tapping in the room next to hers.

The weather changed as they approached Turtle Bay. One day Grimer took off his thick leather traveling cloak, and instead of turning on the gnomish heating box, Mabel opened the window for some fresh air. After that, the sun shone every day. It seemed strange in December, a month Mabel usually associated with woolly scarves and warm fires, but Turtle Bay was hot and humid year-round. The last stage of the journey took them through mountains and then foothills as they passed into Turtle Bay Vale. It was midmorning when Grimer stopped the carriage and banged on the side, signaling them to get out. Mabel's breath caught as she stepped out and saw the view.

"I thought you'd want to see this." Grimer's eyes twinkled in delight.

They could see Turtle Bay sprawled below them from their vantage point on the foothill. The Stone River meandered down into the port city, where gleaming white buildings with terracotta rooftops shimmered in deep red and burned orange shades. Here and there, taller domed buildings and towers stood out among the others. The land tapered down to a point where neat stone docks with wooden jetties played host to vessels loading and unloading. And beyond that—Mabel had never seen the sea before, and it was beautiful. A constant moving, glittering vastness, sparkling in the sunshine. Mabel was sure she could see ships far out on the ocean if she squinted her eyes enough. She wondered how sailing out over that endless expanse so far from land and people would feel.

"Ah, you never forget your first look at Turtle Bay," Alden said. "I hope you won't mind too much if we don't stay here too long? Now that we are so close, I don't want to delay."

"Of course," Mabel said. She jumped into the carriage and held her hand out to help Alden. She stared out the carriage window as they made their way down the busy streets. The houses were different from those in Capital City. The year-round heat permitted light and airy architecture, complete with courtyards and welcoming porches. People seemed to live their lives outside as much as possible. Food stalls attracted queues of people, cafés spilled out onto the streets, tables and chairs seemed to be everywhere and nearly always full. The streets got narrower and more crowded the further into the port they got.

"Here we are," said Grimer, pulling the carriage to a stop. "Moontide Inn. You're lucky I've got such good contacts. Turtle Bay is never busier than Winter's Tide, and tomorrow is Lantern Night." Grimer unloaded their luggage and handed it to a waiting porter but didn't get his own trunk off the coach.

"Aren't you staying here, too?" Mabel asked.

"I'll be staying at the Coachman's Inn on Farrier Lane. It's better for the horses. Come find me there when you're ready to head back to the Capital."

"This truly has been the most pleasant journey I have taken anywhere within the queendom," Alden said. A glint of gold flashed as he pressed a coin into the dwarf's hand.

"Yes, thank you so much," Mabel said, shaking his warm, calloused hand. Although she had no gold coin in her palm, Grimer's smile was just as wide.

"Moontide Inn is near the Trading Square," Alden said. "Thorne's shop isn't far. I hope you don't mind if we head straight there. We can unpack and settle in afterwards."

They had only been walking for a few minutes when the narrow street opened out onto a large square full of colorful market stalls. A tall fountain crested by a large bronze turtle with water spouting from its mouth stood in the middle of the market, and shops with bright awnings lined the edges. Elves, gnomes, dwarves, and humans mingled with races she had never even seen before. A tall, wiry figure with what looked like thin green leaves for hair stood behind one stall selling the most beautiful flowers. *A petalborn?* Mabel also saw a six-foot-tall hare bartering with a quick talking tinker gnome. The rabbitfolk leporiae were common in Capital City, but their taller and more adventurous harefolk cousins were much rarer.

"I could spend a whole day exploring this market, maybe a whole week," Mabel said.

She looked left and right, trying to take it all in. Small carved animals on this stall, colorful hats on another, necklaces with sparkling gemstones, all kinds of fruit and vegetables. They walked through a section that sold only fresh and dried seafood. She had grown up in a rural vale eating river fish and looked in horrified fascination at the weird and wonderful sea creatures on display. She hesitated at a stall with long blobby things, a purple creature that was all tentacles, and a fish with eyes as big as oranges and thick spines down its back, all on ice. A leathery old man gave her a huge, single-toothed smile and held out a wobbly piece of white meat on a stick. He spoke in heavily accented Olio, a patchwork language common in taverns, and second only to Shar, the language of Queen Liana's court and the most widely spoken in the queendom.

"For free! Try some, then you will buy some!"

Mabel shook her head and quickly hurried on.

Alden walked ahead and made steady progress through the crowds, largely thanks to his enchanted walking cane. The curved stick gave him incredible stability when planted on the ground, but the silver cap at the bottom stored up magic and would give a little zap to anyone who touched it. Mabel had given herself a jolt several times while brushing past it in the carriage. The cane moved constantly, probing out in front of the old alchemist, giving a little tap to the feet and shins of those who jostled or bumped into him. Startled, they would move aside quickly, wondering what had just happened.

Very soon the smells, the colors, the heat, and all the tightly packed bodies made Mabel feel quite dizzy. She was relieved when they stepped into a side street. Just a few shops down, she could see the alchemist's symbol of a vial hanging from an iron bracket.

"It's closed," Mabel said, as she approached the glass-fronted shop.

"How very strange." Alden shook his head. "There's a way in around the back. Thorne lives above his shop." They walked a little further along and went through an unassuming wooden door. It opened onto an alleyway that ran behind all the shops. Alden led them to a red-painted door. Alden raised his walking cane and used the curved end to rap smartly at the door. There was no answer, but the door swung open slightly.

"This isn't right," Alden muttered.

He gently pushed the door open further, calling out for Thorne as he did so. Mabel's mouth opened in surprise when she saw the room inside.

It was a complete mess.

MABEL STEPPED INSIDE AND LOOKED AROUND, AGHAST. IT WAS obviously a workroom, not unlike the one she shared with Brianna at the Alchemists' Guild, but this one looked like someone had picked it up and turned it over several times.

"What on earth has happened here?" Alden said, his voice soft. He leaned on his walking stick and looked around, frowning, and shaking his head.

Broken glass littered the worktops and the floor from smashed bottles and equipment. There didn't seem to be anything in the room that hadn't been knocked over. Papers were strewn about everywhere. Mabel picked up a few sheets. They must have been wet at one point because the ink had run, making them illegible, but the paper had since dried out and become wrinkly.

"It's like a storm has passed through here," Mabel said, walking further into the room. She looked up at a cupboard. One door was open, the other ripped off completely. Jars were smashed, and tins were knocked over. Mabel winced when she thought about the cost of the ingredients gone to waste. She sniffed the air. She could smell chemicals and herbs from the smashed pots, but no musty smell, which was surprising if it had been wet enough to ruin all those papers.

"Who could have done this? Oh, my friend," Alden said. "You don't think . . ."

Mabel felt her stomach sink. She didn't know what had happened. It looked like some kind of terrible robbery, but valuable equipment and ingredients had been smashed, not stolen. Her practical mind raced, turning the situation over. Alden might be thinking the worst, but if his friend had been hurt, you would expect some blood, bad smells, that sort of thing. Her brow wrinkled with concern as she looked at her mentor. His eyes were roving the room, unable to settle on any one place. Mabel hesitated, waiting for Alden to take charge of the situation like he always did, but when she saw him start to sway slightly despite his magical cane, her worry took over and she stepped towards him.

"Perhaps you should take a seat for a moment," Mabel said, picking up a stool from the floor and dusting it off. She bit her lip while waiting for Alden to tell her he was fine. Instead, he stood there, looking lost. She gently pressed him down onto a stool, feeling him trembling slightly beneath her hands. Alden had always seemed larger than life to Mabel, but just at this moment, he looked quite small, and old.

"Please, stay here for a little while. I'll check to see if Thorne is in the shop, or upstairs. I'll be back in a minute."

Mabel walked quickly over to the internal door and pushed it open before she could change her mind. Whatever had destroyed the workroom didn't seem to have affected the shop, which for the most part was neat and tidy and full of interesting things. A rosewood counter stretched across the room, its surface polished to a rich shine. Behind it stood a towering cabinet full of large and small drawers, each one carefully labeled. Some drawers had been left open, and the contents were gone. Next to the counter was a rack full of potions and a range of colors, some swirling in the vials all by themselves. A long, hooded cloak hung on a mannequin in the center of the room. At first glance, it was nothing special, but if you tried to look right at it, the shadowy colors seemed to shift. Mabel's eyes started to water as she stared directly at the dark material. Her eyes wanted to slide right off it. The shelves around the rest of the room were filled with strange and familiar objects. Ordinary warming mugs were next to a globe filled with smoke and a shelf full of metal objects under that. Mabel longed to look through all of it and ask questions of their creator. She hoped to one day have a shop like this of her own.

It was confusing. All these items were incredibly valuable and easy for a thief to take and sell, but they were untouched. Mabel checked behind the counter and found a money box that was still locked.

A spiral wooden staircase leading upstairs was at the far end of the room. Mabel took a deep breath and climbed the stairs quickly. At the top she found a pleasant set of rooms, just right for an alchemist living by himself. A comfortable chair was by the fireplace, and a small kitchen was situated right by the window, from which you could see the comings and goings of the Trading Square. Like so many other houses in Turtle Bay, a little balcony was on the window. The one closed door must have been a bedroom. She hesitated, her hand raised to knock, remembering another time, another door. She squeezed her eyes shut and made herself knock. Nothing. She wanted to turn around and run downstairs, but she thought of Alden and drew the courage to open the door. It was just an empty bedroom that seemed untidy in the ordinary way. A cloak on the bed, slippers kicked off, books piled up on the bedside cabinet. No sign as to what might have happened. She took a moment at the kitchen window to pull herself together before going back downstairs. Alden had gotten off his stool and was using his cane to poke around in the broken debris on the floor.

"There is no one in the shop, or upstairs, and it's not been turned over like this room," she told him. Alden looked a lot better than he had just a few moments before. The vulnerability had vanished, replaced by the curious and vital energy of the mentor she was used to.

"Thank goodness. For a moment I thought you might find, oh, never mind what I thought. I've been looking around in here, and it makes no sense."

"I know. I thought it might be a burglary, but the money box is still behind the counter, and everything seems to still be on the shelves. Some drawers have been emptied, though."

"They have? I'll take a look." Alden tapped his way briskly into the main shop. "Can you write these down in your notebook, Mabel?" Mabel quickly found her notepad and pencil, while Alden shuffled up and down the cabinet of drawers checking the labels. "I see serpent moss has gone. Also, gorgon clay, sealing solution, willow bark, dragon salt, iron dust, and safflower crystals, all missing."

"Do you have any idea why these things were taken?" Mabel asked, scanning the list.

"They don't immediately seem to be connected. They certainly weren't the most valuable." Alden shook his head. "We had better visit the local Whispering Vials Alchemists' Guild House. If they don't already know what has happened, someone should tell them, and if they do know, they can tell us. It's just the other side of the Trading Square."

Mabel packed her pen and notepad in her bag, but she hesitated.

"Actually, would it be okay if I stayed here? I could speak to the shopkeepers on each side. Perhaps they know what happened?"

"That's a very good idea. Don't forget, we are staying at Moontide Inn—I'll meet you there afterwards."

Mabel worried for a moment about Alden heading to the Whispering Vials by himself, but he seemed to have recovered from his earlier shock. She remembered all the legs that his cane had lightly assaulted on the journey through the market and decided he would be just fine.

MABEL STEPPED BACK AND LOOKED AT THE BUILDINGS ON EITHER SIDE of Thorne's shop. Maritime Macarons, with delicate biscuits and pastries in the window, was on the left, and a souvenir shop with no sign that seemed to be an explosion of knick-knacks was on the right. There were baskets and wooden tubs outside packed with odds and ends, including one full of canes with little hooks on the end, a sign saying *10 Coppers Each* nailed to the tub. She was just about to enter when the door opened and a gnome with a long brown beard came bustling out, hurriedly taking the baskets inside.

"Rain soon," he said, pointing up at the sky. Mabel looked up. It had been so dry since they approached Turtle Bay that she was surprised to see there were indeed dark clouds passing over. Mabel picked up the tub of sticks and carried them inside the shop.

"Many thanks," the gnome said, as he closed the door. Mabel was just about to ask him something when he put his fingers to his lips and then pointed at the door. The first rain-drops hit the glass, just one or two, and then the sky seemed to empty onto the street. He laughed.

"How did you know? About the rain, I mean," Mabel said.

"A weather box, of course," he replied.

The gnome pointed to a wooden box on the wall. It had a painted wooden cloud on one side, and a sun on the other. A little bell on a chain hung above each one. The cloud had risen high enough to touch the bell, letting the gnome know rain was coming.

"Very useful here in Turtle Bay. It doesn't rain quite as much in December, but you wait till May. It will rain every day, only a little, but every day. I'm Tibbit. Have a look around. There's something for everyone here!"

Even as they were talking, the rain cloud was making its way back down the face of the wooden box, and the sun was creeping up. The rain was slowing outside. Mabel looked around. There were shelves lining all the walls, and they were all overflowing with bits and pieces. Little statues, purses, beaded mirrors. She walked over to a rack with colorful hats on display.

"A hat is just what you need!" Tibbit said.

"They're so thin and light," Mabel said, feeling the material between her fingers. She tended to buy thick felt hats and had never seen any made of this material before.

"It's never cold here. These hats keep the sun off. If you don't have one, you should get one for your stay."

Mabel was still wearing her high-buttoned traveling dress, better suited to the colder weather of Capital Vale than the warm, sticky heat of Turtle Bay. Having something to keep the sun off her head would be welcome. She picked one up and tried it on. It was the color of the purple-pink orchids that used to grow in her grandmother's garden. Most of her clothes were black and practical, all the better to hide alchemy stains. Mabel didn't often buy new clothes, but she liked this hat very much.

"I will have it, thank you." She dug four silvers out of her purse and handed them over. "I'm really here to ask you something though. I'm here with my mentor, an alchemist. He is an old friend of Thorne Emberwald who runs the shop next door. He's not there, and we are a bit worried about him. Do you know where he is or what has happened?"

"The shop's been shut for about three weeks now, but I've seen his apprentice coming and going a few times. Taking stuff out of the shop and locking it back up again. I tried to catch him the last time to ask what's happening, but he looked at me like I was a ghost and just ran away." Tibbit shrugged. "That's all I know. Try Maritime Macarons on the other side. I don't live here, upstairs is full of stock, but Driel lives above her bakery. She might know more." Just as he finished speaking, the wooden sun rang the small bell on the gnome's weather predictor.

"Rain's over. Everything outside again!" Tibbit declared. He opened the door and started taking his baskets of goods back out onto the pavement. Mabel carried the bucket of sticks back out again. The street was still wet with rain, and it was really humid now. People started emerging from shop doorways. Two children who looked like brother and sister ran up and took two of the sticks out of Mabel's bucket before she had put it back on the ground. They paid Tibbit and walked away chattering excitedly, comparing their sticks.

"What are these for?" Mabel asked.

"Ha, you really are from out of vale. They are for tomorrow's Lantern Night parade. Everyone makes a lantern, or buys one, and hangs it on one of these sticks. Each one has a light crystal inside. At sunset the whole of Turtle Bay will gather on the docks to watch the sun go down. At the last flash, magicals will walk through the crowds lighting lanterns, and then everyone parades them back through the town. Then it's tables out in the street, food out, and dancing until first light! It's lucky for the year ahead if your lantern stays lit all night. Would you like a lantern stick?"

"Oh, we have floating lanterns where I come from, or standing ones with candles in so we don't need sticks. I'd love to make one, but I don't think I'll have time."

"Not to worry, many will be sold on Lantern Night. You won't miss out!"

Tibbit wished her goodbye and hurried back into his shop, other customers having gone inside.

Mabel walked a few paces over to Maritime Macarons. There was a beautiful display in the large glass window. A large cake in the shape of a turtle was surrounded by smaller turtle cakes in pretty paper cases. Meringues in swirling colors were suspended from threads to look like lanterns. The shop was busy, and she joined a queue that went out the door. A young elven woman about the same age as Mabel with dark hair swept up into a delicate bun was smiling and serving. An older elven woman with equally dark hair came in several times, filling up gaps in the display on the counter. It smelled wonderful. Mabel bought two small turtle cakes.

"I would like to ask something, too," Mabel said, putting the cakes in her bag. "Tibbit suggested I speak to Driel. It's about your neighbor Thorne."

"Driel is my mother," the young elven woman said. "You'd better come through to the kitchen." She unlatched a half wooden door on the counter edge and ushered Mabel through a door. The kitchen was a marvelous place. A large bank of three ovens was at the back, a pot full of red fruit was boiling on the stove top, and little cakes and fancies were everywhere. The older elven woman was bent over the table carefully placing small chocolate eyes onto a new batch of turtle cakes with a pair of tweezers.

"Mother, this lady is asking about Thorne. I'd better get back to the counter." The young elf grabbed a tray of lantern-shaped biscuits from the table and disappeared back into the shop.

"I'm sorry to take up your time," Mabel said.

Driel put the tweezers down and stood straight, stretching her back.

"Oh, don't worry about that, I'm glad for the break. These turtle cakes are a best seller, but very fiddly to get right! I've not seen Thorne for a while, but why are you interested?" There was something kind about the elf's face, and Mabel found herself pouring out all that had happened. She told Driel all about her mentor, the strange note, and the terrible state of the workroom next door.

"Well, it must have been upsetting for you, and you say you found his workroom like that just now? Here, sit down." Driel pulled out a stool and moved the boiling fruit mixture over so she could put a kettle on. "I always say something sweet helps after a shock." Driel placed a plate full of tiny almond cakes with some kind of piped cream in front of Mabel. "I'll also put a spoon of honey in your tea." The elf seemed to enjoy fussing around her, and Mabel felt herself relax. It was nice to be mothered for a little while.

Driel poured two cups of tea and passed one to Mabel.

"Drink up, you'll feel better," Driel gave Mabel an encouraging smile, and sat down at the table with her own cup.

"You said you haven't seen Thorne for a while. When did you last see him?" Mabel asked. She took a sip of her tea and nearly spat it out again. It was incredibly sweet.

Driel's forehead creased. "Hmm, let's see, it must be three weeks, maybe a little more. But it was quite unusual, even for Thorne."

"Unusual how?"

"It was nearly midnight, and I couldn't sleep. I made myself a lavender tea and sat on the balcony. It was such a pleasant night. There was a bit of a commotion coming from Thorne's workroom, banging, crashing that sort of thing." Driel sipped her tea.

"Weren't you worried?" Mabel asked.

"No, odd sounds and smells come out of that workroom all the time. I remember once an orange foam leaked out from under his door and filled half his courtyard. It smelled of rotten eggs for days afterwards." Driel's nose wrinkled, as if she could still smell it.

"Is that when you saw him? Late at night?" Mabel leaned forward in curiosity.

"Yes, the back door creaked open shortly after I stepped

outside. Thorne came out, and Robert, his apprentice, was right behind him. Between them, they were holding some kind of contraption. It looked like they had tied a tea tray to some sticks and were carrying it the way healers carry a stretcher. On it was something not too big, maybe the size of a number three cake pan, and it was wrapped in a blanket. They kept arguing with each other, but quietly. Then the blanket started flapping, all by itself. An odd chill crept over me, which was strange because it was so warm. Whatever it was started shaking so much they had to put it on the ground. It seemed to settle down, and they picked the sticks back up and went off down the road, arguing in whispers all the way." Driel shrugged.

"We thought someone else might have come in and smashed up his workshop. It's a relief to know that Thorne left of his own accord, but it's all very strange," Mabel said. She wondered what could have been in the blanket.

"I haven't seen Thorne since that night, but I have seen Robert. He's been back several times, collecting things and shutting the shop up again. I thought they might have gone to the Alchemists' Guild house."

"My mentor has gone there now to see if there is any news. Maybe everything's sorted out then." Mabel considered trying to find the Guild House herself, but a lot of time had passed. She didn't want to arrive there and find Alden had already left. "I told Alden I would meet him at the Moontide Inn, so I'll head there now."

"Finish your tea first, and I'll put some of these cakes into a bag for you," Driel said, getting up and bustling about again.

Mable forced down a few more mouthfuls of the sweet tea to be polite. Luckily it had cooled, and she could drink it quickly. Driel handed her a brown paper bag that smelled of almonds.

"Thank you so much for the cakes and for telling me about

Thorne. Knowing that makes me feel better, and I know it will comfort Alden too." Mabel said.

"When you find out what's been happening, come back and let me know. If I see Thorne or his apprentice, I'll send a message to the Moontide for you."

Mabel thanked Driel and hurried back through the Trading Square to see if Alden had returned to the inn.

MABEL WAS CURLED UP IN A LARGE, COMFORTABLE CHAIR BY A downstairs window at the Moontide Inn. She held the glass orb in her hand and was practicing channeling aether into it when she heard the tap of Alden's cane. She looked up eagerly, hoping for good news from the Alchemists' Guild, but Alden shook his head.

"They haven't seen him in over three weeks," he said, easing himself into the chair opposite her. "Thorne had been working on something special for Winter's Tide. He'd been keeping it under wraps, working on it secretly for months. Then he came in and told everyone he'd had a great success, and that they wouldn't believe their eyes on Lantern Night. After that, he stopped popping into the Whispering Vials, and they noticed that his shop was closed. They thought that his invention hadn't worked after all, and after all his boasting, he was too embarrassed to face anyone. No one was worried about him."

"His neighbors weren't worried, either," Mabel said. She told Alden everything she'd discovered. Alden raised his eyebrows when she got to the part about Thorne carrying something out of his shop at night, but he let Mabel continue to the end. He steepled his fingers and looked to the sky, as if hoping for inspiration from above.

"What should we do now?" Mabel asked.

"I really don't know. I'm not as worried as I was, knowing he left his shop voluntarily. For a while I thought that someone might have taken him, or worse. Clearly, something is still very wrong." Alden sighed and rubbed at his forehead, squeezing his eyes shut. "It's been a very long day. Let's have dinner."

Mabel ordered the Moontide Inn's most famous dish, treasures of the sea soup, although the treasures mainly seemed to consist of white and chewy wobbly bits or things with suckers. After the first few spoonfuls, she tried not to look too hard at some more interesting pieces floating under the surface. As long as she carefully suppressed memories of the fish stall that afternoon, she found it did taste very good, and at least the white, fluffy bread was familiar. She looked over at Alden's plate, full of steaming white fish and green sea vegetables, and decided to order that next time.

"I was thinking, no one has seen Thorne for weeks, but they have seen his apprentice, so he must still be nearby. Perhaps if we asked around about him, we might get some idea about where they have gone?"

"That's a good idea, Mabel. The market would be a good place to start. It's the beating heart of Turtle Bay, and market traders like to gossip. Let's make a start on that first thing in the morning." Alden rubbed his eyes, the dark circles underneath more pronounced than usual.

"I've been meaning to ask, are you not sleeping? I sometimes hear you walking around in the night," Mabel said.

"No, I don't sleep very well, but I'm used to that."

"My Grandmother used to make a special tea for sleeplessness. Have you tried anything like that?"

"I have potions too, but they either don't work or work too well and leave me sleepy the next day or cause other problems. At my age, you need to get up several times a night if you drink anything just before bed." He gave her a weary smile. "I have, how can I put it, difficult dreams that I am glad to wake from. It is very hard to get back to sleep when they are over."

"I'm sorry Alden. I didn't mean to pry."

"Please don't worry, it's nice you're concerned." He leaned forward and reassuringly patted her arm. "Really, I'm fine. It's just been a very long day, and an upsetting one too."

Mabel smiled at Alden, although she still felt worried for him. She mopped up the last of the soup with her bread and sat back with a heavy sigh. The meal had been an experience, but she felt better for it. It was still far too early to go to bed, and the air in the busy restaurant was hot and stuffy.

"They have a rooftop bar upstairs. Why don't we sit out in the fresh air for a bit?" she suggested.

The Moontide Inn was several stories higher than the surrounding buildings, and the open air rooftop bar had a view that took in the bay. They watched the sun sinking towards the sea, and the comings and goings at the docks. Alden tried an opaque drink with a frothy topping which smelled fairly alcoholic to Mabel. She couldn't tolerate even the smallest amount of alcohol. It made her flush bright red and gave her a terrible headache. She tried a cold herbal tea, which was just right for a warm night. They shared the cakes Mabel had bought from Driel's bakery.

"Can I see the note again that Thorne sent you?" Mabel asked. Alden took it out from a pocket inside his robe. Mabel read it over and over.

"What does he mean by 'remember the old days'?"

"We were best friends, but I was always the sensible one. Our friends joked that he was the Thorne in my side. Whenever we got in trouble, it always seemed to stem from one of Thorne's good ideas. He was an incredibly talented alchemist who was innovative and unafraid to try new things. But that bravery sometimes bordered on recklessness, and I can't help but wonder if that has happened now."

Mabel returned the note. She got her own notebook out of her green leather satchel and started writing down her thoughts about the day. She flipped to a page titled *Masterpiece Ideas*, underneath which were a few crossed-out entries. Her pen hovered over the next blank line.

"Hoping for inspiration?" Alden said, peering over at her book. "Coming up with the idea will be the hardest part for you. Once you know what you want to do, you will very quickly discover a way to make it happen or figure out that it can't be done. You are a problem solver at heart, Mabel. You need a problem to solve."

Mabel grimaced, but considered this. She had been trying so hard to come up with a grand idea, a brand-new invention, instead of thinking about how she could make life better for people. She wrote *Problems* at the top of a new page and then tapped her pencil against her nose as she thought. In a world full of problems, she couldn't think of a single one to tackle.

"Thank you, Alden. I think that's going to be helpful. Would you like another drink?" She asked, finally looking up from her notebook, only to see Alden had fallen asleep in his chair. She wrote *Sleep difficulties* down in her book.

MABEL STIFLED A YAWN AS SHE DECIDED WHAT TO WEAR THE NEXT morning. She didn't have many clothes to choose from, and most were too warm for the humid heat of Turtle Bay. Finally, she chose a light blue dress that was also her smartest. It was Lantern Night, after all. Mabel twisted her long dark hair into a bun and perched the orchid-colored hat at a perky angle. It had little hair combs that kept it in place, probably because of the frequent sea breeze that blew through the port town. She put her notebook and her glass orb into her green leather bag and headed downstairs.

Alden was already sitting at a table in the common room, having breakfast. He smiled when Mabel joined him and poured her a cup of coffee from the pot. Mabel helped herself to some spiced fruit bread from the basket on the table. Soon they were heading out again into Turtle Bay market. It was not so hot this morning, and Mabel wished she had nothing to do but browse all day.

"I thought it would be busier, as it's Lantern Night tonight," Mabel said, as they moved easily through the market.

"Many people will be preparing food, or making lanterns with little ones today. Tonight, it will be chaos! You will see."

"Where do we begin?" Mabel asked, looking around the bewildering array of stalls.

"I thought we would start with the stalls that sell alchemical goods. If Thorne's apprentice has been back to the shop to collect things, he may have come to buy supplies from the market too."

They spent most of the morning asking at various stalls, all while the temperature rose. Mabel's nerves began to fray. She hadn't had time to get used to the warm weather, and the market was getting busier. The hat was doing a good job keeping the sun off, and she was glad she bought it. She eyed some of the cooler dresses on display, billowing silks and fine thin linens, and hoped to have some time for personal shopping later. Alden was leaning on his cane and fanning his face. Mabel put a hand on his arm.

"Why don't we sit down with a cool drink for a while?" she asked.

"Yes, perhaps you could ask at this stall, and I'll do the one next door, then we will take a break," Alden said.

Mabel approached a stand with a chalkboard sign that said *Tide's Bounty Alchemy Supplies.*

Various shells, algae, mermaid's purses, and seaweed in all different colors were presented neatly in wooden compartments. A tangy, salty smell rose from the display. Mabel reached out to touch a clump of spongy orange frilled leaves. They felt rubbery under her fingers. A crinkled old woman behind the stall gave her a huge smile.

"Ah, you like the siren's spongefrill? Only six platinum."

"Six platinum!" Mabel pulled her hand back as if it was burned. "What is it for?"

"If you grind it, you can make a tea that will compel a person to tell the truth for a short time. The only problem is that they will tell you all kinds of true things, not necessarily the one you were hoping for. They babble like crazy! Still, alchemists and herbalists keep buying it, hoping to refine it into an effective truth serum." The old lady leaned over and spoke quietly from behind her hand, as if sharing a secret. "Personally, I think you get the same effect from several good glasses of whiskey!" She stood back and laughed loudly. Mabel grinned, too. The old lady's good cheer was infectious.

"I really came over to ask you something. My mentor and I are a bit worried about Thorne the Alchemist, and I was wondering if you have seen him or his apprentice in the last few weeks? I just want to be sure he's okay. Do you know them at all?"

"Yes, of course. I know Thorne, cheeky old devil that he is, and his apprentice, Robert. I haven't seen Thorne for a while, but Robert was here last Tuesday. He brought a whole bag of weatherweed." The old woman lifted some stringy green seaweed with long twisting fronds.

"What's that?" Mabel asked, not daring to touch in case it cost six platinum.

"Sailors use it to predict the weather at sea, and alchemists use it to make those fancy weather boxes. Popular around here because of the afternoon rain."

"Yes, I've seen one of those. Did Robert say if everything is all right?" Mabel fished her notebook out of her green bag and made some quick notes about what the lady had said so far.

"Hmmm. Robert did look a bit flustered. I offered to deliver the weatherweed to Thorne's shop, because Robert was already carrying a lot of packages, but he said no because he had to take it to the docks." The old woman shrugged. "I hope everything is okay. Even though Thorne is a rascal and barters my prices down to the bone, he is a good customer."

"We hope so. I'm sure we'll find him soon. Thank you for your help."

"You are very welcome. You seem like a nice girl, and you have a lovely hat. I'd hate to see it get ruined. You should take some weatherweed." Despite Mabel's protesting hand gestures, the old woman tore some fronds from the long twisted seaweed and started putting them in a bag.

"You only need a little bit. It'll tell you when it's going to rain. See how it's crisp and dry now? That means dry weather. But if the weatherweed goes soft, then it's going to rain. Make sure to take that hat off. It'll lose its shape if it gets wet! If the fronds roll into a tight tube, the wind will be strong, so make sure your hat is pinned on well." The woman spun the bag around, twisting the top securely. "If it's soft and rolled up at the same time, there will be a bad storm, and I've been told the fronds curl outwards towards the spine if it's going to snow, but I've never seen that. There has never been snow in Turtle Bay. For you, just two silver." The old woman held her hand out for the money. Mabel was relieved it wasn't several platinum. She handed the silvers over and accepted the paper bag.

"Thank you," Mabel said, turning to go.

"You're welcome. Keep it in your pocket and check it every now and then!" The old woman called out as Mabel hurried away to tell Alden what she had discovered.

AFTER A COOL DRINK AT AN OUTDOOR CAFÉ, MABEL AND ALDEN treated themselves to an open carriage ride to the docks. The smell of the sea became stronger the closer they got, and the shouts and calls of men working the boats and handling cargo got louder. Shops and houses gave way to large warehouse buildings. Mabel couldn't stop staring at the tall ships lined up at the wooden docks, their gangplanks swarming with people carrying things up and down. As a child in Medlar Vale, she often sat at the inland moorings in Riverhaven and watched the barges arriving and leaving. She had thought some of those ships were impressive, but they were nothing compared to the oceangoing vessels she saw here. They were huge, with masts as tall as trees, ornate carved bows, and so many ropes and sails. A nervous horse whinnied and shied as it was led down a gangplank onto the docks. Large warehouse doors were open, and carts lined up ready to take the boxes, barrels and sacks that came off the ships. Although at first it looked like chaos, Mabel realized that actually it was all very organized, and everyone seemed to know their part in the complicated dance of crates and barrels.

"Any ships that arrive tonight will have to wait to be unloaded, because you won't be able to move for people," their carriage driver said. "Everyone will be down here on the docks by dusk. There's nothing like the sunset here on Lantern Night! You're my last customer today. I promised the kids we would finish their lanterns together, then walk down to get a good spot. So, where do you want to be dropped off?"

"Is there a tavern here, one where everyone will know the latest gossip and news?" Alden asked. The carriage driver laughed.

"You want The Barnacle over on the east dock." He flicked the reins, and the horse started to turn left.

They found themselves standing outside a rather rough-looking tavern a few minutes later.

"Do you think it's safe in there?" Mabel asked Alden.

"I'm sure it will be. This is still the queendom, although many in Turtle Bay are from outside it. You don't have to come in, of course."

Mabel looked around. She didn't think she would feel much better about standing outside.

"Let's quickly ask inside and move on, then." She straightened her hat, clutched her bag tightly, and followed Alden through the battered door.

It was gloomy inside, the light filtering through thick, dirty glass windows in the front and flickering from the old ship's lanterns inside. The stools by the bar had rope work around the seats, and the tables were made of old planks. Mabel looked up at the yellow ceiling—old saws and other ship-building tools hung from the beams, along with sprigs of weatherweed and decorative knotwork. It was mostly empty, but a few drinkers settled in for the day. The lady behind the bar looked like she could easily lift any beer keg with one hand. She dried glasses as she talked with the regulars until she noticed them.

"The lantern parade isn't until this evening," she told them, "and these seats are for customers only."

"I'm looking for some information about a friend," Alden said. The barkeeper relaxed, put down her glass and cloth, and leaned forward with her elbows on the bar.

"Aye, we've usually got the scuttlebutt around here. If

you've got enough coins and you don't mind buying a drink or two, I expect someone will be willing to share their news."

"We will, of course, buy a drink." Alden looked at the bewildering array of bottles behind the bar. "Perhaps I could have something that can be shared with everyone?"

The woman grunted, wiped her hands on her apron, and fetched a square bottle with a clear spirit inside. The label said *Dawn's Dread*.

"This'll loosen some lips," she said, opening the bottle. "It's named after the hangover you get the next day,"

Mabel could smell the alcohol from where she stood. The barkeeper grinned as she poured the clear liquid into thumb-sized glasses. The air shimmered above each one. Mabel shook her head as one was pushed towards her.

"I'll just have some water, thank you."

Alden picked up a glass and took a sip, coughing a bit as his eyes watered.

"It certainly clears the sinuses!"

The uncorking of the bottle drew drinkers from all corners of the tavern. No one had any immediate information on Thorne or his apprentice. After some conversations between the regulars, a dwarf with a scar on his forehead and a thick leather belt approached them.

"I'm Ornon, and I've been working the docks all my life." The dwarf gave them a warm smile and took a seat at the bar. "On the queen's docks, we all know each other and keep an eye out for each other. If you're worried about your friend, I can send a runner to ask around."

"Yes, please. I'd be very grateful," Alden said. He gave Ornon a description of Thorne and his apprentice. The dwarf smiled and went to talk with a rangy-looking boy in the corner, who nodded several times before scuttling out of the door.

"You can wait or come back tomorrow," Ornon said when

he returned to the bar. "Jack will do his best, but most folks will be off to meet with family and watch the sunset soon."

"I'd very much like to see the sunset," Mabel said. "If there isn't any news by then, perhaps we could watch the lantern parade and come back tomorrow?"

Alden pursed his lips for a moment as he thought it over. "Yes, I would like to wait in case there is any news, and the Turtle Bay celebrations are wonderful. I wouldn't want you to miss out on that, Mabel." He turned to the scarred dwarf and smiled warmly. "Thank you for all your help, Ornon. I appreciate it more than I can tell you."

"Now, maybe you can tell me why you are so worried about your alchemist friend?" Ornon asked.

They told their tale, and Ornon continued to sit with them at the bar, telling stories that made Mabel laugh. The Barnacle looked rough, but everyone inside was friendly, and Mabel found she was enjoying herself more than she had in a long time. The barkeeper brought out a large tray of flatbreads and a round-bellied clay pot of vegetable stew.

"Eat up!" she called out to the room at large, then she leaned over to Mabel. "If I don't give them something to soak it up a bit, they'll all be impossible later. It's on the house, so help yourself."

Mabel could see the sun getting lower in the sky out of the small, dirty windows. People with lanterns were gathering on the docks. She nudged Alden, who was looking rosy about the cheeks and finishing a third flatbread.

"It looks like people are getting ready for the celebrations," she said. "Do you think we could go outside and watch?"

"Yes, let's. If we haven't heard anything by now, I don't think we will tonight." Alden brushed some crumbs off his robe and stood up. "It looks like we're not the only ones."

Mabel hadn't expected the denizens of The Barnacle to be

taking part in the parade, but lanterns started appearing out of nowhere. There were lanterns shaped like fish, Ornon had one shaped like a ship, and even the lady behind the bar brought a moon-shaped lantern out from the back room. Mabel had just started to open the door when the young lad Jack came bursting through it, almost knocking her back into Alden. Jack took his hat off in apology and gripped it as he spoke.

"Sorry about that, miss. I've just been talking to the loaders on the west side, and they've seen a young man who might be your apprentice alchemist," the boy said. He paused for a moment to catch his breath before continuing. "He's been coming back and forth from the Trading Square, carrying boxes and bags of stuff, and always in a hurry. They saw him going inside one of the warehouses before I arrived. I ran all the way back to tell you." His face was still pink from the effort, but he looked pleased.

"It could be Robert," Mabel said. "The lady at the market did say he was carrying lots of packages when she sold him the weatherweed, and the gnome in the gift shop said he saw Robert taking things out of the shop too."

Alden looked relieved. "It's worth a try. Would you show us the way, Jack? I'd happily pay you a silver for your trouble."

IT WAS DIFFICULT TO WALK QUICKLY THROUGH THE PEOPLE. ELVES, dwarves, gnomes, and humans were crowding the docks, many clustered in family groups. Everyone's lanterns were bobbing in the breeze from the sea. Children sat on their father's shoulders, and grandmothers praised clumsily decorated efforts made by small hands. Mabel saw a huge red crab-shaped lantern that was so large two elves had to hold it up. They were followed by a band of drummers and a dwarf playing a trumpet. Pop-up stalls punctuated the crowd like rocks in a stream, selling food, shells, colorful garlands, and lanterns. There was still an hour or so until the sun would set.

"Here we are," Jack said at last. "I'm not going in there, though. That place is weird."

They had stopped in front of a warehouse one street from the docks. There were no crowds because there was no view of the sea.

"Thank you so much, Jack. I hope you won't miss any of the celebrations on our behalf," Mabel said.

"Don't worry. My Da's been working the dock today. I'll join him and Ma there now, and they will be very happy with the silver you gave me." Jack gave them a wide grin and ran back towards the crowds.

Mabel looked up at the building. Blue paint peeled on the large double cargo doors, and the upstairs windows looked like they had been papered over years ago. It was a contrast to the other warehouses on the street that looked neatly kept. A shabby side door was visible at the far end of the building. From the distance, music drifted over from where crowds were watching the beautiful sunset, and Mabel wished she were there instead.

"Let's go knock on that side door," Mabel said reluctantly.

As they walked closer, in-between the tap, tap sounds of Alden's cane, Mabel thought she heard a *tick . . . tick . . .* noise coming from her bag. She opened the green leather strap and looked inside to see the copper wheel in her magic practice orb slowly rotating.

"That's so strange," she said. As she reached in to get it, she saw the paper bag with the weatherweed had torn. The leaves inside weren't dry and crispy anymore. They were soft and leathery.

"Oh no, not rain," she said, taking the weed out. She put a

hand on her hat. Then she felt rather than heard a low rumble as if it was coming up through her boots. Thunder maybe? She looked up at the clear sky, her forehead wrinkled.

"That's odd. It's changing again." Mabel held the weather-weed out to Alden so he could see. They both watched as it curled up into a tight tube and then it uncurled in her hand and flicked itself over, the fronds curling inwards on the other side towards the thick spine running down the back.

"It makes no sense. That's supposed to mean snow, but it's boiling!"

"I think someone's been having a little joke with you," Alden said.

"I've been taken for a fool by that market seller," Mabel said, her cheeks hot. She shoved the weed into her pocket, feeling it turn crispy again as she did so, and strode quickly towards the door. As she reached out to knock, Mabel could feel the hairs on the back of her neck rising. The ticking noise from her bag was fast and insistent. She took a step back and turned to face her mentor.

"Someone or something is using a lot of magic in there, Alden."

"We knew Thorne took something from his shop. Maybe it's that," Alden replied. "Your sense for the aether has always been stronger than mine, but even I can feel it now that we are closer. Perhaps you should walk back to the docks. I can check on Thorne and meet you at The Barnacle afterward."

"I don't want to leave you to go in alone. I'll go in first. If I sense anything really bad, I'll let you know."

Mabel tried the handle, expecting the door to be locked, but it swung open, revealing a musty, disused office. Chairs were messily gathered around old desks. Yellowed paperwork lay in piles here and there. Dust gathered thickly, but Mabel could see feet had recently tracked a path into the other room. Her heart thumped as she felt the rumbling sensation coming up through her boots again. She drew in a deep breath, squeezed her fists tight, and followed the footsteps in the dust. They walked through several smaller rooms filled with old sacks, oars, ropes, and fishing nets.

Finally, they came to a blue door larger than all the others. Every hair on Mabel's body stood on end. Goosebumps covered her skin, and the stinging metallic tang of magic was so strong in the air that she could taste it. Cautiously, Mabel nudged the door open just a sliver. A deafening roar came out, accompanied by shouting voices. Mabel immediately pulled the door shut, and it was quiet again.

"A noise-containing spell!" Alden said. "It's not easy to keep one of those going."

"Good gods, what's going on in there?" Mabel said.

"Oh, Thorne, my old friend. What have you been up to now?" Alden said, shaking his head. "It was definitely his voice I heard, and a younger one too, his apprentice, I assume. Let's go in and find out."

Mabel pushed the door open again and stepped through into a gale.

Mabel's skin prickled painfully. It felt as though one of her failed experiments was about to explode. She had to bend almost double to make any headway into the large warehouse, plodding forward with heavy footsteps. She glanced behind her to see Alden planting his enchanted cane firmly on the ground and using it to pull himself along. Mabel felt her new hat tear away from her head despite the combs, taking a few hairs with it. Squinting into the wind, she could see a bearded figure in a billowing alchemist's robe shouting to a tall young man in a brown shirt and trousers. Behind them, a sphere with an iridescent sheen was suspended in midair. Then, in an instant, everything changed. Mabel staggered a step or two as the wind completely dropped. The temperature started to rise. Even though the noise of the wind had stopped, the alchemist and his apprentice still shouted at each other. Mabel wiped her brow; it was hotter now than at midday. Her practice orb whined in her bag. The wheel must be spinning off its axis with all the magic in the air.

"Thorne!" Alden shouted.

The alchemist turned, shocked, and then his exhausted face broke into a smile.

"Alden, thank the gods, you came!" Thorne ran over and clasped Alden's free hand in both of his, shaking it warmly before pulling him into an embrace. "But you must get out of the warehouse! It's not safe in here anymore. I can't leave with you, I'm afraid. Things got worse so much faster than I expected."

Thorne's apprentice, Robert, walked over to them slowly, hands thrust deep in his pockets. He looked at them both with a wary expression. Mabel saw strings of weatherweed tightly tied to a pillar behind him. She put a hand into her pocket and pulled out her own bunch. It was curling back towards the spine again.

"What has happened, Thorne? Is this why you sent me the note?" Alden placed a hand on his friend's shoulder and looked worriedly into his face.

"I was working on something special, Alden, for the lantern parade. It was going to be the masterwork of my life, the culmination of all my studies. It needed a lot of magic to set the spark; at first, everything was perfect. Then it became unpredictable, and the area of effect kept growing and growing, and no matter what I did, I couldn't seem to contain it."

"But what is it, Thorne? What have you made?"

The temperature in the room plunged. Ice formed on the

floor beneath the floating sphere, and big fat snowflakes began to fall from nowhere.

"It's a weather stone, like from the children's stories. I wanted to make a real one," he said, gesturing to the snow. He looked embarrassed. "I was going to present it at the Lantern Night feast in the Trading Square. I thought the kiddies would enjoy playing in the snow underneath. It was only supposed to cover a few yards. Most of the children here have never seen snow. But on Lantern Night, where I come from, it snows every year. I thought it would be fun . . . " he trailed off.

Alden rubbed his eyes.

"A weather stone indeed! Thorne, you know better than anyone something of that complexity is almost guaranteed to fail."

"But I did it! It worked! I was storing it in my privy until Lantern Night, and it was perfect. But after a few days, I noticed that the snow was spreading outside the privy door, so I brought it into my workroom to tweak it a little, and that's when things started to go wrong. When I channeled aether into it a second time, the stone cracked, just a little, the size of a hair."

"It stopped doing just snow then," Robert chimed in. "There was a big whirlwind, and it broke everything in the room, then it rained, and all our research papers got wet."

Mabel shivered and hugged her arms around herself. She wasn't dressed for cold weather. The snowflakes were melting into her hair and settling on her clothes.

"Yes, that's when I knew I had to move it." Thorne continued, his own teeth chattering. "I asked around, and a friend of a friend let me rent this place. We brought it here at night so we could fix it."

The weatherweed was changing in Mabel's hand again, curling into a tight tube.

"Not the wind again," she said. The snowflakes started to peter out, and a breeze blew them around. The wind grew stronger, whipping at Mabel's clothes and driving the snow into drifts. Thorne had to shout again to be heard over the roaring wind.

"I've been here ever since trying to contain it, but I'm afraid, Alden. I'm losing control." He turned and gestured to the opal-colored stone in the center of the room. "The crack is growing, and I don't know how far the effect will spread."

"Thorne, you utter fool. Why didn't you build safeguards to limit how much aether it could draw? I'm amazed you have kept it contained this long." Alden shouted to be heard, holding his hat on his head, his stick keeping him rooted firmly in place.

Mabel covered her eyes. The wind was whipping snowflakes into her face and stinging her skin. She gripped the weatherweed tightly in her fist so it didn't blow away. Then she felt the fronds soften in her grasp and knew what was coming next. The wind died down, and mercifully, so did the noise. Then the rain started. It quickly melted all the snow but soaked Mabel to the skin. She pushed wet strands of hair out of her face.

"How have you been able to stand it?" Mabel asked Robert. She had only been in the warehouse a short while, and she was already miserable. Robert looked like he wanted to cry. Both he and Thorne appeared utterly drained.

"We take it in turns," Robert said. "When Thorne sleeps, I keep an eye on it. I've had to go out for supplies and food and things. It's been hard," he said. The rain plastered his hair to his head and ran in rivulets down his face, making him look even more miserable.

"Is it safe to get closer? Can you show me?" Mabel asked. She could feel the magic thrumming in the air, but she wanted a better look at the weather stone. It was dangerous but also fascinating.

"Don't touch it," Robert said, "but you can get quite close. The magical effect area has been increasing. I don't think we can keep it inside the warehouse much longer. Do you think Alden will be able to help?"

"I don't know. I hope so."

Although the weather stone looked pearlescent from a distance, as she got closer, Mabel could see it was a large smooth rock made up of pink and white stone swirled together, sparkling slightly. The stone was about the size of a small loaf of bread. Mabel saw the crack and could feel the raw power coming from inside. Suddenly, her stomach heaved; she felt as if she was falling, and her ears popped. The rain started falling upwards.

"Oh no, not this again!" Robert moaned.

"It only started doing the backward rain today," Thorne said, moving to stand behind Robert, putting a hand on his shoulder. "It's becoming more unstable. What am I going to do? Alden, this is why I wrote to you. If anyone can figure this out, it's you."

Alden spent some time examining the stone, asking Thorne questions about its creation, and scratching his head in thought. Eventually, Alden's chin dropped to his chest, and he slowly shook his head.

"I'm sorry, old friend. I'm not sure I will be able to fix it this time."

The raindrops rising towards the sky disoriented Mabel, so she closed her eyes and concentrated on what she could feel. Wild fluctuations in the aether meant the stone was beyond unstable, making her very afraid. Her eyes snapped open.

"Alden, the weather stone is reaching a breaking point. The crack is too large now. The stone is going to fail. There will be a huge blast of released magic when it breaks in two. I'm very worried. What happens if the stone is in a heat phase when it goes? We are right next to the docks. Docks that are currently packed with people . . . " Alden looked concerned, but Thorne put a hand up to stop her talking.

"Even if it goes into a heat phase, I don't think it would do much worse to anyone standing on the docks than give them a mild sunburn, singe some hair perhaps, maybe set fire to a lantern or two. Probably." Thorne ran his hand through his beard as he spoke.

"Probably!" Mabel actually choked on her anger and was unable to speak for a moment.

"It wouldn't be very good for us in here, though, either way, would it? Can't we put it on a boat and row it out to sea?" Robert asked. He crossed his arms huffily. "I've been telling Thorne to do that all week."

"I didn't know it was going to go critical!" Thorne exclaimed, his voice rising as his cheeks flushed. "If we dumped the blasted thing at sea, it could end up anywhere. It might sink a ship by whipping up a storm or wash up on some unsuspecting fishing village. How in the queen's name are they supposed to stop it if we can't?"

"Now is not the time for arguing," Alden said, putting his hands up. "But I don't think we dare to move it if it's so unstable—it might be the last straw."

"When experiments go bad in my workroom, I throw a magic-dampening blanket over them," Mabel said. "Can't we just wrap it up in one?"

"That's how we moved the stone from my shop," Thorne said. "We wrapped it in a magic-dampening blanket and carried it on sticks so we didn't have to touch it, but the blanket could barely contain the magic even for that short trip; it kept blasting out."

Robert nodded. "When we got to the warehouse, we thought we'd keep it wrapped up for a bit, but the blanket just disintegrated." Robert used his sleeve to wipe his nose, which had started running due to the upward rain. "When the blanket fell away, we saw the crack had doubled in size, and the stone had become much more unpredictable."

Mabel rubbed her temples as she thought. She looked around the warehouse. Stone pillars held up the high ceiling, covered by a network of ropes and pulleys designed for moving and stacking heavy crates. The weather stone was going to fracture, and soon. There was no way around it. An idea itched at the back of her mind. If they couldn't stop a critical failure, maybe they could time it? Perhaps they could provoke the stone to explode on a rain cycle rather than a heat one. She didn't want the children on the docks to suffer even a mild sunburn or have their lanterns catch fire, assuming that Thorne was correct. She imagined poking the stone with a broom handle or throwing something at it, but there had to be a better way. A raindrop fell directly up her nostril, making her snort, but even that wasn't dislodging this train of thought. The ideas started to snowball. Maybe they could direct the blast, too? The upward rain petered out, and the room began warming up again. They were running out of time, but Mabel felt a fizz of excitement mix with her fear. She didn't have a solution, but an emergency salvage measure would be enough.

Mabel hurried out of the main warehouse, with Robert tagging along behind her. They had left Alden and Thorne in the other room, doing their best to stabilize the stone just a bit longer to buy Mabel some time. She gathered up a large sack, some sail-mending thread, a needle, and a length of rope and bundled them into Robert's arms as they went.

"You can put it all down there," she said, pointing to a spot next to a small wooden barrel. "Do you still have alchemy supplies left?"

"Yes, but some things we used up all together. What do you need?"

Mabel flipped through her notebook, looking back at the list of ingredients from the empty drawers in Thorne's shop. "I see you brought gorgon clay, iron dust, and sealing powder from the shop," she said to him. "Do you still have them?"

"I'll go check." He hurried off and returned a few moments later clutching a leather alchemist's supplies bag. He started laying out jars and packets.

"There's plenty of gorgon clay, and we didn't use any iron dust. There's not much sealing powder left, though," he said, holding up a jar with only a few teaspoonfuls of white powder in.

"We don't have time to get any more. It'll just have to do. Is there a set of measuring steels?"

"Yes, at the bottom of the bag." Robert rummaged until he brought out a set of metal spoons connected by a leather strap. "I still don't understand why you want to turn a sack into a magic-dampening blanket. It didn't work last time." Robert looked exhausted. He sagged against the wall and wiped his arm across his forehead.

"There's no way to stop the stone from failing now," Mabel said. She opened the gorgon clay and measured a single scoop into the barrel. "But if we can force the stone to explode on a rain cycle, it would be much safer. If we can pull the sack up over the stone, all that magical energy will be directed right back at it, and then . . . " Mabel made an explosion gesture with her hands. Robert swallowed. "We just have to time it right. Do you have any water?"

"Yes, it's the one thing we've had a regular supply of," he said gloomily. Robert pushed himself off the wall, disappeared into the other room, and returned with a clay pitcher a few moments later.

"It's going to be very bad for whoever puts the sack over the stone, though, isn't it?" Robert said.

Mabel measured three large spoons of iron dust into the barrel. "I've been thinking about that, too. We can use that pulley system in the roof, you know, the one used to stack crates, so no one has to go right next to the stone. We wait until it's raining, then hoist the sack and stabilize it using ropes. Then, we can tie it off and hide behind the pillars. If we close the top up a bit, but not all the way, then there's a chance the magic will go up instead of out. I'm hoping that's better than what might happen if we leave it."

"It could work," Robert said slowly. A small amount of hope leaked into his face for the first time.

Creating a magic-dampening blanket was one of the first assignments new students at the Whispering Vials Guild House were given. Each student made their own to take from class to class in case their experiments went wrong. It was not hard to do, although the ingredients were expensive. First, the material would be soaked in gorgon clay and iron dust. This helped absorb and reflect the magic. Then, it was stabilized with sealing solution before being infused with a small amount of aether.

Mabel poured the water in and asked Robert to stir the ingredients until the powder dissolved. Meanwhile, she sewed down the lip of the sack with the tough sail thread and a curved needle, using large bounding stitches for speed. Mabel left openings for ropes to pass through and made a channel at the bottom of the sack, too. Then she put it into the barrel and used the blunt end of an oar to pound the fabric.

"I'm hoping this will work it into the fibers faster," she said.

"I can do that," Robert said. He took over while Mabel looked at the jar of sealing powder. She bit her lip. The longer she left the sack to soak, the better, but the stone could give way at any moment. She hesitated, then poured the whole jar of sealing powder into the barrel. Robert pounded it in. She pulled the sack out, and they wrung it dry, twisting it between them.

"We just need to activate it now," Mabel said.

"We should do this together; it will be faster," Robert said. Mabel nodded reluctantly, and they both started infusing aether into the sack. For a moment, Mabel thought she could manage, but as soon as she felt her magic fluctuate, she quickly pulled her hands back. Robert looked up at her quizzically but carried on. Soon, a slight silver shimmer developed on the surface of the rough fabric. It was done. They rushed to the blue door. Mabel pushed it open and jumped back at the sound of a crack of lightning. Robert made a groaning noise.

"This one is even worse than the upwards rain. Can we wait a few minutes?"

"We might not have a few minutes!" Mabel walked into the warehouse without waiting for Robert and saw Thorne and Alden sheltering together under an arched pillar. Thorne had his arms outstretched as he tried to contain the magic. Mabel could feel static electricity building in the air. She saw all Thorne's hair standing on end, his robe floating oddly. Alden gripped his enchanted cane tightly.

"What's happening, Robert?" she asked, turning back, but Robert crouched near the doorway, urgently beckoning her to come over. Mabel felt her hair and skirts starting to swirl and lift. Broken crates and old barrels started floating. She tried to make her way over to Robert, but her feet lifted off the floor after just a few steps, leaving her walking helplessly on air as the pressure built and built. There was a crackling sound, and then a bolt of blue lighting seared through the air and struck the floor near the stone. The magic in the air was gone, and her feet hit the floor with a thud, the barrels and crates landing with a crash. The atmosphere changed, and the stone started to heat up again.

"It's never been that bad before," Robert said, coming out from the doorway.

"We have to get this done quickly. Robert, can you lower one of those pulleys?" Robert found a rope hitched to a metal pike and unwound it, lowering a metal hook attached to a movable pulley. Mabel attached the sack and handed out guide ropes to Alden and Thorne.

"Can you wind your ropes around those pillars, but just loosely for now? We can use them to position it, and when the sack is over the stone, pull your ropes tight and tie them off. I'll pull on my rope to close the neck of the sack." Mabel placed the sack as close to the stone as she dared, and they used the ropes to slide it directly underneath.

After a few moments, everything was in position. They waited. Sweat trickled down Mabel's back. She held her rope taut and watched the weatherweed tied to the pillar. It curled towards the spine. *That will have to do*, she thought to herself. The heat dissipated, and she called out when the first snowflakes fell.

"Lift!"

Robert pulled on his rope, the pulley in the ceiling squealing as he did so. Alden and Thorne used their guide ropes to ensure the sack stayed directly under the weather stone as it rose. As the sack eclipsed the stone, Mabel could feel the magic in the room lessening, and the snowflakes dwindled to a column directly above the sack.

"Tie your ropes off. I'm going to close the top," she called out. Alden and Thorne pulled their ropes tight and knotted them off on the pillars. Then Mabel stepped backward as she pulled on the thin rope that closed the top of the bag. She could hear a whining noise inside the bag—the stone must be going critical. She wound her own rope around a metal loop set into a pillar. How far should she close the top of the bag? Too far and the whole bag might explode; not far enough, and it may not be enough to force the blast upwards. When a hand-span of space was left at the top of the sack, the whining noise became unbearable. Mabel tied her rope off.

"That's it, that's all we can do," she shouted over the noise.

"Then let's get the fizz out of here!" Robert cried.

The sack bulged and bucked as they ran towards the door, but the ropes seemed to hold fast.

"Here it goes!" called Thorne. Everything went completely silent for a moment, and then there was an almighty crack. The top of the sack erupted with a powerful, pure white jet of snow that blew right through the warehouse roof.

FOR A MOMENT, THEY ALL FROZE IN PLACE AND STARED AS SNOW continued to erupt from the bag, a thick, white, unending column that disappeared through a rather large hole in the roof. Robert had his hand on the door, ready to run for the outside, but Mabel made a motion for him to wait.

"I can feel the magic draining," she said. The intense buzz of aether in the air pressing on her senses was fading quickly. "It doesn't feel dangerous anymore, not like it did before." Mabel took the glass practice globe out of her bag and showed it to Alden. The copper wheel inside, which had been a whining blur before, now spun at a steady pace, ticking gently.

"Hmm, perhaps we should take a closer look, Thorne?" Alden said.

Thorne looked as keen as Robert to be out of the door. He puckered his mouth as if he had eaten something unpleasant but huffed an agreement and followed Alden over to the stone.

"Do you really think it's safe now?" Robert asked.

"I can't say for sure, but the aether has dropped to near-normal levels," she said. The wheel inside her globe had slowed to every other heartbeat. Mabel's hands, which had been steady until now, started to shake. She quickly put the globe back in her bag and folded her hands beneath her arms, hoping that Robert wouldn't notice. She had been worried earlier when it looked like they might all get blown to bits, but she had also felt grounded and clear. Now that they were safe, it was as if someone had drained all the blood out of her. She felt cold, light-headed, and clammy. She looked up and saw Alden and Thorne returning from the stone. Thorne had cheered up considerably.

"It seems the worst is over! The snow will continue to erupt as the weather stone uses up its energy. When we return to clean up, I expect we will find an empty sack." Thorne's eyebrows furrowed as he looked at Mabel. "Are you quite all right, my dear? You look as though you are about to be sick?"

Mabel didn't trust herself to speak. Alden gently took her arm and steered her towards the door.

"I think we could all do with some fresh air after this evening's excitement," Alden said gently.

Mabel felt better as soon as she was on the move. By the time she stepped onto the street and took in a deep breath, her hands had stopped shaking. She forgot all about herself as soon as she looked up. Piercing through the warehouse roof was a gleaming white column of snow rising higher than the tallest spire in the city. Her eyes followed the snow's path into the sky.

She thought it would never stop, but eventually, the uppermost snow fanned out and fell slowly and gently like a graceful but enormous fountain.

"Cor blimey, look at that!" Robert said, coming to stand next to her. "How long do you think it'll do that, Thorne?"

"It could go on for half an hour, an hour, maybe even longer," Thorne said, looking impressed at the sight of the snow fountain. "Definitely not longer than a week. Hopefully."

They could hear the sound of trumpets, drums, and singing just one street over. The eruption had obviously not stopped anyone from enjoying the party at the docks. Mabel suddenly longed to join them.

"Shall we go join the celebrations?" she suggested.

"Why not? There's nothing else to be done here," Thorne said cheerfully. "This is the quickest way."

He led them to the end of the street, where they took a turn and suddenly found themselves among the celebrating crowds. The trumpets and drums were so loud that they could be felt as much as heard. The music had likely muffled the noise of the weather stone exploding, but many still pointed and stared at the column of snow spiking into the sky. People laughed and nudged each other, seeming to take it as just another part of the entertainment. The first flakes had yet to reach the ground, but it was still a very impressive sight. Most eyes, however, still looked out over the sea. The sky was an amazing wash of oranges, pinks, and purples, and the last gold curve of the sun was just visible above the horizon. As she watched, the sun dipped below the horizon, and the crowds cheered. People hugged and exchanged greetings. Children danced, holding their lanterns up high.

A gnome in a vivid blue hat, holding lanterns for sale, headed straight for Mabel.

"I was going to say, may your lantern last through the night, but you haven't got one!" the gnome said. "We can't have that. One for you, miss, and one for your nice young man."

"He's not—" Mabel began, but the seller thrust a starfish-shaped lantern into her hand and an acorn one into Robert's arms. Robert reached into his pocket for coppers, but the seller held up a hand.

"No charge! I can't see two lovely young people without a lantern. Get them lit before the magicals leave for the feast." He gestured towards the docks, where they could see lanterns lighting up in meandering patterns as magicals moved among the crowds.

As Robert and Mabel stepped forward, the seller blocked the path of Alden and Thorne.

"You two gentlemen, now, you need lanterns as well. I have just the right ones for a serious-looking pair like yourselves." He handed Alden a plain round lantern and Thorne a similar one that looked like someone had sat on it. "That'll be a gold each."

"But that's extortionate!" Thorne spluttered. "Anyway, I just saw you give two away for nothing."

"Those two youngsters look like they have been dragged through a hedge backward. You two don't look much better, but I know good quality alchemist's robes when I see them. I think you have more than enough gold tucked away in there. Come on, pay up. It's very bad luck not to have a lantern tonight!" The gnome smiled widely, his hand stretched out, ready to receive payment.

"Oh, very well," Thorne grumbled, pulling out enough gold to pay for his and Alden's lantern. "We definitely don't want any more bad luck." He waved a hand irritably, and all their lanterns lit.

Mabel felt a snowflake land on her cheek. The first flurries had finally reached the ground. People turned to each other in surprise, holding their hands out and looking up into the sky.

More and more people turned and pointed at the majestic column of snow behind the docks. Children ran around in delight, lanterns bobbing, trying to catch the delicate flakes.

An alchemist, with the emblem of a senior guilder from the Whispering Vials embroidered on his cap, came up and shook Thorne warmly by the hand.

"So, this is what you've been working on, you sneaky old goat. Oh my, you weren't joking. It's spectacular! Everyone will be talking about this for years to come. I haven't seen snow since I was a boy—wonderful!" Mabel watched as Thorne performed an exaggerated bow and lapped up the praise, her mouth forming a perfect "O" of indignation.

"I thought it would be very well-received, especially by the kiddies, you know. Much better to keep it as a surprise."

Mabel turned to Alden, who shrugged wearily.

"I hoped he might learn some humility after this," Alden said, "but I should have known better."

Couples danced in the snow, twirling around and around. Then, the trumpets and drums changed tempo, and people formed themselves into a column, ready to parade back into the main streets of Turtle Bay for the feast.

The odd snow flake was still falling when Mabel, Alden, Thorne, and Robert found themselves outside Thorne's shop. Driel had kept Maritime Macarons open; the windows were blazing with light, and the door was crowded with people. Families sat together at mismatched tables dragged from shops, houses, and taverns into the street. Music played, and children ran around laughing. Buckets of sand had been placed along the pavements, serving as holders for lanterns of every shape and color. Mabel pushed the wooden stick of her starfish lantern into a bucket that had space and joined the others at a wobbly table. She perched on a crate that someone had thoughtfully put a cushion on. Candles burned in curved glass jars on the tables, creating even more light. Plates and trays had been laid out with traditional seafood pastries, stuffed rolls, biscuits, and cakes. Robert reached for the food as if he hadn't eaten properly in weeks.

Thorne had been soaking up congratulations on his wonderful addition to the festival all evening. With every compliment he accepted, bow he took, and mock, humble smile he made, Mabel became more furious. When another guilder slapped him on the back and walked off, raising a glass to him and miming snowfall with his fingers, she couldn't keep it in anymore.

"How can you sit there and accept praise like that? You put both yourself and Robert at risk—for weeks! You could have ruined the entire lantern parade this evening, and if things had gone really bad . . . " Mabel gestured to take in all the families eating, laughing, and enjoying themselves in the light snowfall. She didn't want to think about what might have happened.

Robert looked shocked and shrank down in his seat. Alden sat back, cradling his wine, smiling, and looking as if he was enjoying Mabel's outburst hugely.

Thorne's face drew into a frown. "Young woman, who are you to lecture me? You are not even a full alchemist! How dare you speak to a senior guilder like that." Thorne's voice boomed, deep, resonant, and outraged. He paired it with a stern glare from under furrowed brows. This combination made Robert sink even further down in his chair. Just a few weeks ago, it would have made Mabel shrivel up, too. But by this point, Mabel was so angry that she found she was completely immune. She glared right back, just as piercingly, righteous indignation making a magnificent shield, and a pretty good sword, too.

"I'm the person who stopped you from being blown to smithereens by your own invention! You should be ashamed of yourself. If you're so experienced and wise, then you should know better."

Thorne's eyebrows raised, his mouth quirked into a smile, and then he sat back in his chair and laughed deeply, slapping his leg and spilling his drink.

"Ha, she's wonderful, Alden! I see why you brought her to Turtle Bay on this little adventure."

"You are wasting your time, Mabel," Alden said, leaning forward and patting her hand. "Thorne feels no shame. Never has, never will."

"This can't possibly be the same girl you mentioned in your letters, Alden. The complete doormat, doing all her friend's work," Thorne said, mischief crinkling his eyes. Alden raised his hands as if he could ward off the words.

"I did not write that, Thorne! You old scoundrel," he turned to Mabel, who now shone her full glare on Alden. "Believe me, that's not what I wrote at all. But if you give Brianna one of those looks, I don't think she'll bother you about doing her work again!"

Robert laughed but stopped dead when Mabel scowled at him.

"He's not wrong, though. I can't imagine anyone telling you what to do," Robert said. Mabel crossed her arms and settled back onto her cushion, only slightly less angry.

Thorne looked down into his drink. It was some kind of coconut affair with large chunks of fruit floating in it. He swirled the pineapple and mango around thoughtfully.

"I was so close, Alden. I mean, I actually did succeed. Just for a short time, everything was perfect." He looked up, and three horrified faces looked back.

"Don't worry! I won't be making any more weather stones any time soon. A nice bit of peace and quiet is what's needed after the last few weeks. It has been very wearing."

"That's putting it mildly," Robert said. He still looked too pale, although he had eaten enough food for three people in the few short minutes they had been sitting down. "I'll write to you, Alden, if he starts doing anything else crazy. I'm not going through that again."

"Ah, a spy in my own workshop! You see, you can content yourself, Mabel. I'm sure I will be kept a very close eye on."

Somehow, Mabel didn't think oversight by an apprentice would be enough to keep Thorne out of trouble.

"There's one thing I don't understand, though," Alden said thoughtfully to Thorne. "If you wrote to me after taking the weather stone to the warehouse, why didn't you tell me where to meet you? We wasted a whole day trying to find you."

"But I did! It was all in the letter," Thorne said. Alden pulled the letter out of his inner pocket and opened it up. The same black scrawl was at the top of the paper, with no mention of warehouses or weather stones.

"You mean you didn't get it?" Thorne said, surprised. "I even mentioned Rumbalow's class. Look."

Thorne held the letter over a candle in the center of the table, just enough to catch the heat. In the large blank space under the original note, new writing appeared in a burned brown color.

Meet me at the docks, warehouse 4 on Squid Street. Weather stone created for the festival gone badly wrong. Stone cracked. Magic effect area grown exponentially. Please think over the problem on your journey.

I hope you can help me.

T.

"We wrote secret notes to each other in class all the time, and Rumbelow never had a clue! Why else would I mention that old codger in a letter?"

Alden's cheeks turned quite pink. "Well, having that information from the beginning would have been very useful. You could have written it in normal ink, you know."

"Alden, you know how nosy alchemists are. News of my failure would have spread faster than your journey. I wouldn't be basking in glory so much as suspended from the guild right now!" He let the paper fall to the table, and Mabel picked it up, turning it over curiously.

"Is it written with a special alchemical ink?" she asked.

"No, it's just lemon juice," Thorne snorted.

Mabel dropped the letter and rolled her eyes. "A child's trick!"

"I'm very proud of you, Mabel. It was a good idea to direct the magical expulsion like that. I was thinking of only how it could be stopped." Alden said.

"I was worried about expansion of the weather patterns when I should have been more concerned about the crack," Thorne said.

A flush swept across Mabel's cheeks at the praise. "I've had so many disasters in my own work over the years. I'm used to dealing with magical crises. This one was just on a much bigger scale."

"I hope you will go back to the Whispering Vials with a new sense of confidence," Alden said. "You are perfectly capable of the work and will succeed in time." Thorne nodded in agreement with his friend.

Mabel did feel better about things. The weather stone had been terrifying but inspiring, too. Not only that, she was pretty sure she had an idea for a possible masterpiece. She looked over at Alden, who was yawning in his seat. Maybe she could help both herself and her mentor at the same time.

Robert cleared his throat.

"Would you like to dance? It's kind of traditional," he said to Mabel. He stood and held out his arm to her, looking hopeful.

She looked around at all the people dancing in the streets, lit by the warm glow of hundreds of lanterns. Each person held a lantern in one hand, linked arms, and span around and around. It didn't look too hard.

"Yes, I think I will!" She gave Thorne a sharp look to let him know he still wasn't forgiven, grabbed her starfish lantern from the sand bucket, and took Robert's arm, ready to spin and twirl under the stars of Turtle Bay.

HAVE YOU EVER WANTED TO OWN A PET DRAGON? EXPLORE DEEP DWARF mines? Find a wand that talks? Bonnie Axton has too! She loves reading and writing fantasy books. It's the best way to visit magical realms and meet mythical creatures while waiting for a portal to appear at the bottom of her garden. Find out more about Bonnie on her website: bonnieaxton.com

Look out for *The Alchemist's Return* in the summer of 2024.

About Cozy Vales

Cozy Vales is a cozy fantasy shared world. Originally created by Scott Walker (writing under the pen name L.A. Scott), several authors have expanded the world through contributions to the world of Cozy Vales and to the growing list of stories in the Cozy Vales Collection.

While the stories themselves may by mysteries, adventures, or slice-of-life tales, they all have one thing in common: they're cozy.

To learn more about this world, subscribe to The Golden Acorn, the most popular broadsheet in the vales and the best source of information and news about the queendom!

cozyvales.com

facebook.com/cozyvales
x.com/cozyvales
instagram.com/cozyvales

Printed in Great Britain
by Amazon